Summer in the South

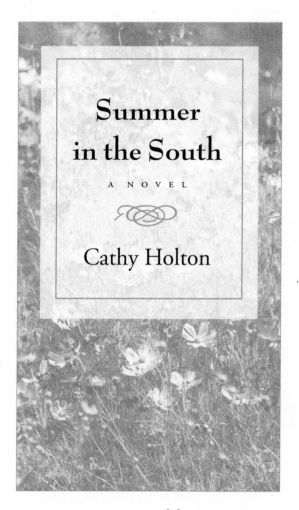

Summer in the South

A NOVEL

Cathy Holton

BALLANTINE BOOKS   NEW YORK

Published in the United States by Ballantine Books, an imprint of The Random House Publishing Group, a division of Random House, Inc., New York.

BALLANTINE and colophon are registered trademarks of Random House, Inc.

LIBRARY OF CONGRESS CATALOGING-IN-PUBLICATION DATA
Holton, Cathy.
Summer in the South : a novel / Cathy Holton.
p.   cm.
ISBN 978-0-345-50601-6 (hardback) — ISBN 978-0-345-52634-2 (ebook)
1. Domestic fiction. 2. Southern States—Fiction. I. Title.
PS3608.O494434S86 2011
813'.6—dc22   2011000708

Printed in the United States of America on acid-free paper

www.ballantinebooks.com

2 4 6 8 9 7 5 3 1

FIRST EDITION

Book design by Laurie Jewell

Title-page photograph: © iStockphoto

To Mark

Acknowledgments

Many thanks to Kristin Lindstrom and to the entire team at Ballantine, most especially my editor, Kate Collins, and Kelli Fillingim. Thanks to Sam Holton, Lauren Holton, Jordan Holton, and all the girls of the Birthday Lunch Club for their unfailing source material (none of you are in this one, I promise.) To Randal, a very special thanks for a weekend I'll never forget, and for sharing with me tales of her illustrious family.

And, as always, thanks to Mark, my partner in all things.

Summer in the South

1931

Woodburn, Tennessee

The body was lying on a table in the basement of the Purdy Funeral Home. The town was too small to have need of a morgue. The few accidental deaths or homicides that occurred within the town limits were brought here or to McClendon's.

Josephine stood just within the doorway, steeling herself for what she must do. The heat in the room was stifling. The worst summer heat in ninety years, the newspaper said, but not a drought. It rained nearly every day so the land was like a swamp, a jungle. Strange insects dropped from the vine-strangled trees, and bizarre fungi bloomed on the walls of the houses like exotic flowers. A summer like no other.

The body was covered by a sheet. Two naked lightbulbs hung from long cords above the table. Across the room Sheriff Gillespie stood talking in a low voice to two deputies. They were chuckling and jostling each other like men at a barbecue, but when they saw her they rose quietly, dipped their heads, and left the room.

The sheriff took his hat off and walked over to her, his gun creaking in its holster.

"Good evening, Miss Woodburn."

"Good evening, Sheriff Gillespie."

"I'm sorry to have to ask you to do this but Mrs. Woodburn

seemed . . ." He hesitated. "Well, she seemed not herself, and you were the next of kin. Procedural matters and all that."

"Yes, yes, of course." She moved closer to the body before he could take her arm. He followed behind, creaking softly.

"It's not a pretty sight," he said gruffly. His demeanor changed, becoming all businesslike and brisk as he lifted a corner of the sheet to expose the face.

Josephine had a sudden sensation of falling from a very great distance. She swayed on her feet. The sheriff put his hand out as if to steady her, but she ignored it.

"That swelling is usual in cases where the body's been in the water for a while. And those bruises and lacerations to the face." He hesitated here and she was aware again of the change in his demeanor. It occurred to her that he was trying to impress her. "Well, that could have been caused by rocks or debris in the river."

Maitland had moved up on her other side. She had not heard him come in. His youthful face was pale, and she could see that his hands were trembling, his cuff links blinking under the lights. He glanced at the face and then quickly averted his eyes and Josephine saw in that glance all she needed to know. She felt a quick stab of guilt and despair. She had sent the letter that brought him here, to this.

She turned and laid her gloved hand protectively on the sheriff's arm. "I'm not sure what to do. I'm not sure what to say. You'll have to guide me, Sheriff Gillespie."

He blinked and cleared his throat. He looked down at her hand. "Is this the body of Charles Woodburn?" he asked in a stern, officious voice.

"Yes," she said and he dropped the cloth, easing back into his former affable self. She let her hand rest on his arm a few seconds longer than was necessary and then withdrew it.

There was a faint scent of whiskey and unwashed linen in the room, and underneath it all a sweet, fetid odor. She had not noticed it before, or if she had, it had not registered consciously. The shock of seeing him had driven everything else from her mind, the dreadful swollen face, once beautiful, so monstrous now. The inner man finally re-vealed.

"We found a bottle of whiskey in his pocket and surmise that he fell into the river near your place, intoxicated, and drifted downstream past the Haskell Bridge," the sheriff said.

She said nothing. He continued, "That would explain the lacera-tions. There are many rocks, and the current is swift."

She stood staring down at the swollen, shapeless thing that had been Charlie Woodburn. So much tragedy in life. So much cruelty.

Beside her, Maitland stirred. He said, "Will there be anything else, Sheriff?"

She heard the quaver in his voice. She thought, *Some things can never be forgotten. Some things can never be forgiven.*

"No, that's all. There'll be an inquest but we'll keep as much of it out of the papers as we can in deference to the family."

"Thank you," she said.

Maitland took her arm and without another word, the two of them turned and walked out.

1998

The Traveler

When Ava was small, Clotilde told her stories of ghosts and ruined castles and lonely moonlit roads. Most children would have been afraid of such tales but Ava welcomed the shivers of fear and trembling possibility they sent up her narrow spine. She preferred the gnomes and changelings and lonely, misshapen creatures because they seemed more familiar to her than the beautiful princesses and handsome princes that wove themselves in and out of Clotilde's rambling tales.

"Tell me a story," Ava would say, climbing sleepily onto Clotilde's lap, and Clotilde's girlish face would go still and then brighten as the words came to her.

They owned few books in those days, not because they were poor but because Clotilde liked to travel light. She preferred rented rooms furnished with the cast-offs of other people's dismal lives to possessions of her own.

"I'm a traveler!" she always said, and when Ava was older and asked her morosely, "But why?" Clotilde's face, still girlish, softened for a moment. "Because when you leave one place and move to another, you get to start over. You get to become whoever you want to be."

To help in this metamorphosis, Clotilde sometimes changed her name. Over the years she was Dharma and Abrielle and even (ironically) Magdalena. But it was the name Clotilde that she most often used.

"Clotilde was the Queen of Sardinia!" she exclaimed, grinning sheepishly at whatever man was currently in her life. "Besides, the name means 'famous in battle.'"

Clotilde saw no more harm in changing her name than she did in moving every six months. "What's in a name?" she liked to say.

Ava, who had been born Summer Rayne Dabrowski, inevitably responded, "Everything."

Around the time she was in third grade, not long after they moved to Cincinnati and just before they moved to Cleveland, Ava had jettisoned Summer Rayne in favor of Margaret, after the name penciled into her well-worn copy of *Grimm's Fairy Tales,* Margaret Anne Govan. And later, not long before she started high school, she had abandoned Margaret in favor of Ava, still foolishly believing, like Clotilde, that she could leave her girlhood behind just by changing her name.

"Tell me a story," she would say when she was still small enough to believe in Clotilde's tales. "Tell me a story about my father." And she would snuggle down in her narrow bed and wait for Clotilde to begin, wait for the words to form behind the smooth mask of Clotilde's girlish face, and come tumbling out of her sly rosebud mouth.

"Once upon a time there was a handsome prince of the Underworld, and he fell in love with a beautiful princess. But she was betrothed to someone else, and when her father found out that she had been tarrying with the prince of the Underworld, he had the two of them locked up in a tower behind a pair of huge paneled doors.

"'You cannot live apart,' cried the angry king. 'Let's see how you shall live together, day after day, night after night, with only each other for company!'

"And although the two were given water, slid through a panel in the massive doors, they were denied food.

"'Live on your love for each other!' roared the cruel king.

"'Give us bread!' they wailed, shut up in their tower tomb. 'We are hungry!'

"Their pitiful cries went on for days and weeks, becoming ever weaker and more pitiful as the days went on. Finally they stopped. When the villagers crept close there were no sounds but the growls and slurps of voracious eating, the sharp clatters of teeth against bone, the sound of flesh being torn and devoured."

It was one of Ava's favorite stories. Years later she would remember it and, closing her eyes, would see the youthful images of her parents entombed behind paneled doors, waiting like tragic ghosts for her to come and free them.

When Will Fraser called and suggested that she spend the summer in Woodburn, Tennessee, Ava thought the idea preposterous. What little she knew about the South had come from bad cinema and the stories of Flannery O'Connor, and it had always amazed her that someone as cultured as Will could have come from the land of monster truck rallies and corn bread festivals.

It wasn't the first time he'd invited her. They had gone to college together at Bard, and had kept in touch over the past seven or eight years through emails, phone calls, and the occasional visit. Communication between them was sporadic and due mostly to his efforts. Ava considered them to be casual acquaintances. He'd come to Chicago several times on business and had looked her up. Each time he'd asked her to spend some time in Tennessee, she'd laughed. She had made the mistake of telling him that she wanted to be a novelist—he had a manner that invited confidences—and he insisted that his sleepy little hometown would be the perfect place for her to write her first novel. He didn't seem to understand that, unlike him, she had to work for a living. She had school loans to pay and a job in a prestigious Chicago ad agency that it had taken her some time and effort to land.

But this time when he called, things were different. Her life was undergoing a series of cataclysmic upheavals. In less than six months her estranged mother had died of a brain aneurysm, her career had stalled, her affair with her boss, Jacob, had wound down to its inevitable conclusion, and most disturbing of all, she had received a condolence letter out of the blue from a man purporting to be her father. Coming one on top of the other, these events had left her shaken, confused, and understandably depressed.

Sunk in a dense fog, she hadn't had the strength to pretend that things were fine when Will called.

"Are you all right?" he asked her.

"I've been better," she said truthfully.

On his last trip to Chicago a few months before, she hadn't seen him. He had called and left a message saying he was in town, but she had planned a rendezvous with Jacob that night and so pretended she hadn't gotten the message in time, calling Will later to apologize. She felt guilty for weeks about standing him up, and yet the truth was, they had only known each other for a short time in college. He was two years ahead of her in school, and was friends with her first love, Michael. In those days Will was a tall, dark-haired boy, very well mannered but shy, with a slight Southern accent.

"Another trust-fund baby," Michael had called him dismissively and it was true. There were plenty of those at Bard, although Will didn't seem like old money. He shopped at thrift stores like the rest of them and drove an old battered Volvo station wagon. The truth was, Ava hadn't really paid much attention to him; she had been so caught up in her tumultuous love affair with Michael, and Will had simply been a quiet backdrop to all of that. A silent witness.

Once she and Michael had quarreled in a bar several miles from campus and Michael, in a fury, abruptly left, taking the car and leaving her stranded at two o'clock in the morning in an unfamiliar part of town. Will, who had been watching from the bar (he had grown accustomed to their violent arguments and no longer intervened), insisted on driving her home. She was dismayed to find herself crying, and raged against Michael on the ride home while Will listened silently. He insisted on seeing her up the rickety stairs of her Victorian apartment building to her front door.

"Would you like me to wait?" he asked.

"No. Thank you." She knew Michael would return later and there'd be another row, and she didn't want Will to see it. She was embarrassed suddenly that he'd already seen so much of their dysfunctional relationship.

"All right. Good night." He touched her briefly on the arm and a faint tinge of color appeared along his brow. Ava realized then that he had a crush on her.

"Good night," she said.

She never told Michael how she'd gotten home and he never asked, but a few weeks later he mentioned rather casually that Will Fraser was engaged to a girl he'd gone to boarding school with. After that, there was a wariness between Will and Ava whenever they met, something that Ava noted at first with mild regret and later didn't notice at all. By the time Will and Michael graduated a year later, the two had drifted apart and Ava rarely saw him.

She saw Will briefly at graduation. He was standing on the lawn among a small knot of friends and family. He'd grown very thin and pale, and when she remarked on this to Michael he smiled unpleasantly and said it had something to do with the fiancée. A broken engagement or something like that.

"Women," Michael said, shaking his head. "God knows why we put up with you."

"You've got spinach in your teeth," Ava lied, and while he hurried off to check, she strolled over to congratulate Will.

He smiled when he saw her and introduced her to his family. His parents had died in a car accident when he was a child, and he'd been raised by two great-aunts, Fanny and Josephine. They smiled politely at Ava. They were both elegantly dressed, with pale skin and clear gray eyes. Very attractive, both of them, although they must have been in their sixties. The smaller one, Fanny, smiled shyly and took Ava's arm.

"So you're Ava," she said. She wore a silk dress belted tightly around her narrow waist and a short little jacket.

Josephine, the taller one, let her eyes flicker coolly over Ava. "Goodness, Fanny, don't clutch her so." She was dressed in a gray suit that matched her eyes, and she seemed rather reserved, like Will, only in him this reserve came across as shyness, while in her it seemed cold and distant. "You'll have to excuse my sister," she said to Ava. *Sistuh.* "As you can see, she's never met a stranger."

It was an odd thing to say, and yet spoken in that beautiful accent it sounded like music.

"What lovely hair you have," Fanny said.

Ava smiled. "Thank you." It was her best feature and she was rather proud of it. She had left it down today, and it fell in red-gold waves around her shoulders.

"Aren't you chilly?" Josephine asked, noting her sleeveless dress.

Ava laughed. "After Chicago, this is nothing," she said.

"So you're from Chicago?"

"Pretty much."

"Ah," Josephine said in a tone that could have indicated surprise or disapproval or resignation.

A faint bloom of color appeared in Will's face. He raised his head and looked around the crowded lawn. "I wonder what's happened to Uncle Maitland," he said.

Somewhere south of Owensboro the landscape changed, became more rolling and green. Great clouds of yellow pollen hung in the air. The light in Chicago had a sharp, clear quality but here it came in at odd angles, filtered by tall trees and masses of greenery lining the roadway.

They had thrown her a going-away party at work, a *Deliverance* theme party complete with dueling banjos and white-trash martinis. Colleen, drunk, had stood up and given a nice little speech, ending with the warning, "And whatever you do, don't get off the expressway! For Christ's sake, stay on the expressway." Everyone at work thought of the South as a place of hillbillies and moonshine, and Ava had to admit (although only to herself) that she felt the same way. Perhaps this was why she had forced herself to get off the expressway just north of

Louisville, and, buying a map, proceeded to drive bravely along curving picturesque county roads past small-frame farmhouses and tall-steepled churches and mobile homes with elaborately attached decks and discarded appliances rusting in the yards.

Beside her, buckled safely into the passenger seat, Clotilde rested quietly in her enameled urn like a genie waiting for someone to come and rub her lamp.

They passed a wide field and a weathered barn with *See Rock City* painted on its sagging roof. There was something insubstantial and airy about the shimmering light and the varying shades of green, like a landscape from a dream or a long-forgotten fairy tale.

"It's so green," Ava said to Clotilde.

A hawk circled lazily above the tree line. Far off in the distance, a rim of blue mountains rose into the hazy sky.

She had told Will everything: about her mother, about Jacob, about her job that she detested. She unburdened herself to him like she once had about Michael, droning on and on while he listened quietly. It was the alcohol, she told herself later, that had made her so garrulous. That and the fact that she wasn't sleeping well.

"You can quit your job and move down here and write your novel," he said when she'd finished, and she'd laughed disparagingly. He had continued in a placid voice as if trying to soothe a fussy child. "No, really. Woodburn is a sleepy little town. Nothing much ever happens around here. There are no distractions, and you can stay with Josephine and Fanny. They live in an old house near the town square, and you'd have a suite of rooms to yourself. You wouldn't be disturbed. It's a large house. I tease them that they should turn it into a bed-and-breakfast one of these days."

"Do you live with them?"

"No, I live at Longford."

"Where's that?"

"The family farm. Out from town. I inherited it when I turned twenty-one. I'd ask you to stay with me but I'm renovating the house and it's pretty primitive right now."

"Shouldn't you ask your aunts before you offer to move me in?"

"Actually, they were the ones who suggested it."

"Really? Why?"

He cleared his throat. "Well," he said, "they remembered you from that day at Bard, the day I graduated. 'Your little friend Ava,' Fanny calls you. 'The one with the lovely hair.' I told them you were looking for a quiet place to write your first novel and they said, 'Oh, tell her to come down here. She can stay with us.' "

"That's very generous of them."

"You sound surprised."

"It's just that I got the feeling the stern aunt, the tall one . . ."

"Josephine?"

"Yes, Josephine. I got the feeling she didn't like me."

"That's just her way. The Woodburns are Scottish, and they tend to be reserved."

"And you're a Woodburn?"

"On my mother's side. My grandmother Celia was Josephine and Fanny's sister."

"I can't quit my job," Ava said. "I need to work to eat."

"It's free room and board. Think of it as a writing retreat. One of those communes where artists spend the summer."

Despite her gloomy mood, Ava was flattered by his enthusiasm. He was kind and considerate, the sort of man she didn't usually fall for. Unfortunately, she and Clotilde had shared more than their hair color; they both had bad judgment when it came to men. Ava was determined to remedy this in the future.

"I don't know."

"What do you have to lose?" he asked.

The road rose slightly, following a low ridge. A line of pink-blossomed trees with fringed leaves swayed in the breeze. On the other side of the highway, trailing vines mounded over distant pines and telephone poles, and dangled from utility lines, creating a series of undulating green hills. The whole landscape was lush and alien; Ava had the feeling that a seed tossed haphazardly from the window of a speeding car would take root in the rich soil and blossom to monstrous proportions.

What do I have to lose? she thought. *Nothing. Everything.* She turned her head and glanced at the ceramic urn in the seat beside her.

"Isn't that right, Mother?" she said.

She had moved back to Chicago after she graduated from Bard. She knew the city; she and Clotilde had landed there her sophomore year of high school. They'd lived at first in a ratty walk-up in Rogers Park before moving to a more promising neighborhood on the outskirts of Wicker Park.

By then her nomadic lifestyle with Clotilde had paled. They were always starting over, always fleeing some creditor or landlord, always packing their meager belongings into the car in the dead of night.

"I'm a gypsy!" Clotilde would crow, her long red-blonde hair falling around her shoulders, her silver-ringed fingers clutching the steering wheel.

Often fleeing some jaded boyfriend, too. By now Clotilde herself had begun to pale. Ava fantasized about getting her driver's license and driving away from her mother, leaving her stranded in some gray-skied industrial city. But then they had landed in Chicago and Ava had refused to leave until she had finished high school. She took a test, was accepted at a good Catholic school, got herself a scholarship, and for the first time in her life Ava had friends and did things normal kids did; she went to movies and parties and even dated a little. Chicago began to feel like home.

But living in Chicago after college graduation was different. For one thing, Clotilde had moved away, hooking up with a ski bum who was headed to Durango, Colorado. And the friends Ava had made in high school had gone away to college and settled elsewhere or else they'd stayed, married, and started families. Ava kept up with one or two friends from Bard who had left New York and moved back to Chicago, occasionally meeting for drinks in a small sports bar near the Loop; it was through one of them that she had landed her first job, as a writer for a local entertainment magazine. This led to a stint at a start-up public relations firm, which led to a position as a junior copywriter with a small ad agency, which eventually led to a job as a copywriter with a large, well-known agency. Each professional advance was accompanied by a raise in salary that bumped her standard of living accordingly so that by the time she landed at the large agency and met Jacob, she was living in a fifth-floor one-bedroom on Lakeshore Drive, the kind of apartment she could only have dreamed of living in during her days with Clotilde.

But regardless of her promising career, she was always broke. She never seemed to save any money. With each step up the professional ladder, she felt more and more trapped, knowing that she'd never be able to go back to living on what she'd made before. Knowing that she'd never be able to do the thing she most wanted to do, which was to stop working at the ad agency and write novels full-time. She'd wanted to be a writer her whole life, ever since third grade. On career day, all the kids had stood up and said that when they grew up they wanted to be astronauts and firemen and ballerinas, and Ava had realized, in a sudden flash of insight, that she could be all three (well, maybe not a ballerina, that wasn't her style). She could be whatever she wanted to be just by using her imagination and writing stories. From that point forward, she had never questioned her destiny, studying creative writing at Bard, and sending out an endless stream of unpublishable short stories to various literary magazines.

But after college she found that making a living as a writer was difficult. Freelance work was unreliable, magazine work was competitive, and the pay, at least for beginning writers, was poor. She had been lured into advertising by the promise of a steady paycheck and the hope that a higher salary would enable her to save enough money to eventually quit and write novels full-time. But that wasn't how things worked out.

First there was the car payment and then the new apartment and the new furniture. And always there were the clothes and shoes and handbags necessary to convince everyone, to convince *herself*, that she was a professional woman. Her writing began to take a backseat to her ad agency work until it became more of a hobby than a career.

To make matters worse, she was lonely. She and Michael had finally broken up her senior year of college, having given the long-distance relationship one year before calling it off. Although she dated sporadically once she moved to Chicago, none of those affairs lasted longer than six months.

And then she met Jacob.

She hadn't even liked him at first. He was difficult to work for. He was loud and brash and told inappropriate jokes, so she was not surprised, one day over lunch eight months after she'd joined the agency, when he suggested a sexual rendezvous as casually as if he were pitching a proposal to a client. She wasn't surprised at Jacob but she was surprised at herself. She accepted.

No one in the office guessed that they were sleeping together. Ava was attractive enough, with a trim figure and large, dark eyes. Still, she was not a bombshell. She was not the type anyone would have pictured Jacob with. She did not wear low-cut blouses or her skirts too short. She did not color her hair. Her face, in some lights, could be almost plain. Perhaps it was the fact that none of the other women in the office thought he could find her attractive that drove her into Jacob's arms.

Or maybe it was just that he was coldly inattentive, and Ava had a bad habit of falling for unpredictable men who gave her very little attention.

Jacob was in his mid-forties, divorced, with two children. Ava told herself that the affair would be nothing more than a brief fling. A brief respite from her loneliness until she moved on to something more promising.

The sex was good at first, and later less so. At the office they were cordial but professional. He made sure they were never alone together; there was never any hint of impropriety, no fevered glances or hurried embraces in the conference room, no stealthy touches in the corridors.

After nearly a year, the unthinkable had occurred, the thing Ava had promised herself would not happen; she had begun to fall for him. It amazed her that she could fall for someone whom she didn't really like, that she could wait all night for his phone call, listen for the sound of his voice in the hallway, the tread of his footsteps on the stairs. Whatever slight confidence she had once displayed around him was gone. Now she found herself listening jealously while he flirted with other girls, feeling ugly and awkward. Jacob's spirits seemed to soar the longer the affair went on, while she grew more and more despondent. She realized now the mistake of sleeping with someone she worked with, someone she had to take orders from. She fantasized about leaving but she'd only been at the agency a short time, and she needed a position on her resume that had lasted longer than twenty months.

If Jacob guessed that she was unhappy he gave no sign of it.

"Take your hair down," he said once, when they were alone. Her hair was long and thick, and she wore it up at work or pulled back into a sleek ponytail. "You look like one of those pornographic Victorian postcards," he said, running his hands through the long curls.

Ava said she wouldn't know anything about that.

He laughed. "I can't stay," he said. "I have an early-morning meeting."

Her friend at work, Colleen, was always trying to fix her up. Because Ava had never talked about a boyfriend, because she had never brought a date to any of the office functions, the rumor was that she was gay. Colleen refused to believe it.

"How about that guy in the building next door to you?" she asked Ava one morning over coffee.

"The one who sits in a lawn chair in the snow reading Dostoyevsky?" Ava had not heard from Jacob in several days and she was irritable and depressed.

"Yeah, him. He seems like your type."

"Just because I read Russian novels doesn't make him my type."

"Was he wearing a wedding ring?"

"I doubt it."

"Then I'll restate my question. What are you waiting for?"

"For all I know he could be a serial killer."

Colleen considered this. "Not in that building," she said.

Through the glass walls of the soaring atrium, Ava could see the towering skyscrapers of the Loop silhouetted against an ashen sky. They sat at a small table near the entrance to the coffee shop, stirring their lattes.

"How's Dave?" Ava asked, trying to change the subject. She had run into Jacob on the elevator this morning, and he'd seemed more distracted than usual, giving her a swift, puzzled glance, as if he didn't recognize her.

"Who?"

"Dave. The guy you're dating."

"Oh, Dave," Colleen said, waving her hand dismissively. "I'm bored with Dave." Colleen seemed to have a new boyfriend every week; she changed men the way some women change purses, a different one for each outfit.

She ducked her head and gave Ava a sly smile. "Guess what?" She crossed her arms on the table and leaned forward, glancing around to make sure she wouldn't be overheard.

"What?" Ava asked, sipping her coffee.

Colleen giggled and put one hand over her mouth. She smirked at Ava, lifting her eyebrows comically.

"Come on," Ava said. She stared at Colleen irritably over the rim of her cup. "Tell me. It's too early in the morning for guessing games."

"I'm sleeping with Jacob."

Ava sputtered and choked, spitting coffee all over the table. Colleen's eyes widened. She leaned over and thumped Ava on the back. "Are you okay? Did you swallow wrong?" She took a napkin from the metallic container and mopped up Ava's spilled coffee. "I know it's crazy but I couldn't help it," she said, avoiding Ava's eyes. "We were having lunch together and something happened. Something totally unexpected. He says he's had a thing for me since the beginning but hasn't been able to bring himself to tell me. We spent the whole afternoon at the Hyatt Regency. We didn't even come back to the office."

Ava coughed into her fist. She said, "Our boss Jacob?"

"It's a huge secret. You're the only one who knows, and you can't tell anyone."

Two days later Clotilde died unexpectedly of a brain aneurysm. Ava flew to Colorado to make the final arrangements, which consisted of having her mother cremated and donating her few possessions to the local Goodwill. There was no memorial service. The ski bum had long since disappeared, and Clotilde had been living alone in a small duplex off the main street and working as a desk clerk at the Strater Hotel. Ava found a boot box filled with Clotilde's important documents: several tax returns, an affidavit signed by two people with the unlikely names of Doobie Moonshine and Skye Rain, and her own birth certificate. Her birth name was listed as Summer Rayne Dabrowski, and her father was listed as Frank Dabrowski. He was a shadowy figure known only to Ava in myth. He had left when she was still a toddler and, according to Clotilde, had died in an ice-fishing accident on the Detroit River when Ava was ten years old.

Her mother was listed as Margaret Anne Govan, aka Dharma Dabrowski.

There were also photographs: several of a chubby blonde Ava and Clotilde on a beach, in front of a merry-go-round, or posed (dangerously close) to the edge of a scenic overlook. There was one of Clotilde with a handsome, long-haired boy (her father, Ava guessed) and one of Clotilde in a multicolored granny gown standing in front of a purple bus decorated with peace signs.

Also enclosed was an envelope containing Ava's baby teeth and several locks of bright blonde baby hair tied up with a ribbon.

All the meaningful highlights of Clotilde's short life distilled into a reliquary the size of a shoebox.

It took about a week to tie up all the loose ends of her mother's death, and when she returned to Chicago, Ava went immediately to the office. She sailed past Jacob's receptionist, closing the door behind her. He was sitting with his feet up on his desk, and when he looked up and saw her, an expression of alarm spread swiftly across his face. (She wished then that she'd carried something in her hands, a letter opener or a three-hole punch, anything he might view as a potential weapon. She was enjoying the look of fear on his face, his mouth stretched into a grimace, eyes darting like a cornered rodent.)

She told him that it was over between them, that she knew about Colleen, and that if he ever told Colleen about the two of them, she would see to it that his partners got a full report of his activities. She told him she expected their working relationship to go on as before, cordial and professional, and she intimated, without ever actually saying it, that should this not occur she would certainly look into filing a sexual-harassment suit that would probably prove fruitless but would, no doubt, open him up to a career-ending scandal and expose him as the worthless son of a bitch that he was. He listened, speechless (the only time she had ever seen him speechless), while she spoke, his only signs of distress a faint flush of color along his brow and a furtive squint to his eyes as he glanced from her to the door and back again. When she had finished speaking she turned and left, leaving the door open behind her.

She floated along the corridor as if in a dream. Halfway to her office she was overcome by a feeling of relief so intense she thought her knees might buckle.

Several weeks later, Will Fraser called her and asked her to come to Tennessee. She was sitting by her apartment window wrapped in a blanket, her slippered feet slung over one arm of the chair, a glass of red wine and a book in her hands. It was a Saturday evening, and a fresh blanket of snow lay over the city. The lights of the apartments across the way gleamed wetly, and the distant lake was a pale, vaporous fog. She was reading *Wuthering Heights* and daydreaming of a savage, other-worldly lover, wondering at Emily Brontë's ability to tell such a brutal, magnificent tale.

When the phone rang she almost didn't answer it. But she was glad later that she had, glad for the confession Will allowed her, although she could not shake the feeling that there was something else required of her, some act of contrition, some sacrifice.

The feeling of relief she'd felt after leaving Jacob's office had not lasted, of course. It had swelled into a feeling of hopelessness and despair, a sense that, up to now, she had wasted her life on things that weren't important. A childhood spent being the responsible one, making sure the rent was paid and the bill collectors were kept at bay, had formed her. Had crippled her. She had planned her escape from her mother all those years ago, had followed that plan persistently, and yet here she was at twenty-eight, sitting alone in her expensive apartment with her expensive furniture wondering what purpose her life had. It was ridiculous, really, and pathetic.

Perhaps it was grief over her mother's sudden death swamping her finally, guilt and regret that they had not spoken in more than a year. Who knew how swiftly and unexpectedly death could come?

Or perhaps it was the letter.

It lay crumpled in a ball on the floor, and she leaned over and scooped it up. Will was telling her tales of the quirky inhabitants of Woodburn, trying to entice her with stories of his cousin, Fraser Barron, who dressed up as Edgar Allan Poe and did recitations of "The Raven" at cocktail parties.

"He must be a lot of fun," Ava said.

"You have no idea."

She smoothed the letter on her lap. It was written in a childish scrawl. *I was so sorry to hear about your mother,* he had written. *She loved you very much.* He had signed it, *Frank.* Not *Love, Dad* or *Your father* but just plain *Frank,* exhibiting a refreshing lack of sentimentality. She could relate to that; respected it, actually.

She picked up the flap of the torn envelope, looking at the return address. *1645 Hennipen Street, Garden City, Michigan.* Her father, who she'd thought dead all these years, had lived only a few hours away.

She felt a stab of anger at Clotilde for lying to her, for depriving her all those years of the fiction of a living, loving father.

Will repeated his offer of a change of pace, a new beginning in Tennessee. He seemed to be weighing each word, coaxing her along like he would a timid bird with bread crumbs. "Just come for the summer," he said.

Ava was surprised to find that she was weeping. "I'll think about it," she said.

She stopped for gas at a cinder-block convenience store, a short, squat building with a hand-lettered sign out front that read *Guns. Bait. Day Care.* The store looked old but the pumps were new. Ava swiped her card and then stood waiting for the tank to fill. She stretched her arms above her head and leaned back slightly, gazing across the road at a field of soybeans. Or at least she assumed that they were soybeans. A man in overalls at the last gas station had told her that soybeans were the staple crop in this area.

The green fields, the glittering road, the hard-baked grass of the clearing all seemed flattened and diminished beneath the weight of the noonday sun. Cicadas sang in the stillness. Far off across the fields, a distant fringe of forest stood outlined against a bleached sky. Ava ran her fingers through her short, spiky hair. Behind her a screened door slammed, and a moment later a woman's voice said, "Oo-ee, it's a scorcher. I'll bet its 90 in the shade and here it is only May. Hot as road tar in July, as my daddy used to say, and he should know, he lived through enough heat spells in his time." Ava turned around to see who the woman was talking to and was surprised to see that it was her.

"Excuse me?" she said nervously.

"Hot as a June bride in a feather bed," the woman continued, chuckling softly and patting her top lip with a Kleenex. She was an elderly woman in a flowered dress with a large black purse shaped like an anvil strapped to one arm. "And he should know, 'cause he got the sunstroke on a day like this, working on the barn roof with his brother, Dooly." Ava glanced anxiously at the store. The woman appeared to be unsupervised. There was no other car at the pumps, and no one had followed her out. She opened her purse and dropped the Kleenex inside, then snapped it shut. She reminded Ava a little of the deranged Bette Davis character in that old movie about the elderly sisters.

The woman tilted her head up at the sky, remembering. "It was a hot, sunny day in nineteen thirty-six, a Tuesday, I believe it was, or no, no, a Thursday. The wind was from the southeast, and he and Dooly were up there on the barn shingling in the heat. All of a sudden Daddy stood up and took off his hat and said, 'Dooly, there's a goat in the horse trough,' and then he fell off the roof. His eyes just rolled up in his head and he went over backwards like a snake-handling Pentecostal. Would have killed himself, the doctor said later, if he hadn't gone all limp before he fell."

The woman, whose eyes were bright and curious as a little sparrow's, had moved up close enough to the car to see Clotilde strapped into the front seat. "That sure is a pretty vase," she said.

Ava stopped pumping gas. She screwed the cap on and closed the lid with a thud. "How close to Woodburn are we?" she asked.

"Woodburn? Oh, about thirty-five miles, I'd say. You have business in Woodburn, do you?"

Ava hung the nozzle back on the pump and didn't wait for a receipt. "I have to go now."

The woman folded her arms across her stomach. She smiled. "You aren't from around here, are you," she said.

A few miles down the road Ava began to sneeze, so she put the windows up and turned on the air-conditioning. She passed a sign that read *Woodburn—30 miles* and she realized she would be arriving early. She'd have to stop in one of the small shops in town to kill some time, to pick up a gift for the aunts.

"Try to arrive by Toddy Time," Will had told her. "That's around five o'clock."

"What's Toddy Time?"

"Cocktail hour."

She'd been surprised, this far south in the Bible belt.

He laughed. "You do realize this is the home state of Jack Daniel's?"

She glanced at herself in the mirror, running her hand through her spiky hair. She'd never worn it short before and she was still getting used to the look. She had cut it the night Will called, the day she got the letter from her father, going into the bathroom and clipping great handfuls while tears streamed down her cheeks. When she finished, her head felt lighter; she could see patches of scalp glimmering through the wispy curls.

"My God, what have you done to yourself?" Jacob said when he saw her.

"I'm leaving," she told him. "Consider this my two-weeks' notice."

"Leaving to go where?"

Gripped by a sudden desire to make herself seem less pitiful, she said, "I'm spending the summer at a writers' colony."

He said carelessly, "I didn't know you were a writer."

"There's a lot you don't know about me."

He didn't come to the Deliverance Party and Ava was relieved. Later she drank too much and pulled Colleen aside and told her everything.

It was the last bit of unfinished business she felt she had before leaving Chicago.

She took her time heading south, driving first to Detroit and then meandering down I-75 in her used Saab. She spent the first night in a bed-and-breakfast outside of Cincinnati, where she lay awake listening to the clattering din of the crickets. She finally fell into a restless sleep but awoke some hours later to one of her night terrors, lying motionless and sweating until the spell passed. A trail of moonlight lay across the bed. She could hear the steady ticking of a clock somewhere deep within the house but she could not sleep again, tossing and turning until the clock chimed six and the first rosy fingers of daylight pushed themselves through the blinds.

As she prepared to leave, she thought of the characters in Russian novels who always said a prayer of protection before a journey. Even Tolstoy during his period of late-life despair would, she imagined, have prayed before fleeing his estate. Organized religion was something else Clotilde had thought unnecessary for Ava to experience, although she had espoused a kind of new-age spirituality: crystals and karma and past-life regressions.

As if this life hadn't been traumatic enough. A sudden defiance swept Ava. She bowed her head and prayed aloud, "Lord, bless this journey and keep me safe from harm." And holding the vase aloft and giving Clotilde a sly grin, she said, "And bless this one, too, and forgive her her many sins. Amen."

Another road sign appeared, announcing *Woodburn—20 miles*. She passed a group of cows standing motionless beneath the shade of a spreading tree. A shimmering pond reflected the metallic-colored sky.

Despite Will's reassurances that she would like Woodburn and she would fit in fine, Ava felt like a stranger in a strange land. And it wasn't just the dappled quality of the light, the small shotgun houses with their overgrown lawns and cement statuary, and the railroad crossings standing like sentries in the dusty little towns that made her feel this way. The people, too, seemed odd, almost frightening, with their overt displays of friendliness. Chicago was a friendly city, but people didn't wave to one another as they drove down the streets, and they didn't reveal their family histories to strangers at the gas pump.

She thought of Will, whom she hadn't seen in years, a man who was almost a stranger to her. She pictured Josephine, the tall stern woman with the piercing eyes whom she had met at Will's graduation. She thought of the bridges she had burned, the career she had left behind in ruins so she could pursue some wild dream she might never be able to attain.

For the first time since leaving Chicago, a vague sense of misgiving bloomed in her chest.

Woodburn

Ava had pictured Woodburn as a sleepy little crossroads with Will's home perched like Graceland at the end of a long avenue of oaks. She was surprised to find a neat, quaint little town with tree-lined brick streets laid out around a square of prosperous shops. The houses, a mixture of antebellum, Victorian, and neoclassical architecture, stood back from the streets across broad landscaped lawns in neighborhoods that formed ever-widening squares around the center of the town.

She stopped at a gourmet kitchen store and bought a gift basket of assorted coffees, ceramic mugs, and tea towels to give to the aunts. All the stores on the square had green awnings and window boxes filled with geraniums. They all faced the statue of the Unknown Confederate Soldier that stood on a pedestal in the middle of a neat lawn scattered with trees and park benches. Ava sat for a while on one of these benches, sipping an iced coffee and watching the shoppers who trolled the storefronts. The town was close enough to Nashville to look prosperous. Will had told her many of the country music millionaires were settling out here.

She also bought a map and spent some time driving through the pleasant neighborhoods. The Woodburns' house was on a street a few blocks from the square. It was not as grand as she had envisioned it;

there were no white columns but instead a deep porch that ran across the front and down one side. Long shuttered windows stood on either side of a graceful mahogany door crowned by a fanlight. The lawn was trimly cut, crowded at the edges with dogwoods and long banks of pink and white azaleas. A graveled drive curved along one side of the house toward a detached garage in the back. A Ford pickup truck was parked in the drive.

Ava drove slowly past, not wanting to appear earlier than the five o'clock Toddy Time. Will had promised to meet her at the house so she wouldn't have to face the aunts alone.

There were only a few houses along this street, all with expansive lawns and well-maintained exteriors. Each house had its own historical plaque tacked to the front, and the one in front of the aunts' house read *Woodburn Hall, c. 1821.* The street sign read *River Road,* and Ava discovered why when, a block from the house, the street curved sharply to the left and continued along a narrow, swiftly moving river. It was all woods and heavy undergrowth here; the town ended abruptly. Ava followed River Road for perhaps a quarter of a mile, until it intersected a two-lane county highway that crossed the river over a narrow bridge. She turned right onto the highway, crossing the Harpeth River, and drove for a mile or two. It was all farmland here; wide green fields, hazy beneath the afternoon sun, ran along both sides of the highway. She passed a sign that read *Longford Plantation—8 miles.*

She turned around and headed back, wondering if she might meet Will on the road. She would recognize him immediately, although she hadn't seen him in nearly four years. She glanced at her closely cropped hair in the mirror. He, of course, would be less likely to recognize her.

William Woodburn Fraser. When they were in college she had teased him once about his middle name being the same as his hometown.

"Why were you named after a town?" she'd asked.

He laughed. "It's the other way around," he said.

The truck was still parked in the drive beside Woodburn Hall, and Ava wondered if it might be Will's. She felt a slight cramp of nervousness in her stomach. Driving slowly along River Road toward the house from this angle, she could see that it was actually quite deep, with a long wing that extended back from the less-imposing facade.

She was tempted, for a moment, to drive past. To keep going. At the last minute she swung into the drive and pulled slowly up behind the truck. She parked and sat staring up at the house.

Will had explained to her that it was his great-great-great-great-grandfather's summer cottage, built in the early years of the nineteenth century as a retreat. The planters and their families had come to town to socialize and to escape the yellow fever that raged on the plantations in July.

"Some cottage," she said now to Clotilde.

The apprehension she had felt on the road caused her stomach to quake. She thought, *What am I doing here?*

Staring up at the house, she found herself wondering why Will had asked her to come, why he had seemed so intent on having her visit him in his own surroundings. It bothered her that she had not posed this question before. She had been so befuddled over her own life that she had not stopped to think about him: his motivations, his desires, the way he might see her. She hoped he had not misread her acceptance of his invitation. She hoped this would not be the end of a perfectly good friendship.

But then the back door swung open and he was coming down the steps to greet her, broad-shouldered and smiling, and she grinned and thought, *It'll be okay.*

He had filled out in the four years since she had seen him last. The change suited him. She had forgotten how good-looking he was, or perhaps this was something she had never, for some reason, noticed. She was sorry now that she had cut her hair. *He'll think I'm plain,* she thought.

"I like your hair," he said, giving her a brief, fierce hug.

"I had a moment of insanity," she said, running her fingers self-consciously through the short spikes.

"No, really. It suits you."

She went around to the trunk of the car to get her suitcase.

"Here, let me get that," he said. He had noticed the vase in the passenger seat; she saw his eyes flicker curiously over Clotilde's final resting place, but he said nothing.

She stood with her hands shielding her eyes, staring up at the house. "This is some cottage," she said. Her attention was caught by a slight movement at one of the upstairs windows, an arm drawing aside a curtain, but when she looked again, it was gone, and the curtain was still.

He closed the trunk. "We can get everything else later, once you're settled." He wore a blue shirt, rolled at the sleeves, and his hair curled damply against his collar.

"They're all waiting for you in the library," he said, and she thought she detected a slight nervousness in his voice.

She followed him up a brick sidewalk and a short flight of stairs, into a narrow screened porch that ran across the back of the house. A door to the left opened into the kitchen, and a door to the right opened into a small bedroom that had once served as the cook's room. All this Will told her as they climbed the stairs. He seemed to be trying to put her at ease, speaking in that low, pleasant voice he used with her sometimes. Or perhaps it was himself he was trying to put at ease. He explained that Fanny and Josephine were waiting for them, as was Fanny's husband, Maitland. All three she had met at his graduation from Bard. They had also invited Clara McGann and Alice Barron, both childhood friends and neighbors of the aunts, to come over later.

"You'll like them," he assured her.

"How long does the drinking go on?"

He grinned at her over his shoulder. "You mean Toddy Time? It ends precisely at six o'clock and then there's supper."

She grinned. "Served by liveried footmen, no doubt."

"You've been reading too many romance novels. There are no liveried footmen, no servants at all, I'm afraid." He opened a pair of French doors that led into the main hall. The doors were quite tall, and the top halves were made with long wavy sheets of heavy glass. They looked like they might have come from a country house in Provence.

"Gracious, you're not bringing her in the back way, are you?" someone called out.

Will closed the doors behind them. He put his hand on her back as if to steady her. His touch was warm, pleasant, mannerly. Authoritative in a quietly masculine way.

They stood in a center hallway that ran from the front door to the screened porch at the back. The hall was wide enough for various pieces of heavy antique furniture. Stepping into the house was like stepping into Alice's looking glass; all scale and proportion seemed off. Viewed from the outside the house did not seem so extensive and imposing, but the interior was very large and grand, with high ceilings and spacious, ornately furnished rooms opening off the expansive center hallway. Scattered oriental rugs deadened their footsteps as they walked along the darkly polished, wide-planked floor. The house was very stately and well cared for, and yet there was a certain chill to the air, Ava noticed, an uneasy sensation that old houses sometimes convey, of ancient tragedy and loss.

"They're here, they're here!" someone cried, and a moment later, Fanny burst through one of the doorways and came hurrying down the hallway, her hands fluttering around her skirt like a covey of rising doves. Her red-gold hair was cut in a stylish bob, and she looked even younger than Ava remembered, with her pale skin and large gray eyes. Ava had no time to examine her further, for she found herself pulled suddenly into a fragrant embrace. "We're so glad you've come," Fanny said in her ear, then stepped back, squeezing Ava's hands before letting them go.

"Thank you for having me," Ava said. She suddenly remembered the gift basket. "Oh, wait, I have something for you in the car."

"Don't worry about that right now," Fanny said, taking Ava's arm and steering her down the hallway.

"Come and have a drink," Josephine called.

She was sitting on a long sofa in the library and she rose, smiling, her eyes resting lightly on Ava's face, and yet managing to encompass all of her in that glance, from the tips of her toes to the ends of her short spiky hair. "We're so glad you could come," she murmured, putting her hand out to Ava. Her skin was cool and smooth to the touch. Like her sister, she was slim, and her hair was cut stylishly, although she did not color it, and it curved like two snowy wings on either side of her handsome face.

"And who's this pretty thing?" Maitland bellowed, standing beside a tall sideboard laden with decanters and glassware and a silver cocktail shaker. He strode quickly across the room, pulling Ava into a clumsy embrace and kissing her loudly on both cheeks.

"Oh, Mait, don't crush her!" Fanny cried but he only laughed and said, "I kiss all the pretty girls!" His accent was nearly unintelligible to Ava, much more hurried and softly rounded than the aunts', as if he spoke through a mouthful of marbles. He was stylishly dressed in pleated trousers and a blue shirt. He wore a sport coat and a tie, and a pair of leather loafers.

He rubbed his hands together fiercely. "Now, what can I get you?" he said to Ava, indicating the decanters on the sideboard.

They were drinking something call a Gin Rickey, which Ava gathered from their conversation they had learned to drink in the twenties up at Vanderbilt. "We made it in the bathtub," Fanny said gaily, lifting her rocks glass.

"We didn't make it," Josephine said mildly. "We bought it from bootleggers who did. It was during Prohibition."

Ava looked around the room in astonishment. "You went to college in the nineteen-twenties?" she said.

"I was sixteen when I went up to Vanderbilt in 1927," Josephine said. "In those days you finished high school at sixteen."

Ava stared blankly at Josephine. "But that would make you—"

"Oh, I know. Don't say it," Fanny cried.

"Eighty-seven," Josephine finished serenely. "Fanny is eighty-five and Maitland is eighty-seven."

"But none of you look a day over seventy," Ava said, and Will laughed nervously.

"Up at Sewanee we drank Singapore Slings," Maitland said, and it was not too hard to imagine him as a college boy dressed in white bucks and a coonskin coat. He had the look of a perpetual college boy about him, jovial and outgoing. He was perched on the arm of a low sofa, sitting next to Fanny, who had her knees crossed, her drink resting on her lap. She had remarkable legs for a woman her age, astonishingly good legs. Josephine sat at the opposite end, the hand holding her drink resting lightly on the raised arm of the sofa. Both aunts wore tailored skirts and blouses and, looking down at her jeans and flip-flops, Ava felt badly underdressed.

She sat down in a wingback chair, trying desperately to drink her Gin Rickey, and looked around the spacious library. All her life she had wanted a room like this. Floor-to-ceiling bookshelves of a light blonde color stood along three walls, and a massive fireplace stood in the middle of the fourth paneled wall. All the furniture in the room was pulled away from the walls so one could reach the shelves unimpeded. There were literally hundreds of books; a sliding ladder on a rail allowed access to the very top shelves.

"What a wonderful room," Ava said.

"Are you a reader?" Josephine asked.

"Oh, yes."

"So was Papa," Fanny said. "He and Josephine used to sit for hours in here on a rainy day with their noses buried in some dusty book. Now Will and I," she said, looking fondly at Will, who was seated in a leather club chair across from Ava. "We were never too fond of reading. Board games and jigsaw puzzles were our favorite ways to spend rainy days."

"And what do you do on rainy days?" Ava asked Maitland.

"I mix the drinks."

She smiled and lifted her Gin Rickey in acknowledgment. Ava was not a big drinker—she preferred red wine when she drank anything—but she didn't want to hurt Maitland's feelings. He seemed to take his duties as cocktail master seriously.

"So Vanderbilt accepted women in the twenties?" she asked. Despite the cheerful appearance of the rows and rows of books, she was struck again by an odd, fleeting sense of melancholy. Houses have personalities just like people, she had learned in her years of traveling, and this one felt somber and dispirited. More like Thornfield Hall than Pemberley House.

"Oh, before that," Josephine said. "In the eighteen-eighties, actually. They were very progressive."

"Although women were not awarded degrees," Fanny said. "At least not initially. They were allowed to audit classes but no degrees were conferred."

Ava pretended to sip her drink. "It must have been unusual for women in your generation to attend college."

"It wasn't unusual for women of our—" Fanny began and then stopped, and Josephine finished smoothly, "It wasn't unusual for women in our family, our friends, to attend college."

"It's amazing how much has changed over the last hundred years," Ava said. "Women's liberation, the Civil Rights movement, the improvements in science and technology." She was rambling; she always did that when she was nervous, and it often ended badly, with her saying something inappropriate or pointless.

The others stared past her, their faces fixed in polite expressions.

"I often feel that our forefathers must be turning in their graves," Josephine said, lifting her glass to Maitland, who was pouring refills.

Fanny, who had been smiling at Ava with a dreamy expression, said, "You have the loveliest hair. Were your people Scottish?"

"My people?" Ava said.

"Your family," Will said.

"Oh. Well, actually, I don't know a lot about my family. My parents came from Detroit originally. I think. My mother's maiden name was

Govan, which sounds Irish, but I really don't know. She never spoke of her family. Dabrowski has to be Polish." She smiled at Maitland but indicated that she didn't need a refill.

"Polish!" Fanny said. "How lovely! I don't think I've ever known anyone who was Polish."

Ava turned her attention to one of the framed photographs on the coffee table. They seemed to be waiting for her to say something else and when she didn't, Josephine turned her head and spoke to Maitland in a low voice about supper.

There were photographs everywhere, on all the tables in the room and on the bookshelves; the paneled wall around the fireplace was covered in them. Ava stood up and slowly made her way around the room clutching her unfinished drink in her hand, stopping to peer at the images. Some were in color but most were in black and white. A good many were of Fanny and Maitland in their younger days: standing in front of Niagara Falls, landing in a seaplane on Puget Sound, on the beach at Cannes, sitting in a café in Provence. Their life together seemed to have involved a great deal of travel. And drinking. There were photos of them in the Adirondacks, a cocktail table displayed prominently in the foreground; Maitland dressed in evening clothes holding a cocktail shaker and two glasses; Fanny, in a very short skirt, balancing a martini glass on her nose. Mixed in with the gay travel photos were Victorian family portraits: sepia-tinted prints of somber, bearded men and women in long white dresses and huge hats. Ava picked up a photo of three young girls, startling in their prettiness and resemblance to one another. They wore white dresses and large bows in their hair, which fell in ringlets down their backs.

"My sisters and I," Josephine said. "Celia, the baby, was Will's grandmother. She died when Will's mother was still a girl."

"She was lovely," Ava said. "You were all lovely."

"Oh, don't look at those old things," Fanny said. "It was so long ago I can scarcely remember."

"Not so long ago as all that," Maitland said gallantly, and Fanny, pleased, gave him a coquettish smile. They were so sweet with each other, married all this time and still acting like newlyweds. Ava hoped she would be so lucky. As if reading her thoughts, Will, sitting across the room with his empty glass resting on one knee, caught her eye and smiled.

She picked up another photo, this one of a young woman dressed in a shimmering dress, her hair parted smoothly and coiled at the nape of her neck. She was very slender and lovely, but her eyes were cold, and there was a haughty expression on her face, as if she knew and disapproved of the photographer. Ava recognized Josephine, a much younger Josephine, her chin tilted slightly upward, eyes heavy-lidded, caught somewhere between an expression of boredom and reproach.

At that moment there was the sound of a door closing and then a female voice called out, "Hello! Anybody home?"

"We're in here," Will called; he and Maitland stood and a moment later two women appeared in the doorway. They were both well dressed and appeared to be roughly the same age as the aunts, and Ava was struck again by the smooth, beautiful complexions of these Southern women. It made her wonder if there was a mysterious Fountain of Youth hidden somewhere on the grounds, something secretive and transforming known only to the women.

Will introduced Ava to Alice Barron and Clara McGann. Alice was Maitland's widowed sister, and she lived next door with her son, Fraser. "I grew up with these two," Alice said, indicating Fanny and Josephine. "We were girls together."

"We were all girls together," Clara said. Her skin was a pale mocha color, and her eyes were green. She held Ava's hand for a moment, gazing at her curiously. "The resemblance is remarkable," she said.

"I noted it when she first came in," Josephine said.

"What?" Fanny said, excited by their tone. "Her resemblance to whom?"

"Delphine," Alice said.

"Who's Delphine?" Ava said.

"My great-great-great-great-grandmother," Will said.

They took her into the dining room to show her the oil painting of Delphine Woodburn. She was dark-haired and dark-eyed, and Ava saw little resemblance between them but she was too polite to say anything.

"She was French," Alice said to Ava. "Are you French?"

"No," Josephine said. "Polish. And Irish."

"Well, I don't really know what I am," Ava began lamely, feeling her face flush. "I didn't know it mattered."

"It doesn't," Will said quickly.

"Randal married her in 1816 and brought her here from New Orleans," Josephine said. Behind Josephine's shoulder, on the wall facing her, Ava could see the portrait of Randal Woodburn, the patriarch. He was an exceedingly handsome man, with pale eyes beneath heavy brows and a wide, sensuous mouth. His hair was worn long over a high, starched collar, and his shoulders were wide beneath his buttoned coat. He was the very picture of masculine virility, yet there was something about his face, a hint of cruelty about the eyes, that Ava didn't like.

"They were devoted to each other," Josephine said, gazing at Randal's portrait.

"She bore him sixteen children," Alice said.

"Oh, everyone loves a good love story, don't they?" Fanny said brightly, her eyes resting briefly on Maitland.

"Look at us, chattering like a bunch of old women while this child is probably bored to tears," Clara said, sliding her arm around Ava's waist and leading her back to the library. "That's all we old folks have left, our stories."

"Oh, I like stories," Ava said.

Behind her, Josephine said quietly, "You've come to the right place then."

After supper Will showed her to her room and helped her get her things settled. He brought in her box of books and her laptop, and she brought Clotilde, setting her on the mantel beneath a painting of red-coated hunters on the trail of a fox. The horses were all drawn with the small, sleek heads and long, tapering limbs common to the nineteenth-century style, and the human figures, too, seem disproportionate.

Will noted her careful positioning of Clotilde's vase on the mantel, but again he said nothing, sliding his eyes away politely as he began to unpack her books. She liked that about him, that although he seemed curious about her, he did not push her to confide in him. He was patient. He seemed content to let her make the first move.

The aunts and Clara and Alice had no such qualms. They had questioned Ava relentlessly over supper, although they were so good at it, so discreet at making inquiries in an offhand, roundabout way, that Ava did not realize until the interrogation was over that she had been thoroughly cross-examined. She was not one to spill her guts to strangers, yet in the space of less than an hour she had confessed much of her dysfunctional gypsy childhood, the fact that she had been raised without religion, had never known her father, had had a series of unfortunate love affairs, and although relatively well educated, had wound up in a job she detested. By the time they rose from the table, Ava felt as if she'd been prodded and poked by unseen fingers. She also felt that Josephine and Alice, in their subtle investigation of her past, had found her somewhat lacking.

"Through that door is a small office I thought you might use," Will said, pointing to a door she had mistaken for a closet. It stood between the fireplace and a glass-fronted secretary filled with rows and rows of leather-bound books. The room they stood in was far grander than any bedroom Ava had ever slept in. A tall four-poster bed flanked by a mahogany armoire and a lowboy chest stood against one wall, opposite the fireplace. At one end, long shuttered windows overlooked the garden.

"Actually, I thought I might set my laptop up here," Ava said, pointing to a table and a pair of leather chairs that stood in front of the windows.

"The light will be better," he agreed. "And you'll have a nice view of the garden."

"Yes." Ava strolled over, peering between the slats. She had noticed the wrought-iron fence when they came up the back steps, but in the dim light of early dusk she could see now that it surrounded a garden that was very wide and deep, set back from the side porch across a patch of lawn.

"Your great-aunts must have green thumbs," Ava said. Swift black shapes flitted across the lawn. *Bats,* she thought.

"It's mainly Clara. She loves to garden."

"Oh?" She turned and looked at him in surprise. "Does she live here, too?"

"No. She lives in a cottage behind the property." He set her laptop down on the table and stacked her books on one corner. "The closet is here," he said, opening a corner cupboard. "It's small, of course, because these old houses were built without closets. They were all added later." He walked over and opened the door to the adjoining office. "Feel free to store anything you don't need in here. My great-grandfather, Colonel James Woodburn, used it as an office. He was Josephine and Fanny's father."

She followed him into the narrow, paneled room. At one end a long window overlooked the garden and at the other end, a door opened into the center hallway of the house. An old-fashioned desk with a drop front and various cubbyholes stood along one wall, topped by a glass cabinet filled with large leather-bound books.

She was aware suddenly of the close atmosphere of the room and the fact that the two of them seemed to fill it so completely.

"It's claustrophobic in here," he said apologetically, stepping aside so she could edge her way over to the desk. "I hadn't realized that. It was used as an office, although at one time I'm guessing it was a dressing room. I thought it would be a quiet place to write."

She opened the cabinet and took out one of the books, realizing that they were journals, each with dates written in a flowing script.

"Those are the farm journals," he said, "kept by the owners of Longford, the first Woodburns in the county. In those days farmers kept journals to use as guides for planting and harvesting." *Farm. Farmers.*

She noted how careful he was not to use the words *plantation* and *planters*.

The date on the first one read *1826*. "Oh, my God," she said, opening it reverently. "I can't believe you have treasures like this just lying around."

He grinned. "It's my aunts' doing, I'm afraid. The whole house is like a museum, but they won't part with any of it. They like their old things around them."

"I don't blame them."

"No?" he said, giving her a mocking, tender smile.

She peered intently at one of the entries, trying to read the archaic script. The words came suddenly into view, seeming to leap off the yellowed paper.

November 4th. Clear and cold. Commenced digging slips around 8 a.m. Got in 4 banks of leathercoats, pumpkin, Spanish and reds.

The baby was quite sick this morning. Gave her a little vitriol. Captain D. Sinclair stopped and took tea with me. Heard that James Fraser's child died of scarlet fever.

"The ledgers used to be kept at Longford, but after Reconstruction the family moved into town. Longford was rented out to tenant farmers and that's why the books were moved here."

"When am I going to see Longford?"

"Tomorrow, if you like. I thought we'd go after breakfast."

She looked up at him, returning his smile. "I'd like that." She closed the ledger and slid it carefully back onto the shelf. "You don't mind if I read some of these, do you?"

"Of course not. Read anything you want, although you'll probably find more to your liking in the library."

"Trust me, I'll see plenty of the library. The trouble will be pulling me away so I can get some work done."

"I'll do my best to keep you on track." He leaned over and kissed her cheek, a very chaste and brotherly kiss. She followed him out into the bedroom, shutting the office door behind her.

"If you get bored there's a TV in the library," he said.

"Thanks. But I'll be too busy exploring this incredible house to get bored."

He stopped in the doorway, his hand on the jamb. "And don't worry about the aunts. They know you're here to write and they'll leave you alone. No one will bother you."

Despite her intention to explore the house, Ava was tired, and after Will left she went into the bathroom at the end of the hall to get ready for bed. Coming out into the darkened hallway, she stood for a moment listening to the gentle sighs and creaks of the old house settling around her. The front porch lights were on, falling through the fanlight and dimly illuminating the front half of the hall. The back half was cloaked in shadow. Above her she could hear the distant thuds of Maitland and Fanny and Josephine readying themselves for bed.

She went into her brightly lit bedroom, wandering around and peering at the treasures she found there, snuffboxes and ceramic thimbles and oil paintings of ancient hunting scenes: dogs with brightly feathered birds in their mouths, and men on horseback in pursuit of some hapless fox.

She stopped at the mantel, looking around her.

The room reflected pleasure and comfort and social prominence. It reeked of old money.

"I wish you could see me now," she said aloud to Clotilde.

Not that Clotilde would have been impressed, of course. Clotilde was never impressed by material possessions. "They're just things, Ava," she always said when Ava exclaimed over some rich classmate's house. "They don't matter in the end."

And yet some things had mattered. Clothes, for instance. No matter how broke they were, Clotilde always saw to it that they were well dressed. She disdained bargain department stores in favor of Junior

League thrift shops, where they could pick up last year's good-quality clothes, some barely worn, for a fraction of what they cost new. Anyone looking at them would never have guessed how they lived.

It was the heavy material trappings that Clotilde had cared nothing for: a house, furniture of their own, a car with less than 200,000 miles. She had died with a closet full of beautiful clothes and less than two hundred dollars in the bank. She had left behind a rusty Subaru, a stack of unpaid bills, and a shoebox filled with relics.

She had died alone.

Ava felt a sharp cramp in her stomach. She stretched her hands out on either side of the vase, grasping the mantel and looking down at her feet, waiting for the spasm of pity and remorse to pass.

She dreamed that night that she was skating on a frozen lake. The air was cold and prickly against her face, and she was flying over the ice like a bird, hurrying away from some danger she couldn't see but could only vaguely sense. Behind her the ice was cracking, shifting, and she knew that whatever was chasing her was near. She could feel it breathing on her neck. Startled, she pressed on, but she found now that her legs felt heavy and her feet felt as if they were being slowly encased in ice. She struggled with the rising chill that seemed to be overtaking her, and as she did, she looked down in horror at her feet.

There beneath the rippled surface of the ice, a face stared back at her.

She awoke with a start. Moonlight flooded the room, falling between the slats of the shuttered windows. In the distance, a train rumbled mournfully. The horror of the dream gradually faded, and she turned her head repeatedly, assuring herself that it was just a dream and nothing more. Only a dream.

She turned her head and studied the massive mahogany furniture of the room. "Made by the people on Longford," Josephine had told her.

Not *slaves,* but *people.* The word *people* down here carried some kind of tribal significance. What was it they had asked her? "Where do your people come from?" As if Ava, who barely knew her own mother, who knew nothing of her father, should be able to explain the whereabouts of her ancestors. Southerners, who had stayed in the same small town for generations, seemed to take it for granted that the experiences of the rest of the country would mirror those of their own narrow world. No, not Southerners. She knew too few of them to be able to make such sweeping generalizations. Woodburns. *Landed gentry.* She had read about them in English novels but had never, until this evening, understood exactly what the term, with all its historical and socioeconomic connotations, meant. The Woodburns were like something from a Jane Austen novel.

No, not Austen, she thought, remembering the face under the ice.

One of the Brontë sisters, more likely.

When she awoke again it was nearly nine o'clock. Sunlight flooded the room, falling between the window slats and making geometric patterns on the dark floor. There was a scent of coffee and frying bacon in the air, and Ava could hear movement deep within the house, the clinking of china and silverware.

Coming out of her room, she stood for a moment in the sunny hallway, listening to the muffled sounds of the house. The lingering sense of melancholy she had felt yesterday seemed to have dissipated in the bright sunlight. The house seemed even more splendid than it had last night. Will had given her a tour, and she had passed in openmouthed amazement from room to room, but seen now in the brilliance of a summer morning, the shutters open, light flooding the large rooms and pooling against the darkly polished floors, Ava was amazed anew at the stunning elegance of the old house.

The ceilings on the first floor were twelve feet high and trimmed with ornate plasterwork. At one end of the wide central hallway, near the front door, a graceful staircase rose to the second floor. The rooms opening off the central hallway were expansive and filled with antique furniture, most of it in the Empire style. Oil portraits of dead ancestors hung on the walls. All the interior doors were massive, eight feet tall and nearly four feet wide. ("Wide enough so ladies in their hoop skirts could pass through," Josephine had told Ava.) They were solid mahogany and, like the furniture, had been made at Longford. Oriental carpets covered the dark heart pine floors. A massive French gilt mirror graced one of the walls of the hallway, a place where the women of the house used to stand to check their wide skirts before venturing out. "If only that mirror could talk," Fanny had said gaily to Ava, "what stories it could tell!"

She walked slowly through the dining room beneath the watchful eyes of Randal and Delphine, stopping to look at the many objects of interest. Along one wall, built-in glass-fronted cabinets housed an extensive collection of sterling silver. Several smaller sideboards held silver tea trays, jam pots, and ornate obsolete utensils. She stopped and peered at a gilt-framed letter hanging on a wall between two long windows. The script was barely legible but the signature was vaguely familiar.

As if sensing her presence, Will came through the butler's pantry, whistling cheerfully. "Good morning," he said.

"Morning." She turned her attention back to the letter, tapping the glass with one finger. "Thomas Jefferson," she said. "I recognized the signature. This is a very good replica."

He smiled faintly, an apologetic yet vaguely defiant smile. "That's no replica," he said. "He and my great-grandfather Randal were friends."

She stared in amazement, then turned and followed him through the butler's pantry into the sunny kitchen.

Josephine was standing at the sink, an apron tied around her narrow waist. "There you are," she said, as if she had been waiting for Ava. She was wearing a pair of yellow rubber gloves. "Are you hungry?"

"Yes," Ava said, surprised. "I am." She never ate breakfast in Chicago—she usually wasn't hungry until lunch—but the delicious smells had awakened in her a ravenous appetite.

"There's a plate for you on the stove. And coffee in the percolator." Josephine nodded at the gleaming pot on the counter, glancing at Ava's bare feet.

"Good morning!" Fanny called brightly. She, Clara, and Alice were sitting in the small sunny breakfast room off the kitchen. A large tabby cat slept on Fanny's lap. Ava poured herself a cup of coffee and, collecting her plate, went to join them.

Will pulled out a chair for her and then sat down beside her. He seemed shy around her this morning. Attentive but unsure of himself. She was awkward, too, looking at the long-limbed man beside her and trying to remember the boy she'd known in college. She remembered the brotherly kiss he had given her and the jaunty way he had said goodnight.

"We're being lazy," Fanny said, stroking the cat, but Ava noted that they were all dressed except for her. Fanny wore a blue dress and Clara wore a pair of jeans and a red sweater. Ava was still in flannel shorts and a faded T-shirt, her usual sleeping attire.

"Sorry," Ava said, running her fingers through her hair and glancing around the table. "I'm not really a morning person."

"You're on vacation," Will said. "You're entitled to sleep in if you want to."

They had set a place for her, although it was clear that everyone else had finished breakfast some time ago. The table was cleared except for their coffee mugs and a pair of silver jam pots that Alice placed in front of Ava with a faint smile. Alice wore a coral-colored tennis warm-up with a flower-shaped diamond brooch on one lapel. Her dark blonde hair was cut close around her narrow face.

"As long as I don't make it a habit," Ava said. She had planned on rising early and finishing the outline for her new novel, a coming-of-age story about a girl and her mother traveling around the Midwest, before heading out to Longford with Will.

"It's going to be a scorcher," Fanny said, staring out the window. "Why, I can't remember a time when it's been this hot in May unless it was that summer all those years ago when the strange insects dropped out of the trees and the river was swollen with the rains. You remember, Sister. The summer of—" She stopped, a curious expression on her face.

"Yes," Josephine said quickly. "I remember."

"We thought we might take a drive," Will said to the table at large. "Out to Longford."

"Such a pretty day for a drive," Fanny said. Alice and Clara looked at Fanny and she blushed suddenly, a deep crimson color.

Josephine stood in the doorway, wiping her hands on her apron. "Try the blackberry jam," she said to Ava. "It's made locally."

Ava ate while the other four women talked quietly about an upcoming barbecue. Will stared out the large windows, his hand curled casually around an empty coffee cup. He had told her last night that he was renovating Longford, trying to update the house while remaining true to the architectural period. Upon being further pressed as to what he did for a living (she gathered from his demeanor that this wasn't something she should have asked), he admitted that he flipped the occasional house and had been involved for some time in a local company that manufactured parachutes. He had sold that business, he told her, when he began the renovations on Longford. The reality, of course, was that he didn't have to do anything and they both knew it.

"It won't take me long to get ready," Ava said to him, spreading her toast with blackberry jam.

"I'm in no hurry." He gave her a brief smile and then glanced up at Josephine, who remained standing in the doorway. "Aunt Jo, do you think those blueprints might be up in the attic?"

"The plans for Longford? Possibly. I know there was a set that was given with the family papers to Vanderbilt. But there are still several old trunks and boxes I haven't had time to go through."

He rose, touching Ava lightly on the shoulder. "I'll be back," he said. He walked through the butler's pantry into the dining room and a moment later they could hear his footsteps on the stairs.

"The attic?" Ava said, looking around with interest. Outside the breakfast room window, a profusion of hydrangea blooms pressed against the glass panes.

"Don't go up there," Fanny said, shuddering so that the cat opened its eyes and regarded Ava lazily. "It's a morbid place."

"One of our ancestors was a doctor," Josephine said before Fanny could say anything else. "You can still see the outline of the staircase that once stood at the rear of the house. He used to occasionally see patients up there."

"He was an anatomist," Alice said. "A vivisectionist."

"He was a man of science," Josephine said. "Of natural curiosity. And in those days anatomy was a relatively new field of study. An unpleasant thing to be talking about at any time but especially over the breakfast table." She glanced severely at Alice and Fanny as if to put an end to the discussion.

"I can't imagine why he was allowed to perform his grisly experiments in the house," Clara said, ignoring her. "That's the part I've never understood, why Randal and Delphine would have allowed that."

"Experiments?" Ava said.

"Dissections." Fanny shivered again and the cat arched his back and yawned.

"It was illegal in those days," Alice said. "Dissection. He had to pay grave robbers to bring him bodies in the middle of the night."

"Resurrection men," Clara said.

"Oh, for goodness' sake!" Josephine said, one of the veins in her temple showing blue against her pale skin.

"He was one of Randal and Delphine's two sons who survived," Fanny explained blithely to Ava. "Great-Uncle Jerome. Out of sixteen children, they only had four who lived to adulthood. Great-Uncle Jerome, Grandfather Isaac, Great-Aunt Louisa, and Great-Aunt Sophia."

"That's terrible," Ava said.

"Not so uncommon in those days," Alice said.

"I was terrified of the attic," Fanny said, stroking the cat and staring pensively through the window. "Papa used to keep it locked. We weren't allowed to play up there. It was above the nursery where Josephine and Celia and I used to sleep as girls, and at night I could hear things moving around up there."

"Oh, Fanny!" Josephine said, glancing sharply at her. "You were always so fanciful as a girl."

Fanny tilted her head with a mildly surprised expression. "Was I?" she said.

Ava chewed her toast, aware suddenly of an undercurrent of tension in the room. She thought of the nightmare that had awakened her in the middle of the night, but like all nightmares it had already begun to fade, and she could remember only snatches of it now, a fleeting impression of fear and speed and glittering water.

"Listen to us going on about things that happened so long ago as if it were only yesterday," Josephine said briskly, taking off her apron and folding it neatly over the back of a chair.

"You'll have to get used to that in this house," Clara said to Ava, patting her hand. "The past mixed up with the present."

"I don't mind," Ava said.

As if to change the subject, Josephine said, "Will tells us you're a writer."

Ava coughed lightly and put her fist to her mouth. It was the moment she had come to dread, her stilted confession of being a writer, followed by the inevitable moment of silence and then the bright retort, "Oh, really! What do you write?" She could never seem to pull it off.

"I'm working on a novel," she said. "A coming-of-age story set partially in Chicago."

"How wonderful," Josephine said.

"I do love a good English mystery," Alice said. "Murder in the rose garden by the crazy vicar, that sort of thing."

"Agatha Christie is good," Clara agreed. "But Zora Neale Hurston, now she could tell a story."

Fanny, who had been sitting quietly, said abruptly, "You know Zelda

Sayre was a writer." They all looked at her. She smiled at Ava. "She was a distant cousin of ours on our mother's side. Zelda was such a lovely girl, so full of life and laughter and high spirits! Sister visited them in Paris in '29"—here Fanny glanced at Josephine—"and found Zelda very much changed."

"I shouldn't wonder," Alice said darkly. "Married to that scoundrel."

"Wait just a minute." Ava held up one finger. She shook her head delicately. "Zelda Sayre? Are you talking about Zelda and *F. Scott Fitzgerald*? As in *The Great Gatsby*? As in *Tender Is the Night*?"

Fanny put the cat down and stood up, and a few minutes later she was back with a photograph of an unsmiling Josephine dressed in a fur-collared coat and a cloche hat, standing next to Zelda and F. Scott Fitzgerald in front of a Paris café. The Fitzgeralds looked small and chastened beside the tall and somber Josephine, as if her presence diminished them in some way. Ava stared at the photograph in amazement, trying to fathom the Woodburn legacy: a house filled with antiques and memorabilia most museums would envy; a family history of wealth and privilege tied to the same landscape for generations; dazzling family connections.

Once, in a moment of unexpected candor, Clotilde had told Ava the true story of how she and Ava's father, Frank, had met. She had told Ava a hundred different versions of this event but somehow this one felt like truth. They had met on a Boblo boat during a cruise on Polka Night. The boat was on its way to Boblo Island, an amusement park in the middle of the Detroit River, and her mother had gone with a friend to hear Mitch Ryder and the Detroit Wheels. Frank was there with friends from the line at Ford where he worked and he asked her to dance and later escorted her around the park, where they rode the Wild Maus and the Super-Satellite Jet. Clotilde told her, "I didn't even like him at first. He had big feet, and his hands smelled of lemon soap. But he was persistent and he wore me down eventually."

It was that detail of the lemon soap that had given the story its authenticity. Clotilde was a palm reader, and Ava could imagine her flipping Frank's hand over to peruse its secrets. Picturing this, Ava had felt a sudden dizzying awareness of her parents as they must have been at that time in their young, hopeful lives. She had visualized the two of them, good-looking and wary, the whir of the giant machinery, the lights glittering on the water, the distant strident sounds of the band.

At that moment her imagined life, intertwined with the lives of these two strangers, had felt fateful and expansively heroic. But now, looking down at Josephine standing next to Zelda and F. Scott Fitzgerald, she could see what a small, inconsequential thing her family history really was.

"Zelda was the better writer of the two," Alice said. "That was the tragedy of the whole thing. She was the better writer, and his jealousy drove her to have a series of—spells."

"Nervous spells," Fanny said.

"Spells?" Ava said, looking from one to the other.

"All the old families are prone to them," Josephine said serenely.

The Tale-Tell Heart

It was a beautiful morning, sunny but not too warm, when they started out for Longford. Will drove so that he could show her "the scenic route." The farther they got from Woodburn Hall, the more his mood seemed to lift. They drove through the shady streets of the old town, the very streets Ava had driven just a day before, and he pointed out sites of interest: the first African-American school in the county, a house with a cannonball still visibly lodged in its outer wall, a leftover from a Civil War skirmish known as the Battle of Harpeth Hill. From time to time, in between showing her the elementary school he had attended or the creek where he first learned to fish for crawdads, he remarked quietly, "It's a great place to raise a family."

He was proud of his hometown, Ava could see, and she regretted now the times she and Michael had teased him at Bard about being from Hambone, Tennessee, the Chitlin' Capital of the South. He had taken their teasing with a great deal of good-natured resignation but she realized now, having witnessed the courteous way Southerners treated one another, that he must have been appalled by their lack of manners and knowledge of geography.

They turned onto the highway and crossed the bridge over the river, following the route Ava had taken earlier.

"This is the old road to Longford," he said. "It used to take almost a day of hard traveling by wagon to get to town. Now it only takes ten minutes."

She stared at the green fields and the distant rim of blue mountains. "What's a vivisectionist?"

He glanced at her and then back at the road, his expression a mix of annoyance and mild amusement. "I see you've been talking to the aunts about Great-Uncle Jerome."

"They've been filling me in on some of the sordid family history. So what's a vivisectionist?"

"Someone who dissects living organisms to see how they work. In the 1840s dissection of a human body was illegal, so doctors had to make do with what they could scrounge up—dogs, cats, birds."

Ava said, "Isn't that what serial killers do?"

He laughed, and she was glad to see laugh lines crinkling the corners of his eyes. She was anxious to recapture some of the free and easy camaraderie she had felt with him at Bard. He had seemed like such a good sport to her then: shy, self-conscious, but intelligent and quietly humorous, too. The kind of guy she never would have fallen for in college.

In college she and Michael had teased each other cruelly. He insisted that he could always spot a girl with "daddy issues" because she invariably kept cats. (Ava didn't particularly like cats but she had rescued a big black-and-white feline named Figaro her freshman year). She claimed she could always spot a "good" man by how he treated his mother. (Michael sulked and refused to speak to his mother when she denied him anything. He could go months without talking to her.)

Their relationship had been less like a love affair and more like a fight to the death.

Will had laugh lines around his eyes, but Ava had no way of knowing how he had treated his mother. She had died when he was six. Josephine had been a surrogate mother, he once told Ava. After his parents died and he came to live with the aunts, it was Josephine who helped him with homework, played ball with him in the yard, and volunteered as a den mother for his Cub Scout troop. Fanny and Maitland were always away, traveling the world.

And his conduct toward Josephine, Ava had noted, was one of courteous and respectful affection.

"And why in the world didn't you tell me you were related to Zelda Fitzgerald?"

He gave her a mocking, martyred look. "Oh, God," he said.

"Despite the fact that it is universally accepted that Zelda was crazy as a loon, they seem to prefer to call her breakdowns 'nervous spells.' "

He laughed again. "It's all a matter of perspective," he said.

They had stopped at a railroad crossing at the edge of a soybean field for a slow-moving train. He put the windows down and they sat for a minute listening to the pleasant rumbling, feeling the warmth of the sun on their arms.

He put his head back and closed his eyes. "How do you picture it?" he asked.

"Picture what?"

"Longford."

"Oh, I don't know." She slipped her feet out of her sandals and put them up on the dash, hugging her knees. "Kind of like Tara, I guess. A big white house with columns across the front and girls in hoop skirts on the lawn."

He smiled indulgently, keeping his eyes closed. "Everyone expects Tara," he said.

The train passed and the crossing guard went up. They drove on.

"I hope you won't be disappointed," he said.

In college he had spoken with an almost neutral accent but down here he lapsed into the soft accents of his youth. When they passed a car or truck on the road, he lifted his hand off the steering wheel and waved. It was a small gesture, really, a slight lifting of a couple of fingers, but everyone did it.

"Is that like some kind of secret handshake?" Ava asked him, after they had passed an old man standing at his mailbox and the two of them had exchanged the "wave."

"Just being friendly," Will said. "You'll get used to it."

She told him about the crazy old woman at the gas station who had shared the rambling tale of her father falling off the roof.

He grinned and shook his head. "Down here we don't say 'crazy,' " he said. "We say 'eccentric.' "

Despite his obvious pleasure in showing her the house, he seemed in no particular hurry to reach Longford. They turned off the highway and drove aimlessly down country roads that meandered past fields, roadside vegetable stands, distant farmhouses, and every so often, a new brick ranch house set back from the road in a patch of green lawn. The sun had reached its zenith, and the light had changed to a hazy yellow-green, shimmering and rising off the asphalt in the distance like a mirage. In between the fields and clearings, tall trees lined the road, covered in some type of broad-leafed ivy. The ivy draped from power lines and mounded over the trees and greenery, and Ava was reminded again of the fantastic landscapes of fairy tales and dreams.

"What is that stuff?" she said.

"Kudzu. It covers everything in its path, growing up to a foot a day. They originally brought it in from the Orient to use as cattle feed and for erosion control, and now it covers the South."

"How do you kill it?"

"Goats."

"Goats?"

"They eat it. Frost also kills it. It dies back in the winter, thank God. When I was a boy we used to build forts in there. You can stand up under it and walk for miles. It's like a big green circus tent."

He had left the windows down, and the air was fragrant with the scent of newly mown grass. She had always loved long drives in the country. When she was in high school in Chicago, she had befriended a girl who lived in a large rambling Victorian house close to the University of Chicago. Margaret Stanley's grandfather had started Sentry Insurance, and although they attended the same private Catholic school

(Ava as a scholarship student), Margaret was head and shoulders above Ava, socially and financially. They had met in honors English, bonding over *Beowulf,* and Ava would spend weekends and go for long drives in the country with Margaret and her parents.

Mr. Stanley didn't work. He spent most of his days on the golf course, and Mrs. Stanley spent most of hers shopping or playing bridge or drinking martinis in the kitchen with the maid, Frances. Margaret was an only child. ("Adopted," she confided in Ava, "because Mother is barren.") They giggled over this, making up tragic stories about Margaret's "real" parents, who they called Mr. and Mrs. Ortho Slogett. Mr. Slogett was an alcoholic with a wooden leg who couldn't find work, and Mrs. Slogett was so immensely obese she couldn't get out of bed, and that's why they had given Margaret up for adoption. Ava was good at this; like many children who spend a lot of time alone, she was a natural-born storyteller. And she had by this time settled on her dream of being a writer, although she didn't tell anyone of this, not even Margaret, keeping her dream wrapped up and locked away where she could take it out in private and marvel at its cool, redeeming brilliance.

Ava loved the Stanleys. She loved the casual elegance of their lives: Mrs. Stanley wrapped in a fur coat sipping endless martinis, Mr. Stanley coming in from the golf course with grass stains on his pants and his face ruddy with health and happiness. Trouble did not seem to darken the Stanleys' door; misfortune seemed incapable of finding them. They never worried about debt collectors or paying bills or being evicted. And it seemed to Ava that this was the wonderful thing about having money; not that it could buy you things, but that it kept the wolves at bay. It gave you security and stability. Freed from worry and care, it allowed you to live your life with oblivious abandon, taking everything for granted, even good fortune.

And, oh, what a life they led!

"Daddy, let's go for a ride," Mrs. Stanley would call to Mr. Stanley when he came in from the golf course. Wrapped in her fur, clutching her martini glass with jeweled fingers, she would climb into the front seat of the Lincoln Continental beside Mr. Stanley, and Ava and Margaret would climb into the back. They would drive out into the western suburbs and beyond, out into the country past dairy farms and Catholic shrines, and Mrs. Stanley would pour martinis from a little silver shaker for her and Mr. Stanley, and he would tell them stories of his youth. Sometimes they wouldn't return home until late in the evening and Clotilde would be furious, threatening not to let Ava go anywhere with those "arch-Republican Stanleys." But under Ava's relentless pleading she would eventually give in.

Mrs. Stanley had sized Clotilde up pretty quickly and she would have nothing to do with her, but she seemed genuinely fond of Ava. Ava had the feeling that she would adopt her, too, if given the chance, and she spent a lot of time fantasizing about becoming one of the fabulous Stanleys.

Ava stuck her arm out the window and let it undulate in the wind like a snake fighting a swift current. All along the road were masses of greenery: tulip poplars and hickory trees and wild azaleas. They passed small shotgun houses with cars rusting in the yard and a lone trailer set back from the road beneath a sodium vapor lamp. They passed a boy riding a four-wheeler along a dusty road, and a flock of goats standing in the shade of a sycamore tree.

"All this used to be Woodburn land," Will said.

"It doesn't look very prosperous now."

"The town grew to the north and the west. I suppose that's why the family stopped living out here after the Civil War."

"But they held on to the property?"

"Yes. They rented the land first to sharecroppers and later to big farmers, but after a while the taxes and upkeep got to be too much. The aunts didn't want to sell it. They were afraid it would be snatched up by some big developer and turned into McMansions on postage-stamp-sized lots and that's why they gave it to me."

"Wow. Some gift."

He seemed amused by her reaction. "I inherited it when I turned twenty-one. It was in trust, and as the Colonel's only remaining male heirs, it could have gone to either Sumner or me."

"Who's Sumner?"

"Fanny's son. Her only child."

"So you got the family farm and Sumner didn't? He must really like you."

He smiled ruefully and glanced in the rearview mirror. "He doesn't like any of us much, I'm afraid."

She turned her face to the window. The scattered farmhouses and trailers gave way now to wide rolling fields of alfalfa and soybeans. Far off in the distance the land rose gradually to a prominent ridge crowned by a grove of tall trees.

"Longford," Will said, pointing to the grove.

She couldn't see the house. Even after they turned off the main road onto a narrow paved drive, it was still hidden by the trees. A white fence ran along both sides of the drive, flanked by a row of old oaks.

"This used to be a dirt road," Will said. "They've only recently paved it."

The sun glittered along the windshield as they broke from the trees into a wide grassy clearing. The house was not what she had expected, no thick white columns, no ornate antebellum splendor. Instead it was a rather simple-looking two-story brick house with a white portico across the front. The windows were bare and shutterless.

It was one of the most beautiful houses she had ever seen.

Seeing her expression, Will laughed. "I told you it wasn't Tara."

"It's beautiful," she said.

They got out of the car and stood in the yard. The drive circled in front of the house and ran around the western side to a small graveled parking lot. Beyond the parking lot Ava could see a barn and several scattered log outbuildings, and farther on a grove of trees.

"Come inside," Will said.

A brick sidewalk ran from the parking area to the front of the house. It was very quiet here; no sounds from the modern world broke the stillness of midday. She climbed the stairs and stood beside Will on the porch while he fumbled with the lock, listening to the gentle sighing of the breeze through the trees, the steady chanting of insects in the grass. He turned the key and swung open the front door, stepping aside for her to enter.

Like Woodburn Hall, the house was bisected by a wide central hallway. A graceful staircase coiled upward from the first floor. The rooms opening off either side of the hall were large, with high ceilings and long windows overlooking the fields, but because they were so sparsely furnished, and the windows were clear of shutters and drapes, the light fell through unimpeded. It was marvelous, really, the quality of light slanting through the house. Whereas Woodburn Hall had a slightly damp, melancholy atmosphere, Longford felt bright and welcoming.

I could be happy here, Ava thought.

The walls were painted in various shades of slate blue and cream or covered in faded French wallpaper. Every room contained a fireplace and a marble mantel, and overhead a large brilliant chandelier.

"I'm especially proud of those," Will said, flipping a switch so that the chandelier overhead glittered suddenly with light. "They're original to the house. They were made to hold candles, and I had them taken down and shipped to a place in Memphis that electrified them. It took almost nine months but it was worth it, I think."

"Incredible." She stood in the middle of the room, turning slowly, admiring the way the large gilt-framed mirror over the mantel reflected the light. It seemed to Ava that she could imagine the house as it must have been two hundred years ago, the endless days and the quiet, because that's the thing modern people with their constant noise and hurrying couldn't imagine, the quiet stillness of places like this.

She closed her eyes, struck suddenly by a memory of her mother standing in an empty room. "Do you think that houses soak up the energies of the people who have lived there?"

He stood watching her with an amused, baffled expression on his face. "What do you mean?"

"Do you think there's some kind of residual energy left behind? Voices, emotions, images?"

He laughed. "Do you mean like ghosts? Remember, I was a chemistry major. We have our feet firmly planted in the soil of scientific skepticism."

"You could have just said no," she said.

None of the rooms on the first floor were furnished but upstairs in one of the bedrooms overlooking the fields he had arranged a platform bed and several chests and chairs. A small television sat atop a tall dresser in the corner.

"I pretty much live up here," he said. "In these three rooms."

Despite its collection of furniture, the room still felt large and grand. The bed was very neatly made, and there were no clothes or books or used dishes scattered about. The energy here was slightly different, very left-brained and orderly.

A door to the left led into a large bathroom. At the opposite end of the room was another closed door.

"What's in there?" Ava said, and he hesitated just long enough to make her curious, standing with his hand on the knob. As she approached, he leaned suddenly and threw open the door.

It was a recording studio, complete with several guitars propped on stands, and various amps and speakers scattered around. A computer sat on a narrow table crowded with monitors and microphones, and beside it stood an electric keyboard.

"Wow," Ava said.

"It's just a hobby," he said. "A way to pass the time." He seemed shy again, his face beneath his summer tan flooded with color. Ava guessed he hadn't told many about his music.

"What's that?" she asked politely, pointing.

"An electronic drum kit."

"Do you play all these instruments?"

"Yes. I write the music and then record it."

"Everything?"

"I lay down one track at a time. It gives me more control, and I don't have to depend on anyone else to show up and play." He watched her move around the room. "What are you thinking?" he said.

"I'm thinking you're a very interesting guy."

He wouldn't play anything for her but he did give her a CD, sliding it into her purse. "Listen to it later," he said. "When I'm not around. And then give me your honest opinion."

They went back downstairs into the kitchen, which was the only room in the house that seemed to be undergoing renovation. The walls were stripped down to the lathing, and he had left the old brick of the fireplace exposed. A bank of dilapidated cabinets stood along the back wall, crowded beneath a window overlooking the porch and the distant fields.

"This was added later by one of the tenants, and they did a terrible job," he said, standing in the doorway with his shoulder against the jamb. "When the house was originally built, the kitchen was a separate building out back. They did that to prevent fires."

"When was it built?"

"Randal started construction in 1806 and finished in 1810. There was an old log cabin just to the east of here where he lived until then. There's nothing left now, just an indentation in the earth and what remains of an old stone fireplace. A group of archeology students from Harvard came down a couple of summers ago and excavated the site, as well as some of the other outbuildings. They found all kinds of interesting things: iron nails, buttons, broken pieces of pottery and china."

"I like the way you've left the brick exposed," she said, running her fingers across the rough surface. She went over to the old farmhouse-style sink and flipped on the tap, letting the water run before shutting it off.

"Are you thirsty?" he asked. "Would you like some lunch?"

She turned and leaned against the sink, giving the kitchen a doubtful look. "Should we go back to town and pick something up?"

He grinned and walked over to the back door, swinging it open. Outside on the porch was a table covered by a white linen tablecloth, set with a picnic lunch.

A two-story white columned gallery ran across the back of the house. The bottom floor held a line of rocking chairs and several large pots of flowering plants, as well as the small table where Ava and Will sat enjoying their lunch. Beyond the scattered outbuildings a patchwork of rolling fields, hazy beneath the noonday sun, stretched beneath a wide blue sky.

"This is delicious," Ava said, chewing slowly with her eyes closed. She didn't know what else to say. No one had ever made her a picnic lunch before.

"Uncle Mait made the chicken salad," he said. "It's his grandmother's recipe."

"He's quite the gourmet chef."

"It's his hobby, the way music is mine." He had finished eating and sat watching her with a bemused expression, two fingers tapping softly against the table.

Ava had been surprised that Maitland did most of the cooking. She would have expected a cook or a housekeeper in a house as large as Woodburn Hall, although perhaps Will was right; she had read too many English novels, had watched too many old movies. The aunts had a cleaning service that came once a week but Maitland prepared all the evening meals. He was addicted to the food channel, and would spend long hours watching Bobby Flay whip up Fried Chicken with Ancho Honey or Black Pepper Biscuits with Orange-Blueberry Marmalade. Josephine handled breakfast and lunch.

"And the woman who lives behind the house?" Ava asked hesitantly.

"Clara?"

"Yes. Clara. She never worked for the aunts as a housekeeper or a cook?"

He seemed surprised by her question, a faint frown appearing above his brow. "No. Clara grew up with the aunts. Her mother, Martha, was the cook and her father, John, was the chauffeur for their parents. But Clara was a schoolteacher."

"So Clara and her parents lived in the little yellow cottage behind the garden?"

"That's right."

"Clara and the aunts were girls together?"

"Yes."

He stood and began to gather the dishes from the table. A shaft of sunlight illuminated his face, the strong chin, the fine clean line of his jaw. "When you're finished," he said, "there's something I want to show you."

After lunch they packed the leftover food in the old Philco refrigerator and stacked the dishes in the sink.

"I have a surprise for you," he said, and she followed him out the back door and across the yard to a small barn. The afternoon had warmed considerably, but there was an occasional breeze, and in the shade it was not unbearable.

The old barn was filled with a treasure trove of discarded machinery and farm equipment. A tractor sat in one corner beneath a wall hung with various tools and gardening implements. Sunlight slanted through the weathered boards, hazy with pollen and dust. He walked over and pulled a plastic tarp off a monstrous four-wheeler.

"Would you like to take a ride?" he said, and without a moment's hesitation, she grinned and climbed on behind him.

She had never ridden a four-wheeler before and so she was unprepared for how exhilarating it was, flying up and down the green rolling hills, the wind in her face, rolling along darkly forested trails. He was a cautious driver, taking just enough risks to make her scream with laughter without fearing that they might flip over. They roared through gullies and creeks, up steep inclines and down steeper ones. She held tightly to him, resting her face against his shoulder when the climb became too steep or perilous. He took her all the way around the boundaries so she could see how far Longford stretched. They climbed to the top of a small rise, where he switched off the engine and they sat for a while, enjoying the quiet. To their left rose a tall stand of forest. Birds sang in the brush, flitting through the gloom like brightly colored wraiths.

Below them a wide field sloped down to a narrow wash before rising again to the distant ridge where the house sat. From this rear angle it did indeed look like Tara, with its white-columned gallery gleaming in the sun. The prospect was so pleasing that Ava couldn't help smiling, having thought of Elizabeth Bennett's comment upon being asked when she first loved Darcy. *I believe I must date it from my first seeing his beautiful grounds at Pemberley.*

"What's so funny?" he said, leaning to one side so he could see her better.

"Nothing." She raised her hand and pointed to the far field, to a distant island of gravestones surrounded by a wrought-iron fence. "What's that?" she said.

"The family cemetery. Randal and Delphine and all of their children except for Isaac and Jerome are buried there."

At the bottom of the ridge, behind the house, she could see the place where the slave cabins once stood. A grassy gully ran behind the staked plots, the remains of an ancient drainage ditch. She wondered where the slaves were buried. She wouldn't ask him. She had seen from his expression when she asked about Clara that race was not something openly discussed down here. She felt like a blind woman feeling her way along a rocky precipice. She would have to go slowly. She would have to learn to keep her mouth shut.

He turned his head. "What do you think?"

She could smell the scorched cloth scent of his T-shirt, the faint fragrance of his cologne. "I think it's beautiful."

"Come on. There's something else I want to show you."

And restarting the quad, he accelerated, and they headed down to the river.

They rode for a while through the dappled woods until they came to a strip of sandy beach spread between a jumble of large boulders. It was at a bend in the river where the water widened and slowed.

"My swimming hole," he said, holding her arm so she could climb off the back.

"Are there snakes?"

"Probably."

He laughed at her expression. After a few minutes of awkwardness, they stripped down to their underwear, Ava flinging her clothes atop a flat boulder while Will folded his carefully. He took her hand and they walked to the edge of the water. He was very tanned, with a slight sprinkling of freckles across his shoulders. The fact that he was attractive had not registered with her in college. Caught up in her dysfunctional relationship with Michael, she had hardly noticed what went on around her.

He let go of her hand, grinning. "I'll go in first and scare off the snakes." He dived, a pale swift shape in the clear green water.

She smiled, watching him surface.

Amazing how a few years of maturity could change your view of the world.

They swam for a while, laughing and splashing each other like exuberant children. He showed her which rocks were safe to jump from and which ones were to be avoided. Afterward they stretched out on their backs in the hot sand.

"Do you come here often?" she asked him. She could feel the warmth of the sun creeping through her drowsy limbs.

"Every day."

She turned her head and looked at him, shielding her face with one hand. "So what's a typical day in the life of Will Fraser? I'm trying to figure out how you spend your time."

He kept his eyes closed, lying on his back. "It's not that exciting. I rise pretty early, around seven o'clock, and then I work on the house until lunch. Then I spend a couple of hours in the studio before coming down here to swim. After that I get dressed and drive in to join the aunts and Maitland for Toddy Time."

"The life of a country gentleman. It sounds pretty idyllic to me."

He grinned. "It's not too bad," he said.

"And do you do the work yourself? On the house, I mean."

"Some of it I subcontract but a lot of it I do myself. It's a labor of love."

The sun had begun its slow plummet in the western sky. The edge of the beach was bathed in shade. Will sat up, resting his arms on his knees.

"What about you?" he said. "What's it like to be Ava Dabrowski?"

"Endless boredom followed by moments of intense anxiety."

"Have you considered medication?"

"Constantly."

She thumped him playfully on the back, and that's how it began. He leaned and tickled her around her waist, and she laughed and squirmed, and he pulled her against him and kissed her. Perhaps it was the slumberous spell of Longford that made her return the kiss. Or perhaps it was gratitude for the wonderful day, the first she had spent in a long time not thinking about her mother.

She didn't mean for it to go any further than a kiss. Even now she could feel herself withdrawing, retreating.

"I don't want to ruin a perfectly good friendship," she said.

"We won't."

She sighed. What she took for a mild flirtation, he would take for something else entirely. She knew this about him, could see it in his earnest expression, in the slight trembling of his hands. "Look, Will, I just got out of a bad relationship."

He let go of her. "I know that, Ava."

"I'm sorry if you thought . . ."

"No. Of course not. It was my fault." He rested his arms on his knees and stared at the glistening water, his hair curling damply against his ears.

A row of tattered clouds sailed across the pink sky. She had not consciously planned for this to happen and yet she had known it might. She had known last night in the hallway when he touched her back.

She slapped the sand off her legs. She had gone into the woods earlier and she now noticed several red welts around her ankles. "I hope I don't show up at your aunts' house with poison ivy on my ass. That might be hard to explain."

"You're more likely to show up with chigger bites on your ass."

"What are chiggers?"

"Blood-sucking insects the size of fleas that live in tall grass."

"Great," she said. "Now you tell me." She hoped things wouldn't be awkward between them. She thought of everything she had given up to follow this dream. She couldn't just turn around and go back to Chicago.

As if to reassure her, he nudged her with his shoulder and she smiled in relief and said, "So tell me this, Will Fraser. How has a guy like you managed to stay single?"

He stood and leaned to help her up. "I'm a sprinter," he said. "No one can catch me." His eyes were more blue than gray in the slanting light.

"I'm sure they've tried," she said. She grinned, tilting her head and tapping her chin with her fingers. "But wait, there was someone. I remember now. A fiancée. In college. Michael told me you were engaged, although I never met her. What happened?"

His face changed suddenly; the happiness went out of it as swiftly as the falling of a curtain. Behind his head, a bank of feathery clouds drifted slowly across the sky.

"We'd better go," he said, turning and leaning to pick up his clothes. "They'll be waiting for us."

He took her back to Woodburn Hall, staying for cocktails but not for supper. Ava felt wretched in the awkward silence that had fallen between them, wishing she could take back what she'd said about the fiancée. But later, when she was alone, getting ready for bed, she felt a quiver of anger. How was she to know that the broken engagement was a sore subject? It had happened eight years ago. Shouldn't he be over it by now?

She was always saying the wrong thing, always wounding male vanity in some small unintentional way. It was a pattern she had followed in all her previous relationships. She didn't know how to talk to men, how to flatter. But then, why would she, when she had grown up without a father, when it had been only her and Clotilde against the world?

She turned off the lamp and lay down in bed, listening to the sounds of the old house settling around her. Strands of moonlight pushed their way through the shutters. On the bedside table, the letter from the man purporting to be her father glimmered palely. She reached out and touched it with a tentative finger. She kept it there so that she could see it every evening when she went to bed and every morning when she woke up. The paper had gone frail and gauzy with her continued reading of it. *I was so sorry to hear about your mother. She loved you very much.* She had kept the envelope, too, turning it over and rereading the address until she had it memorized.

All the time she was talking to Will on the phone and trying to decide whether to come south, she had been weighing what to do. He had signed his name, *Frank.* The envelope return address read, *Frank Dabrowski, 1645 Hennipen Street, Garden City, Michigan.* The father on her birth certificate was listed as Frank Dabrowski. It must be the same person.

But how could she be sure? Would she know him if she saw him?

She had the photograph she had found among her mother's belongings, the one of Clotilde with a tall, long-haired boy. On the back of the photo, "Frank," written in Clotilde's beautiful script.

By the time she accepted Will's invitation to come south, she had decided.

Before Ava headed south to Tennessee, she first took a detour to Garden City, Michigan. She took her time driving from Chicago to Detroit. The fields were flat and brown, still swollen with the spring rains.

From time to time she passed a barn painted with a black-and-white portrait mural: Ben Franklin, Beethoven, Paul Revere.

Ava had no recollection of her father; according to Clotilde, they had broken up not long after Ava began walking. "It was no big deal. He was a nice guy, but we just didn't get along. He wanted someone who could stay put and I couldn't. Besides, we figured it would be best for you, not being around all those bad vibes." Ava would have liked a say in what was best for her, but she never got one. She stopped waiting soon after her tenth birthday for cards and Christmas presents that never came. When she was ten, Clotilde told her that Frank had been killed in an ice-fishing accident on the Detroit River. "He was drinking," she said, "and fell into the fishing hole he'd cut. They found him later, several miles downriver, staring up through the ice."

They were living in Stevens Point, Wisconsin, at the time, house-sitting for a professor at the university where Clotilde had gotten a secretarial job. Clotilde had awakened one night to find Ava standing at the foot of her bed like an apparition, and when she swore and flipped on the lamp, Ava had stared for a moment, and without a word, turned and walked back to her bedroom. The next morning she remembered nothing.

"You scared me to death," Clotilde said. "You were sleepwalking."

"No, I wasn't," Ava said.

But the episodes became more frequent. Clotilde would hear her padding through the house, or awaken to her small dark figure standing eerily beside the bed. And when they moved to a big Victorian house it was even worse, because then Clotilde would hear her walking up and down the tall staircase in the dark. Ava never stumbled, she never lost her footing, although if Clotilde flipped on the light she would stand like a zombie, and then, blinking, turn and head back to her room. She never said a word, never responded to questions, and in the morning she had no recollection of the episodes.

Clotilde did what she always did when one of them was sick. She went to the health food store, bought a bunch of foul-tasting herbs, and brewed a tea that she made Ava drink daily.

"Can't I just see a doctor?" Ava asked belligerently.

"The body will heal itself," Clotilde said sweetly, "given the proper nutrients. If this doesn't work we'll try a hypnotherapist," she added.

For a while the sleepwalking episodes did become less frequent. But that was only because the disorder was changing, metamorphosing into something more terrible, as Ava discovered not long after their move to Indianapolis. She was in the seventh grade when she had her first attack of sleep paralysis and awoke to what she perceived as a room full of small dark men touching her arms and legs with long spidery fingers.

This time Clotilde had no choice. She took Ava to a doctor.

The doctor asked Ava if she began dreaming immediately upon falling into sleep and if she dreamed in color. Ava responded, "Yes." Didn't everyone?

"Are you sleepy during the daytime?"

"Of course," Ava said.

"Narcolepsy," he said resolutely. "With symptoms of hypnogogic sleep paralysis." He ordered a sleep study and put her on medication that made her nervous and forgetful, or dull and zombie-like, depending on the dosage.

The daytime sleepiness and medication issues made school difficult, and she had to work twice as hard as everyone else to compensate. It also made sleepovers with friends difficult, as Ava was always nervous about having an episode in front of someone. When she moved to Chicago and began high school, the episodes gradually became less frequent, and she slowly weaned herself off the medication. By the time she graduated from college they had become an unpleasant memory, like so much else that she took pains to overcome and hide, and throughout most of her twenties she had been able, for long periods, to forget about the sleep disorder entirely.

She stopped for a cup of coffee at a fast-food restaurant just off I-94. The skies above the landscape were gray and wintry. The closer she got to Detroit, the more nervous she became. What would she say to Frank? What if he didn't want to see her?

Her stomach lurched suddenly, and she pulled to the side of the road and was sick.

Garden City was a neat little blue-collar suburb of small houses and big trees. She drove slowly down the narrow streets, crisscrossing Hennipen until she gathered the courage to turn onto the street.

It was a tiny green cement-block house nestled beside a towering hemlock tree. A swing set and colored plastic toys littered the yard, which surprised Ava, because it meant some of his children were young. She sat for a long time staring at the house, trying to work up the courage to knock on the door.

While she sat waiting, the door opened and a large heavyset woman stepped out onto the stoop, eyeing Ava suspiciously. The two stared at each other for a brief moment and then Ava looked away, pulled slowly into the street, and, without a backward glance, drove away without ever having met her father.

The day after their trip to Longford, Will showed up for Toddy Time with a bouquet of wildflowers. Ava was in her room, sitting at her desk overlooking the garden. She had spent the day reading through the Longford plantation journals, an occupation she found much more agreeable than working on the outline for her novel. She was beginning to understand that daydreaming about writing a novel and actually writing it were two very different things.

He tapped lightly on the door and when she said, "Come in," thinking it was one of the aunts come to check on her, he opened the door and stepped inside.

"For you," he said. He had already put the flowers in a vase and he set it down on the nearest dresser. He seemed jovial and relaxed, and Ava was glad to see that whatever trouble had passed between them yesterday seemed to have been forgotten. She stood, going over to the mirrored armoire to check her appearance.

"You look pretty," he said.

"Do I?"

"Yes."

He clasped her wrist, delicately yet exactingly, as if preparing to sweep her into a dance.

She said, "Behave."

He kissed her lightly and let her go. She ran her fingers through her hair until it stood up in short curling tufts around her face. He sat on the edge of the bed watching her with such a look of frank admiration and respect that Ava averted her eyes in embarrassment. It wasn't in her nature to be so openly amazed and worshipful.

"I came to remind you that today you meet my cousin Fraser, Alice's son."

"He's the one who dresses like Edgar Allan Poe?"

"Right."

She smirked, and was rewarded by a faint flush of color in his face. "And why does he dress like a dead poet?" she asked innocently.

"It started in college. He was asked to join the Raven Society up at UVA. They're the ones who keep Poe's room as it was when he was there, who leave a glass of cognac and three roses out every year on his birthday. It's really a big deal to be asked to join. It's one of the oldest societies on campus, and Fraser picked up his interest in Poe while there. Plus he double majored in history and drama."

"That would explain it."

His manner was casual, complacent. He acted as if nothing had happened between them yesterday, which she found somewhat jarring. She had the impression that she should not mention it at all. So much of what happened down here seemed to pass beneath the surface: thoughts, desires, hurts trolling like icebergs beneath a placid sea. She wondered if she had the subtlety for it.

"There'll be a crowd today," he said. "In addition to Fraser, several of the neighbors are invited round for drinks."

"More cocktails?" she said. "Good God, they don't drink every day, do they?"

"Every day but Sunday."

"How is it they're not all alcoholics?"

"They drink less than you might think. And I've never seen any of them drunk. It's a generational thing, a social ritual, like the English drinking tea."

"Right. Eighty proof tea."

"How's the work coming along?"

"It's not, I'm afraid."

He looked around the room, mildly alarmed. "They haven't been bothering you, have they?"

"Who?" She stared at him in the mirror. "The aunts?"

"They promised to leave you alone to write."

"They've been lovely. No noise. No interruptions. They left breakfast on the stove with a note, and lunch was chicken salad on the verandah, just the four of us."

He seemed relieved. "I knew you'd like them," he said.

"Josephine is a bit cool. I'm not sure she likes me."

He shook his head. "You mustn't read too much into her manner. She's that way with everyone. Very reserved and private."

She turned to face him, smoothing her skirt with her hands. "What's her story, anyway? She never married?"

"No. There was someone. A long time ago. I don't know who, I've just always heard that she was unlucky in love."

"That's a nice way of putting it."

"Yes," he said. "I thought you'd like that."

Later, standing in the library with a glass of red wine in her hand, Ava was amazed at Fraser Barron's resemblance to Poe. He had come in with Alice, and was dressed in a long black frock coat and carried a gold-headed walking stick. He was a small man, no taller than five feet three or four, and he wore his hair in damp curls around his face.

"You've got to be kidding me," Ava said to Will in a low voice.

"I told you."

Fraser advanced across the room toward them with a strange, high-stepping gait, his hand extended, and Ava fought a sudden desire to giggle. Will leaned against her, as if to check the impulse.

"William," Fraser said in a slightly effeminate voice, firmly shaking Will's hand.

"Fraser." Will turned to Ava. "This is my friend, Ava."

"Yes, yes, I'm so excited to meet you," he said, taking Ava's hand in his small, soft one. "My mother's said so many wonderful things about you."

"I like your walking stick," Ava said.

"Thank you." Pleased, he held it up for her review. "I order them specially from the UK. They're so hard to find in the States."

"Fraser, we were just talking about the time Edgar Allan Poe spent up at UVA. Ava was questioning why he'd left without graduating." Fraser immediately launched into a lengthy discourse on the poet, and Will excused himself, giving Ava a slow grin, and went to refill his drink. Most of what Fraser said was interesting. Ava had read Poe's literary criticism in college, and was a fan of the gothic genre, preferring Poe's fiction to his poetry, but after a while her attention began to drift.

Across the room, Maitland and Will were discussing baseball, while over by the sideboard Fanny and Alice stood talking to a couple of neighbors. Alice turned her head, noting Ava with Fraser. She smiled and went back to her conversation. She was an attractive woman but somewhat domineering. Her husband had died young, leaving her to bring Fraser up on her own, which she had done admirably, the aunts agreed. No one mentioned Fraser's eccentric dress and preoccupation with a dead poet; he was family (in addition to being Fanny's sister-in-law, Alice was also a distant cousin) so that excused any censure they might have heaped upon an outsider.

As far as Ava could tell, *eccentricity* in the Woodburn family was not necessarily frowned upon. What was frowned upon, however, were members who didn't appreciate the family's history and standing, "sell-outs" who promoted progress that threatened the "old ways."

Disloyalty in any form was never tolerated.

She could see Josephine sitting on a long sofa, deep in conversation with Clara. One fair, one dark, they were a striking contrast; yet there was something similar in their profiles, something kindred in their height and bearing and grace. Ava had been curious about Clara from that first night at Woodburn Hall, pelting Will with questions. But in that teasing manner he had with her, slightly amused, mildly offended, he'd told her just enough to make her more curious. Clara lived on the block behind the aunts. Her parents had worked for the family when Josephine and Fanny were girls. She had grown up with the Woodburn girls as a sister might. "As part of the family," Will had told her.

"Only she didn't go to Vanderbilt," Ava had remarked innocently.

"No," Will said, his smile fading. "She didn't go to Vanderbilt."

Sunlight fell in large bands across the library's faded Oriental carpet. The sofas, seen in the bright slanting light, seemed somewhat threadbare and worn, although the room was scrupulously clean, the woodwork newly painted and gleaming.

Beside her Fraser droned on about Poe in his soft little singsong voice. Will, noting that Ava's attention had wandered, lifted his glass and motioned for Fraser to join him and Maitland.

"Excuse me, I'm being summoned," Fraser said breathlessly. He put one small hand lightly on Ava's arm. "I'm so looking forward to Mother's barbecue. It'll be such fun to introduce you around because I can assure you" (and here he leaned toward her, glancing around the room) "we're not all this stodgy!" He giggled and walked off in that odd, straight-backed manner he had, like a tiny soldier on parade.

"Ava, come sit with us," Clara called, patting the sofa between her and Josephine. Ava sat down, smiling at Clara, who squeezed her hand gently, then let it go. There was something warm about Clara, something so welcoming that you couldn't help but feel comfortable in her presence. Fanny, too, made her feel instantly at home, and Maitland was like a charming, overindulgent grandfather. Josephine, on the other hand, seemed cordial but distant. There was something of Miss Havisham in Josephine. You had the feeling that beneath her polished exterior beat the heart of a woman capable of anything.

Alice was loudly telling a joke. "How many Episcopalians does it take to change a lightbulb? Ten. One to change the bulb and nine to say how much they liked the old one."

The room exploded in laughter but they were all Episcopalians and you could see that they were proud of it.

"You know what they say," Maitland said, lifting his glass. "For every four Episcopalians you'll find a fifth."

Fraser whooped with laughter, then stopped and checked his appearance in the heavy gilt-framed mirror above the sideboard. Beside him, Will stood smiling at Ava, his back to the glass.

Josephine said, "He's a handsome young man, isn't he?"

"Yes," Ava said. She finished her wine.

"I see something of my father in him, although he's dark like all the Frasers." Josephine was quiet for a moment, her eyes fixed fondly on Will. As if guessing that they were talking about him, he excused himself to Fraser and Maitland and came across the room to join them. "My father was stern, but he was very loving," Josephine continued. "Unusual in a man of those times."

"He was a good man," Clara said. Will stopped in front of them, smiling.

"He loved my mother, and when she died, soon after Celia's birth, he never remarried. And he could have, if he'd wanted to! He was the most eligible widower in town, young, handsome, a man of property." She stopped abruptly, looking down at her glass. "Well, he had everything, and many were the women who set their caps for him and tried to catch him."

"But he was too wary for that," Will said. He had obviously heard this story many times before.

"People who've been wounded in love are often wary," Josephine said, lifting her chin. She and Will exchanged a long look, and Ava saw something pass between them. He leaned over and reached for Ava's glass.

"Let me get you another drink," he said.

1919

Woodburn, Tennessee

Papa and John were in the stable killing rats. Papa had told Sissy and Fanny to stay away, so Fanny was sitting on the kitchen steps like he had said but Sissy was squatting behind a camellia bush spying on them. She had a big white bow in her hair that fluttered among the greenery like a bird. Tom Penny sat on Fanny's lap. He was purring as she stroked him, his claws coming in and out against her leg. Cicadas droned in the heat. They were feeding castor beans to the rats, mixed up in bowls of suet pudding. Fanny knew not to go near the bowls. She knew not to go near the castor bean plants even though their flowers were like little India rubber balls covered in spikes, and their beans were speckled like tiny bird's eggs. "Don't ever touch them," Papa had told them sternly. "They will kill you quicker than a cobra."

Across the wide lawn she could hear the thin wailing of her baby sister, Celia. Mother had gone to be with the angels not long after Celia came. The angels had brought Celia and taken Mother, and now Celia stayed in the house across the backyard where John and Martha lived with their dear little baby Clara. Martha took care of Celia and Clara. When she came to the house to cook for Papa and Sissy and Fanny, she brought both babies with her, laying them on a clean quilt on the floor.

Sissy stood up and motioned for Fanny to join her but Fanny shook her head no. She always did what Sissy said, but Papa had said stay away with his face all sad and stern like it was these days since Mother went away, and Fanny could not bring herself to disobey him.

She wondered if the angels would come for the rats like they had come for Mother.

Fanny cried all the time for Mother but Sissy said, "Don't be a baby." Sissy never cried, but at night, in her sleep, she made little mewling noises like a kitten. This was in the nursery where they slept at the top of the stairs. They had always slept together, in two little spindle beds on either side of the long windows, and at night the big house creaked and moaned around them and the moonlight fell across their beds like fairies. Sometimes the fairies would lose themselves in Tom Penny's fur, blinking wildly until Fanny giggled.

"Don't be daft," Sissy said. "There's no such thing as fairies." Sissy was a Big Girl now. She was too big for fairies and grief.

Sissy was eight years old, and she was turning into a boy. Any day now she would grow an appendage between her legs like a third arm. This is what she told Fanny. Any day now she wouldn't have to sit down to pee.

Sissy was too big for fairies and grief, but she wasn't too big for magic.

Down in the big kitchen Sissy liked to pour pepper into her palm and hold the hand out to Fanny. "Sniff it," she'd say.

"No, Sissy, I don't want to."

"Sniff it."

She always did. Later, when she was snuffling and blowing her nose into a clean starched handkerchief, Martha would shake her head and cluck her tongue.

Once, when they were alone together in the kitchen, Sissy pointed to the big cookstove and said, "I'll bet you can't do a cartwheel from the stove to the table." It was a big thick farmhouse table with a marble slab top. Fanny almost made it, catching her forehead on a corner of the marble slab and opening a long gash that bled terribly while Sissy applied a makeshift tourniquet made out of a flour sack towel. Another time they decided to make a swimming pool out of an old iron washtub they found in one corner of the garden. They filled it with water and then made a diving board out of a cinder block and a pine board perched against the edge of the tub.

"You first," Sissy said, pushing Fanny out along the board.

It teetered and dropped into the water, throwing Fanny forward so that she caught her knee on the edge of the iron tub, splitting the skin down to the bone.

They built a fort under Papa's bed, rolling around on the dusty floor, careful not to disturb the four legs standing in their little lids of kerosene, set out to discourage the bedbugs. It was dark under the massive bed, and Sissy lit a series of matches so they could see. Papa's dusty bottles of moonshine gleamed in the darkness against the far wall. His "snakebite medicine," he used to tell Mother teasingly. When Fanny was bitten by a chicken snake out by the stable, Sissy carried one of the bottles down to the garden and dosed Fanny so liberally she couldn't stand.

And when Papa sold the horses and carriage and came driving up in a gleaming new ReVere Touring Car, they "fed" Papa's new "pet" with sand and rocks stuffed into the gas tank. Not long after that, their cousin Humphrey came visiting from Nashville, pulling up the drive in a Fleetwood Phaeton with a convertible top. He and Papa went into the library to talk, and Sissy decided the convertible top looked an awful lot like the trampoline they had seen used by the trapeze lady at the circus. So while Humphrey and Papa were inside talking business, Fanny and Sissy were jumping up and down on the landau top until their feet went through and they were stuck and pinned like flies on cheesecloth.

Later that night, when she was putting them to bed without supper, Martha said to Fanny, "Lord, child, why do you always have to do what your sister tells you to do? Why do you let her torment you so?"

But Fanny just smiled and sucked her thumb sleepily because she knew something that Martha didn't know, something that only she and Papa knew.

Pain was part of love.

After that the family had a meeting to decide what to do about Fanny and Josephine. They drove to the house in a caravan to meet with Papa, following him into his library with solemn faces, while Fanny and Josephine crouched on the verandah outside the window, listening.

Papa needed a new wife, they told him. Those girls needed a stepmother or a governess. They were growing up wild and untamed as spring colts. They needed a firm female presence in their lives. If they continued on the same path they were on, they were sure to bring shame and disgrace to the family. Papa listened and thanked them quietly, then sent them on their way. He never said a word to Fanny and Josephine but several weeks later a new governess arrived.

She was a French woman from New Orleans; her name was Madame Arcenaux. She called Josephine and Fanny "cherie" or "ma petite," when Papa was around, and when he wasn't, she called them "Hey, you, girl." If she heard Papa's voice in the house, she would hurry them through their lessons and go downstairs to smile and lay her hand coquettishly upon Papa's arm.

Fanny liked her well enough, but Josephine had no intention of allowing a stepmother into their lives, much less a French one. She set about figuring out a way to get rid of Madame Arcenaux.

The woman had a fear of dark enclosed spaces. Josephine overheard her telling Martha about this, complaining that the room she occupied at the top of the stairs was "dark and airless as a wardrobe," insisting that she be moved to the back bedroom downstairs (closer to Papa's room). A few days later, in the middle of a history reading, Josephine let it drop that Papa had had all of Mother's things moved to the attic, where they were stored in large trunks, boxes and boxes of hats, shoes, and lovely dresses.

Fanny watched in horrified amazement as Sissy spun her lies.

"Don't be ridiculous!" Madame Arcenaux cried. "Why would your papa put all of your mother's things in the attic?"

"He thought the jewels would be safer there," Josephine said.

"Jewels?" Madame Arcenaux said.

The next morning was market day. They stood at the window watching as Martha, dressed in a hat and a long coat, pushed Clara and Celia in the big pram on her way to town. Papa had left earlier to meet his lawyer.

"What are you doing?" Madame Arcenaux said querulously behind them. "Come away from that window at once and get back to your lessons."

She waited a few minutes and then went to the window, peering down at the sidewalk where Martha had disappeared just a short time before. "Stay in your seats," she said, hurrying out of the nursery. "I'll be back shortly to check on your progress."

They heard her steps along the wide hallway and they stood and followed her, Josephine leading the way and Fanny trailing behind. They peeked around the doorway, watching Madame Arcenaux as she stood in front of the attic door. She put her hand out and touched the knob hesitantly, turning it so that the door opened with a slow creak. She leaned forward and pulled the light cord, standing illuminated against the dim glow of the bulb. Still, she hesitated. They could hear her breathing. With a sharp intake of breath, she squared her shoulders and started up, clutching the railing with both hands. They heard her footsteps, loud and clumsy on the wooden steps, and then the sharp sound of her heels striking the floor overhead.

Josephine darted forward. She stood on tiptoe and pulled the cord, and the attic was plunged suddenly into darkness. She swung the door shut and locked it.

There was a sudden howling like the sound of a dog that's been run over in the street, and then a wild clumping as Madame Arcenaux made her frantic descent. She was crying, pleading with them to open the door. Fanny began to cry.

Josephine said, "Hush. Wait."

At the sound of her voice, Madame Arcenaux began to scream, "Open this door, you horrible child!" followed by "I'll tell your father!" then, "I'll strangle you with my own two hands!" and finally a string of profanity so blue and explicit as to be unintelligible to the girls.

It was at this point that Papa arrived, unlocking the attic door and swinging it open to the raging, disheveled Madame Arcenaux, and without a word, he went to his library and wrote her a final check, then called to John to bring the car to drive her to the train station.

Sleeping Dogs

Over the next week Ava gradually adjusted to her new life. The occupants of Woodburn Hall, she soon discovered, followed a rigid routine. They rose early (everyone except for Ava) and breakfasted together, then Maitland would leave for his "Gentleman's Club," a stalwart group that met every morning at the downtown diner, while Josephine and Fanny drank their second cups of coffee in the breakfast room. Occasionally Alice or Clara would join them. Ava would stumble into the kitchen around nine, bleary-eyed and drowsy, drawn by the scent of freshly brewed coffee, just as the others were preparing to go about their day. Several times she stumbled in to find the kitchen empty, a note propped against the percolator to indicate where her breakfast might be found.

Some mornings the women would linger over coffee, although they were always dressed when Ava joined them. Josephine was partial to tailored pantsuits and tea-length skirts or, if she was home, a pair of neatly pressed khaki pants and a pastel oxford cloth shirt. Fanny favored brightly colored dresses that showed off her legs. Clara most often wore a pair of jeans and a sweater. Alice, however, wore a never-ending supply of brightly colored tennis warm-up suits. She was partial to Keds and diamonds, which she never went anywhere without; she probably slept in diamonds.

She would come through the kitchen door in the mornings towel-drying her damp hair and shouting, "What's for breakfast?" in a loud, genial voice. Ava assumed it was from a morning shower, but no, Alice admitted one morning that she liked to swim nude in her pool every day for exercise.

"*Nude?*" Ava said.

"You've been warned," Josephine said drolly.

"It's good for the skin!" Alice cried, slapping the underside of her chin.

"Oh, Alice, really," Fanny said, giggling over the rim of her newspaper. "Aren't you afraid one of the neighbors will see you?"

"If they do they're in for the shock of their life," Alice said.

"I'll say," Josephine said.

"Because I've got the body of a fifty-year-old!" Alice crowed.

Fanny flattened the newspaper on the table and stared down at a full-color spread of a local garden party featured on the society pages. "Who are these people?" she said, looking closely. "I don't know a one."

"The nouveau riche and their garden parties," Alice said. "They do like to make a spectacle of themselves."

"This from a woman who likes to swim nude in her backyard," Josephine said.

Fanny stared thoughtfully out the window. "Papa used to say a lady should have her name in the papers only four times in her life. Her christening, her engagement, her marriage, and her death."

"He was right," Alice said.

Ava poured herself another cup of coffee. "What exactly is new money?"

"Anything made after the War of 1812," Josephine said.

Lunch was usually tomato sandwiches or leftovers from the night before, served in the breakfast room, or if the weather was good on the side verandah. A nap always followed lunch, a holdover, Fanny said, from the old days before air-conditioning, when the downtown stores and businesses used to close for "siesta" at noon so people could go home and sleep during the hottest part of the day.

Television in the house was limited to PBS, the History Channel, Turner Classics, and, of course, the Food Channel. Occasionally, Maitland would watch CNN but Fanny found the news "unpleasant."

"Doesn't watching the news just make you want to kill yourself?" she asked Ava cheerfully one day. "If I watched too much of it I'd be tempted to jump off a tall building or ram a knitting needle through my temple."

"Who in their right mind kills themself with a knitting needle?" Josephine said.

Monday mornings were reserved for hair or dental or medical appointments. Tuesday morning Maitland played golf with a group of friends while Fanny attended one of her church or garden club meetings. Wednesday mornings the housecleaner came, and Josephine and Fanny and Maitland did the food shopping. Thursday mornings Josephine played bridge with a group of cutthroat card sharks called the Trump Queens, while Fanny and Maitland, one day a month, went downtown to collect rents from the shopkeepers along Main Street operating out of the Woodburn Building. Friday mornings were reserved for what Fanny cheerfully called Visiting the Dead, which meant taking fresh flowers out to the cemetery to adorn the graves of deceased family members, an occupation that, owing to the number of dead Woodburns and their kin, usually took most of the morning. Saturdays were for sleeping late, puttering in the garden, and supper clubs. Sundays were for going to church and golf.

Ava found that, true to Will's promise, the aunts left her alone during the day. They were either gone, working in the garden, or napping. Ava would wander the house like a disconsolate ghost, picking up silver snuffboxes and antique porcelain vases, pressing her nose to the glass display cabinets in the dining room that housed the extensive sterling silver collection, bowls and platters and archaic utensils collected for generations, rows and rows of biscuit boxes and tea caddies and engraved wager cups. The house would be quiet except for the low hum of the central air-conditioning system and the steady ticking of the parlor clock. She would stand in front of the oil portraits and the framed documents and maps from the eighteenth century that covered the walls of every room, squinting to read the ornate antique script. The whole house was like a museum, every nook and cranny filled with items of historical significance. Each time she looked she found something new to marvel at.

And always there was the feeling of other lives lived here among the antiquities, the eerie presence of the hovering dead, cold spots on the stairs, a fleeting shadow out of the corner of one eye.

Her relationship with Will, too, fell easily into a routine. He never showed up at Woodburn Hall before Toddy Time, although he suspended this rule on the weekends, coming early in the morning to take Ava out to Longford or for a drive in the country to show her some site of historical or natural interest.

He was attentive and coyly persistent. He seemed to take for granted that Ava would eventually relent and look upon him as more than a friend, abandoning whatever hesitation she felt about beginning a physical relationship with him. There were times when, sitting beside him on the porch swing on a sultry evening or noting his handsome profile as they traveled down some dusty back road, she had to wonder why she didn't. It seemed to her then as if she was dreaming, as if she was floating, all time suspended, the image of her and this man as hazy and insubstantial as a mirage.

But then she would remember why she was here, the unwritten novel still lying dormant inside her head, and she would feel a clutch of guilt, tinged with anger that he would expect her to give herself up so easily. As if he found her dreams of being a writer nothing more than a bluff, an idle hobby to fill her days while she waited for something better to come along.

"Come out to Longford and spend the night," he said one evening.

They were out in the pergola in the garden. It was a moonlit night. The sky was clear and dotted with stars.

"I can't," she said mildly. "What would the aunts say?"

"They don't have to know."

"What do you suggest? Climbing out the window?"

"We could just tell them."

"Imagine the scandal," she said.

He kissed her lightly on the neck. "I may have to make an honest woman out of you yet." He was teasing, yet there was something in his voice, some element of hopefulness that she chose to ignore.

The truth was, she didn't want anything more permanent than what they had now, the taunts, the helpless thrashings, the feeling that something wonderful waited, if only she could be patient.

One night after supper she and Will walked downtown to see a movie, *Mrs. Dalloway.* It was a warm balmy night, and when they walked outside from the small theater the sky was still filled with light.

A few people stood outside under the brightly lit marquee.

"Vanessa Redgrave was made for that role," Ava said. They stood for a moment looking up at the faint stars. "Did you like the movie?"

"It was interesting." He hesitated, choosing his words carefully. "You certainly felt like you were there, in postwar London, although, I have to say, I've never been a fan of Virginia Woolf. I'm never quite sure what it is she's trying to say."

"She was talking about choices, I think, and how those choices influence who we become. Clarissa could have chosen Peter and been one person but instead she chose dull old Mr. Dalloway and became someone else entirely."

"But that's a romantic view of life, don't you think? We're all pretty much who we were meant to be regardless of whom we marry." He seemed distracted, almost irritated, standing with his hands shoved deep into the pockets of his jeans.

She laughed. "Now you sound like a Calvinist."

"And if she hadn't been married to Dalloway she wouldn't have been planning a dinner party anyway. He gave her the safety and stability she needed to plan dinner parties. Peter would have been too busy having affairs and running through her money."

"But that's the whole point. She took the safe choice."

"And now she regrets it?" His voice rose, deep and affronted.

They seemed to be talking about something else now. Several people standing near them turned to stare.

Ava spread her hands, trying to calm him. "I don't think she regrets her choice, but she does wonder what it might have been like if she'd chosen Peter. Because, you know, she's become kind of dead inside, she's become Mrs. Dalloway instead of Clarissa. And you're right, choosing Peter would probably have been disastrous but she can't help but wonder if it might have made her feel more alive."

His expression changed, becoming still and attentive. "Feminine logic," he said. He was staring across the street at a dark-haired man leaning against the tailgate of a pickup truck. The man seemed to be studying the two of them, his arms crossed over his chest, his legs stretched out in front of him and crossed at the ankles. While they watched, he nodded his head, slowly and deliberately, in greeting.

Will took her hand and, turning, they began to walk home.

"Who was that?"

"No one," he said.

Halfway home, he let go of her hand. Neither one spoke. They walked now without touching. Something had happened at the theater: she had offended him in some way, and now he would punish her with his silence.

A pale moon sailed over the trees. Insects flew in crazy circles around the streetlamps. Ava wished his feelings for her would fade, but love wasn't like that. It came on with sudden, terrifying clarity. She'd seen Michael across a crowded cafeteria and known, without even talking to him, that he was for her. With Jacob it had been more subtle.

It was like the steady ticking of a clock; one tick, there was nothing, the next tick, something bloomed.

The following Friday, Fanny asked Will to accompany her to the cemetery and Will surprised everyone at the breakfast table by saying yes. He had come in unexpectedly while they were finishing their last cups of coffee. Ava was in the library reading when he stuck his head in to ask her if she wanted to come.

Since she couldn't seem to force herself to write, Ava had taken to spending her mornings in the library, reading. She had found a well-worn copy of *Anna Karenina,* and despite the fact that she had read the novel several times in college, she quickly found herself immersed in Tolstoy's sweeping tale of illicit love and tragedy. It was one of the characteristics of good fiction, she had found, that rereading only enhanced the story rather than detracting from it, and so she found herself once again caught up in the passionate love affair between Anna and Count Vronsky, even though she knew that Vronsky was no good, that despite his charm and good looks he would betray Anna in the end.

"What are you doing?" Will asked. He was standing in the doorway with his shoulder against the jamb, regarding her with a lazy, amused expression.

"Research," she said, embarrassed that he had caught her reading when she should have been writing. She was lying on one of the long sofas, and she sat up quickly, holding out the book, which featured a rather lurid dust jacket drawn in the style of a nineteen-fifties romance novel. "Tolstoy." She wondered how long he had been standing in the doorway watching her.

"I'm going with Fanny to visit the dead. Do you want to come?" He didn't ask her how the work was coming, which she thought was rather pointed and brought a faint flush to her face.

"Sure," she said, rising and carefully folding the book flap over to mark her place. "I could use a break."

She went to get ready and when she came into the kitchen, Maitland and Will were standing in front of the small television set watching Alton Brown mix up Butternut Dumplings with Brown Sugar and Sage.

"He's kind of a smart-ass," Maitland said. "But the boy knows his way around a pastry bag."

They rode out to the cemetery in Maitland's old Mercedes, Maitland driving with Fanny beside him on the front seat, and Will and Ava settled into the back. The sky was a dark metallic gray. Pear blossoms littered the lawns and drives of the neighborhood. The car was a diesel, and rattled like marbles in a tin plate each time they stopped at a light or a stop sign, shooting out a plume of faint black smoke as they accelerated. It was an older-model sedan, Ava was guessing at least twenty years old, but you wouldn't know that from looking at it; Maitland kept it in nearly perfect condition.

It was one of the things Ava found amusing, the fact that the aunts lived in one of the largest houses in town yet drove a twenty-five-year-old Rambler. Alice and Maitland were the same.

"It's like Havana around here," Ava had remarked to Will, "with all the old well-cared-for cars."

"If something works you don't replace it."

"Yes, but I would have expected BMWs and Jaguars. Or chauffeur-driven limousines along the lines of *Driving Miss Daisy.*"

He smiled and said gently, as if explaining something to a child, "You don't draw attention to yourself. You aren't flashy. It isn't—polite."

Maitland was telling them tales of his Phi Delta Theta days up at Sewanee in that jovial manner he had, and they were all laughing because what else could you do but laugh when Maitland started in on one of his tales? He was the amiable grandfather everyone longed to have, a cross between Santa Claus and Colonel Sanders, a big, white-haired bear of a man who made his own mayonnaise and spoke in a nearly unintelligible dialect. Although, curiously, after the nearly two weeks that she'd been in Woodburn, Ava found that she was understanding more and more of Maitland's speech, much like a child dropped suddenly into a strange culture eventually begins to understand the language.

In addition to her fondness for Maitland, Ava had grown close to Fanny and Clara, too. They fussed over her like she was a child, making sure that she got enough to eat, that her room was comfortable, that her skin was protected when she went out into the sun. For the first time in her life, Ava felt pampered and spoiled.

In the front seat Maitland continued his wild stories, accompanied by Fanny's relentless giggling.

Ava had asked Will once what Maitland did for a living and Will, after some hesitation, had replied vaguely that he "looked after his investments." Will was very polite, yet he seemed to imply that she was being vulgar asking such a thing. He told her that Alice had inherited the family home, but Maitland had inherited the family money and Ava deduced that Maitland's sole occupation in life seemed to be taking care of Fanny. Certainly they had traveled the world, as the wealthy so often do, and they had socialized with celebrities, as the many photographs lining the walls of the Woodburn house attested to.

The cemetery sat up on a hill overlooking Woodburn. It was a pretty place, filled with large trees, shaded benches, and tall, mossy monuments. In the distance, the blue-gray ridges of the Cumberland Mountains rose against an endless sky. A narrow road wound its way past iron gates, bisecting the cemetery into old and new areas, and off this main road ran other less-traveled paths. The Woodburn plot was toward the back of the older section surrounded by an ornate iron fence that stood chest high.

Maitland parked slightly off the road, got out, and went around to open the door for Fanny. He was always courtly and respectful in his treatment of her, and Fanny was always gracious and affectionate toward him. Their marriage seemed a testament to true love and devotion, and it made Ava wistful to see the care they took of each other. Their son, Sumner, may have been a disappointment to both of them, but they never spoke of him in other than tender terms; they kept whatever pain he had caused them private.

Ava had overheard Josephine discussing Sumner with Clara and Alice, and she had gathered from their conversation that he was the family black sheep, although no one ever came right out and said why. He was an engineer for the state highway department and was married to a woman Fanny detested, someone who "hadn't had Sumner's advantages," as Fanny euphemistically put it. ("White trash," Will translated.) Sumner rarely visited the aunts but Fanny spoke to him by telephone every Thursday afternoon, calling him at his office so she wouldn't have to talk to the trashy wife.

Ava didn't wait for Will to open her door; she climbed out, although he would have come around and opened it if she had sat patiently as Fanny did, if she had expected it of him. Like Maitland, his manners were impeccable; he opened doors for women, stood when they entered a room, performed all the small courtesies that modern women so often found archaic and chauvinistic, and yet in Will, perhaps because of his good looks and self-deprecating manner, these courtesies seemed charming.

Fanny had brought enough flowers to fill a vendor's cart, and when Maitland opened the trunk, she laughed in that airy way she had, and said, "Goodness, I'll have to start using silk. They're cheaper and they last longer, and you can't tell the difference now!" She and Maitland were both formally dressed, he in a sports coat, good slacks, and a shirt and tie, and she in a black dress and low-heeled sandals.

Ava and Will helped them carry the flowers and distribute them where Fanny indicated. She walked cheerfully among the gravestones, chirping like a little bird, and Ava was struck by how animated Fanny seemed here in this tragic place, almost like a girl at a school dance. After a while, Ava and Will wandered off to leave the elderly pair to their careful work.

They strolled along the narrow paths, reading the headstones. The smell of rain was in the air; the sky gradually darkened. Behind them, Fanny and Maitland kept up a steady chatter.

When they had walked far enough to not be overheard Ava said, "I always thought a Southern accent was a Southern accent, but really there are several different dialects. The aunts, Clara, and Alice all speak differently from some of the shopkeepers in town."

"They speak what used to be called 'Old Nashville.' "

"So you mean it's a class difference?"

He smiled indulgently but didn't look at her. They had stopped at a tall monument that read *Crawford* in large carved letters.

"But you and Fraser don't speak 'Old Nashville.' I mean, you don't talk like me, but you don't talk like the aunts either."

"Really?" he said teasingly. "I don't talk like you?"

She threw a pinecone at him.

"Unfortunately, the Old Nashville dialect is dying out." He pulled her suddenly into his arms and began to mimic the aunts' pleasant voices. "Why, Ava, my dear, how lovely you look this fine morning with your beautiful hair and your eyes the color of pecan shells."

She pinched his waist and he let her go. They walked along a tree-lined path, stopping at a stone that read, *In memory of our dear daughter, Hester Anne, who fell asleep in Jesus, 12th April, 1882, aged 16 years. He hath done all things well.*

"Sixteen," Ava said. "How sad."

"We forget how quickly people died back then. You could wake up in the morning feeling fine and be dead by sundown." Behind his head a line of gray clouds drifted like smoke.

"Speaking of history," she said, as they began to walk again, "I'm curious. I was thinking about Clara and that little cottage she lives in behind your aunts' house."

She had been sitting on the kitchen steps this morning, drinking a cup of coffee and marveling at the garden that stretched beside the house and half a block beyond. A narrow alley ran behind the garden and the carriage shed, bisecting the block, and on the other side of the alley sat Clara's little yellow house. A paved street ran behind Clara's house. It was odd that the cottage faced the back of Woodburn Hall and not the street. The significance of this had slowly dawned on Ava.

"You said that Clara's mother and father worked for your family. Has her family always lived in that house, the one that Clara lives in now?"

"For generations. It was given to her ancestress, Hannah, by my ancestor Randal." He was quiet for a moment as if considering how much to say. "Hannah married a freedman, a carpenter named McGann. They went to New Orleans and had three daughters, and when Hannah and McGann died, Randal went to New Orleans and got the three children and brought them back to Longford."

"Why would he do that?"

"They were orphans. They had nowhere else to go."

"That was generous of him."

"He was a generous man."

A sudden gust of wind rattled the leaves. The sky seemed to be descending, pressing against the tops of the tall trees.

"Damn," Will said. "I left my tools in the yard."

They could see Fanny and Maitland behind the iron fence, Fanny squatting beside a grave and Maitland standing above her. She was laughing at something he'd said. They had started at one end of the Woodburn plot and were making their way slowly among the headstones, stooping to remove dead flowers and replace them with live ones.

"They seem made for each other," Ava said. She and Will were sitting on a bench under a spreading oak tree. The sky was ominous but the rain was holding off. "I've never seen two people more in love."

Will seemed to have fallen into some kind of brooding introspection. He had his eyes closed, leaning his head back against the trunk of the old tree. "They grew up together," he said. "They were childhood sweethearts. The Sinclairs and the Woodburns have been neighbors for generations."

"Well, theirs seems a love match. I can imagine that that didn't always happen when there was money involved. I'm sure there were plenty of arranged marriages in those days."

He stretched his legs out in front of him and crossed them at the ankles. It was apparent from his expression that he thought she was being vulgar again. "The Woodburns don't have money. Not anymore, anyway."

"Oh, come on," Ava said. "With that incredible house filled with all those historical treasures? The stuff alone must be worth millions."

"If they sold it."

"Right."

He opened his eyes and tilted his head forward, regarding her intently. "But you see, that's the thing, they never would. It's been in the family for generations, and they'd never sell any of it, no matter how much money it would bring. How do you put a value on a silver goblet once touched by your great-great-grandmother's hands?"

Ava tried, for a moment, to understand this, but it was difficult. She'd been raised to travel light. Material possessions, her mother had tried to teach her, were not important. They were not important when you'd never had any, but Ava imagined that it would be quite different if you had.

"They're caretakers," Will said. "They've kept it together through flood, and tornadoes, and war. That's how they look at it. And that's why Sumner is left out of Fanny's will, because they know he'll break it up into pieces, all that family history, and sell it off bit by bit."

"So they're leaving everything to you?"

"God, I hope not." He leaned forward, rolling his shoulders and resting his elbows on his knees, letting his hands dangle. "There's been some talk of donating the house and most of the collection to the State Historical Society. They'd turn it into a museum, and that way everything couldn't be sold off piecemeal."

"Would you want that?"

He looked down at his feet. "It's a lot of responsibility, caring for all that history. I'd rather it go to the museum so my children and grandchildren can come and look at it together in one place the way it was meant to be."

Ava said, "Your children?"

He turned his head, grinning at her. "All twelve of them."

"I knew you were a masochist."

"I've always wanted a large family." He hesitated, still looking at her. "How about you?"

She shook her head. A faint breeze stirred her hair. "I have enough trouble just looking after myself," she said.

Ava had never thought seriously about having children. She had spent her entire adolescence fantasizing about being on her own, about having only herself to care for. Being Clotilde's daughter had made her like that.

All the girls she met in school were enamored of her mother. They developed crushes on her, imitated the way she talked, the way she laughed.

"Your mother is so young," they said. "She dresses like we do."

They didn't understand that having a mother who was more like a sister than a mother was a hard burden to bear. Who took on the adult responsibilities when the adult wasn't willing, or capable? Who worried whether the bills would get paid, who made excuses to the landlord? Ava did.

"You're an old soul," Clotilde always said to Ava as she stood wringing her hands in the doorway. "But you need to lighten up. You need to learn to trust in the universe."

But where was the universe when the rent came due? When the car needed repairs or the utility company came to shut off the lights?

Ava was ten when she realized completely and irrevocably that Clotilde wasn't like other mothers, would never be like other mothers. It was parents' night at one of the many schools Ava had attended over the years they spent on the run. Clotilde sailed in wearing a short, brightly colored dress, and all the other mothers, sedate and matronly, took one look at her and closed ranks. Clotilde laughed her tinkling laugh and said to Ava, "Show me where you sit," as if it was some kind of game they were playing. She smiled brightly at the fathers, who smiled back, their foreheads glistening with sweat.

"Is that someone's mother?" a voice behind her hissed, and Ava felt a sudden wash of shame so intense she thought she might be sick. There was something wrong with Clotilde, as she had always suspected. She saw her mother then as the others must see her: Clotilde's too-short dress, her hair that fell in thick waves down her back, her pale lipstick, her reckless, absurd little laugh. Why could she not have thick ankles and doughy legs like the other mothers, women who rose every morning to make their children hot breakfasts before bundling them off to school? Mothers who put down roots and built nests and made sure their children never had to worry about lunch money or overdrawn bank accounts?

As a small child Ava had seen her mother as a playmate, someone always ready with a story or a bit of fun, but now that she stood on the cusp of adulthood she saw Clotilde as a continuous source of humiliation and embarrassment. She was just so different.

Clotilde didn't seem to feel embarrassed at all. She laughed and twittered and smiled at all the adoring children and fathers who gathered around her like bees around a fragrant flower.

Flighty. Ava would later read the word in a book and understand instantly that it described her mother.

Later that same year Clotilde went to the hospital for a hysterectomy and Ava stayed with a neighbor, a staid, sedate spinster. A librarian. They ate microwave dinners on metal trays in front of the TV, and Ava slept on the sofa. The apartment was dark and dank, and it smelled of cat. But everything was tidy. Everything was in its place, the lace doilies on the backs of the chairs, the dishtowel on its little hook, the silk flowers in the middle of the kitchen table.

"It's a shame," the librarian said that first night, tucking Ava in. "Your mother is a young woman and now she won't have any more children."

She said it with a peculiar expression on her face, a faraway look of longing and loss, and Ava understood that the woman was mourning her own childlessness. Ava pictured Clotilde lying bandaged head to toe in a hospital bed, and she felt a sudden pang of homesickness for her mother and for the lost siblings she would never have.

But even then, it was her own loss she was thinking of. It would have been nice to have someone to share the burden of her childhood with, a playmate, an ally, a witness.

Fanny had almost finished in the family plot. There was only one grave left to decorate, tucked away in the corner beneath a small neat headstone. She stepped forward, holding a bouquet of delphiniums against her breast. Maitland followed her but she lifted her hand and waved him away, and something in her dismissive manner, in the respectful way he dipped his head and stepped back, made Ava ask, "Whose grave is that?"

"Charlie Woodburn's."

"Who is Charlie Woodburn?"

"Her first husband."

Ava watched as Fanny tenderly plucked the dead flowers from the vase on top of the grave and replaced them with fresh ones. There was something in her slow, imposing movements that made Ava think again of icebergs. Everyone thought the South a land of jovial, open-faced people but there was much here that was hidden away, dark and dangerous.

"Fanny was married before Maitland?" she said. "No one told me that."

"We don't talk about it."

At his tone, Ava swiveled her head and looked at him. An insect whined in her ear. A ridge of swiftly moving clouds hung over the distant mountains. "But Maitland and Fanny were childhood sweethearts. You said so yourself."

"Yes, they were." Will sighed, as if realizing she wasn't going to let this go. "But then Fanny met Charlie Woodburn up at Vanderbilt and they eloped against the family's wishes. It was a painful time. That's why we never discuss him. That's why there aren't any photos of him in the house."

"What happened to Charlie?"

"He died."

"How?"

"I believe he drowned."

"And then after she was widowed, Fanny married Maitland?"

"After a while, yes. After Sumner was grown."

She looked at him in astonishment. "So Sumner was Charlie's son?"

"Yes."

Ava was quiet for a moment, considering this. There was something here, she could feel it, something in the way Maitland had stepped away contritely to let Fanny tend the grave, something in Will's reticence to speak of the matter. She, of all people, recognized evasion when she saw it. She said, "Charlie's name was Woodburn?"

He hesitated, looking at his hands. "Yes," he said finally.

"So he was related to your family?"

"Fanny and Charlie were very, very distant cousins. He came from a different branch of the family from Josephine and Fanny and me." He took her hand, trying to draw her against him, but she resisted.

"Come here," he said mildly.

"She must have loved him very much to have tended his grave all these years. The father of her only child. A man she was willing to run away with against her family's wishes."

He let go of her hand. It was obvious that he was unwilling to speak further of Charlie Woodburn. But Ava had a stubborn, perverse streak, and once her curiosity was aroused there was no stopping it. She said, "I understand Fanny not wanting to talk about him, but what about the rest of you? Why so secretive?"

His expression changed then, became flat and distant as it had that day at the river. "Because that's what families do," he said coldly. "We keep each other's secrets."

He rose and walked off toward the Woodburn plot. She watched him go, his hands thrust deep in his pockets, his shoulders rounded as if against a cold wind at his back. She had always been a watcher, a chronicler of other peoples' lives.

It was easier sometimes to guess at other peoples' secrets than it was to face her own.

All the way home from the cemetery, Maitland and Fanny chattered as if they'd just come from a cocktail party. Will stared moodily out his window. No one mentioned Charlie Woodburn.

Ava put her forehead against the glass, aware of Will's silent brooding presence beside her. She felt that she had disappointed him. He had given her the chance to be incurious, deferential, and she had failed. She would always fail. Perhaps he was realizing this now as he had not realized it before, with fatal certainty and clarity.

The storm, which had held off all morning, finally broke. In the front seat Maitland and Fanny chattered and teased each other like a pair of young lovers, as if they were the only two people in the world. Ava tried to picture Fanny as a girl, running off with a handsome scoundrel and leaving Maitland to nurse a broken heart. It was hard to imagine.

When they arrived at the house, the rain was falling steadily. Josephine had made a quick lunch of tuna sandwiches and sliced cucumbers and tomatoes, and afterward, she and Fanny and Maitland went upstairs to lie down for a siesta while Ava and Will cleaned up the kitchen. He was quiet but humorously attentive. Whatever disappointment he might have felt in her at the cemetery had obviously been tidied and put away. Smiling, he promised to take her four-wheeling tomorrow before Alice's party.

Alice Barron was throwing a barbecue so that Ava could meet some of the "right people." "And I promise they won't all be as old as Methuselah like the rest of us," she had assured Ava. She was standing in the library holding a Gin Rickey in her hand when she said this, surrounded by the afternoon cocktail crowd. It was a few days after Ava first met Fraser Barron and learned more than she cared to know about Edgar Allan Poe.

When they had finished in the kitchen, Ava and Will walked together out onto the back porch. The rain had diminished to a fine drizzle. Ava crossed her arms over her chest and followed him down the steps.

"Do we really have to go to this barbecue?" she said.

He raised his eyebrows in mock alarm. "You're the guest of honor. Unofficially, of course."

"Oh, shit."

He laughed. "It won't be bad, I promise. They aren't going to run you out of town on a rail if they don't like you."

"That's encouraging."

He kissed her and walked out into the yard. "I'll be back at Toddy Time. Try to get some writing done," he said, and walked off whistling.

It was easier said than done.

She spent the next half hour observing the contents of her room, and then she went online and checked her messages, spending nearly an hour writing emails. Finally, with an act of sheer will, she signed off and pulled up a new file on her screen. She sat for a long time staring at the glaring brightness of the empty page.

The trees outside the window were filled with a silvery light, and the sky beyond was a vivid glaring white. The rain had stopped, and in the noonday heat, the landscape seemed still and slumberous. Ava forced her attention back to her computer and wrote "I watched as my mother's boyfriend spread a map on the kitchen table. 'Pick a spot, any spot,' he said cheerfully. 'Wherever you choose is where we'll move, kid.' "

She sat back in disgust, massaging her forehead with her fingers as if to loosen the words she knew lay buried there. They stayed blocked, awaiting some magical incantation from her, some spell. She could see now why well-known authors were often alcoholics, why they used stimulants and alcohol to force the flow of words, to entice their muses like children leaving cookies for Santa Claus.

The idea of writing a coming-of-age novel about a girl and her flighty mother, which had seemed so brilliant in Chicago, now seemed sentimental and unmanageable. What had she been thinking? Every word she wrote felt like a guilty confession, personal and humiliating, as if she was exposing herself, naked, to the world. She would have to begin again, writing this time from a third-person perspective to distance herself from the main character, Lorna.

She let her eyes wander about the room, coming to rest finally on the copy of *Rebecca* she had found in the library. It was leaning against the lamp on the bedside table where Ava had left it. She had read Du Maurier as a girl, had spent one whole summer entranced by the Cornish coast with its windswept halls and lonely ghosts. She rose, went over, and opened the book, reading one random passage after another. Du Maurier made it look easy.

"It isn't easy," she said to Clotilde, who watched impassively from the mantel. She had never known Clotilde to suffer from writer's block. All her stories had begun with, "Once there was a girl," or "In the middle of a dark wood there lived a witch/troll/ogre," and from there they'd spooled out with ease.

Ava went back to her computer, rereading what she had written, and then deleting it. She sat staring at her screen, trying to imagine Lorna and her mother, Margaret, but all she could see was herself and Clotilde. After a while even those images flickered and petered out. It was no use. The words wouldn't come.

The only other novel she'd ever attempted had been a rambling historical romance that she'd never finished. Perhaps she'd been kidding herself all along about being a writer.

She yawned and lay down on the bed. She felt limp, discouraged, devoid of all energy and ambition, as if the heat and humidity had combined into some kind of unseen entity that was slowly draining her of life.

The bed was soft and fragrant. The room was cool and quiet. She slept.

When she awoke nearly two hours later she was surprised at the length of time she'd slept. It was one of the symptoms of her sleep disorder that her dreams were always vivid and in full color. She'd been dreaming again of water, cold and deep and green. Only this time there'd been a bridge of lacy ironwork and, in the sky above it, a silvery moon that filled the sky with light. There was a sense of melancholy and loss about the dream, and she found herself in a blue mood when she arose, dispirited and irritable. She went into the bathroom and splashed her face with cold water and then combed her hair. That helped a little. She could hear Fanny, Maitland, and Josephine out on the side verandah, the distant murmur of their voices interspersed with periodic laughter.

Through the long windows of her bedroom she could see Clara in the garden, trimming roses. She hesitated a moment, then turned and walked down the wide hallway and out the back door. The sky was a hazy blue. As she walked across the grass she could see Clara's hat moving slowly along the curved wrought-iron fence separating the garden from the front lawn.

The garden ran parallel to the house and was surrounded on three sides by a tall wrought-iron fence covered in trailing vines. Along the back, facing Clara's little yellow cottage, ran a boxwood hedge, and in the far corner equidistant between Clara's house and the Woodburn house stood a columned pergola covered in wisteria. The garden beds were set out in rectangular patterns, with masses of flowering shrubs and perennials along the front and side, facing the street and the house, and neat rows of vegetables on the interior. A raised bed of herbs stood in the corner closest to the kitchen. A series of stone paths crisscrossed the garden, with small wooden benches scattered throughout, and in the corner closest to the pergola stood an old oak tree, its massive limbs providing a shady respite from the summer heat. An ornamental pond filled with goldfish and a small fountain curved along one side of the pergola and filled the garden with a pleasant splashing sound.

"Hello," Clara called when she saw her, stopping to wipe her forehead with the back of one gloved hand.

"You know it's nearly Toddy Time," Ava said to her.

Clara made a dismissive gesture toward the house. "Some days I make it and some days I don't," she said.

"I'm still trying to wrap my head around the idea of cocktail hour in the Bible Belt," Ava said, falling into step beside her.

Clara chuckled. "It was different back when we came of age. During Prohibition everybody drank."

"Did the aunts' father drink?"

"The Colonel? Oh, no. Not him." She shook her head. "He was a very upright old gentleman, very proper and well-mannered. He wouldn't allow so much as a drop of brandy in his house. It was the girls, Josephine and Fanny, who learned to drink up at Vanderbilt and then brought the habit home with them. And later, after he died, and it was just the three of them shut up in the house, then the parties got so wild." She stopped for a moment, staring at the house, her eyes distant with the murky vision of the past.

"The three of them?" Ava said. "You mean Josephine, Fanny, and Celia."

Clara startled, picking up the shears from the basket she carried on her arm. "No, not Celia. She'd gone to live with a cousin after her papa's death."

"Who then?"

Clara hesitated. "Charlie," she said.

"Charlie Woodburn? Fanny's first husband?"

"Yes." She'd stopped to clip one of the pink roses growing along the fence, and Ava was hopeful that she'd continue with her story of Charlie but instead she held up the rose for Ava to sniff. "Souvenir de la Malmaison. Isn't it lovely? It's a bourbon rose named by Empress Josephine from specimens sent back by Napoleon."

"It smells wonderful. The whole garden smells wonderful."

"That's because it was planned so that the prevailing winds would blow the fragrance toward the house."

"Really?" Ava knew nothing about gardening, recognizing only a few of the flowers she saw.

"See," Clara said, pulling forward the tip of a shrub covered in white flowers. "Tea olive. And this is myrtle, and this is mock orange." Ava obediently sniffed each of the plants Clara indicated, murmuring her approval. "And here in this bed are the peonies and the pinks and the sweet violets."

"What's this?"

"Clematis," Clara said. "Although you shouldn't touch it because it causes skin irritation for some people." Ava quickly drew her hand away. "And of course you know that foxglove and nightshade are poisonous, as well as all varieties of rhododendron and azalea."

"I guess that explains why you wear gloves when you garden," Ava said, and Clara chuckled, bending above a pot of sweet peas and marigolds. Ava trailed behind her, working up the courage to speak. There was so much she wanted to ask about Charlie, and it had occurred to her that Clara might be willing to talk, but now that she was here, she wasn't sure how to start. Finally she began, blurting out portions of their strange trip to the cemetery. When she finished Clara was quiet, clipping shoots off the branches of an old gardenia. Ava knew from Clara's silence that she had blundered, but her curiosity got the better of her. "So who was he? This Charlie Woodburn."

Clara continued snipping, and then said quietly, "He was a man best forgotten."

"So he was a bad person?" When Clara didn't answer Ava said, "How did he die?"

Clara eyed her from under the brim of her straw hat. "What did Will say?"

"He says he drowned."

"Well, then," Clara said, sliding her shears into her basket. "I guess he drowned."

Ava walked to the end of a row of summer squash and stood staring at Clara's yellow cottage, visible through an opening in the tall hedge. She had been schooled in the art of listening. Clotilde had had a knack for befriending lonely people, and it was not unusual for Ava to come home for dinner to find a stranger seated at the table. Sometimes they were neighbors and sometimes they were people she had found God knows where. The thing Ava had learned listening to old people talk was that their age allowed them a particular farsightedness when it came to examining their own lives. They could look back with the benefit of regret and experience and see where they'd gone wrong. They could say, "I should have done that," or "It was wrong that I did that," with a cold, clear certainty.

It was for this reason that she knew that once she got Clara talking about Charlie Woodburn, she would find out the truth about who he was and what had happened to him. But it was getting Clara started that was going to be the problem.

"It was more than sixty years ago," Ava said. "I don't understand why no one wants to talk about it."

"Have you ever heard the expression 'Let sleeping dogs lie'?"

"Yes."

"Well, down here we say 'You don't have to be a chicken to know a rotten egg.' "

Ava turned around and looked at her. "I don't know what that means."

"It means some things are best left forgotten."

"But nothing ever stays forgotten. It just festers."

"Well, I wouldn't know about that," Clara said, shading her eyes with one hand and gazing up at the house. "Down here, denial is always best."

That night Ava had an episode of sleep paralysis.

She was tired; she had slept poorly the night before, waking several times to find the room flooded in moonlight. On this evening she awakened three times, the last time to a feeling of dread so pervasive she couldn't move, lying in terror, her body heavy and stiff, her mind agile and fully awake. From somewhere deep in the house she could hear a clock ticking, and she forced herself to concentrate on the steady rhythmic sound as the therapist had taught her to do, drowning out the unreal sensations with the real.

Gradually the thumping of her heart subsided. She lay on her back and stared at the moonbeams rippling across the ceiling. After a while she found that she could move her eyes, and so she did, shifting them to the left and feeling her heart clutch again in horror.

Someone was sitting in the chair beside the window, a tall, dark figure, smoking.

After that, she switched on the lamp and lay in bed, rigid with terror, until falling into a restless sleep sometime after four o'clock. When she awoke again it was morning and sunlight flooded the room. In the cheerful light of day it was often difficult to remember the terror of the night before. She felt that old familiar dread, curled in her stomach like an embryo. The episode last night, coming so soon on the heels of the other nightmares, left her feeling uneasy and apprehensive. It had been years since she had suffered from nightmares and waking hallucinations, and yet now, in the space of less than three weeks, she had suffered two narcoleptic events.

She hoped it wasn't a sign of things to come.

Twins

The last thing Ava wanted to do was attend a party with a group of strangers, especially one that included the "right people," but she knew Alice Barron's barbecue was not something she could avoid. She was very nervous, knowing she would be on display: Will Fraser's Yankee friend come south for the summer.

"I hope I don't get drunk and make a spectacle of myself," Ava said.

"Whatever you do, don't drink too much," Will cautioned. "And don't drink any of those local cocktail creations. Stick to beer or wine." For some reason he seemed as nervous as she was.

He picked her up around ten o'clock on Saturday morning to take her out to Longford and then brought her back to Woodburn Hall to get ready around three o'clock. She was hot and tired, and she had a rash on her arms from the hay. They had spent the morning riding around the farm on the four-wheeler and then had a picnic lunch down by the river. Afterward they had gone swimming. It was when they were putting away the four-wheeler that the trouble began.

Sleepy from the sun and the swimming, Ava sat down in a pile of hay to wait for Will while he covered the quad with its tarp. She curled on her side and closed her eyes in the heat. She opened them later at the sound of rustling hay as he lay down beside her. He had mistaken her drowsy posture as an invitation.

She sat up. "Will. Stop."

He lay back with his arms behind his head, gazing rigidly at the ceiling.

"You're very sweet."

"Don't," he said.

"It's not you," she said. "It's me."

When she came through the back door at Woodburn Hall, irritable and tired, Josephine looked at her as if she knew very well what Ava had been up to out at Longford. She and Fanny were sitting at the breakfast room table while Maitland leaned across the kitchen counter in front of the television set, writing down Food Channel recipes on a yellow legal pad.

"There she is!" Fanny said brightly as Ava came in.

"Hey there, Sugar," Maitland said, glancing up briefly from his legal pad and giving her a broad wink.

"We were all getting ready to go upstairs and dress for the barbecue," Josephine said, looking her over.

Ava pushed her damp hair off her face. "What should I wear?" she asked. "What's the dress code?"

"Oh, I don't know, anything that's comfortable, I guess," Fanny said breezily. But then she went on endlessly about how pretty sundresses were on young women and Ava, taking the hint, tried to remember if she'd brought one. She had learned, in the short time she'd been here, that no one ever came right out and spoke directly. There were always hints and vague suggestions, double entendres and Freudian slips that were meant to be taken literally so that when you carried on a conversation, you had to listen not only to what was said but also to the tone and, through slight facial expressions, to what was *implied*.

Ava had a scratchy feeling in her throat. She put one finger to her nose, warding off a sudden sneeze.

"God bless you!" Fanny cried.

Josephine stared at Ava's waist and, looking down, Ava saw several pieces of hay caught beneath the waistband of her shorts.

Behind them Maitland said, "We can't be out late tonight. Bobby Flay's making Cedar Plank Salmon."

Ava sneezed again.

"Goodness!" Fanny said.

"Hay fever," Josephine said mildly.

The heat of midday had begun to wane, and the sky was a violet color as they walked across the lawn to the party. Behind Alice's large house a brick barbecue grill belched smoke, and along one end of the patio, beside the pool, a long buffet table stood covered by a white cloth. The lawn was dotted with round tables and canvas chairs *like a wedding party,* Ava thought curiously. There was a large crowd already gathered on the lawn, and as they approached several people stepped forward to greet Will and be introduced to Ava. They were very friendly and kind, but there were so many of them, and Ava knew she'd never remember all of their names. Maitland and Will went off to find drinks, and Ava let herself be shepherded from group to group by Josephine and Fanny. In spite of the crowd's friendliness Ava was nervous; she felt herself the object of much sly and murmuring attention, and she was thankful when Will returned and thrust a glass of red wine into her hand.

He whispered in her ear, "All right?" and she said, "Yes."

He introduced her to a group of his prep school buddies and their wives. A young woman in a faux tuxedo came around to get their drink orders.

"I'll have another Donnie Miller," a man in plaid shorts said.

"Me, too."

"Make that three."

"What's a Donnie Miller?" Ava said.

Everyone laughed politely.

"It's a homegrown cocktail," the man in plaid replied. "Whipped up by one of Woodburn's finest." He put his arm around a sandy-haired man in wire-rim glasses.

"Hey," the man said, stepping forward and putting his hand out to Ava. "I'm Donnie."

"Donnie Miller?"

"That's right."

"Wow," Ava said. "I've never met anyone with a cocktail named after them."

"Well, in the South, if you're lucky, you get either a cocktail or barbecue sauce named after you."

"Here," one of the women said, handing her glass to Ava. "Try it."

It was very sweet and very fruity. "It's good," Ava said. "What's in it?"

"Rum," Donnie said. "Two kinds. And lemonade. Orange juice. Peach nectar."

"I'll have one of these," Ava said, holding the drink up and smiling at the waitress, already forgetting Will's warning not to drink the local cocktails.

The sun had begun to set, and long shadows lay across the lawn. A scent of citronella drifted on the warm air. Ava found herself entranced by the scene, the smoky globes of candlelight on the tables, the softly glowing Japanese lanterns dangling from the branches of the trees like golden fruit, the gradual fall of dusk across the landscape. It was her favorite time of day, she'd discovered, that point where day met night and everything grew still. Will had told her that as a boy he'd run barefoot through the summer dusk with the neighborhood children, scooping fireflies into mason jars and playing flashlight tag when it grew too dark to see. It had sounded so idyllic, so perfect a childhood that Ava had felt a stir of envy.

She drifted over to a group of young matrons wearing sundresses and stacked-heel sandals that showed off their lean, tanned legs, and Ava realized now why Josephine had indicated, by her tacit refusal to look at Ava's feet, disapproval of her flat, boyish sandals. The women were friendly and close to her in age, but most had been no farther than the University of Alabama, and they talked of sorority events and babies and au pair girls until Ava, growing bored, excused herself and walked off.

In the trees, the cicadas made a pleasant chorus. Ava settled herself under a crape myrtle, where she could sip her drink and watch the crowd unnoticed.

Woodburn was broken up into social classes that resembled Victorian England. At the very top were the old families, those who had been intermarrying for generations, the first settlers who came originally from Virginia or Maryland, and before that, England or Scotland. They sent their sons to boarding school and private colleges, and presented their daughters annually at debutante balls in Nashville, Atlanta, and Birmingham.

This class was presided over by a group of sharp-eyed dowagers who Will cheerfully referred to as "the dreadnoughts," women who could recite pedigrees and family lineages down to the smallest and most trivial detail. They could look at a child and know if he was a Robinson or a Sinclair; they kept an almost-encyclopedic memory of family traits, ailments, and characteristics—the "Whaley nose," the "Eldridge forehead," the "Clairmont tendency toward suicide." Josephine, Fanny, and Alice were clearly of this class.

"So you mean they could pick you out of a lineup because of your nose?" Ava had asked Will. "Even if they didn't know you?"

"Yes."

"That's fascinating."

"I used to long to live in a big city where no one knew who I was, where I could blend in like everybody else. Be one of the masses."

"Trust me, you wouldn't like being one of the masses."

Ava hadn't liked it either. In high school she had developed a careless, impertinent facade, a biting, caustic wit that made her popular with her peers but less so with their parents, who always asked the same tired questions.

"What was your last name again?"

"Dabrowski."

"Where are you from?"

"All over."

"What does your father do?"

"He's dead."

"And your mother?"

"She's not."

Their questions seemed sly, cunning assaults on her carefully constructed adolescent self. She felt their disapproval but couldn't dispute it. She didn't much like who she was either.

How much better to be a sweet, generous girl like Margaret Stanley, with her big house and carefree, loaded parents; her mother with her furs and martinis, her father with his grass-stained golfing pants. A world of safety and ease.

The Woodburn sisters would have known that same world. It was easy to picture them as girls, pretty and spoiled, going off to dances at the country club, letting well-bred young men rest their damp hands on their narrow, corseted waists.

She could see Fanny and Josephine now, standing in a group of other dreadnoughts across the lawn. Ava sighed and sipped her Donnie Miller. It was difficult to imagine herself growing up in such a world, freed from the constraints and worries of ordinary life.

Across the lawn, Will caught her eye and raised his glass. She smiled and raised hers in return, a glimmer of hopeful optimism stirring suddenly in her chest. He looked so handsome and sincere standing there in the lamplight. Perhaps she had been wrong about him. Already she could feel herself beginning to soften.

"Ava!" She turned to find Fraser Barron advancing quickly across the grass. He was wearing a maroon vest over a white shirt, rolled at the elbows, and a pair of dark pants and leather boots. Ava was struck again by the odd way he moved, like a wind-up toy or a slightly misfiring mechanical device.

"I *love* your dress," he said. He took her drink from her, set it down, and took her hands in his, motioning for her to spin around.

"Thanks," she said. "I think I blew it on the shoes, though. I'm the only woman in flats."

He crossed his arms in front of him, then rested his chin in the palm of one hand, regarding her thoughtfully. "Yes," he said. "The shoes don't do the dress justice."

"And you look very—literary."

"Do I?" he said, pleased, adjusting the rolled sleeves.

"But aren't you hot in all those clothes?"

"No, that's the amazing thing, you get used to it. When I first started dressing like this I used to sweat like a whore in church." He giggled. "But over time I got used to it and now I hardly perspire at all." He was wearing mascara and a slight smudge of eye shadow. "What's that you're drinking?"

"A Donnie Miller."

"Oh, God, don't drink that swill." He took her glass and dashed the contents on the ground. "You need a real drink at your debut, honey, and not one of those fruity-fruity, sweety-sweet things." He beckoned for a waitress and told her to bring two vodka martinis.

"My debut?" Ava said.

"Didn't you know you were coming out?" Fraser made dramatic sweeping gestures at the crowd. "You're Will Fraser's *friend* and you're being introduced to society. You're having what we like to call a debut."

"Does that make me a debutante?"

"Of course."

"I always wondered what that felt like."

"Well?" He raised one eyebrow rakishly. "What does it feel like?"

"I'll let you know as soon as I finish the vodka martini."

"See," he said. "You're a natural."

Later, he tucked one arm under hers and propelled her across the lawn to an empty table. "I hear you're a *fiction* writer," he said in a low voice.

Ava smiled wryly and sipped her drink. "I'm trying."

"Well, you're in the right place. My God, the stories I could tell you—madness, murder, unrequited love, ghostly apparitions."

"Ghostly apparitions?" Ava said.

He waved at someone he knew, then leaned close to her, ducking his chin like a conspirator. "They're all haunted," he said, "each and every house along this street. You know how it is when people have lived and died in a place for more than two centuries. Now, some of the ghosts are more pleasant than others, of course. We have, excuse me, we *had*, one of the nastier ones. The Captain." He shivered dramatically and took a long pull from his drink. "He rode with Forrest during the War of Northern Aggression."

"The War of Northern Aggression?"

"The Civil War."

"Oh. Right."

"He was a truly despicable character, despite the fact that he was one of my revered ancestors, rumored to have beaten the help and, of course, he was there during the Fort Pillow massacre. Anyway, I used to see him when I was a child. I'd be playing in my room and I'd feel a brush of cold air and all the hair would rise along my arms and I would know he was there. He didn't scare me at first—children don't question such things—but I could tell he wasn't a pleasant thing, and after a while I didn't want him around. Mother didn't mind, of course; she said he was family and we mustn't be ashamed of him, but we mustn't talk of him in public either. No airing of the family linen and all that rot. As I got older I saw him less and less.

"And then Mother remodeled the kitchen and one of the upstairs bedrooms, the room where the Captain used to sleep—she made it into a bathroom—and when they opened the walls, they found old whiskey bottles and French postcards hidden there, the old perv. Then things really got crazy. Pictures flying off walls, the workmen's tools being moved, faucets turning off and on by themselves. Let me tell you this: if someone was spiteful in life, you can be sure they'll be spiteful in death!

"After a while the contractors all quit and Mother was so afraid that it would get out, that people would be talking about the family, as if every family on this street doesn't have their own ghosts to deal with." He sipped his drink and rolled his eyes as if expecting her to acknowledge the truth of this statement. "Anyway, after college I had this friend who lived in Atlanta. He was an architect and he'd had a lot of experience remodeling old houses and chasing off the family ghosts, so he arranged for a psychic he knew to come to the house when Mother was away and do a cleansing. And after that everything stopped. It stopped just like that." He snapped his fingers to emphasize his point. "And do you know what Mother did? A few weeks after things got quiet she said, 'I miss the Captain,' all sad and depressed, as if she wasn't grateful at all that I'd gotten rid of him. But I can tell you when her damn Wedgwood plates were flying off the shelves she didn't miss the Captain!"

Ava was quiet for a moment, sipping her drink, and then she said, "Is Woodburn Hall haunted?"

"Oh, yes. By the Gray Lady. Supposedly, she's the ghost of Delphine Woodburn. She walks up and down the stairs in a long black dress. She was always mourning the death of one of her children. They used to die off like flies in those days. They say you can hear her crying at night."

"Have you ever seen her?"

"No, but Will has. He used to see her when he was a boy. Hasn't he told you?"

She looked across the yard to where Will stood talking to a woman in a low-cut flowered dress. She remembered that day at Longford when he'd ridiculed the idea of ghosts. "No," she said. "He hasn't mentioned it."

"I'm surprised. He used to be terrified as a boy to go anywhere near the stairwell."

The woman in the low-cut dress appeared to be an old friend of Will's. She stood talking to him for a long time, laughing loudly and touching him from time to time on the shoulder. Drawn by her loud laughter, Fraser looked across the lawn and said, "Sweet Jesus, who invited Darlene Haney?"

"I did," his mother said, coming up behind them. She had strolled over with Josephine, Fanny, and Clara to check on Ava. They all held rocks glasses in their well-manicured hands. "And I want you to be nice. She's a guest."

"What were you thinking?" Fraser said. "I don't remember seeing her name on the list."

"Well, I was over at the Debs and Brides Shoppe where she works and she mentioned the party. She said she so wanted to meet Ava, and really," she looked at Fraser helplessly, "what was I to do?"

"You mean she invited herself."

"Now, Fraser," his mother said, wagging her finger in his face. "You be a gentleman." Her cheeks were pink from the heat and the gin, and she seemed slightly tipsy. She slid her arm around Ava's shoulders and said, "Having fun?"

"Yes. Thank you. Great fun."

"Oh, look, Fraser, her glass is empty. Be sweet and run up and get Ava another martini."

"I'm fine," Ava said, remembering Will's warning not to drink too much. She was trying, belatedly, to pace herself.

"Are you sure? Well, maybe some iced tea then."

"Dear God, Mother, don't fuss," Fraser said.

Across the lawn, Will had excused himself from Darlene Haney and walked away, stopping to speak to a young couple Ava hadn't met. Darlene stood for a moment, sipping her drink and looking around the yard, then, noticing the group of young matrons, she set off unsteadily to join them. She was wearing high heels that sank into the soft earth with each step so that she walked with an odd lurching motion.

"I taught Darlene in school," Clara said, watching her navigate the lawn. "She was such an interesting character. Darlene Smollett, she was back then. Before she married Eddie Haney."

"Oh, now, *that* was a match made in heaven," Alice said, and Fraser snorted.

He leaned over and said in a stage whisper to Ava, "Eddie was bad to drink." And when she looked at him blankly he made a motion like someone tugging on a bottle. "He was the quarterback up at UT where Darlene was a cheerleader and he was rumored to be a top NFL draft pick. No doubt Darlene thought she'd won the lottery when she landed him."

"That's right," Alice said. "Chased him until he caught her."

Fraser snorted again and looked at his mother appreciatively. They were like a couple of schoolgirls. Ava imagined them sitting around at night with their cocktails gossiping about the townspeople, each trying to outdo the other in outrageousness.

"They came back here and had one of the biggest, tackiest weddings Woodburn has ever seen," Fraser said. "And then Eddie blew his knee out his senior year and had to come back and go to work in his daddy's body shop and that was the end of Darlene's dreams of grandeur. I guess being an auto mechanic's wife was not nearly as glamorous as being an NFL quarterback's wife. The marriage didn't last. Eddie ran off with a cocktail waitress—imagine that—leaving Darlene with three boys under the age of six."

"Poor thing," Ava said. "That's terrible."

"You don't know her," Fraser said darkly.

"Yes," Fanny said, shaking her head sadly. "I hear those boys are quite a handful."

"You don't know her yet but you will," Alice said in a sweet, cautioning voice. "Because here she comes." Darlene had seen them and was waving wildly. She launched herself and began to cross the lawn in their direction, her large bosom jutting before her like the prow of a ship.

"Quick," Fraser said bleakly. "Run. Hide."

"You be nice," his mother warned in a low voice, and as Darlene got closer she smiled and called, "Come and meet Will's friend."

They watched her come and Ava, afraid she might stumble and fall against the table, stood up to greet her.

"Oh, my God, you must be Ava," Darlene squealed, opening her arms wide. She held Ava out in front of her, looking her over. She was smaller but with her high heels they were almost the same height. Darlene was blonde and very pretty in the way that beauty pageant contestants and TV commentators are pretty, with their perfect makeup and hair and trim figures. "How *are* you?" she said, pumping Ava's hand. A cloud of perfume billowed around her like smoke.

Ava, feeling suddenly tongue-tied by this effusive welcome, stammered, "I'm well, thank you. And you?"

"Oh, aren't you *precious?*" Darlene pulled her into another flowery embrace. "I just know we're going to be *good, good* friends," she said.

"Which translated means, 'I just know we're going to be enemies for life,' " Fraser said darkly.

"Now Sparky, don't be ugly," Darlene said, pulling away from Ava and letting her feline eyes sweep over Fraser.

He flushed a dull red. "Don't call me that."

Darlene ignored him. "I am just so happy to meet Will Fraser's Chicago friend," she said, smiling to show her perfect teeth. "I hear you're real smart. And so pretty, too!"

Ava noted that her accent was more nasal than the slow, deep-throated accent the aunts and Clara and Alice used. The older women's voices were like water bubbling in a brook, while Darlene's was a discordant twang.

"Who would have thought that you and Will went to college together?" Darlene said blithely, her eyes scanning Ava. "Who would have *thunk* it, as we say down here."

Fanny giggled. "That's right," she said. "We have our own language."

Darlene gave Ava's arm a little shake. "If someone down here says 'bless her little heart,' about someone—well, that means they're mortal enemies."

"Kind of like saying 'we're going to be *good, good friends,*' " Fraser said.

"And we don't *push* a button," Darlene said. "We *mash* it. We don't *take* someone to the store, we *carry* them." She giggled again and put one hand to the side of her mouth. "And if someone down here says your baby is *sweet,* well, then, you know it's ugly."

Ava shook her head. "Someone needs to write all this down for me. I'll never remember it."

"Isn't she *darling*!" Darlene cried and Fraser said, "Another adversarial statement."

"You know, you're really starting to bug me," Darlene said.

"Fraser, why don't you refresh everyone's drink?" Alice said pointedly.

"What, and leave Ava alone with the succubus?"

Josephine said, "Oh, Fraser, really."

Darlene said, "What's a succubus?"

"Now that you mention it," Ava said, giving her glass to Fraser. "I think I will have another drink."

Later, Ava asked Will, "Why do they call Fraser 'Sparky?' "

"It's just a nickname some of the town kids gave him. They liked to tease him because of his—uniqueness."

"You mean his gayness?"

"Who called him Sparky?"

"Darlene Haney."

"That figures. They always fight like cats."

"Why?"

"I don't know," he said. "Jealousy, I guess."

Darlene Haney had invited Ava to lunch, so on Tuesday she walked the few blocks from the house to downtown Woodburn. It was a hot, sultry day. Cicadas hummed in the trees, and bits of yellow pollen floated on the air like duck down. The sidewalk was old and buckled where the tree roots had pushed through, upending the bricks. All along the street the few people she saw waved to her from their yards and shady porches. "Good morning," they called, and she said, "Good morning." Her manner was brisk. She was embarrassed by their attention, wishing she had paid more attention to the names of those she had met at the barbecue.

The Debs and Brides Shoppe faced the town square with its large fountain and ubiquitous statue of the Unknown Confederate Soldier. Large oak trees surrounded the square, with benches scattered beneath their shady branches. Everywhere there were masses of blooming shrubbery, and from the old-fashioned light posts lining the street hung baskets of ivy geraniums, petunias, and verbena. Most of the shops lining the square sported striped awnings and hand-painted signs, and the whole effect was quaint and charming and looked like something from a turn-of-the-century movie set.

The shop was crowded with debs arraying themselves for the Gardenia Ball. Darlene, looking flustered and overworked, raised her hand when Ava came in and shouted, "I'll be right with you."

They walked next door to the Kudzu Grille to order lunch. "Whewee," Darlene said, lifting her hair off her neck with one hand and fanning herself with the other. "It's hot enough to boil spit on a sidewalk."

They sat at a small table near a window overlooking the square. "What's good?" Ava said, looking down at the menu. "I'm really not sure what to order. I'm still getting used to Southern food. I'll have to order the fried green tomatoes, of course, because I've never had them and hey, when in Rome."

"There's really only one thing to order and that's the blue plate special," Darlene said, closing her menu and reaching for Ava's. "Collard greens, corn bread, black-eyed peas, and squash casserole for two," she said to the waitress. "Oh, and a small plate of fried green tomatoes. And two sweet teas." They watched her walk away.

"Well," Ava said, looking around. The restaurant was beginning to fill up, and Ava was glad they'd found a table. She'd agreed to meet Darlene for lunch because it had occurred to her that Darlene might be willing to share information about the Woodburns. Specifically, Charlie Woodburn.

Darlene gave her a tight, fierce grin and slapped Ava's arm. "I am so glad you came!"

Ava as always, disarmed by Darlene's direct, friendly approach, said, "I'm glad I came, too."

Darlene patted Ava's hand. "I just know we're going to be good, good friends. I knew it from the moment I first set eyes on you. I knew it right here," Darlene said, thumping her chest like she was trying to dislodge something trapped in her trachea.

Ava smiled nervously. She looked around the restaurant. "Do you eat here every day?"

"Sure," Darlene said. She crossed her arms on the table and leaned forward, examining Ava closely. "I wish my eyelashes were as long and thick as yours! Why, if I went without mascara like you do, my eyes would just disappear in my face."

"Is it open for dinner, too?" Ava asked, smiling at the waitress who brought their iced teas.

"I could never get away with wearing my hair short. It looks good on you but if I went around not fixing my hair or my face nobody would give me the time of day!"

Ava coughed politely. The tea was good, very cold and very sweet, served in a frosty mason jar. Ava tried to think of something pleasant to say. "So do you like your job?"

"Oh, hell no," Darlene said. "But it pays the bills and puts food on the table, two things my ex seems incapable of doing, bless his little heart." And she launched into a long tirade about her deadbeat ex-husband and Ava listened, thankful to have Darlene's attention off her for a while. A short time later the waitress brought their food. Darlene was still going on and on about Eddie Haney. "Listen to me," she said finally, giving another bright fierce smile. "Going on and on about my loser ex-husband when you're attached to just about the most perfect man in the whole wide world!"

Ava looked at her blankly. "Who?"

"Why, Will Fraser, silly."

"Oh, right. Will's a nice guy."

Darlene leaned forward and lowered her voice. "So is it true you two are actually—dating?"

"Who told you that?"

Darlene chewed slowly, her eyes fixed steadily on Ava's face. "It's common knowledge," she said.

"It's true that Will and I are good friends. We went to school together." Ava's voice trailed off. She glanced around the restaurant, took a long drink of iced tea. "We're just good friends."

"Oh, really?" Darlene said, and it was clear that she wasn't convinced.

Ava turned her attention to her plate. "The food is good," she said and it was true, everything except the fried green tomatoes, which looked pretty and smelled good but tasted kind of bland.

"This is country-style cooking," Darlene said, pointing at her plate with her fork. "You probably don't get a lot of this at the Woodburn table."

"Oh, no, they eat a lot of vegetables. And Maitland makes corn bread from time to time, although he puts jalapeño peppers in his."

"Really?" Darlene said. "Jalapeño peppers? Huh."

"Listen, there's something I wanted to ask you," Ava said.

Darlene put her fork down and leaned forward. "Go ahead. Shoot. Ask me anything."

"Charlie Woodburn." Ava stopped. Saying his name sent an odd tremor down her spine. A week ago she had never even heard of him and now she couldn't stop thinking about who he was and how he had died.

Darlene stared at her curiously, a slight smile pulling down the corners of her mouth. "What about him?"

"What do you know about him? I know he was married to Fanny before Maitland. A long time before Maitland. I know he and Fanny eloped and then he died."

Darlene pushed her plate away and crossed her arms on the table. "Well, of course that was long before my time," she said, letting her eyes slide over the diners at the tables closest to them before shifting back to Ava. "But you know how these little towns are. Everybody's known everybody else's secrets for generations. And everyone loves to gossip about the high and mighty Woodburns."

There was something secretive about Darlene, something damp and cloying that spilled out of her like an overfilled glass. Ava could sense it now. She remembered Fraser's tale of Darlene's glory days up at UT, how she'd dreamed of marrying a rich man and instead found herself saddled with three children, working long hours in a dress shop frequented by snotty adolescent girls. Ava supposed this was why Darlene seemed so eager to gossip about the Woodburns; it took the focus off her own dreary life.

"High and mighty?" she said.

"Oh, sure," Darlene said, rolling her eyes mockingly. "The Woodburns have been gentry for generations, ever since old Randal Woodburn crossed the Cumberland Bluff back in 1799. On his way to Nashville, they say, to study law with his old friend Andrew Jackson. The Woodburns were an old Virginia family, gentry even back that far, before the Revolutionary War, and Randal was the younger son who had to seek his fortune on the frontier. They say he stopped at Piney Creek and saw the rich bottomland churned up each year by the floods and figured if he could find a way to divert the creek he'd have the makings of a fine plantation. Of course, there was nothing there in the way of civilization at the time, just the occasional fur trader making his way up from Natchez, and a Chickasaw town decimated by smallpox.

"Anyway, he drove off the few Chickasaws who still had the gumption to fight, enslaved the rest, and set about clearing the land and diverting the creek. His father sent a gaggle of black slaves to help, and when they were done he had a well-built stockade to keep the slaves and animals in, a cabin to sleep in, and two thousand acres of rich bottom-land to grow cotton. He called the plantation Longford after their homeplace in Ireland or Scotland or wherever it is the Woodburns came from."

"But how does Charlie Woodburn fit into all this?"

"Hang on, I'm getting to that. It seems Old Randal got lonely back there in the wilderness and took up with a Chickasaw woman who bore him a number of little brown-skinned, black-eyed children. That's where the Black Woodburns come from."

"The Black Woodburns?"

"That's right. They all descend from Randal and this Indian woman, and they're called that because of their dark eyes and black hair. To distinguish them from the True Woodburns, whose eyes are always blue-gray, in case you haven't noticed."

"And Charlie was a Black Woodburn?"

"Black as the devil. Now don't look at me like that, I know it sounds crazy, but you can always tell a Woodburn just by looking at them. They all look like they were stamped out of a cookie cutter, kind of like the royal family of England, only half of them are dark-eyed and dark-haired and the other half are light-eyed and fair. And the ones who are dark are poor as a sawmill rat."

"Will's hair is dark."

"Yes, but he's a Fraser, too. His grandmother, Celia, was a Woodburn, but the male line of True Woodburns died out with Will's great-grandfather, Miss Celia and Miss Josephine and Miss Fanny's father. Maybe that's why the Colonel took such an interest in Charlie Woodburn, offering to pay his way through Vanderbilt. Charlie looked just like Old Randal—you've seen that oil painting of him in the dining room of the house—only with the dark eyes and hair of the Black Woodburns."

"So Miss Fanny's father took Charlie in and raised him? He approved of Fanny marrying him even though they were distant cousins and Charlie had no money?"

"Oh, hell no," Darlene said, shaking her head and looking at Ava like she couldn't believe how naive she was. "Charlie was a Woodburn but he wasn't highborn. He wasn't a True Woodburn. He was born here but raised in New Orleans. The rumor is, his father was a gambler and Charlie took after him. Came riding into town in a big car and fancy clothes, making all the girls' hearts flutter like that actor from the silent movies, the one who always dressed up in veils and turbans."

"Rudolph Valentino?"

"Yeah, him. Fanny's father was happy to send him to Vanderbilt, but he never intended for Charlie to marry one of his daughters."

"So what happened?"

"The old man dropped dead and suddenly Celia and Josephine and Fanny were orphans. Rich orphans. Celia was still a child, but Josephine and Fanny were up at Vanderbilt with Charlie, and that's where he got his hooks into her. He eloped with Fanny right under the Woodburn cousins' noses, not to mention Maitland Sinclair's, who was Miss Fanny's childhood sweetheart. They say Charlie did it for the money."

"So Charlie Woodburn eloped with Fanny, and the rest of the family got angry because they felt he was taking advantage of an orphaned girl?"

"That's right, and that's why they killed him."

Ava stared blankly at Darlene.

Darlene's eyes grew round. She clamped a small, plump hand to her face. "Oh, dear," she said through her fingers. "I've said too much."

"Don't even think about stopping there," Ava said, leaning to peel Darlene's fingers off her mouth. "Continue."

Darlene looked around the restaurant and dipped her head, dropping her voice. "That's just a story," she said. "No one knows if it's really true. There are probably a half dozen stories about how Charlie Woodburn died. And who killed him."

Ava was quiet for a moment, remembering Will's hesitation in the cemetery. "Tell me," she said finally.

"Well, some think it was Maitland Sinclair. He had the most to gain because he and Fanny had been sweethearts since childhood and they married after Charlie died."

"But not right away."

"Oh, hell no. Not until after Miss Fanny's boy, Sumner, was grown. And then some. Sumner was born the same year Charlie died, and he must have been about forty when they finally married."

"Fanny and Maitland waited *forty* years to marry?"

Darlene shrugged. "Yeah, but still, they married."

Ava sat back with her hands in her lap, thinking about all this. She thought of the framed photographs of a youthful Fanny and Maitland hanging on the walls at Woodburn Hall. They may not have married right away but they had certainly traveled the world together, they had certainly acted like husband and wife. Or had they? Perhaps they had only been friends, not lovers. Fanny must have been crazy in love with Charlie Woodburn to mourn him for nearly forty years.

She thought of big jolly Maitland with his homemade mayonnaise and apron that read *Kitchen Bitch*. Poor man.

"Maitland is a sweetheart," she said. "I can't imagine him murdering anyone."

Darlene gave her a dismal look. "You never know what people will do," she said darkly, "if they're pushed to it." They were quiet for a moment, each lost in her own thoughts, and then Darlene roused herself and added, "Personally, I always thought it was the McGann woman."

"Clara? What about her?"

"Who killed him. From what I've heard anyway."

"Wait a minute," Ava said, holding up one hand. "Start at the beginning. How exactly does Clara fit into the Woodburns?"

Darlene frowned and tapped one finger against the edge of her iced-tea jar. "I don't know. Her people were slaves at one time, I guess, but no one around here ever talks about stuff like that."

"Will says Clara's people were freed before the Civil War."

"Oh, well, he should know, then." Darlene yawned, then hesitated as if something else had occurred to her. "One story I always heard is that Clara is related to the Woodburns somehow."

"How?"

Darlene shrugged. She gave Ava a sly smile. "Maybe you should ask your good friend Will."

Ava imagined that a question like that would go over about as well as her questions about the fiancée and Charlie Woodburn. "Why do you think Clara had something to do with Charlie Woodburn's death?"

"Her mother was a healer. People used to come from far and wide to have their fortunes told, and she knew how to use herbs and wildflowers. I'm sure she taught her daughter. I'm sure Miss McGann knows how to use plants, which ones are poisonous and stuff like that. She could've poisoned him and no one would have known the difference."

"But why would Clara McGann have poisoned Charlie Woodburn?"

Darlene shrugged and stifled another yawn. "I don't know," she said. "Maybe she didn't like him."

Coming out of the Kudzu Grille, Ava's attention was drawn by a man loading lumber into the back of a pickup truck. He was standing across the narrow brick street with his back to her, and for a moment Ava thought it was Will. But then he turned and she stood staring at him in amazement. He bore a striking resemblance to Will, tall and dark-haired, although he was sturdier, more heavily built. He stood staring intently at her, the sunlight glinting on his hair. Beside her, Darlene stiffened.

"Good morning," he called and his voice was not like Will's. "Who've you got there?" he said, talking to Darlene but still staring at Ava.

"Wouldn't you like to know?" Darlene said. She took Ava's arm. "Come on," she said. "We're risking our reputations just talking to him."

He laughed as they walked off. Ava turned and glanced at him over her shoulder. He was leaning against the truck watching her, and she suddenly remembered that night outside the movie theater when she and Will had been silently observed by a dark-haired man. He was that man. She was sure of it.

"My God," Ava said, letting Darlene pull her along the sidewalk.

"No. Jake Woodburn," Darlene said.

"One of the Black Woodburns?"

"Black sheep more likely," Darlene said. "He makes Charlie Woodburn look like a saint."

"He and Will could be twins! Well, maybe not twins, but certainly brothers." Ava could feel the heat beating down on the top of her head, seeping through her, settling in her bones.

Darlene stopped, letting her hand drop. "I wouldn't mention to Will that you saw Jake if I was you."

"Why?"

"They don't speak. They're estranged."

"But why?"

Darlene let her face go blank. "Something about a girl," she said.

"A girl?" Ava said stupidly.

Darlene clamped her hand over her mouth, her eyes blue and sharp as ice picks.

"Oh, dear," she said. "I've said too much."

Burn Barrel

Darlene Haney left the clueless Yankee girl Will Fraser was dating, told her boss she had to make a bank run, then drove over to the wrong side of town to visit her mother and brother. She was in a foul mood; being around Ava had done that. Darlene couldn't quite put her finger on what it was about Ava that was so attractive. She was pretty enough in that careless, affected way some smart girls adopted, as if the way they looked was secondary to what went on inside their heads. But she certainly wasn't pretty in the conventional sense of the word, not in the sense that Darlene, raised on beauty pageants and reruns of *Charlie's Angels,* had been taught to appreciate. Her hair was too short, she wore very little makeup, she obviously didn't care a thing about fashion, and yet there was something compelling about her.

Darlene guessed she was different enough from the Southern girls that Will Fraser had been raised with to seem like a novelty, although Darlene was just as certain that Will would eventually tire of all that naturalness and come looking for a woman who kept breath mints on the bedside table, who went to bed wearing full makeup, and never left the house without fixing her hair and wearing a pair of six-inch heels. It was only a matter of time before you came back to what you were raised with.

This thought took root in her mind, but instead of cheering her only served to deepen her depression as she pulled up in front of her mother's peeling little shotgun house. A pair of kitchen chairs sat out on the sagging porch, and the overgrown yard was decorated with a couple of painted plywood cutouts, one showing a spotted hound dog lifting his leg on a daisy, and the other a little girl in a petticoat and a short dress leaning over to water the grass in a disturbingly provocative way. A rusty wind chime stirred listlessly in the slight breeze. This part of town sat down in a depression and was always foul smelling and airless, choked from the south by a dense swamp and from the north by the railroad stockyards. Darlene had spent her childhood and adolescence trying to figure out how to get as far away from here as possible.

And now here she was back again, although she wasn't living with her mother; thank God, she hadn't sunk that low. Yet.

Darlene's seventy-seven-year-old mother, Snowda, was a chain-smoking diabetic who had already lost one leg and a lung to her vices, and spent most days hooked up to an oxygen machine. She kept her thermostat set on eighty-five, even during the hottest days. Darlene's sixty-year-old brother, Richard, lived with Snowda. Richard had a heart condition and failing kidneys that left him puffed up like a blowfish. He was deaf in one ear but refused to wear a hearing aid, which may have been a blessing in disguise, as his ex-wife, Deb, had been a loud-mouthed shrew. Deb had recently absconded with the proceeds from the sale of their trailer and most of Richard's railroad pension, leaving Richard with nothing more than a molting, mean-tempered parrot named Fred who spent his days screeching, "Ri-chard! Ri-chard!" and "You want a piece of me?" in exact mimicry of Deb's shrewish voice.

When Darlene opened the front door they were just sitting down to what Snowda liked to call "her programs." The cable was out, and they were reduced to watching Spanish television soap operas even though neither one of them spoke the language. Through the dining room window of the tiny house Darlene could see her three sons in the back-yard flicking lit matches into a burn barrel.

Neither Snowda nor Richard seemed to have noticed her arrival, their eyes glued to the flickering television set. "Guess what," Darlene said to her mother. She sat down gingerly on the sofa, smoothing her skirt. "Guess who sold more cotillion gowns this month than any other salesgirl at the Debs and Brides Shoppe!"

At the other end of the sofa, Richard scratched listlessly at his crotch and said, "Mama, turn it up some. I can't hear."

"Don't make no difference if I turn it up or not," Snowda said. "You can't understand none of that gobbledygook they're saying."

"Me! That's who!" Darlene said brightly.

Snowda slid her eyes from the screen to Darlene, then back again. "What?" she said. "Were some of the regular salesgals out sick?"

The house was as sweltering as a jungle. Waves of heat rose off the TV and hung in the air like thunderclouds. In the background the parrot screeched, "Ri-chard! Ri-chard! Ri-chard!" in a crazed, endless loop.

"No, they were not out sick," Darlene snapped, but she knew she was fighting a losing battle. She'd gone her whole life without her mother's approval, and she wasn't about to get it now. Snowda had been nearly fifty when she had Darlene, a surprise up until the very moment the birth pangs began, and as a child Darlene used to imagine that she'd been kidnapped from a large white-columned house on a hill and plopped down in the middle of these poverty-stricken circus freaks.

"Mama, you got any Pepsi?" Richard said.

Snowda pointed behind her with a large flat thumb. "Them boys of yours need a good whipping," she said to Darlene. "They cut the blooms off all my Crimson Glory roses."

Darlene stared through the window at her sons, who had managed to ignite the burn barrel and were dancing around it now like a tribe of savages. She left the boys with her mother because she couldn't afford decent child care with the wages she made at the Debs and Brides Shoppe. She sighed. "I'll buy you some new roses, Mama."

"Them boys need a daddy."

"I'm working on it," Darlene said grimly, and, rising, she went into the kitchen to hunt for the fire extinguisher.

By the end of her third week in Woodburn, Ava was growing accustomed to the routines of the house. The sameness of their days, broken only by the one daily planned activity, the punctuality of meals, the afternoon nap, light gardening or reading followed at five by Toddy Time, all had a soothing effect on her. She found herself being lulled into a kind of stupor by the somnolent quality of the place: the steady ticking of the mantel clock, the low hum of the air-conditioning, the ceaseless whirring of the cicadas in the trees, so loud you could hear them through the window glass.

Some days she would wander out on the verandah after lunch while the others slept, stretching out on the old porch swing or along one of the settees with a book on her lap, a frosty glass of iced tea resting on the table beside her. They made it by the pitcher down here and loaded it with sugar and fresh mint. *Sweet tea,* they called it, and Ava had never tasted anything so good. She would sip her tea and gaze out at the garden and the lawn, hazy beneath the midday sun. Everything in the landscape seemed to move in slow motion, drowsy with the heat. She would look up into the tall trees shading the house and think, *This is heaven.*

Lost in her reveries, it was not hard to imagine how it must have been when the house was first built, men on horseback passing out front, the muffled clop of hooves on the dusty road, the jangle of mule-drawn wagons on their way to town. In the old days this would have been fields and forest, all except for Woodburn Hall and a few other summer "cottages" scattered along the road. Half closing her eyes and squinting up into the tops of the tall trees, Ava could imagine herself in another time and place, with no sound but the clatter of cicadas, birdsong from the dense thickets, the occasional creak of wooden wheels or the rattling of bridle bits.

She had always been an imaginative person. Reared on Clotilde's fantastic stories, Ava had turned naturally to literature. Whole worlds opened to her between the covers of a book. Whatever her other failings as a parent, Clotilde had always made sure Ava had a library card, and she had gone once a week to prowl the shelves of the public library in whatever city they found themselves marooned in. Ava never got over the sense of sanctuary she felt in a library, the fragrance of cloth and old paper, the reverence she felt when holding some dusty book in her hands. It was the same feeling she got now, shut up in the library of Woodburn Hall. The house, the whole town, was like living inside an old novel.

Yet despite the quiet peacefulness of the place, she had not written one word since she arrived. She had not entered one sentence onto the glowing computer screen.

Since college, she had written only in the evenings, being forced to support herself by a series of dismal day jobs. None of the produced work had been promising; few of the short stories were ever finished, and those that were were never accepted by the literary magazines she sent them to. But she had persisted with a stubborn tenacity, an overwhelming belief that she was meant to be a writer and that one day her luck would change. The sale of her mother's old Subaru, as well as the extra income from her sublet apartment, had left her with enough to get by on for a few months this summer, and yet now that she had time and quiet and was free of the need to make a daily wage, she found herself unable to sit down at her computer and plink out more than a few halfhearted attempts at an outline.

Write what you know or what you'd like to know, one of her professors in college had told her. What she had known, what she had experienced, was a nomadic childhood with a mysterious mother who collected odd characters the way some women collect spoons. And yet when it came time to write about such promising material, she felt stymied, blocked, unable for some reason to immerse herself in the story.

As if guessing that she was having trouble starting, Will asked her one day, "Do you want me to brainstorm with you?"

"No, that's all right. Not now anyway." It irritated her that he always seemed eager to fix her problems, as if he had little confidence that she could do it herself. This was on a Friday afternoon and she was putting on some makeup for Toddy Time, while he sat and watched.

"Really," he said. "I don't mind."

"No. Thanks."

She caught his expression in the looking glass. He looked amused and dubious, and it occurred to Ava that he was only being polite, that he really didn't care if she ever wrote a novel or not. She had listened to his CD and had been surprised at the quality and sophistication of his music, something of a cross between Radiohead and Pete Yorn. But when she asked him why he didn't try to land a recording contract, he said coolly, "It's just a hobby. Just something I do for myself. Trying to make a living out of it would only spoil it."

"Who's coming today for cocktails?" she asked.

He told her. She fluffed her hair with her fingers, glad now that the short spikes had lengthened and were beginning to lie flat against her scalp. He stared at her in the glass, smiling. She hadn't told him about seeing Jake Woodburn on the street, and yet now it seemed as if she should.

"You look nice," he said.

"Do I?" The time for confession was past. She avoided his gaze, turning swiftly from the mirror.

Cocktail hour, she had learned in the weeks that she had been here, was as ritualistic as a Japanese tea ceremony; it began at five o'clock and ended promptly at six. Maitland was in charge of the silver cocktail shaker, and took his duties seriously. Everyone dressed for Toddy Time; Maitland always wore a prep school tie and a blazer over a pair of dress slacks and a shirt, while Fanny and Josephine invariably changed into light summer dresses. Will was partial to collared shirts and khaki shorts. Even Ava would change her shorts or jeans for a skirt. There was always a silver tray of sliced cheese and crackers and sometimes an assortment of olives sitting on the coffee table. It was impossible to tell how much anyone actually drank, as Maitland continued throughout the hour to discreetly refill glasses.

"You asked me that first day out at Longford about my broken engagement," Will said suddenly, without warning, and she was so surprised she could think of nothing to say. He went on slowly, carefully choosing his words. "I was engaged," he said. "To a girl I met in boarding school. Her name was Hadley."

"Hadley? How very aristocratic." She kept her tone light, teasing. She waited to see if she might feel even a twinge of jealousy but she felt nothing.

"We got engaged our second year of college, which I realize now was entirely too young. She was up at Sewanee, and we had been dating for nearly four years and, I don't know, it just seemed like the right thing to do. At the time."

"Look, Will, you don't have to . . ."

"It seemed like the right thing at the time," he said. "But it wasn't and I realize that now. I just didn't want you to think I was still grieving over that relationship."

"No, of course not," she said.

He seemed so sincere, so mannerly, and she felt bad that she had ever teased him about his engagement, and that he seemed so determined to explain something she really cared nothing about.

She couldn't stop thinking about Jake Woodburn. She knew that it was wrong, that it would only wind up complicating her life when she was intent on simplifying it. The aunts had never mentioned him, and Ava felt certain there was a reason for that. And Will had made it clear that evening outside the movie theater that he disliked Jake. Ava didn't want any trouble. She wanted a quiet summer where she could work undisturbed, and she was grateful to the Woodburn sisters, and to Will, for giving her this opportunity. She made up her mind to stop thinking about Jake Woodburn and start thinking about the novel she had so little time left to write.

But, as often happens when a conscious decision is made to avoid someone, she seemed to run into Jake everywhere.

The first time she was coming out of the small bookstore on the square and he was passing on the sidewalk. He stuck out his hand and said, "Hello, Ava. I'm Jake Woodburn."

"Yes, yes, of course. Nice to meet you," she said, taking his hand, briefly, and then hurrying away.

The second time was coming out of the Piggly Wiggly. He drove by in his truck and waved, but Ava turned her head and pretended she hadn't seen him.

The third time was at the hardware store.

She had spent the morning listlessly prowling her bedroom. Determined to work on her outline, she had risen earlier than usual, and after a breakfast of cereal and fruit, had brought her coffee back to her room. She opened the shutters and made the bed, and then she sat down at the computer, facing the long windows. Sunlight flooded the room, lying in bands across the Oriental carpet and the dark polished floor. She ran her fingers over her favorite books, all neatly arranged on the wide desk between two bookends: her well-worn thesaurus, her copies of *Beloved, Jane Eyre, Love in the Time of Cholera,* and *The Turn of the Screw.*

Outside in the garden, Fanny was feeding the cats. They were feral, and no one could get near them but her. She brought them scraps of food and milk, which she placed in saucers around the garden, and they followed at her feet mewing and rubbing themselves against her legs for all the world like a troop of tame house cats. But if anyone else entered the garden, they would take off like so many streaks of color, and if anyone else brought scraps, they would wait until the stranger reentered the house before they crept forth warily to eat.

Ava yawned and looked at the clock, wondering what Josephine might be making for lunch. She had grown accustomed to regular meals, and now she found herself looking forward to breakfast, lunch, and supper. It gave a pleasant order to the day and filled the house with delicious smells. Freed from her usual habit of eating restaurant food and takeout, she had begun to feel healthier than she had in years. She had even managed to lose a little weight. Now, if only she could sleep at night, her transformation to good health would be complete.

She yawned again and stared, bleary-eyed, at the garden. Fanny had disappeared around the corner of the house along with her coterie of cats. Ava shifted her eyes to her scrolling screen saver. She picked up her mouse but nothing happened and, flipping it over, she saw that the battery was dead.

She rose immediately and went into the kitchen.

"Where's the best place to buy batteries?" she asked Josephine, who was standing at the counter slicing cucumbers.

"The hardware store has them. Or Walmart. The Piggly Wiggly." Josephine pointed with her knife. "There may be some in that drawer over there."

"That's okay," Ava said. "I'll go to town. I need a break anyway."

She parked outside the hardware store and went in. There were only a few people in the store, mostly contractors who stood around making small talk with the clerks, and now that she was here Ava felt foolish buying a package of batteries. She went over and inspected a collection of garden tools.

"Can I help you, ma'am?" a short, red-faced man asked her, and she said quickly, "No thanks, I'm just looking."

A knot of men lounging at the cash register watched her. She would have to buy something else now, something besides the batteries. She stopped at the battery display and then took a slip of paper out of her purse, pretending to check a list, and walked slowly along the paint aisle.

It was silly but now that she'd begun this charade, she'd have to finish it. Men in groups always made her nervous. Unlike women, they made no attempt to hide their scrutiny, speaking in loud, clear voices that were easily overheard. One of them said, "Like what you see, Bill?" and the others snickered.

She picked up a couple of paintbrushes, determined to stop this foolishness and get back to work, and as she wheeled around, she ran headlong into Jake Woodburn. He had come up behind her while she stood examining the brushes. He put his arms out to steady her.

"I thought that was you," he said.

"Excuse me," she said, clutching the brushes to her chest.

He dropped his arms. He was tall like Will, but broader through the shoulders, and his hair was longer, falling just below his ears. His eyes, slightly almond shaped and dark, were set above sharply jutting cheekbones. He wore a kind, bemused expression. "Do you need some help?"

The others watched them quietly. "No, I've got it," she said and stepped back with an odd, graceless movement, knocking over a cardboard display of painters' tape.

He helped her clean up the display, then followed her outside.

"Well, that was embarrassing," she said.

"Happens all the time. Contractors are a clumsy lot." She had the feeling he was laughing at her, although his expression was neutral, courteous. "Are you hungry?" he asked.

"Yes," she said. "I mean, I'm not sure."

"There's a really good barbecue place down on the river."

She tried to imagine what she would tell the aunts and Maitland if she didn't show up for lunch. She imagined Josephine's pale gray eyes flickering over her, ferreting out her secrets.

"You can follow me in your car, if you like," he said. "It's not too far."

"I can't."

"Aren't you hungry?"

"Yes."

"If we get there early enough we won't have to wait for a table."

"All right," she said.

———

It was only a short drive, but when she pulled up in the half-filled parking lot, she knew it was a mistake. Someone was bound to see her and report her to the aunts. Someone had probably seen them standing in the street outside the hardware store and was already on the phone to Josephine. Ava imagined phone lines all over Woodburn lit up like warning flares. It amazed her that she had only been here a short time and already she was beginning to care what others thought.

He was waiting for her under a sign that read *Battle Smoove Barbecue Joint,* and when she saw him standing there she stopped caring about the phone lines.

"Order the brisket," he said as they waited to place their orders.

It was early, but already the tiny restaurant was crowded with construction workers, lawyers, and clerks. You placed your order at a long counter in the front, then took a number and sat at one of the small tables covered in red-checked tablecloths, waiting for them to call your number.

"Out or in," the surly countergirl said.

"Sorry?" Ava said, fumbling with her wallet.

The girl sighed and stuck a pencil behind one ear. "You want it to go or here?"

"Here," Jake said, handing the girl a twenty.

"No," Ava said in embarrassment, but he laughed and said, "You can buy the dessert."

They made their way through the crowd to a small table in the far corner. Ava didn't recognize any faces but she had met so many people at Alice Barron's barbecue that she couldn't remember everyone. She saw a table of women near the front who seemed to take note of them as they came in.

"Why is this place called Battle Smoove?" she said, sitting in the chair he'd pulled out for her.

"Battle Smoove was a World War II veteran, a pilot with the Tuskegee Airmen who came back and opened a restaurant using his mother's recipes. When I was a boy we used to ride our bikes out here to eat barbecue."

"So you mean there really was a person named Battle Smoove?"

"There was. He's dead now. His granddaughter runs the place."

He went to the counter to get their sweet teas. His clothes were dusty in the back, as was his dark hair, and Ava remembered that someone, Darlene Haney probably, had told her he was a furniture maker.

"What do you think?" he said, sliding back into his chair and setting her tea down in front of her. He seemed completely unconcerned about his appearance, as though it were perfectly natural to go around with wood shavings in his hair.

She sipped her tea, which was strong and sweet. "About what?"

"About anything."

"I think it smells good in here."

"Best barbecue in Tennessee," he said, pulling a straw out of a wrapper. He glanced around the room, nodding at someone he knew.

"Are you a furniture maker?"

"I am." He dropped the straw in his glass. "I have a shop over on Hanover Street. When I dropped out of college, I went out to California for a while and when I came back here, I had to figure out something to do. I've always been a carpenter of sorts. I worked summers during high school and college on a construction crew, and I like working with my hands. So I started building furniture in my garage. Chairs and tables, simple stuff like that at first, that I sold at craft shows around the area. And then, over time, more and more people started calling me to do custom pieces, and my business kind of took off from there. Now I have a shop and do most of my sales on the Web, selling to dealers in New York and LA."

"So you're living the dream."

He smiled and shrugged, and Ava marveled at the powerful force of attraction, how it could make someone ordinary seem extraordinary. "I guess you could say that." He crossed his arms and leaned forward against the table. "What about you? What brings you to our fair city?"

She told him about her job in Chicago and how she and Will had gone to school together, and he had suggested that she come South for the summer to work on her book.

"Now, I'm just doing a little writing," she added vaguely, looking around the crowded restaurant.

"Fiction or nonfiction?"

"Fiction."

"Cool."

He didn't look at her the way others did when she told them she was a writer. A *fiction* writer. There was no stunned silence, no look of surprised embarrassment.

"So you're staying with the Woodburn sisters?"

"That's right."

"How are the old girls?"

There was really nothing ordinary about him, she decided. She would have noticed him anywhere, even on a crowded city street, his height, his black hair, the almost Oriental slant of his dark eyes. "They're fine. Fanny's a hoot. And Josephine, well, what can I say about Josephine? She's an interesting character."

He laughed. "She is that." He turned his head and stared out the window and she was struck again by his resemblance to Will. Thinking of Will brought a slight tremor of guilt, a feeling of disloyalty that was swiftly and smoothly cancelled out.

"They used to be quite fond of me," Jake said.

"Really?"

"When I was a boy," he said mildly.

The girl at the counter called their number and Jake went to get their food. Ava thought about calling the aunts to tell them she wasn't going to be there for lunch but she was afraid she might get Josephine and have to explain where she was. And then she was angry with herself because she was a grown woman and she didn't need to explain herself to anyone.

She picked up her phone and called Woodburn Hall. Maitland answered and she explained that she had stayed in town for lunch and would be back in a little while.

"Hell, take your time," Maitland said. "There's nobody here but us old folks and we'll see you when we see you."

She hung up and slid the phone back into her purse. Jake set the plates down on the table. "Do you want extra sauce?"

"No, thanks. Do you need some help?"

"Nope. I got it." He returned to the counter and brought back a basket of condiments and several large paper napkins. "How's Uncle Mait?" he asked.

"He's great," she said. She had ordered the brisket and a side of coleslaw and he'd ordered the pork sandwich with fries and slaw. She was glad now that she hadn't ordered the sandwich because she could see that it was going to be difficult to eat. "Does he remind you a little bit of Colonel Sanders in a sports coat?"

He grinned, opening his sandwich and piling his coleslaw on top. "I never really thought about it," he said.

They were quiet for a while, turning their attention to their food. From time to time he would turn his head and stare thoughtfully out the window. *He's moody,* Darlene had told her. *He has a dark side.* Ava was comfortable with his long silences. She had always been attracted to men with a touch of melancholy.

"You know the aunts paid for my schooling. I've always been grateful to them for that." He gave her a long, searching look.

"So you grew up with Will?"

"No. Not really. We ran in different circles," he said, and she thought how attractive his smile was, the way it pulled the corner of his mouth up higher on the left side than the right. "Early on, Will went to private school and I went to public. And then when they decided to send him off to boarding school in eighth grade, Fanny showed up one morning at my mother's place to see if maybe I wanted to go, too. I was a couple of years older than Will and I really didn't want to go off to school but I'd already gotten in a little trouble with the law, nothing serious, just high-spirited, boys-will-be-boys stuff, and my mother thought it'd be best if I got out of town for a while."

Ava chewed slowly. She had the feeling he was trying to convince her of something, to make her see things his way. "Why do you think they did that? Offered to pay for your schooling?"

He shrugged, wiping his mouth with his napkin. "I think Fanny did it out of the goodness of her heart and Josephine—" He was quiet for a moment, as if considering this. "Well, I think Josephine hoped I'd look after Will."

"And did you?"

His eyes flickered over her face, his expression sober, reproachful. "Of course I did."

"So whatever happened between you and Will, the falling-out between you two, didn't come until later? After boarding school?"

"I see you've been listening to the town gossips."

"Just Darlene Haney."

He groaned and shook his head. "The mouth of the South," he said.

"She said it was over a girl."

"Is that what she said?" His gaze remained sober, reflective. After a minute he set his sandwich down, carefully wiping the tips of his fingers. "It was more complicated than that. I did something wrong, something disloyal. Something Will and Josephine are never going to forgive me for." He seemed unwilling to say anything else. He leaned back in his seat, stretching one leg out beside her. "They're not forgiving people, those Woodburns," he added, and there was something soft but insistent in his voice.

All around them was the hum of conversation, the clatter of silverware.

"You're a Woodburn," she said.

"Not the right kind."

She told him then everything she'd learned about the Black Woodburns, including the mystery of Charlie Woodburn's death. While she talked he sat very still, listening.

When she'd finished, he raised his glass, drained it, then set it back down. "Why would you want to dredge all that up? It happened more than sixty years ago."

She was surprised by his reaction. "Why *wouldn't* you? Aren't you related to Charlie in some way?"

He shook his head. "That's what's wrong with this place," he said. "Everyone gets so caught up in living in the past, they don't live in the present."

"But you have to admit it's an interesting story."

"Maybe to a fiction writer."

Outside the windows the river glistened like a sheet of glass. A boy and an old man stood at the edge of the water, aimlessly casting their lines.

"Fraser Barron told me there used to be a ghost in his house."

He chuckled and shook his head. "Fraser Barron," he said softly.

"Do you believe Woodburn Hall is haunted?"

He looked at her as if he thought she might be kidding, but when he saw that she wasn't, he said honestly, "I wasn't there enough to know. I spent some weekends with the aunts when I came home from boarding school. But usually I stayed with my mother. The girl Will dated in boarding school, though, had a different take on it."

"Hadley?"

He looked at her curiously. "Yes, Hadley. She used to come and stay for weeks at the house visiting Will. She slept downstairs in that front bedroom and she used to say a dark man visited her in the night."

Despite the heat, Ava felt a cold chill on the back of her neck. "What did you think of that?"

He stood abruptly and collected her empty plate, stacking it on top of his. His voice changed, becoming curt and businesslike.

"I always assumed it was Will," he said, and turning, he went to take their plates to the counter.

After that their conversation settled on less controversial matters. Jake told her about his days out in Santa Cruz and Ava told him about her time in Chicago. The restaurant gradually cleared around them but neither one made the first move to go.

Jake asked her what her novel was about and she told him, going into great detail about her plans for the book. She was honest with him, too, about the problems she was having getting started. When she was finished he said, "What do you like to read?"

She told him, running down the list of her favorite books, the ones she had displayed on her desk beside her rarely used computer, the classics she had read in childhood and college, as well as her current favorite contemporary artists: Alice Munro, Hilary Mantel, Doris Lessing, and Peter Carey.

"What novels do you have sitting beside your bed right now, waiting to be read?"

She told him. "The first is about an eighteenth-century Irish giant who's paraded on the sideshow circuit in London during the Age of Reason."

"And the second one?"

"It's about a nineteenth-century Anglican priest transported to Australia for gambling who marries an heiress and on a wager builds and moves a glass church from Sydney to New South Wales."

"You seem to enjoy reading historical novels." He said this as if he was trying to make a point.

Later, they got around to talking about their childhoods (he had never known his father either, they had that in common), and after a slow beginning, Ava began to tell him about her vagabond childhood. She told him about her mother's lie regarding her father's death in the icy Detroit River, and she told him about the letter she'd received from the man purporting to be her father, and as she talked, she became more and more amazed, because she'd never told anyone before, and now here she was confessing it all to a total stranger.

"Why don't you call him?" Jake said when she was finished. His hand lay on the table just inches from her own. She could feel a kind of heat emanating from him, a low vibration like pinpricks against her skin.

"Call whom?" she said vaguely.

"The man who sent you the letter." Her expression made him smile.

"Well, I can understand if you don't want to call him, but at least write him. You have his address. Write him and ask him why he never, in twenty-eight years, sent you a birthday card or a Christmas card. It's an honest question. You deserve an honest answer."

When they walked outside the parking lot was nearly empty.

He walked her to her car. "Do you like horses?" he said.

"I used to," she said. "I read *Black Beauty* when I was eight. And I desperately wanted a pony when I was ten. But I've never really been around them." She was rambling again. Now that they were outside in the bright sunlight, she felt a momentary awkwardness, a feeling of constraint.

"My mother raises miniature horses."

"You mean those tiny ones the size of big dogs?"

"They're as smart as dogs, too. They're house-trained, and they sleep with her at night. When she takes them to the mall they wear little sneakers made especially for miniature horses."

She smiled. "You're kidding."

"I'm dead serious." He was quiet for a moment, staring off behind her at the distant river. "Would you like to go with me out to her place?"

She had a sudden vision of Will's face, of Josephine's cold gray eyes, if they should find out. "Oh, I don't know," she said.

"Not tomorrow. One day next week."

Ava watched a flock of starlings careening above a chestnut tree. "I have a lot of work to do."

"My mother knows all about Charlie Woodburn. You can pump her for information if you like."

Looking up into his face, she had a feeling of falling, of the ground opening up beneath her feet.

"All right," she said.

On the drive home, she thought about what Jake had said about her liking historical fiction, his inference that maybe this was something she should try writing. It was astounding to her now, thinking back on their conversation, how much personal information she had shared with him.

As a child, she had clipped photos from magazines and pasted them into little "books" she made out of construction paper, folded and stapled down the middle. She had written stories to go with the photos, filling the pages with her childish scrawl. She never showed the books to anyone, not even Clotilde, storing them in shoeboxes under her bed, and taking them out from time to time to "read." It was one way she had found to fill her solitary childhood, but it was more than that; the act of creation gave substance and shape to her life. It made order out of the chaos. Sitting in school day after dreary day, she couldn't wait to rush home to her little books, her little worlds.

Later, when she went to college and read Flannery O'Connor and Eudora Welty for the first time with understanding, she had become more concerned with technique, dissecting the author's work to see how it had been formed, how the author had used theme, symbolism, meter, all the tools of the trade.

When she landed her first real job, she told herself it was just temporary. She'd do her real work in the evening, working on her novel, a sloppily sentimental historical romance. And she did, for a while, plodding through endless drafts trying to correct the choppy style, the unrealistic dialogue, the clichéd plotlines. But over time she grew bored with the story. Sitting down in the evenings became a kind of torture, a bleak realization of her talents laid out against the bright shimmering fabric of her dreams. Yet she couldn't stop, she couldn't give up so easily. To stop writing completely produced in her a bleak and relentless depression, so she stubbornly persisted, plodding through endless drafts and revisions, telling herself she was learning something each time. She was still working on this rambling seven-hundred-page novel when she met Jacob.

For a time her growing infatuation with him produced in her a kind of restless energy, and she went back to work on her novel with renewed vigor and resolve. But eventually she settled back into the writing doldrums. The drama of her life with Jacob seemed to overtake the drama of her novel, and she found it easier and easier to procrastinate, to spend long hours patching together their relationship rather than writing.

Yet she knew she was a good writer; her high school teachers and college professors had all told her so. Jake's comment, so true in its implication, had shaken her. She knew he was right. She had to find a way to recapture the passion she had felt writing those first childhood stories.

She had to find something to write about that captivated her.

Our Town Is Rife
with Suicides

After Alice Barron's barbecue, the mood in the Woodburn house shifted. The barbecue seemed to have cemented something. There was an air now of accord and delicate expectation, as if everyone was tiptoeing around on eggshells. Even Josephine seemed to warm to Ava.

Ava and Will spent their evenings now going around to parties: supper clubs, cocktail parties, graduation barbecues.

Woodburn was a town of social ritual. In addition to the daily afternoon gathering for Toddy Time in the big houses lining River Road, there were teas, barbecues, birthday clubs, church fund-raisers, supper clubs, and Bunco groups. Ava had lost track of the invitations she'd received. The women were all very friendly and sweet. Regardless of their educations, their lives seemed to revolve around children, husbands, houses, and social events. The women's movement might never have happened here. In addition to enjoying the indulgences of their nineteen-sixties counterparts (cocktail parties, dinner groups, prescription drugs), these women also engaged in something called "me time," which included spa days, shopping jaunts to Nashville, and tennis trips to the beach.

One husband told Ava, "In my next life I want to come back as a Woodburn housewife," but he was smiling indulgently at his wife when he said it, and Ava could see that he felt a certain masculine pride in her for accepting this lifestyle, and in himself for being able to provide it.

It was, after all, a very pleasant, carefree existence, a life of safety and security.

Woodburn seemed to be seeping into her bones like the heat. Accustomed to the hectic pace of Chicago, Ava had, at first, found the slow-moving, slow-talking townspeople hard to take. But gradually, effortlessly, she was succumbing to the languid charm of the place. How lovely to rise when she felt like it, to spend the morning reading in the cool library or beneath a slowly moving ceiling fan on the verandah; how wonderful the traditions of afternoon nap and Toddy Time. The slow pace of the days suited her, Ava realized. Instead of cramming as much as you possibly could into a twenty-four-hour space, you built your day around one daily task; shopping, reading, working in the garden. One day followed another with a kind of slumberous certainty.

And yet there was a worrisome aspect to this lifestyle: the fact that it was so easy to forget work, to put it aside indefinitely in the pursuit of pleasure. There was a slightly addictive quality to the way Will and his friends lived, Ava realized in brief moments of clarity, a quality that might be detrimental to a writer.

"I thought we might have a party," Will said one evening.

It was the day before Ava was supposed to see Jake Woodburn again, to go out to his mother's house, and she was in a very good mood. She was sitting in the library playing Scrabble with Will, Josephine, and Fanny. Toddy Time was over, and Maitland was in the kitchen finishing up dinner.

"Oh, yes, a party!" Fanny said, clapping her hands.

"For the young people, not for us," Josephine said. She smiled serenely at Will. "I think that's a marvelous idea."

"At Longford," he said.

If he had heard about her lunch with Jake, he hadn't mentioned it. Ava had meant to tell him, but as the days wore on and his mood continued to be cheerful and sociable, she hadn't wanted to spoil it. Now, of course, she'd left it too long and there was no casual way to bring it up.

"What do you think?" he said, turning to Ava.

Ava was remembering what Jake had said about writing to the man who might be her father and demanding that he explain his absence in her life. She had been thinking of this, off and on, for days. Yes, of course, he was right; she was owed an explanation. If nothing else, she was owed that.

"Ava?" Will said loudly and she looked up to see everyone at the table staring at her.

"Are you feeling all right, my dear?" Josephine said, not unkindly. "You seem a little flushed."

"I'm sorry," she said. "Is it my turn?"

"Did you hear what I said about the party?" Will's eyes fastened on Ava. His smile thinned.

"Yes. A party. That would be great." She looked down at her tiles, moving them around. She had dreaded the visit, in the days following her lunch with Jake, feeling that she had allowed herself to be manipulated into agreeing to go. But as the day approached, she found herself anticipating tomorrow's lunch. The chance to gather more information on Charlie Woodburn was irresistible. And she had never seen a miniature horse.

"Will you help me?"

She looked up again. "Help you?"

He gave her a cool, studied look. "With the invitations?" he said. "With the planning?"

She smiled faintly. "Of course," she said.

He continued to stare at her.

"There's a stationery shop on the square that does a nice job with printing. Use them," Josephine said. "They have a woman who does calligraphy so you can give your list to her."

Will was quiet now, staring down at his tiles.

"Printed invitations!" Ava said, trying to restore his good spirits. "I don't think I've ever had a party where printed invitations were sent."

"Oh, really?" Fanny said.

"That will change," Josephine said quietly.

Ava thought, *What will change?* She wanted life to go on just as it was. She didn't want to think about what was coming later.

The following morning was overcast, and Ava rose earlier than usual and showered and dressed before going in to breakfast. Fanny and Josephine had gone downtown to see their lawyer but Clara and Alice were sitting at the table in the breakfast room, lingering over their coffee.

"You look nice," Alice said, surprised at seeing her dressed. "Where are you off to this morning?"

Ava poured herself a cup of coffee and sat down at the table. "I've got some errands to run," she said.

"Better take an umbrella," Clara said. "It's going to rain."

Ava stirred her coffee and stared serenely out the window at the ominous sky. She had made arrangements to meet Jake at the barbecue place and follow him out to his mother's in her car. She had been adamant about driving herself, not knowing how the visit might go and not wanting to be dependent upon him for a ride back. Besides, she didn't want anyone to see her riding in a car with Jake, at least not until she'd had a chance to tell Will about befriending him. She glanced at the clock, noting that she had almost an hour before she was to meet him.

"The other morning when we were talking you said something interesting," Ava said, not looking directly at either woman. She had found that although Fanny, Josephine, and Will refused to talk about Charlie Woodburn, she could sometimes coax Clara and Alice to speak of him if the aunts weren't present. That was how she had discovered that the bedroom she slept in, the very bed she slept in, had once been used by Charlie.

"You said Charlie slept in the front bedroom where I'm sleeping now, but Fanny slept upstairs. Was that common in those days?"

Alice coughed lightly, her eyes darting to Clara. "It wasn't uncommon in those days for married people to have separate bedrooms," she said.

"But surely it was uncommon for newlyweds?" Ava tried not to appear too curious, turning to observe a framed photograph hanging on the wall beside her shoulder. It was of a young Fanny and Maitland dressed in pith helmets and standing over a downed water buffalo. Fanny was very petite and pretty, wearing riding jodhpurs and staring at the camera with a look of brash audacity. Maitland was muscular and bronzed and looked a little like Charlton Heston in *The Ten Commandments*. There was a man in the foreground grinning widely, down on one knee beside the buffalo. He looked oddly familiar to Ava.

"He was a night owl," Clara said, glancing at Alice, who snorted into her coffee cup. "Charlie could stay up all night but Fanny went to bed with the sun. At least she did in those days when she was expecting Sumner."

"And Sumner was Charlie's son," Ava said smoothly, still examining the photo.

"Of course," Alice said, as if any other suggestion was preposterous.

Ava nodded her head, wondering how to politely pose her next question. "And how long had Fanny and Charlie been married when she found herself pregnant with Sumner?"

"A little over a year," Alice said quickly.

So it hadn't been a shotgun wedding then. Fanny hadn't been forced to marry Charlie because she was pregnant.

"He liked his cups," Alice said.

"What?"

"Charlie. He was bad to drink," Clara said.

"You mean he was an alcoholic?"

No one said anything. Behind them, the kitchen clock ticked steadily. Alice coughed again, delicately. "Josephine hated him with a passion," she said. "She did everything she could to break up that marriage. He would bring low characters back to the house and sit up all hours of the night drinking and gambling. That's why Fanny had her own room."

Clara gave Alice a direct look. Ava could feel an undercurrent between the two women, some unspoken warning swirling through the room like smoke. She took the framed photograph off the wall and stared at it.

Despite Clara's warning glance, Alice continued. "Maitland was brokenhearted when Fanny married that rascal. He'd loved Fanny all his life. When Mama asked Maitland why he didn't marry someone else, he said, 'Mama, some people are born to love only one person, and I have the fortunate distinction of being one of them.' "

"He was a patient man," Clara agreed. "Waiting for her all those years."

"She wouldn't marry until Sumner was grown," Alice said to Ava.

"But they traveled together?" Ava asked, tapping the photograph with her finger. "Even before they married?"

"Oh, yes. Everywhere. They were great travelers."

Ava dipped her head and peered at the unknown man in the photograph. Why would Fanny and Maitland have traveled the world together and yet waited forty years to marry? She glanced again at the clock. It was when she looked back down at the photograph that it occurred to her who the man was.

"Oh, my God," she said. "Is that Ernest Hemingway?"

He was waiting for her when she arrived at Battle Smoove Barbecue. The sky was a gunmetal gray but the rain had held off. She smiled and waved and he gave her that two-finger salute they all gave each other down here in greeting. He was driving the same old Ford pickup, and she followed him out of the empty parking lot and down a narrow, curving asphalt road.

His mother's place was on the opposite side of town from Longford, and Ava began to relax, realizing she probably wouldn't run into Will.

They drove past several subdivisions filled with small modern-looking houses, surrounded by wide flat fields. A distant forest stood wreathed in fog, and farther on the mountain range rose above a bank of low-lying clouds like islands in a milky sea.

She wondered what his mother would be like. Sally was her name, he'd told her. She raised miniature horses and worked part-time at a local vet's office. "A large, plainspoken woman," Jake had warned her. "Don't expect any of the old-money polish you find with the Wood-burn sisters."

The sun broke briefly between the clouds and Ava took it as a hope-ful sign.

They turned off the paved road finally and followed a sandy dirt trail between boxwood hedges. The hedges had been left to grow wild, and they were taller than the car and covered in trailing vines. Ava bounced along behind Jake as he pulled into a grassy clearing and parked beside a small log house shaded by two overhanging trees. Forest surrounded the house on three sides but to the back, Ava could see a vista of cleared rolling fields.

He climbed out of the truck carrying a large brown paper bag, waiting for her. She parked carefully in the gravel drive. The house was very small, with a steeply pitched roof. A stone walkway led from the drive up to the narrow front porch past a pair of geranium and ivy planters.

"What do you think?" he asked.

"It's very quiet," she said.

He walked ahead of her along the walkway. "She must be out in the barn," he said. She followed him up the narrow steps into the house.

It was a true log cabin, one big room opened all the way to the roof rafters. A tiny galley kitchen ran along the back wall, next to a pair of French doors that opened onto a small deck overlooking the long sweeping fields in the back. A bedroom and bath were tucked into a small wing opening off the side of the house, and a ladder led up into a sleeping loft overlooking the great room, which was sparsely furnished with an L-shaped sofa, bookshelves, a round oak table, and various antiques. Several colorful rag rugs were scattered across the wide-planked pine floors.

"This is wonderful," Ava said, looking around. All the windows were bare and looked out onto the forest or the wide sloping fields.

"Thanks. I built it." He set the bag down on the counter and she realized he had brought lunch with him. "Will and I built it," he corrected himself.

"You and Will?" she said.

He went to the cupboard and took down three glasses. "One summer when we were in college. Mama ordered the kit from one of those prefab cabin places and when the logs came, Will and I put it together. Just like you would a Lincoln Log set, only about a thousand times harder. It took us all summer, which doesn't say much for our skill set, but we learned a lot doing it."

"Where did your mom live before that? Did you grow up in town?"

"I grew up out here," he said. "The land's been in the family for about thirty years but we lived in a trailer before the house was built. I grew up in a trailer." He looked at her when he said it, as if to give her time to understand the kind of childhood he'd had, the kind of people he came from. There was an element of polite restraint in his manner that had not been there the other day at lunch.

They walked outside, down a narrow path to the barn, which was little more than a two-stall lean-to. "Mama, we're here," he called out as they approached, and Sally Woodburn stepped out to greet them.

She was a big woman, not fat but solid, and she spoke in the nasal twang used by Darlene Haney, only her voice was deeper. Her hair was brown and cut short like Ava's, and she wore jeans, a T-shirt, and a pair of muddy cowboy boots.

She gave Ava a quick, bashful hug. "Any friend of Jake's is welcome here," she said.

Ava felt suddenly shy, and she was glad when Sally said, "And this here is Sprinkles and this is Tinker Belle."

The horses were adorable, neither one bigger than a large golden re-triever, and when they walked back up the trail to the house, the two of them followed at Sally's heels. They stood on the deck, their noses pressed against the French doors, watching as Jake, Ava, and Sally washed their hands and sat down at the table.

"Jake says they're house-trained," Ava said, laughing at the little horses' forlorn expressions.

"Oh, yes," Sally said. She had strong, regular features, and Ava real-ized that Jake got his lopsided grin from her. "They come in at night but during the day, when the weather's nice, I insist that they stay out-doors. Horses are prone to respiratory problems, and they need clean fresh air to stay healthy."

She set china plates out for them. Jake took the barbecue out of the bag and put it on the table so they could help themselves, along with silverware and napkins.

Sally smiled at Ava, indicating that she should go first. "Jake says you're from Chicago."

"Yes," Ava said.

"You're a long way from home, aren't you?"

Ava wasn't sure how much Jake had told his mother about her rea-sons for being in Woodburn, so she just smiled and said, "It's been a real adjustment."

"Don't worry, you'll get used to it," Sally said, helping herself to some coleslaw. "Everyone does. Eventually."

They talked for a while about the business of raising miniature horses. A blustery wind blew across the deck from time to time, stirring the tails of the little horses, and far off to the east a line of heavy storm clouds rode low on the horizon, wrapping the ridgetops in fog. Ava could see now how the Smoky Mountains got their name.

She and Jake were quiet during lunch, letting Sally do most of the talking. When she stopped, Ava put her fork down and said, "Jake told me you might know something about Charlie Woodburn." She hadn't meant to launch into it like that, to pose the question quite so boldly, but Jake's continued silence was beginning to unnerve her. He seemed preoccupied today, and restless.

"I know a little," Sally said.

"Was he related to you?"

Sally looked at Jake. "You didn't tell her?" she said.

"Nope."

"Boy, you surprise me." She pushed her plate back and said sternly to Ava, "He has a fondness for the old Woodburn sisters that I don't necessarily share. You should know that up front. Miss Fanny's always been a kindhearted soul, but that Josephine's as cold as a week-old enchilada."

"That week-old enchilada donated a wing to the hospital that treated your kidney disease," he reminded her.

"Blood money," she said ominously.

"So you are related to Charlie?" Ava said, trying to head off an argument. She was avoiding him now, posing her questions directly to Sally.

Sally sighed, as if waiting for him to say something, and when he didn't she pointed at Jake and said, "He's Charlie's grandson." She chuckled, watching Ava's face. "I know, I know, it's like a big old soap opera. I was married to Jake's daddy, King, who was Charlie's son. King's mama was a woman Charlie took up with before he ran off with Miss Fanny. They weren't married or anything, at least not anything legal, but Charlie gave King his last name anyway on the birth certificate."

Jake stood up and collected the empty plates and took them to the sink.

Sally said, "Charlie Woodburn was quite the ladies' man, but I guess you've already heard about all of that."

Ava sipped her iced tea and set her glass down. "Everyone down here seems to have their own version of Charlie and how he died."

Jake stacked the dishes in the sink and turned on the tap. "Why don't you just go with what the death certificate said?"

"What did it say?"

"It said he drowned. Accidentally."

Sally snorted and waved her hand dismissively. "Hell, the death certificate would say whatever the Woodburns wanted it to say. You can't go by that at all."

Later, Sally told them about Clara McGann. How Clara's ancestor, Hannah, had been a slave and bore Randal Woodburn three children. When he married Delphine, he gave Hannah and her children their freedom, and Hannah married and went off to New Orleans with her new husband. But when Hannah and her husband died, Randal went to New Orleans and brought the three children back to Longford, and later he gave them to one of his sons as a wedding present.

"You mean he took three children who were *free* and put them back into slavery?" Ava said.

"That's right. And his own children at that."

Jake rose and went to the refrigerator. He hadn't said a word during his mother's revelations, staring rigidly out the French doors, his fingers tapping lightly against the table.

"So Clara McGann is actually a Woodburn?" Ava said.

Sally pointed at Jake's sturdy back. "She descends from Old Randal just like he does."

"And the Woodburns know this?"

"Of course they do! Nobody talks about it, but everybody knows."

Ava was quiet for a moment. Now that she knew, she felt that she had suspected it all along: the way Josephine and Clara carried themselves, their similar height and graceful manner. Hadn't she thought they looked like sisters?

She leaned forward and rested her arms on the table. "So tell me, Sally. Who do you think killed Charlie Woodburn?"

Jake brought the pitcher of tea and poured everyone a fresh glass. Sally watched him, her lips pursed, a fond, thoughtful expression on her face. "I always heard it was the Woodburn cousins. Josephine and Fanny didn't have any brothers, so the male cousins would have considered it their duty to protect the womenfolk from a scoundrel like Charlie. That's how it was done in those days. They say Charlie's body was pretty battered when they pulled him out of the river. It's a large family, spread out over most of the county. They're all intermarried, you know. Of course, that's the way it was done back then. Look at the royal family of England, look at the family trees of most of the well-to-do in this country. Cousins marrying cousins for generations just to keep the property intact." She glanced at Jake, who stared down at his glass. "It's all about money. Money and property and family honor. They killed Charlie because he was a Black Woodburn, and they couldn't have him getting his hands on any of that money."

Jake rose and put the tea away. He looked at Ava. "I thought we might take a walk," he said.

Sally groaned and flattened her palms against the table, pushing herself to her feet. "My back is acting up. You better hurry before the rain comes."

Ava said vaguely, "A walk would be nice." She was thinking of something she hadn't considered before. She remembered Alice and Clara's admission that Charlie had been an alcoholic. Nothing Sally had told her contradicted that. "You don't think it might have been suicide, do you? With Charlie? You don't think he might have taken his own life?"

"Oh, I don't think so," Sally said. "From what I've heard about him, he didn't seem the type. Still, you never know." She grimaced and put her hands on her back, stretching. "It happens more frequently than you might think. This town is rife with suicides."

There was a smell of rain in the air. The little horses followed them to the edge of the deck, then stood watching soberly as they crossed the field. Jake went ahead of her to open a gate that led into another, larger pasture. As he leaned down, she saw his deeply tanned neck above the collar of his T-shirt, and she imagined herself touching him there, laying her fingers lightly against his skin. When he straightened up, she looked away quickly.

They walked across the field to a fringe of tall trees. There was a path here leading down to a rocky creek. The air beneath the trees was cool and damp, and smelled of leaves and wet rock. She walked beside him, matching her stride to his, so close they occasionally bumped against each other.

He stopped for a moment, listening. Thunder rumbled in the distance. "We've got about twenty minutes before the storm hits. We shouldn't go too far."

They went on, following the sound of the creek.

"Does it make you nervous when I ask about Charlie Woodburn?" she said.

He grinned. "Again with the personal questions."

"Sorry. It must be my Yankee upbringing."

"I like your honesty. It's refreshing."

"I'm not trying to offend anyone, although I have the feeling that I do. Constantly. It's unintentional, though."

Now that they were away from Sally he seemed a little more at ease, although Ava still had the feeling he was on guard about something, holding himself close.

"We're a little sensitive down here about our history," he said. "You see one too many bad made-for-TV movies and you get a chip on your shoulder."

"I'm sorry if my questions seem rude. It's just that I'm curious. It's some kind of strange compulsion I have. If someone has a secret, I have to try to figure it out."

"You might find that we're not as interesting as you think."

"Let me be the judge of that."

The slope became gradually steeper, and they could see the creek now through the trees. He stopped, and let her walk ahead of him.

"If I thought about it, I could be bitter about the Woodburns," he said. He seemed more comfortable talking to her back. She walked slowly, grabbing hold of narrow trees and brush to keep her balance. "But I could be bitter about Charlie Woodburn, too. My father drank himself to death three years after I was born, and who's to say it would have been any better if he'd had a father, if Charlie had lived. Charlie didn't bother to marry my grandmother. He ran off instead with Fanny Woodburn against her family's wishes—he doesn't sound like the kind of man anyone should grieve over. We've got a bad habit down here of allowing patterns of male violence and oppression to continue through generations. I, for one, don't think it's healthy."

"I guess I hadn't really looked at it like that. From your father and grandmother's point of view. I was looking at Fanny and Charlie and thinking it must have been some kind of passionate love affair. Something neither one could deny."

"There may have been some of that. Who knows?"

"That's the interesting question," Ava said.

"I think living in the past is always a mistake. You can't go back and change anything, so let it go and move on."

They were walking side by side, and occasionally he would brush against her. When he did, she felt a strange hum, like a kind of low vibration, run up her bare arm and across both shoulders. She stopped and looked up at him. "But what if we can learn something from the stories people tell?"

He was quiet for a moment, considering this. "The aunts are good people. They've been good to me." He gazed up through the trees at the distant rim of sky. "Everyone has a different story, and you have to ask yourself what motivates people to see reality the way they do. The aunts gave me an opportunity to get an education, to better myself, but from my mother's point of view they took me away from her for six years. They're members of a family that refused to recognize my father as being anything more than illegitimate white trash. So she doesn't see them in a favorable light."

He continued to stare at the sky. When he spoke again it was in a cautious, thoughtful tone. "The way I look at the Woodburn legacy is this: it's not right, what happened, but it's the way it was. Period." He dropped his chin, stared at her intently. "Every civilization has its dark periods. Look at how the Irish were treated in New England. Look at the New York race riots, child labor during the Industrial Revolution."

"Were you by any chance a history major?"

He grinned suddenly, a brief, dazzling smile. "Art history."

"I knew it. She wondered what he would be like as a lover.

He stepped around her, careful not to touch her, and walked to the edge of a steep rise, looking down at the creek.

"Is something wrong?" she said. He would be generous, inventive, and kind, she decided.

"We should probably go back."

"That's not what I meant."

He turned and came back up the slope, stopping several feet below her. He broke off the tip of a pine branch, slowly stripping the needles. "I thought you and Will were old college friends," he said. "Nothing more."

"We are."

"I heard you were engaged."

"Good Lord! Who told you that?"

"Someone who was at the barbecue."

"Well, they're wrong. Will and I are just good friends."

He gave her a long, searching look, pulling the branch through his fingers. "Does Will know that?"

She struggled to hold his gaze, then looked away. "He should. I've told him often enough." They stood quietly facing each other. There was nothing else she could say.

"We better get back," he said.

She turned and walked ahead of him up the ridge. Behind her he said quietly, "There's already bad blood between Will and me."

She realized then that he wasn't going to touch her. Whatever it was between him and Will, he wanted it over with.

The storm, which had held off all morning, finally broke. Rain lashed the tops of the trees and drummed along the roof of the car as she drove home. The weather matched her melancholy mood. Nothing would come of her attraction to Jake Woodburn. She knew that now. He wouldn't do anything to further distress the aunts or Will; he had made it clear that he wanted back in their good graces.

Despite her disappointment she couldn't help but feel a flicker of relief. The last thing she needed this summer was another dead-end love affair. The last thing she needed was another distraction to keep her from writing her novel.

She drove through the rainy countryside thinking over what she'd learned about Charlie Woodburn, what she'd *supposedly* learned, because the truth was, you couldn't trust town gossip, even gossip that had been sifted and honed through over sixty years of telling. Anyone could have killed Charlie. Charlie could have killed himself. It was tempting to let it go, to spend no more time thinking about him.

But she couldn't. Instead, she thought of the way Maitland tenderly kissed Fanny's hand as they sat watching television at night. She thought of the sepia-tinted Woodburn family photographs showing solemn, slightly menacing young men in slouch hats and boots, long rifles nestled in their arms. She thought of austere, taciturn Josephine, the keeper of the family history, the guardian of its honor, a woman who seemed capable of anything, even murder.

And later that night as she eased into sleep, as pale moonlight flooded her room and crickets chanted outside her window, she thought of doe-eyed Clara McGann tending her beautiful poisonous plants in the moonlit garden.

That evening she suffered another attack of sleep paralysis.

She awakened to the sound of someone whispering her name. She could feel a presence in the room with her, although she could not turn her head to look. Her eyes were open and staring at the ceiling but she could not move them; she could not move any part of her body. She lay as if encased in a tomb of ice.

The blackness inside the room was thick, and smelled of smoke and old linen. As Ava stared upward, she became gradually aware of a dark shadow flitting across the ceiling at regular intervals. She was terrified by the fear that a strange face might lean, horrifyingly and without warning, into her field of vision.

The episode went on for several minutes and just as the feeling of dread became too much for her to bear, she found herself quite suddenly able to blink her eyes.

Instantly, as if released from a spell, she was able to move again, and she cried out.

She leaned to switch on a lamp. The room was empty, cheerful and cozy in the lamplight. Gradually her breathing evened. Her heart stopped its wild thudding and beat a calm, steady rhythm. One of the old plantation ledgers was lying on her bedside table and she pulled it into bed and curled on her side, cradling it.

The horror of the episode gradually faded. She opened the ledger and began trying to decipher the old-fashioned script. She read:

> *April 19th. Sunday. Did not go to church. Wind very fresh but no rain. Laramore and Phipps came around noon. Went down to the Negro houses and took five Negroes viz.–Peter, John, Sam, Titus, and Louisa. They are sold to a man near Carthage. They seemed in good spirits but I am loath to part with them through no fault of theirs, but by my own extravagance. This should pay my debts to Barnwell and Cuffy and leave some for the children's tuition.*
>
> *Spent the afternoon reading* Chevalier de Faublas.

It was horrible, the way someone could describe a human being as if they were of no more consequence than a cow. She had admired the Woodburns' collection of artifacts, their wealth and prestige and history, and yet all those things had come at the price of human misery.

> *April 20th. The yard Negroes pulled up the floor of one of the outhouses and killed 60 rats. Clear and hot in the morning. The Negroes at home are disconsolate over the sale yesterday but they know it could not be helped.*

They may yet see their children again. Took a hunt with Sumner
Whitson. Killed a very large buck. Bathed and dressed and rode over and
dined with W. F. Fraser.
    Wife sick again.

She flipped back to the opening page of the ledger. *1832* it read, in flowing script. Old Randal would have been master in those days. These were his words Ava was reading.

April 24th. Clear, calm, and beautiful. All hands planting cotton.
While at supper, Old Judy came in crying that Toby was worse. Went
down to the Negro houses and found him perfectly *dead. They told me*
yesterday he was better and so I did not send for the doctor. Toby was a
good boy, about 15 years old, and will be a great loss to me. He lost an eye
last summer and was not the same after that, very dispirited and low.
Taken sick on Tuesday, died Thursday.

Somewhere deep in the house Ava heard a steady thumping sound, a vague knocking. It went on for a minute or two, then stopped. She closed the ledger and lay back, thinking about the boy, Toby, who had died one hundred and sixty-six years ago. It was easy to imagine him, wounded and disheartened, going about his dreary life.

Had he welcomed death when it finally came?

The Negro houses were where the Harvard students had come to excavate several summers ago. The next time she was at Longford she would ask to see them, to see if she might catch some lingering presence of Toby, to walk where he had walked, to see what he had seen.

She wondered if Josephine and Will had ever read the plantation journals. She wondered how much of their family history they had truly been willing to face.

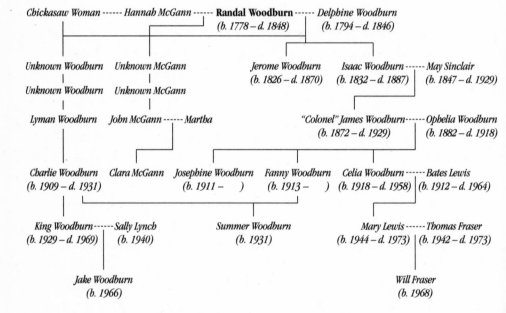

Longford

The following evening, Ava began her novel.

She was taking a bath in the old-fashioned claw-foot bathtub when a sentence came into her head: *He was tall and dark, and when he entered a room all eyes turned his way.*

She climbed out of the tub, dressing quickly, and padded down the hallway. The house was quiet; the others had climbed the stairs to bed hours ago, and she went into her room and switched on the desk lamp. The room, beyond the dimly glowing light, was bathed in shadow. She sat at the computer and opened a new file, waiting as the glowing page loaded on the screen, and then without thinking about it too much, she began to write.

Time passed, but she was unaware of its passing; she was in turn-of-the-century New Orleans with a destitute boy and his mother. A boy she named Charlie Finn. She saw him and his mother step aboard a streetcar, saw them sit at a window and watch the scrolling scene, the ancient oaks draped in moss, the beautiful old houses lining St. Charles Avenue. She saw them climb down from the car and walk along the brick sidewalk to a grand white house that sat like a wedding cake behind a wrought-iron fence, taking up the entire block. She watched as Charlie and his mother, a seamstress, went in through the gate and around to the back of the house and rang the bell. Later they were shown through a series of large cool rooms, and up a back staircase to a room where the lady of the house sat waiting to be measured for new undergarments: lace-trimmed drawers and corset covers and chemises. Ava saw the boy, Charlie, with his large dark eyes and black hair, sitting quietly and patiently, waiting for his mother to finish. She saw his face as he looked around the large room with its expensive furnishings, saw his mother, weary and broken from work and poverty, on her knees before the lady of the house, her worn tape measure in her hands. She felt something stir in his chest then, something determined and fierce.

She saw him as an adolescent and then as a handsome young man, standing in front of his mother's burial vault in Lafayette Cemetery.

And later, she watched as he drove triumphantly into Finn's Crossing, the sun shining brightly on his dark hair and along the gleaming chrome of his Ford Model T Runabout. She saw his face on the day he first laid eyes on the beautiful Fanny Finn, strolling along the downtown street on the arm of her beau, Maitland Wallis. Charlie fell instantly, irrevocably in love with Fanny, determined, despite his lack of prospects and her social standing, to have her.

At three a.m. Ava stopped. She was tired, her eyes were dry, and her shoulders ached. Her whole body felt sore and heavy, as if she had run a great distance. She had written nearly six thousand words, and she had no clear recollection of how it had happened.

She shut the computer down and clicked off the lamp, and, climbing into bed, fell into a deep and oblivious sleep.

In the morning when she awoke, Will was there. He knocked on her door and entered carrying a cup of coffee in his hands. She sat up in confusion, looking around the bright, sunlit room.

"What time is it?"

"Nearly ten-thirty." He set the coffee down on the bedside table.

"My God," she said, yawning. "I had no idea."

He sat down gingerly on the edge of the bed. She pushed herself up against the headboard, pulling her legs up and resting the steaming cup on one knee. Outside the window the trees made a lacy pattern on the screen.

"I came by to show you the list," he said.

She sipped her coffee. "What list?" she said.

He stared out the window, his profile severe in the slanting light. "The invitation list," he said. "For the party at Longford."

"Oh, right."

"You don't have to help if you don't want to." He looked tired; the skin beneath his eyes was dark and dull, and there were lines around his mouth.

"Don't be silly," she said. "Of course I want to help." She wasn't bothered by his moods today. She was happy, remembering that she had begun her novel, remembering the work she had done last night. She smiled and put out her hand. Without a word, he gave her the list.

She looked it over carefully. She recognized very few of the names, although she had, no doubt, met everyone on it. Jake Woodburn, she noticed, was not listed.

She took a pen and added a name at the bottom, then gave it back to him.

He said, "Darlene Haney?"

"She's been nice to me. You don't mind, do you?"

"Invite whomever you like," he said, folding the paper and sliding it back into his pocket. His manner was brusque, irritated.

"I started working last night."

"Working?"

"On my novel. It just seemed to flow out of me, Will. It was incredible."

He put his hands down on either side of him on the bed and looked at her. "That's great," he said mildly.

"And now I don't want to stop. I want to keep going and see how far I can get."

"Well, of course I don't want to interfere with your work," he said, sounding as if he would very much like to do just that.

She sipped her coffee. She was restless, wanting him to go, wanting to read over what she'd written last night to see if it was any good.

"I thought you might like to walk downtown with me to the stationers," he said. "And maybe get some lunch afterward." He hesitated at her expression. "Or not," he added quickly.

She set her cup down, crawled over, and put a hand on his shoulder. "You don't mind, do you? It's just that I've got so much work to do. I want to get back to it while it's fresh."

His eyes in the slanting light were almost blue. There was a childlike quality about him that many women would have found endearing, but Ava did not. She was finished with men who ruled her with their moods and petty withholdings of affection. She had her work now, and that was all that mattered. She had caught a glimpse last night of what it could be like, the intoxication, the dreamlike abandonment.

"I don't mind," he said.

Yet she owed him a debt of gratitude. Her novel, her story was a gift from him, from his family. Not that she could tell him, of course; he would try to put a stop to it. Still, she owed him something. She opened her mouth to speak but stopped, her attention drawn suddenly to the mantel. She stared, feeling a vague sense of unease. She had left Clotilde's vase resting on the left side of the mantel but now it was pushed to the far right.

The cleaning ladies, she thought, *must have moved it.*

He stood abruptly, causing her hand to drop. "I'll see the caterer and take care of ordering the tables and chairs. I thought we'd set everything up in the dining room and front parlor." He stood awkwardly beside the bed, his hands at his sides.

"Yes," she said. "Yes, of course."

His look was bitter, reproachful, as if he'd suspected all along that she'd let him down. "I'll let you get back to work then," he said.

And because she was grateful to him and because she felt guilty that she *had* let him down, she said insistently, "Let me do something! Please. I want to help."

"You can order the table arrangements."

"All right," she said, her gazed fixed once more on the mantel. "I'll order the flowers. Let me take care of that."

And it wasn't until after he had left, his footsteps echoing eerily down the hallway, that she realized, *My God, I sound like Clarissa Dalloway.*

She had an absurd desire to please people. It was something about herself that had always driven Ava crazy.

In the beginning of her love affair with Jacob she had kept part of herself back. He was cheerful and vulgar, and she pretended a kind of bemused detachment, like an overindulgent mother with a spoiled child. But over time she lost her footing. It became a kind of competition between them, and she began to feel herself weakening, while he seemed to grow in strength and confidence. Unable to understand this relationship, she had finally seen a professional.

"I've tried to make myself over to please him and it isn't working. He's bored, I can feel it, and I don't know if he loves me. He says he does but I wonder."

"What about you? Do you love him?" The doctor, a bald and rather paunchy man, watched her with a benign expression.

She was quiet. "I want him to love me," she said anxiously.

"And if he doesn't, how would you feel?"

"Like a failure."

Something had been exposed, a quivering nerve that seemed to run through the core of her.

Later, as she drove home through the rain, the words taunted her, clanging through her head like a fire alarm.

She did not see the doctor again.

Having begun the novel that she tentatively called *Old Money,* Ava found over the next two weeks that her days passed in a frenzy of creative activity. She rose around ten-thirty every morning, and after a quick breakfast and coffee, sat down at her desk to read over and rewrite what she'd written the day before. After lunch she would take a long walk around the garden, thinking about the scene she was preparing to write, and when she felt that she had it right, she would go in and sit down at the computer.

The novel ran through her head like a movie. The characters were so real she could picture the faint gleam of sweat along their upper lips, could smell the burnt-sugar scent of their starched clothes. Sometimes to help her set the scene she played music, Respighi's "The Pines of Rome," or Gershwin's "Rhapsody in Blue," and more recently, Debussy's "Preludes" for piano.

After supper she would return to her computer, writing long into the night when the house was quiet and shifting shadows settled in the corners of the room. She had read once of a historical novelist who wrote only by candlelight, feeling that the flickering light and the trancelike state it engendered transported her back to another time and place. Ava could certainly understand that now. Sitting in her darkened room, lit only by a desk lamp and the glowing screen of her computer, it was easy to find herself carried away.

And yet after two weeks of steady, relentless work, she found herself at an impasse.

Fanny has run away with Charlie and they are living in Finn Hall. But Fanny has begun to feel guilty over her betrayal of Maitland. She has begun to miss his company. And Charlie, too, has begun to feel adrift, living in the big house he has always dreamed of, yet surrounded by a family that despises him. It is only his love for Fanny that sustains him. He is handsome (when she closes her eyes Ava imagines Jake) and sociable, and the many parties he throws are an attempt to amuse Fanny, to bind her to him.

But she had it wrong, Ava realized. The story was too simplistic in a way that life never was. Being poor didn't make Charlie "good" any more than being rich made Fanny "bad." And yet Fanny's upbringing would have influenced who she was, the decisions she made. As would Charlie's. And what of Josephine, Clara, Maitland, and Charlie's illegitimate child, King? What part might they have played in the tragic love story of Charlie and Fanny? A story that was becoming less clear, the morality more clouded, the more Ava wrote.

She couldn't stop now, though. She had come too far. She could only hope that the characters would eventually reveal themselves, that their motives would emerge as she blundered along. She had only been writing two weeks and already she had almost eighteen thousand words. A phenomenal start. And Will, busy getting ready for the party at Longford, trying desperately to finish the kitchen renovation before then, seemed more than willing to let her spend her evenings working. Which was fine with Ava.

Sometimes though, in the middle of a particularly moving love scene, or more often as she imagined Charlie going about his daily routine, the sun shining on his black hair and dark eyes, she thought of Jake. She had not heard from him since that day at his mother's house, although she had not really expected him to call. He had made it clear that he wanted no further trouble with the Woodburns. And neither did she. She could not imagine writing anywhere else but here in this fateful house.

She could not afford to be thrown out now, before the story had fully formed itself, materializing before her like a ghost.

Ava went out to Longford early to see if she could help Will get ready for the party but he seemed to have everything under control. He had obviously done this before. He and the caterer were on a first-name basis, and when he saw Ava he smiled at her distractedly and reminded her to put her things upstairs (she was spending the night). The buffet table had been set up in the room Will called the small parlor, and several large round tables had been set up in the dining room and front parlor. The tables were covered in white tablecloths and a mix of sterling silver pieces. White floral arrangements stood in silver vases in the center of each table: white tea roses, lilies, hydrangeas, and baby's breath (Ava had let the florist suggest the flowers; she knew nothing of such things). Tea light candles were scattered among the flowers, and with the dimmed chandeliers and the faded wallpaper the rooms looked like something out of a *Martha Stewart Weddings* book.

Ava wandered around, amazed at the transformation Will had managed in the kitchen. He had installed a new bank of black cabinets and soapstone countertops, and the walls were covered now with drywall, although none of the finish work had been done. Still, the overall look was pleasing, and she could imagine what the room would look like when he was finished. Three women dressed in chef coats, members of the catering staff, introduced themselves to Ava. She wandered out onto the back gallery where the bar had been set up, smiling at the bartender, who was busily setting up glassware and stocking the shelves.

It was late June. The afternoon sun had begun to settle in the sky, and the heat was slowly waning. Long shadows lay over the grass. Over by the foundation where the old cabin once stood, birds sang in a clump of fig trees. Clusters of muscadine grapes hung from a long white trellis, separating the lawn from the distant rolling fields.

It was all perfect. Tranquil and perfect. Even the old barn, Ava noted, had been given a new coat of white paint.

She would have been fine if she hadn't started drinking Donnie Miller cocktails. Or at least that's what she told herself later. Dinner was good. The food was excellent, and the rooms, spare and lit with candlelight, set a warm, intimate mood. Ava had started out drinking red wine, going from table to table with Will, letting herself be shepherded about with his hand on her back. She was always nervous in social situations. But after a couple of glasses of wine, bolstered by Will's presence and his obvious ease among his guests, she began to relax and enjoy herself. Everyone was so friendly. This was something she hadn't counted on, the way Southerners could make you feel like you'd known them forever. She had never felt so accepted, so welcome as she felt now, roaming among Will's friends.

After dessert she wandered out onto the back gallery to get another drink. The bartender had set up a tray of rocks glasses filled with Donnie Miller cocktails. He smiled at Ava.

"Having fun?" he asked softly.

"Yes," she said, picking up a glass. "I am."

"You aren't from around here."

"How could you tell?"

He grinned, leaning against the bar. "You talk funny."

She sipped her drink. "How old are you?" she said.

"Old enough to ask you to go for a drink with me when this thing is over." He glanced behind her, then stood up and began to wipe down the bar.

"Here you are," Will said.

Ava turned around. "Here *you* are," she said, looking up at him and grinning foolishly. The lights behind his head seemed to glimmer and streak like shooting stars.

"Maybe you should stop drinking for a while," he said smoothly, sliding his arm around her. He stared deliberately at the bartender and Ava giggled. He looked so handsome and gallant standing there. She thought, *What's wrong with me? I should just marry him.*

And although she had not consciously thought of it, the possibility that she might marry him became suddenly quite real to her. *Why not?* She could stay here in this lovely house and write a series of light, humorous tales about a quirky little Southern town. Something harmless and frivolous. A Mitford kind of place where everyone is kind, where the good are rewarded and the bad are punished, and the tragic past is never touched upon. The Woodburns, with their vast network of family and influential friends would, no doubt, be able to help her find a publisher in New York for such a series. And because she would not need the money, fame and good fortune were sure to follow.

He kissed her. "Let's go check on our guests."

"Yes," she said happily.

Later, she found herself cornered at a table with a woman Will had gone to prep school with. The woman's name was Grayson Byrd, and she was tall, blonde, and blue-eyed, the kind of woman who had never, since the age of puberty, spent a Friday night home alone. She introduced Ava to her husband, David, a mild-mannered pediatrician with dark curly hair and wire-frame glasses. Grayson was very outgoing and effusive, while he was very quiet, letting her do most of the talking. They had two sons, Franklin and Caldwell, who closely resembled their father (Grayson carried several photos in her wallet that she was only too happy to pass around). Franklin was in first grade and Caldwell was in second. She put her photos away, then sent David off to talk with some of the men.

"So how did you and Will meet?" she asked, laying her hand lightly on Ava's arm.

Ava told her they had met in college.

"And you kept in touch all these years? How romantic," Grayson said, resting her chin on her palm and gazing wistfully across the crowded room. Her cheeks were very red, and her eyes were bright. "Will has let his hair grow out. It looks good on him. Very Lord Byron." She giggled at her odd comparison. "He was always such a romantic guy. Very old-fashioned, if you know what I mean." She giggled again and her chin slipped off her hand, and Ava realized she was drunk.

"I always thought that he and Hadley would wind up together eventually." Grayson stopped, frowning, realizing she had said the wrong thing.

Ava said quickly, "How long have you and David been married?"

"Ten years."

"Ten years? Wow."

"I know," she said flatly, making a wry mouth. "We got married right after college, before David went off to med school." She gazed across the crowded room to where her shy husband stood quietly listening to Will and another man who were engaged in an animated conversation. "He was such a good guy. David. Not very romantic, but a good guy. You know what I mean?"

Ava said she did.

"Kind of quiet but a nice guy." Grayson sighed and leaned her arms on the table. "I don't know. You reach a point in your life where you have to make a decision. Do you stay with the wild and sexy boyfriend, the one who makes your pulse race and your heart pound, or do you settle for the guy who will always pay the mortgage?" Her eyes were wide, tragic. "Do you settle for regular orgasms or money in the bank?"

Ava didn't know what to say to this. She supposed if you were lucky, you got both.

"My dad was an artist. A bohemian," Grayson said, and Ava, alarmed, sensed a confession coming. "I'd come home from school and he and a bunch of his friends would be smoking weed in the hot tub, listening to Led Zeppelin on the stereo. I didn't want that for my kids, you know?"

One of the caterers stopped by and asked if they wanted a refill.

"No thanks," Ava said.

"Another Donnie Miller," Grayson said.

Compared to Grayson, Ava realized she was stone-cold sober. And growing more sober by the moment.

"Do you know what my dad said to me the night I told him I was going to marry David?" Ava looked around uneasily but Grayson didn't wait for her to reply. "He said, 'He'll never make you happy.' Just like that. As if he knew, or even cared, what made me happy!"

Fraser entered the room from the dining room and Ava quickly raised her hand and motioned for him to join them. She could see Darlene Haney sitting at a table with three other women. Darlene saw Fraser and made a face, turning her head slightly so she wouldn't have to speak to him.

"And now I have these two sons," Grayson continued, waving her empty glass in the air in front of her, "and they're as cute as can be.

You've seen pictures of them?" she asked, and Ava smiled and nodded her head. *Dear God, don't let her take out the photos again.*

"They're as cute as can be and they're sweet, quiet boys just like their father, and they don't have any friends. Well, not very many anyway, not like I did when I was a child. I was very popular." She looked at Ava. "Were you popular when you were a girl?"

"Not really."

"Oh." Grayson frowned, as if struggling to understand this. "What was I talking about?"

"Your sons."

"Oh, yes! Do you know how many kids showed up for Caldwell's birthday?" She put the glass down and held up five fingers. "That's right," she said. "Four."

Fraser had stopped to say hello to someone he knew and Ava stared at him, willing him to look at her.

"Four out of ten invites," Grayson said, sniffing.

"Well, that's almost fifty percent," Ava said bravely. She wasn't trying to make light of Grayson's pain. Clotilde had once thrown a surprise party for Ava's thirteenth birthday for which no one showed up, but it turned out later that Clotilde had put the wrong date on the invitation and everyone showed up a week later. ("Oops!" Clotilde had said, laughing.) So maybe it wasn't the same thing at all.

"Hello, girls," Fraser said. He had come up while Ava had her head down, remembering her dismal thirteenth birthday party. He had toned down the Edgar Allan Poe tonight, wearing a pair of dark slacks and a dark silk shirt opened at the throat to show a simple gold crucifix.

"Hello, Fraser," Grayson said brightly, dabbing at her eyes. "Excuse me. I have to run to the little girls' room."

He sat down and they watched Grayson push her way through the crowd. "Trouble in paradise?" he asked, arching one brow.

"Just girl talk," Ava said.

"Well, then you can tell me, silly."

"Kids," she said. "Don't ever have any."

He leaned forward, smiling smugly. "And speaking of spilling the beans."

"Were we?"

"How was lunch with Jake Woodburn?"

She looked at him uneasily. "How did you know about that?"

"Honey, the whole town knows about it."

She was quiet for a moment, wondering which lunch he was talking about. She decided it had to be the barbecue place. *Battle Smoove.* She sat back, running her hand through her hair, pulling it forward around her face. "It was just lunch. It wasn't sex in the afternoon. It wasn't anything sordid." Despite her insistence that there was nothing wrong with it, Ava felt her face flushing.

Fraser, noting her discomfort, grinned and said, "I'm not blaming you. Isn't he delicious? And so very *bad.* Who can resist?"

"What is it exactly that he's done that makes him such an outcast in this town?"

"Well." Fraser crossed his legs and rested his hands on one knee. "He's kind of a lone wolf, if you know what I mean. He doesn't mix much with the town, doesn't go to parties or barbecues, doesn't date debutantes."

"None of that makes him an outcast in my book."

"The biggest thing, of course, is that he went up against the Woodburns. You know that old saying you don't bite the hand that feeds you? Well, Josephine and Fanny paid for him to go to prep school, they paid for his college. He was living in a trailer with his mother on the wrong side of town and when Fanny found out, she went out there and talked to his mother. She insisted that the Woodburns would pay for his education, and they did. And that's what made it so much worse, later, when he broke up Will and Hadley. He could have had any girl he wanted but he set his sights on Will's fiancée and that's what caused the rift."

Ava felt a little quiver of alarm. She said, "Jake dated Will's fiancée?"

"Well, technically they weren't engaged yet. That came later. I don't know if Jake dated her but he certainly slept with her. They were sleeping together while they were at Sewanee. While Will was up at Bard but before he and Hadley got engaged."

She remembered Jake's face the day she asked him if the breach between him and Will was over a girl. "Was it serious?"

"Between Will and Hadley? Of course it was! They started going together their sophomore year of prep school. He was crazy about her. She wasn't from around here. Birmingham, I think, or maybe Mobile."

"No. Between Jake and Hadley."

Fraser waved animatedly at someone he knew. He turned his attention back to Ava. "Who knows?" he said, shrugging. "It's hard to tell with Jake. Although he must have felt something for her because he dropped out of school and went to California after she and Will got engaged."

She was quiet for a moment, wondering what upset her more, the fact that Jake had lied when he said it wasn't a girl that caused his break with Will, or the fact that he might have been in love with that girl. She supposed she wasn't really surprised. What was it Darlene Haney had said about him? "We're risking our reputations just standing here talking to him." He was obviously the kind of man whom women flocked to against their better judgment.

"So Will didn't know about Hadley and Jake when he asked Hadley to marry him?"

"No. He found out two years later and then he broke off the engagement."

"It was a sleazy thing to do," she said quietly. "But obviously Hadley chose Will over Jake. She got engaged to Will. So maybe Will should have just forgiven everybody and gone on with his life."

Fraser fussed with his sleeves. "Will didn't see it that way, of course. He took it as a personal betrayal. So did Josephine. And you know how those Woodburns are, they can carry a grudge."

"So Josephine was fond of Hadley?"

"I suppose so."

"That figures. Southern girl and all that."

Fraser grinned and made a dismissive motion with his hand. "Now don't be jealous. I'll bet Will hasn't thought of her in years."

"I'm not jealous," Ava said.

"You're as different from Hadley as two girls can be. You're just plain folks."

"Careful."

Fraser giggled. "You know what I mean. You're *comfortable.* And I mean that in a good way. And Hadley, well, she was just a big ol' Barbie doll."

"Oh, thank you very much."

"A cruel-hearted dominatrix in stiletto heels."

"It's time for another Donnie Miller," Ava said.

"Who's a cruel-hearted dominatrix?" Darlene had sneaked up behind them while they were talking.

"Speak of the devil," Fraser said.

She ignored him and turned to Ava, "Hey, are y'all talking about Hadley Marsh? Will's old fiancée?"

Ava said, "We are, but I don't know why."

"I'll tell you anything you want to know," Darlene said.

Fraser snorted. "Well, aren't you sweet?"

She pointed at his face. "Your mascara's running."

"At least I know not to wear blue shadow with melon lipstick."

"It's not melon, you peckerhead," Darlene said. "It's coral."

"Who're you calling a peckerhead?"

"Hey, if the shoe fits."

"Speaking of shoes," Fraser said, staring at Darlene's feet. "What size are those boats you're wearing?"

Darlene said, "You fucker."

Fraser laughed merrily.

Ava said, "Time to make a liquor run." The room revolved around her, reflecting the glittering light of the chandelier. She closed her eyes briefly, trying to get her bearings. Jake's face came suddenly, vividly, into view.

She put both palms on the table and pushed herself up, and while Fraser and Darlene continued with their argument she stumbled off through the crowd, determined not to think of him again.

Two Donnie Millers later, Ava spotted Will across the crowded room. He'd been cornered by Darlene. They had their heads close together. Will was looking at the floor and Darlene had her hand cupped around her mouth and was saying something into his ear. He raised his head, staring into Darlene's face. She shrugged. Then they both turned and looked at Ava.

She was too drunk to do anything but lift her glass in a kind of hearty salute. Darlene smiled and melted into the crowd. Will stood staring at her with an expression she couldn't quite decipher and then, as she began to make her way toward him, he, too, turned and walked off.

They both had too much to drink and after their guests left he fell on her with a ferocity she hadn't expected. It was so unusual for Will that at first she didn't know how to respond. She pushed him away. The room was spinning, and she thought she might get sick.

"Forgive me," he said. There was a hint of malice in his expression that left Ava disturbed and vaguely repulsed.

She passed out on one of the downstairs sofas while he went upstairs to sleep.

But in the morning he seemed composed and aloof. He asked her with exaggerated courtesy how she had slept, and after breakfast, as her car wouldn't start, drove her back to Woodburn Hall.

The morning was bright and lovely but he barely said two words to her and she, after a halfhearted attempt at conversation, fell silent, too. They were both embarrassed by their conduct the night before but he was angry with her for some reason, too. That much was clear. It would never be direct confrontation and accusation with Will, she realized now, but always polite and numbing glacial coldness.

He pulled up in the drive to drop her off but kept the engine running. "Aren't you coming in?" she said.

"No."

That's when she realized that Darlene had told him about her lunch with Jake Woodburn.

Josephine was in the kitchen when she came in. She seemed surprised to see Ava. "You're home," she said. "Where's Will?"

They both heard his truck in the street, roaring off like some raging mechanical beast.

"He couldn't come in," Ava said. She was suddenly very tired. She had a headache and her stomach hurt. "I'm not feeling well," she said. "I think I'll lie down." She turned and headed for the dining room.

Behind her Josephine said, "There was a letter for you."

It was postmarked from Michigan. Ava's hand trembled as she took it from Josephine and slid it into her purse. She had taken Jake's advice and written to Frank Dabrowski two weeks ago, a curt, questioning letter.

Josephine said, "Can I get you anything?" If she noticed Ava's agitation over the letter, she gave no sign of it.

"No. Thank you. I just need to sleep."

"Of course," Josephine said.

Ava went into her room and shut the door. She took the letter out of her purse and stared at the handwriting. She sank down on the bed and opened the letter. It read:

I didn't send birthday cards or Christmas presents because your mother said not to. I didn't think that was right and I told her so. But your mother thought it was best for me to stay out of your life. I'm sorry she told you I was dead. I should have done more. Maybe if you'd been my true flesh and blood I would have fought harder. I don't mean that like it sounds.

                                                     Sorry. Frank.

P.S. It's ok if you write me back.

Beneath it he had scribbled a phone number, as if an afterthought.

1927

Vanderbilt
Nashville, Tennessee

She had only seen him twice before, the first time when he came up to
the house to thank Papa for paying his tuition to Vanderbilt, and the
second time when he brought her flowers on her sixteenth birthday. It
was the summer before she went up to Vanderbilt and she thought,
"What cheek, I don't even know him." His hair was dark, and glittered
with pomade, and his fingers were thick and blunt, not the hands of a
gambler, but those of a red-dirt farmer. When he left, Papa said, "Sister, I'm ashamed of you, treating a guest in our home that way."

She had heard about him, of course. He was the talk of the whole
town, riding around in his Ford jalopy, making all the girls swoon over
his resemblance to Rudolph Valentino. Josephine didn't see it. He was
good-looking, of course, there was no denying that, but he knew it.
Charm seemed to ooze out of every pore but it was a false charm, and
she was surprised Papa had fallen for it. He was usually such a good
judge of character. She supposed it had something to do with Charlie
Woodburn's striking resemblance to Old Randal Woodburn, the Patriarch. He had been downtown at his broker's when Charlie walked by
the window, and the shock of seeing that face had caused Papa's heart
to flutter. He went out into the street and called to the boy, and discovered that he was Lyman Woodburn's son, one of Old Randal's Black

Woodburn progeny. He had been taken to New Orleans by his mother as a boy and raised there, and had only just recently returned to his "Pater's stomping grounds," as he put it. All this Papa told them one evening at supper while Josephine sat curling her top lip and Celia played with her food and Fanny secretly fed Tom Penny tidbits from her plate. It was the fourth or fifth Tom Penny they'd raised; Fanny seemed to lack imagination when it came to naming cats.

"I hear he's a gambler and a drunkard," Josephine said. She flushed under her father's steady gaze.

"There's some that have not had your privileges, Sister."

There was something personal in his defense of Charlie Woodburn, Josephine realized later. Papa was, after all, the last of the legitimate male Woodburns; all the male cousins had different surnames now, and although that might not have mattered to some, it obviously mattered to Papa. It was a year of great floods and cataclysmic events, so Josephine should have been prepared for a world turned suddenly upside down. Still, she was surprised to learn later that he had taken Charlie under his wing, had seen to it that the boy was introduced around town, made sure he had decent and respectable lodgings. And he had taken a fatherly interest in the boy's education, too, writing a letter to Chancellor Kirkland at Vanderbilt offering to pay Charlie's tuition.

When Charlie came to the house to thank Papa, his manners were oily and obsequious, and Josephine was surprised Papa didn't see this. Charlie had the hungry, ambitious look of a man who aims to climb high, and when he glanced at Josephine, she let her eyes rest on him a little longer, as if to say, "I see you for who you are even if they don't," and she was rewarded by a faint creep of color along his brow.

When he brought her flowers on her sixteenth birthday, she took them with an abrupt "Thank you," and spent the entire evening not giving him so much as a glance, yawning and excusing herself halfway through the story of his childhood in New Orleans.

Later, she heard the heavy tread of Papa's footsteps on the stairs, and when he left after scolding her, she lay in the big mahogany bed watching the moon climb the June sky, determined that should she run into Charlie Woodburn at Vanderbilt, she would cut him dead.

Josephine was attractive, although overly tall, and as a good many of the freshman class at Vanderbilt had been her classmates at Mr. Webb's school, she was never at a loss for partners at dances and cotillions. She was known to have a rather dry, sarcastic wit, and was the antithesis of the wild "flapper" but nevertheless was considered a "jolly girl" and a "good sport." She bobbed her hair and smoked Coronas and, as it was still Prohibition, carried around the requisite "Teddy Bear" with its hollow metal stomach filled with gin.

Vanderbilt, in those days, boasted a social calendar nearly as strenuous as its academic calendar. Josephine was a good student and she took her studies seriously but she also enjoyed the club sporting events and the dances and the house parties. Booze was illegal, but they had no trouble getting it, frequenting a Smoky Row bootlegger who went by the incongruous name of Tiny Hammer.

In March of her freshman year, she was one of a select group invited to take the annual pilgrimage to Mammoth Cave, Kentucky. They would take the train from Nashville to Glasgow, Kentucky, and then the Mammoth Cave Special to the Cave Inn, where they had rented several suites. The following day they'd spend touring the cave with its many resplendent rooms and its memorial to Vanderbilt before spending the evening dancing at the Mammoth Cave Ball in the hotel's mezzanine ballroom. Josephine had been hearing about the annual pilgrimage ever since she first began at the Webb School, and she had looked forward to this event almost as much as she'd looked forward to Vanderbilt itself.

She'd only run into Charlie Woodburn a few times; he'd obviously been keeping a low profile, which was a good thing, as no one liked a threadbare social climber, even one with the illustrious name of Woodburn. On the bright morning she left for Mammoth Cave, she had just climbed aboard the train and settled herself in her seat when she heard the opening blasts of a jazz tune and, turning, she saw Charlie Woodburn a few rows back with a clarinet to his lips. He was sitting in the back surrounded by Ben Clement, Miles Crockett, and Jeff Bemis, who were all clapping and thumping him on the shoulders and it occurred to Josephine that Charlie was more intelligent than she'd given him credit for being. He hadn't been lying low at all; he'd been slowly, gradually insinuating himself into her social set. He played "Birmingham Bertha" and "Blues My Naughty Sweetie Gives to Me" and "Let's Sow a Wild Oat" until the conductor came back and told him to stop.

Later, on his way to the dining car, he winked at Josephine and said, "Hi, Toots," and this time it was Josephine who felt her face flush.

Lenora Donelson leaned over and said breathlessly, "Isn't that your cousin?"

Josephine opened her compact and began to powder her nose. "Not really," she said.

After that, Josephine couldn't go anywhere without running into Charlie Woodburn. He was good friends with all the boys she'd attended the Webb School with, and as he was a polished gambler who knew how to cheat in order to let his opponents win, he was considered a "sport." The girls were all wild for him, for his dark good looks and easy charm. He was also an accomplished jazz musician and knew all the jazz lingo from having grown up on the streets of New Orleans, and his vocabulary and manner of speech were much admired and copied. In this he was lucky; if he'd grown up in Woodburn, a boy from his background would have talked with the nasal speech so derided by members of her own class, what the editors of the school newspaper, *The Hustler,* called "that naso-nasal twang." But with his carefully modulated, slightly Creole accent he sounded a little like Madame Arcenaux, Josephine's long-vanquished nemesis.

Madame Arcenaux had been relatively easy to get rid of but

Josephine had the feeling Charlie Woodburn would not be quite so manageable.

The summer after her freshman year she went to Italy with her cousins Minnie and Lamar. It was all she could do; she couldn't stay home. Papa had secured a clerking job for Charlie Woodburn in his factory's office, and he took his noonday meal with the family now, walking from downtown in the dusty heat and returning to his office after siesta. In those days the downtown shops and offices closed for dinner and for an hour afterward, when everyone went home to nap during the stifling heat of midday.

Josephine and the cousins rented a villa in Florence near the Palazzo Pitti and later spent two weeks in Venice, but despite the Ponte dei Sospiri and the Basilica di San Marco, Venice made Josephine feel agitated and restless. The gondoliers along the canals, with their dark good looks and bold, roving hands, reminded her too much of Charlie Woodburn.

Fanny and Celia's letters from home were filled with Charlie. He called them "Little Cuz" and "Sprite," and he made them all laugh, even Papa, with his jokes and tales of Uncle Remus and Bourbon Street. He built Celia a dollhouse out of oak, and when Fanny's old cat disappeared he brought her a dear little gray kitten that she named Tom Penny VI. Papa took Charlie to meetings of his gentleman's club, the Belle Meade Club.

All in all it seemed that the entire family was enamored of Charlie Woodburn; everyone, it would seem, but Josephine.

They sailed from Europe too late to attend the opening of Vanderbilt, and by the time Josephine arrived on campus, classes had been in session for nearly two weeks. She had determined during the long transatlantic trip that her relationship with Charlie Woodburn would, in the future, be cordial but cool. She would no longer allow herself to slip into a pattern of open hostility on her part and amused acceptance on his. It had occurred to her that Charlie was a gamesman, and that her open dislike of him, rather than cooling his vanity, simply stoked it. She wished now that she had not fled to Europe. Her sisters' tales of the long summer spent in Charlie's company left Josephine feeling oddly bereft, as if she'd missed something that could never be recaptured. Papa spoke of Charlie's manly grace, of his natural ability as a marksman. Only the child Clara seemed to have escaped enchantment, becoming oddly agitated at the mention of Charlie's name and wrapping her hands tightly in her mother's apron.

Charlie had pledged Delta Tau Delta, one of the best fraternities on campus, which should have surprised Josephine, but did not. It was an old house whose members were mostly legacies, and she suspected Papa had had a hand in Charlie being rushed. The winter formal was being held in New Orleans, and in November Carlisle Ransom asked Josephine to accompany him as his date. They were to take the train to New Orleans Friday morning, spend Friday night at the Ponchartrain Hotel, and Saturday night dancing at the Creole Ballroom, before returning to Nashville on Sunday. They would take individual cars to the Nashville train station, caravanning, and because Carlisle was a good friend of Charlie Woodburn's, it was determined that Carlisle and Josephine would ride up with Charlie and his date, Marian Cason. The arrangements were made, there was nothing Josephine could do to contest them, but halfway to the station, Charlie swung his head over his shoulder and looked at her and she knew suddenly, as clearly as if he'd spoken the words, that he had arranged for Carlisle to take her, that she was here at Charlie's bidding. This knowledge left her irritated and yet vaguely, faintly thrilled.

By the time they reached New Orleans, however, she'd begun to think she had imagined it all, because not once on the rest of the ride to the station, not once on the long train trip to New Orleans, had Charlie shown her the least bit of attention. She was in a foul mood by the time she dressed for dinner, and was a miserable date for Carlisle, pleading a headache after dinner at Galatoire's and making an early evening of it. On Saturday she determined to do better, dressing herself carefully before the ball in a blue silk gown that echoed the startling gray-blue of her eyes, and carefully painting her mouth a brilliant shade of scarlet.

She was surprised to find Charlie waiting for her at the foot of the stairs. "Your date is hailing a cab," he said to her. His evening clothes were badly tailored, and that gave her a surge of confidence. "Oh?" she said, pulling on her gloves.

"Marian is helping him. I'm here to escort you."

"Are you?" she said smoothly, still fiddling with her gloves, and without a glance in his direction she went out the doors ahead of him.

He did not ask her to dance. It didn't matter—her card was full—but from time to time she sought him out in the crowded ballroom. He danced recklessly, carelessly, his dark hair combed smoothly off his brow, the color rising in his face. Whatever poor impression his badly fitting clothes made was offset by his graceful manner; yet there was something of the dance hall in his movements, too, a style that seemed at times coached and uninspired. His face, when he thought no one was watching, would relax into lines of disappointment and boredom, before changing, just as quickly, into an expression of good cheer and camaraderie when someone came up to clap him on the shoulder.

Josephine's cousin, Minnie, was there from Sewanee. "Ooh la la," she said, gazing at Charlie across the crowded ballroom, "is that The Cousin?" She was very drunk, and later, when they went to a little speakeasy on Frenchmen Street, sat on Charlie's lap and ran her fingers through his hair so that his date, Marian, got up in disgust and wandered over to the piano player. They were drinking bathtub gin, and Josephine's head banged like a bass drum. The air in the smoky, crowded room became too thick to breathe. She stood up and stumbled out into the cobblestone street. She had lost Carlisle, and apparently one of her shoes, too, several juke joints back. She stood for a moment staring at the garish lights blinking along Frenchmen Street, trying to get her bearings. She could see the spires of St. Louis Cathedral rising over the tree line. Behind her the door to the speakeasy banged open and a rush of stale, smoky air swept over her.

"I'll see you home," Charlie said, taking her arm. His hand on her arm made her light-headed, and she leaned against him, hobbling as they walked. The streets smelled of sewer and burnt sugar. A drunken sailor stumbled out of the shadows and said, "Hello, doll," but Charlie pushed him and said, "Shove off."

They caught a cab at the corner and when they got back to the hotel, he climbed out behind her. "I can see myself up," she said, fumbling for her key, and dropping it on the street.

Charlie picked it up and took her firmly by the elbow. "Cousin James would never forgive me if I didn't see you to the door," he said. His face was pale under the flickering gaslights, strangely tense, as if he was listening to the sound of distant music and found it slightly jarring.

When they got to her room, he put the key in the lock and turned it, smoothly shoving the door open with one hand and with the other pushing her up against the wall. He put his hand on her breast and kissed her.

When he had gone, she locked the door behind him and went into the bathroom to be sick. That's how she knew she was doomed.

That's how she knew she was in love with Charlie Woodburn.

Desire. The relentlessness of it, the exquisite agony of waiting for the loved one's presence, his touch, the weight of his mouth. All her beaux up to now seemed like schoolgirl crushes compared to what she felt for Charlie Woodburn. And yet she did not see him for some time after the winter formal. It was as if he was avoiding her, denying what had happened between them. He spent Christmas in New Orleans, and when she returned to school in the spring she saw him at social events, always in the presence of throngs of people, and he was cordial but distant. She became awkward in his presence, tongue-tied and stammering. She couldn't eat, she couldn't sleep.

When her despair became too great for her to bear, he would give her a token of affection, a smile across a crowded room, a light touch at her waist, a murmured greeting in her ear. In February he sent her a Valentine signed —Always, C. At a picnic at the Hermitage he kissed her under a chestnut tree, and at a house party in May he whispered, "Don't forget me this summer."

As if she ever would.

He was spending the summer in Greenville, Mississippi, at a classmate's house, clerking in his father's bank. Josephine, who had spent the spring imagining the two of them together at Woodburn, was disappointed. She spent her days reading novels and writing her name as Mrs. Charles Woodburn. Did he know the depth of her feeling? Probably not. He was surrounded by girls at school and, no doubt, in Greenville, too. And yet she could have him, Josephine knew, she had seen it that night in his face when he first came to call on Papa, that hungry desire to rise above his station, to be, once and for all, a True Woodburn.

But would Papa have him for a son-in-law? That was harder to gauge. True, he was fond of Charlie, and he was always glad to receive his letters. (Charlie never wrote to Josephine but would include little notes for her in Papa's letter—Remember me to my cousins; Tell Josephine the belles in Greenville think college for women is a waste.) But Papa was a proud man, a man who, once crossed, would never forgive. She would have to proceed slowly, patiently. Josephine spent the summer murmuring sweet remembrances of Charlie into Papa's ear, reminding her sisters often of Dear Cousin Charlie, singing his praises loudly and sincerely to all who would listen.

In August he wrote that he would be coming through Woodburn on bank business. Josephine set about getting ready for his visit in a frenzy of excitement. She had the house aired and cleaned until the woodwork shone. She had Martha make chicken and dumplings, his favorite, according to Fanny, for dinner. She bought a new sheath dress and had her hair permed in the latest style.

The day he was to arrive dawned hot and airless, and Josephine rose early and went about her business on trembling legs. At noon she checked on dinner and, assuring herself it was all done according to his liking, she went out onto the verandah to await him and Papa. By twelve-thirty they still had not come, and Celia and Fanny came out to complain that they were hungry. The heat made them all irritable and they quarreled, and the younger girls went back into the house, slamming the door. At one o'clock, Josephine rose and, calling to her sisters, went in to dinner. She couldn't eat, sitting expectantly at the table, waiting to hear the sound of their boots on the verandah. At one-thirty, Fanny and Celia climbed the stairs to their rooms to nap. Josephine sat at the table with her hands in her lap.

She was still there when Papa came in at four o'clock. He seemed surprised to see her, sitting at the table with the electric fan raising little whorls of hair around her face, and he was more surprised still when, explaining that the train had been late and so he and Charlie had lunched at the hotel before Charlie left for Nashville, she rose with a little cry and, covering her face, ran out of the room.

In September, Fanny went up to Vanderbilt with her. Josephine steeled herself for the inevitable period of adjustment that always followed Fanny's leaving home. Fanny was sixteen but she was much more girlish than most girls her age; she still carried her favorite doll in her suitcase, still spoke baby talk to Tom Penny, still cried at night for Martha and home. She had done the same when she went off to the Webb School, even though they were only day students. She had cried and carried a doll in her Gladstone bag every day, and no pleading from Josephine could make her stop. At Vanderbilt it was even worse, as they boarded at Mrs. Stillwell's, and every night Fanny would cry herself to sleep with homesickness, her face buried deep in her pillow and Josephine stroking her back. Josephine had fallen into the habit of protecting Fanny years ago, not long after she realized that Fanny was so loving and trusting that she had to be protected at all costs. Having Josephine as an older sister had not broken her of this habit, it had not made Fanny suspicious or cynical, and so the only thing to do was to protect her.

It was exhausting. But it kept Josephine from spending all her time thinking about Charlie, it saved her from that misery. He had returned to school even more full of himself than before, clapping Josephine fondly on the shoulder when he saw her and calling her "old girl." With Fanny he adopted a slightly more paternal role, warning his fraternity brothers to "keep your grubby paws off my little cousin," and making sure she was not included in any of their wilder house parties.

In October, Papa dropped dead of a heart attack on his way to the bank. It happened on a bright, glorious day when he had insisted on walking to town, stopping in the middle of greeting Mrs. Chesney to grab his left arm before collapsing with a pained, surprised expression on his face. John drove up in the car to get them, and Charlie rode back with Fanny and Josephine for the funeral; the only sound above the smooth hum of the motor was that of Fanny's shuddering sobs.

The funeral was well attended. Afterward Josephine met privately with Papa's attorney, Mr. Atwood, and a few days later the sisters and a large retinue of family retired to Mr. Atwood's office for the reading of the will. The estate was divided between Josephine, Fanny, and Celia, with generous bequests going to Martha, John, and Clara. Surprisingly, there was also a bequest for Charlie, a small trust set up to pay for his remaining terms at Vanderbilt, and several sealed envelopes, letters of reference to help Charlie find a job following graduation.

Josephine told Charlie of the bequest herself. He seemed not so much surprised as disappointed. "How kind of him," he said, and Josephine, hearing something in his voice, looked at him, but his face was smooth and expressionless. He left early the next morning to return to Vanderbilt.

Josephine was a wealthy woman now. Perhaps not as wealthy as she would have been before the Crash, but certainly well-off. She could have anything she wanted, including Charlie Woodburn. And yet now that she was so close to achieving her dreams, she seemed to hear Papa's voice in her head, Careful, Sister. What do you really know of this man? Why saddle yourself with a stranger you barely know? Mr. Atwood seemed to echo these sentiments.

She sent Fanny back to school while she stayed to tie up the loose ends with Mr. Atwood. Two weeks later, she set out for Vanderbilt. She was hopeful for the first time since Papa's death, feeling oddly elated, as if her life were about to change, as if she were at the beginning of a long journey. She was free for the first time in her life. Anything was possible.

When she got off the train it was snowing. The sky was gray and wintry. Mrs. Stillwell had sent a car, and Josephine had anticipated a warm welcome, but when they reached the boarding house she found the windows darkened and Mrs. Stillwell, surrounded by several of the other boarders, crying in the kitchen. She was clutching a creased note in one hand. Josephine recognized the handwriting.

That was how she came to know what Mrs. Stillwell and the other boarders knew, what the entire campus had known since early that morning. Last night, while Josephine was packing her suitcase and preparing for her new life to begin, Charlie Woodburn had slipped into Mrs. Stillwell's boardinghouse and eloped with Fanny.

A Superstitious Kind
of Delicacy

One of Clotilde's favorite fairy tales was "The Tale of the Sleeping
Princess." She told it often to Ava over the years, in many different
forms, but always it was the same story.

Once there was a princess of royal blood named Sheelin. She was very
wise and brave, and when a plague came upon the land, the old king,
her father, sent her to the East to obtain the One True Pearl. With this
Pearl she could cure the land of sickness and famine, and restore her
father to health. But it was a perilous journey, for the Pearl was buried
at the bottom of the sea, guarded by a fierce dragon. The Princess
Sheelin set forth with three companions, all of whom were killed along
the way. When she arrived at the Hall of the Sea God, Sheelin
disguised herself in the sparkling garments of the Sea People. But they
guessed her mission and gave her a potion to drink. When she drank it
she fell into a deep sleep, and when she awoke she didn't remember
who she was or why she was here. Her father, fearing she would never
return, sent a letter in the form of a white bird that perched on
Sheelin's shoulder and reminded her of her noble birth and her destiny.
Then she awoke and kissed the bird. Remembering who she was
and desiring to return to her own kind, she charmed the sleeping

dragon and stole the Pearl. As she hurried from the hall with the Pearl she shed her false clothes, finding that the Pearl directed her home with its shining light.

Remembering this tale in the days following her receipt of the letter from Frank Dabrowski, it was all Ava could do not to lift the vase and throw it against the wall, dispersing Clotilde's dusty remains everywhere. Every time she thought of the letter, she glared at her mother and hissed, "How could you?"

Her true father could have been any one of a number of nameless men. Clotilde may not have known herself, masking this fact in her false and elaborate stories. Her vain attempts, Ava saw now, to throw her off the scent.

But later, after her anger had died down, she thought mournfully, *Who is my father? Who am I?*

Perhaps Frank knew. He had thoughtfully included his phone number, but Ava was not ready to talk to him. She was not strong enough for that yet.

Instead she sat down and wrote him another letter.

Two days after the party at Longford, Jake called her. It was a rainy, dreary Monday morning and she was sitting at her computer, trying to work. She had not slept well the night before, and she was tired despite abundant cups of coffee.

"I've been thinking about you," he said.

"Have you?" she said coolly. Despite her intention to keep her distance, she couldn't help but feel a flutter of pleasure at the sound of his voice.

"I heard you had a great time out at Longford the other night."

"Who'd you hear that from?"

"A little bird told me."

"That little bird wouldn't by any chance be named Darlene, would it?"

"I'm sworn to secrecy," he said.

She regretted now that she had added Darlene's name to the guest list. Ava had dreaded the aunts telling Will about her meeting with Jake but she had not expected Darlene to do it. It seemed disloyal and unfriendly, and not the kind of thing she would have expected from someone she had insisted be invited to a party (not that Darlene knew that, of course). Ava was beginning to understand Fraser's warning that "down here people can be as sweet as a spoonful of honey to your face, all the while plunging a knife deep between your shoulder blades."

"It was quite a party," she said.

"I heard you were a dancing fool."

"I have no recollection of that."

He laughed. "It makes me wish I'd been invited."

"You'll have to talk to Will about that."

"Yeah, that's not going to happen."

A sudden gust of wind rattled the windows. Thunder rumbled in the distance. "Why didn't you tell me your break with Will was over Hadley?" She was surprised by the vehemence of her own voice. She hadn't meant to bring it up at all.

"I thought you knew. You said you'd talked to Darlene Haney and she'd told you."

"She told me it was over a girl. She didn't give me any specifics."

"How was I supposed to know that?"

"And besides, you lied when you said it wasn't over a girl."

"I said it was over something a lot deeper than a disagreement over a girl."

"You implied that it wasn't over a girl at all."

"Did I?"

"Yes."

"Well, then, I'm sorry." He was quiet for a moment and she could hear distant music in the background. She wondered where he might be calling from. "Look," he said finally. "I'm not really proud of what happened between Hadley and me. We were both young and we'd known each other for a long time and it just happened. It wasn't planned. We didn't set out to hurt Will."

"I'm sure that made him feel a lot better."

"Don't take his side without hearing the whole story."

"I'm not taking anyone's side. It's none of my business."

"That's not how you're acting."

"Did you love her?"

The rain fell softly. On the leafy branch of an oak tree, a large black crow sat watching her with dark glittering eyes.

"Can we talk about this some other time?"

"I have to go," she said, and hung up.

She knew she'd been hasty and narrow-minded. It occurred to her that she might have sabotaged the whole thing subconsciously, but she didn't care. The work was what mattered now.

She didn't have time for anything else.

She couldn't work after the phone call. She walked around the room, picking up objects and setting them back down again, sorry now that she'd acted the way she had. She thought about picking up the phone and calling him back but she wasn't sure how to manage it. What would she say to him? What would she tell Will?

Outside the window, a ridge of gray storm clouds rolled in, rattling the glass and splattering rain against the fat green leaves of the magnolia tree. After a while Ava stretched out on the bed to take a nap.

She dreamed of cold dark water. She was floating in a canoe under a starry sky. She had no paddles and she was drifting, being pulled slowly and inexorably toward a dangerous rocky shoal. She could hear the rushing sound of water and she could see the humped shapes of boulders rising out of the white-tipped waves. A black ridge of forest rose behind them, and a three-legged dog ran along the rocky shore barking incessantly. She looked down into the oily glistening river. She knew she could not survive the rocks, so she dived into the water and began to swim toward the opposite shore. She could breathe underwater (she was not surprised by this), and she darted back and forth like a fish, taking in great gulps of dark silty water, and leaping finally to the surface, where a beam of moonlight floated on the waves like a silver coin.

Behind her the dog, cheated of its reward, barked voraciously.

She awoke to thunder rattling the glass. Faintly in the distance, the neighbor's dog, which was afraid of storms, barked a frenzied warning. The room was lit by a watery green light, and a moment later the rain began in earnest, drumming against the roof and the gutters. Ava lay on her side, watching flashes of lightning against the dark gray sky. Outside the windows the old trees bent and swayed. After a while she switched on the bedside lamp and curled on her side, reading, and when she tired of this, she closed the book and lay back with one arm thrown behind her against the headboard, her fingers tracing the whorls and channels of the elaborate carvings.

She had always loved thunderstorms. In college she and Michael had stayed in bed on rainy days, using the weather as an excuse to skip class and roll around under the sheets. Despite their amorous exploits, love with Michael had always felt tragic, illusory. They had lain in each other's arms and talked in a careless way about their "future": the white picket fence around a house in the suburbs, two-point-five children, a life circumscribed by restraint and routine. The whole time they were talking, Ava had known it was false. A fairy tale.

She thought of beautiful Grayson Byrd settling for a safe, predictable life with David the Doctor, settling for the big sprawling house and the skiing vacations to Aspen and the two good-looking but socially awkward children. She had given up spontaneity and regular orgasms for money in the bank, because wasn't that really what she'd been trying to tell Ava, in her reckless and inebriated way? If you settle, it isn't always fair. It isn't always pretty.

Despite the fantasies she had spun around Michael, Ava had never been able to see herself having a future with him. Or with Jacob either, for that matter. She had known she'd never want the same things they wanted, no matter how much she pretended. She had known instinctively that if she had children, writing would become a hobby, something to be taken out and fitted in between nap times and meals and playgroups, and then put away again. She needed more than that.

She was more like her mother than she liked to admit.

Clotilde hadn't been able to settle either. At least not on the American Dream, the one every girl of her generation was raised to expect: matrimony, motherhood, a life of self-denial. Clotilde was a pretty woman and there had been plenty of men who would have liked nothing more than to slip a ring on her finger, to tie her down, but she was always on the move, she was always fleeing . . . what? What had driven her mother all those years?

Ava's earliest memory was of standing at a big glass window, half-hidden behind a filmy drape. It was night and it must have been Christmas because the house across the way was covered in multicolored lights, reflecting off the snow. Ava had her chin resting on the window ledge, that's how small she was, and she was looking out into the street, waiting for someone. Clotilde, perhaps, on her way home from work.

No, that wasn't right. Clotilde was in the kitchen behind her; she could hear her singing as she made dinner. So who was it she was waiting for?

Santa Claus. She remembered now. She was scanning the sky looking for a sleigh pulled by flying reindeer but the only thing moving was a long black car coming slowly along the street. It stopped in front of the house, its headlights glittering on the snowy banks.

"What are you doing?" Clotilde said behind her, and, looking up, Ava saw her stricken face. "Come away from that window at once." She pulled Ava away, standing at the edge of the drape and staring out as the big rumbling car began to move slowly down the street.

Ava's fingers had stopped their exploration of the headboard, had lingered for a moment over an abrasion she could feel with her fingertips, scratched into the smooth surface of the wood in the narrow space between the headboard and the mattress. Curious, she rolled over and pulled the mattress away. She could see several letters carved there but she could not make out the words. She pulled the lamp closer and rubbed the scratches with a wet finger, but still she couldn't make them out.

It wasn't until she had pulled out the small flashlight she carried on her key chain and shone it against the dark wood that she could make out the faint words scratched there.

Help me.

There was a sudden loud clap of thunder and the lamp flickered and went out. The house was silent with the void left by the air-conditioning system shutting down. Distantly, above the roar of the rain, Ava could hear a faint scratching noise as of rodents in the walls. There was another flash of lightning, followed by a boom of thunder, and then a high-pitched yelp. She could hear voices coming from the kitchen, and she made her way there through the shadowy house. She met Fanny in the dining room as she hurried past with her hands clamped over her ears, wincing under each thunderous boom as if from a blow. Fanny was as frightened of thunderstorms as the neighbor's dog, and she spent most stormy days cowering under the covers of her bed with a pillow over her head. She smiled apologetically at Ava but her mild gray eyes were as wide as a frightened child's.

"Oh, dear, oh, dear," she said, as she hurried past. "It's a doozy this time." Maitland trailed behind her offering words of comfort, telling her the storm was nearly over and the power would be back on in no time.

Josephine and Clara were in the kitchen hunting candles and matches. They looked up, startled, as Ava appeared in the doorway.

"Are you all right?" Josephine said. "You look like you've seen a ghost."

"Sorry," Ava said.

Josephine pointed at the dimly lit breakfast room where Alice sat morosely observing the storm. "There's sweet tea in the refrigerator if you're thirsty," she said to Ava. "Or coffee. The percolator's still warm. The power hasn't been off long." She turned and went back to hunting candles.

Ava poured herself a glass of tea and sat down across the table from Alice, who sat with her cheek propped on her hand, her face turned anxiously toward the rain-swept window. "It's at times like these that I hate having all those big trees around my house," she said to Ava. Behind them, Josephine slammed one drawer and opened another. Without the background hum of the air-conditioning, all sound was magnified in the quiet house. "It's funny. All the houses along this side of the street are out of power but the lights on that side are still on."

"Different generators," Ava said.

They could hear footsteps on the back stairs and a moment later Will burst through the kitchen door, shaking the rain out of his hair. His T-shirt was plastered to his wet skin and he went over to the sink to wring it out.

"Can you believe this?" he said.

"It's a real duck drencher," Clara said.

"Should I check the fuse box?" he asked Josephine. He came into the breakfast room and put a hand lightly on one of Ava's shoulders. She had only seen him twice since the party at Longford and both times there had been a sense of restraint between them, a wariness. But the unsettled feeling appeared to have broken with the storm. He seemed almost cheerful today, smiling at her, the rain streaming down his hair into his collar.

"Why bother with the fuse box?" Alice said. "The lights are out all along the street."

"It's probably a good idea," Josephine said, overruling her. "Let me get the flashlight."

She opened the cellar door, a narrow door off the pantry, and she and Will went down together. Clara shivered and joined them at the table. "I hate going down there," she said. "Mama used to keep apples and potatoes in the cellar, and she'd make me go down and get them."

"What were you afraid of?" Ava asked.

"I don't know." She shook her head ruefully and poured herself a cup of coffee. "Something."

Alice said, "I hope Fraser remembered to unplug the TV. Last time we had a lightning strike it blew out the TV and we had to get a new one." As if to prove her point, a sudden bright flash lit the room, followed by a boom of thunder.

"How many times has your house been struck?"

"Just the once that I know of."

Clara propped her elbows on the table and sipped her coffee. "They say the Empire State Building gets hit at least twenty times every year."

"Is that right?" Alice looked at her in mild astonishment.

Ava could hear Will and Josephine moving around down in the cellar. She thought of the words *Help me.* So pitiful and plaintive. She remembered her fingers touching the words, and she shuddered suddenly.

"Someone walk over your grave?" Clara said.

Ava looked into her dark, curious eyes. "Sorry?"

Clara chuckled and shook her head. The storm seemed to be moving off; lightning still flickered in the sky but the rumble of thunder was more distant, and the rain fell steadily but with diminishing force.

Ava splayed her fingers out on the table on either side of her glass. "You say there's no photo of Charlie Woodburn?"

Clara stopped smiling and glanced at Alice. "No," she said, setting her cup down. "Not that I know of."

"I suppose he was handsome," Ava said.

"As the devil," Clara said, blowing her nose into a napkin.

Alice sniffed and ran her finger along the steamy window glass. "They used to practically swoon in the streets as he drove by. And at Vanderbilt, it was the same. He had that effect on women."

"So he liked women?"

Alice frowned and glanced at Clara. "I wouldn't say he *liked* women. He certainly used them."

"He associated with loose women," Clara said, getting up to throw the napkin in the trash. "Saloon girls and flappers and jazz singers."

"He had a child out of wedlock with a woman by the name of Sweeney. Myrtle, I think her name was, or maybe Mabel. Before he ran off with Fanny. That's the kind of man he was, although the family didn't know it, of course. All that came out later. There was something wrong with the child, a son. He was crippled somehow, and when he saw the boy they say Charlie cried like a baby." Alice shook her head slowly, as if trying to imagine this. "You wouldn't expect a man like Charlie Woodburn to be tenderhearted over something like that but he was."

Clara clucked her tongue and said in a less sympathetic tone, "Him and that boy of his, that crippled child he named King. King Woodburn. Can you imagine that? Always riding around in that big car like they owned the world. Like they expected everyone to bow and scrape. Well, pride cometh before a fall, as they both soon learned," she added darkly.

Ava could hear footsteps on the cellar stairs. Josephine and Will were coming up. "What happened to the boy?" she asked quickly.

"Boy?"

"King Woodburn. Charlie's son."

Clara glanced at the cellar door and back at Ava. "Died of cirrhosis of the liver at the age of forty. But not before he'd fathered his own son, that Jake, who's caused Will so much heartache and trouble. That's all Black Woodburns were ever good for. Causing trouble and heartache for decent folk."

That evening Ava wrote long into the night. The novel had taken on a life of its own; the characters were beginning to reveal themselves in ways she'd never imagined. Charlie's love for his crippled son, King, she had already anticipated. And yet despite his simple love for the child there is something hard in Charlie, something she had first glimpsed the day he went with his mother to the grand house on St. Charles Avenue, something she had seen in his face that day at the cemetery when he stood staring at his mother's vault. He is a mysterious character, a man who loves his mother and yet not other women. Even Fanny, he loves fiercely and passionately but not as a woman: as a possession, a symbol. Sweet, vain Fanny who cares only for pretty dresses and parties.

But it is Josephine who is turning out to be the most astonishing character of all. Josephine carries a secret, and Ava glimpses it in her face one night as she sits watching a room of gaily plumed dancers twirl around the front parlor of Finn Hall. Bessie Smith is on the phonograph singing "Gulf Coast Blues." The long windows have been thrown open to the night, and Josephine sits in front of one of them, trying to catch a breeze. She is looking at the crowd with a dazed, inattentive expression. She lifts her gloved hand to mop her brow, and in this vague, unguarded movement she gives something away. Something blooms in Josephine's heart, seeping into her face, her eyes, and Ava, astonished, sees it.

Josephine is in love.

But with whom?

That night Ava had another attack. She awakened to a room so cold her breath left a faint plume in the air. She was lying on her back, stiff and lifeless as a moth pinned to a board. The shutters had been left open but it was a moonless night, and the only light was the faint glow of a distant streetlamp. She could hear deep breathing in the room. The sound came from the chair near the window. She could not turn her head to look but she could hear him, because she knew now that it was a masculine presence, she could hear it in his heavy uneven breathing, she could feel it in the cold, clammy pounding of her heart. There was a faint odor of smoke and whiskey in the room. The paralysis lasted just a few minutes, and when she could finally move, she drew a long, shuddering breath like a woman drowning, and turned her head.

In the dim light from the window, she could make out the dark shape of a man. She gasped and leaned to turn on the lamp.

The chair, illuminated by the faint glow of lamplight, was empty.

House of Hair

On the second Thursday of every month, Darlene Haney took her mother and brother to the Woodburn Medical Center to see their doctors. She did this out of the goodness of her heart and because she was a dutiful daughter and sister, even though it meant that she must take unpaid time off from work and make other arrangements for day care for the boys. Which was not easy to arrange these days, as the boys had been slandered at school, no doubt by other mothers who were jealous of the Haney boys' physical prowess, and most of the paid babysitters in town now refused to sit for them. They were not, of course, *bad* boys; they were just high-spirited. They were just in need of a daddy with a firm hand, and Will Fraser fit that description to a tee as far as Darlene was concerned.

Not that it would be easy, of course. First she must get rid of the Yankee girl. She anticipated no problems in that direction. So far everything was working like clockwork. (Ava was not as dumb as a stump but she *was* as clueless as one.) Once Darlene and Will were married, they would send the boys to that fancy boarding school he and Jake Woodburn had attended. Darlene imagined herself on Parents Day, floating through the school grounds in a flowered Versace, a large Kentucky Derby hat perched rakishly on top of her expensively styled hair.

No more House of Hair dye jobs for her. Once she married Will Fraser, only the most expensive Nashville hair salons would do. And clothes! As Mrs. Will Fraser, she would wear only the best designers. And wouldn't the girls down at the Debs and Brides Shoppe be green with envy when she waltzed in wearing Dolce & Gabbana or Marc Jacobs! (Serve them right, too, the stuck-up old cows.)

Darlene's pleasant imaginings were interrupted by the sight of her mother and brother waiting on the porch of the small, dilapidated house. She tooted the horn impatiently, looking on in annoyance as they rose and began their slow, plodding progress. Snowda was wearing a prosthesis she hadn't even *tried* to disguise with panty hose. She pushed a wheeled walker in front of her, like a geriatric lion tamer, only without the whip. Beside her, Richard waddled along dressed in a pair of tightly fitting black slacks that ended just above his ankles, a white shirt, a pair of white socks, and black orthopedic shoes clamped on his feet. Darlene sighed, wondering how in the world she could be related to these people.

It would be different, of course, once she was married to Will Fraser. Then she could afford to send her mother and brother away to some private and expensive nursing home. Some place a couple of counties over. It was not hard to imagine herself as Mrs. Will Fraser. Darlene had been a dreamer all her life, and she had been dreaming about Will ever since high school. He'd gone to private schools, of course, so she hadn't run into him until the summer after ninth grade, when he'd come home from boarding school with his cousin Jake. The two of them had been inseparable in those days; they'd spent the summer driving around town picking up girls in a 1967 Chevrolet Corvette they'd bought at an auction. Jake was the worst. You didn't dare get into the back with him unless you wanted to come out with bruises and whisker burns all over your face and other places too embarrassing to mention. Darlene had made that mistake just once. Jake was the older of the two, taller and more filled out, and he was a lot more confident with girls, so you noticed him first. But later, Darlene had noticed Will. He was kind of quiet, not really shy but more reserved than Jake and better mannered, too. When you told him "no" he seemed to respect that. He didn't push it like Jake did.

But damn, they were fine, the two of them. Like rock stars, driving around town in that flashy green car and flirting with all the girls at the Sonic Drive-In. Of course, Will was dating Hadley Marsh by then. She wasn't from Woodburn—they'd met at boarding school—but she came to visit that summer, and Darlene met her for the first time outside the movie theater. Well, she hadn't actually met her because Will didn't introduce the two of them. He didn't seem to notice Darlene or her friends at all. He was standing there with Jake and Hadley, and they had their heads together, laughing at something private. Like they knew they were too good to be here with all these small-town rednecks and had just come out to give the locals a show. As if Jake Woodburn, who was nothing more than trailer trash, had a right to be stuck-up. Hadley was dressed in a pair of jeans, a white cotton blouse, and a pair of jeweled sandals, and she looked like Michelle Pfeiffer standing there under the lights of the marquee. Watching the way the lights caught in her dazzling hair, Darlene had known she'd never be able to take Will away from Hadley no matter how hard she tried.

Darlene stared irritably at her mother and brother and then gave the horn another light toot. At the speed they were moving they would never get to the appointment in time. She slammed the car in park and climbed out, going to move them along. Snowda was halfway down the front ramp when she remembered that she'd left the television on.

"Oh, for crying out loud, get in the car," Darlene snapped. "I'll turn it off."

She opened the door and stepped into the sweltering front room, lit only by the flickering television screen. The room smelled of socks and old cheese. Darlene held her breath and went quickly to turn off the set. Through the dining room window she could see the neighbor, old Mrs. Caslin, hanging clothes on her clothesline.

She had spent her entire freshman year of high school dreaming about how to catch Will Fraser but it was no use; he was head over heels for Hadley Marsh, and when Darlene found out years later that they were engaged, she had not been surprised. Still, she often reminded herself, you never know how things might turn out. She herself had married a hometown boy who might have played professional football had it not been for one bad knee. And look how tragically Will Fraser and Hadley Marsh had ended.

Over in the corner, Fred the parrot eyed her despondently and began to screech, "You want a piece of me? You want a piece of me?" hopping from foot to foot and jutting his tattered feathers like a deranged hunchback.

Fate was unpredictable. Anything could happen, which made Darlene all the more hopeful that she'd be able to separate Will from his Yankee girlfriend—a woman who rarely wore makeup, never fixed her hair, and went around in cut-off shorts, T-shirts, and flip-flops. A woman who didn't know enough to recognize an enemy when she saw one.

Darlene smiled a sly little smile, squared her shoulders, and walked confidently across the crowded room. She paused at the front door, leaving it open a crack. With any luck, a gust of wind would blow it open and the wretched parrot would make his final and irrevocable escape.

Returning later from the medical center, Darlene let Snowda and Richard off at the curb. She'd run an hour over the time she'd said she'd be back at work, and SuSu Dilworth, the owner of the Debs and Brides Shoppe, was sure to make her pay by working inventory. Snowda and Richard clung to the curb like a couple of giant fungi, watching as Darlene's car pulled away, tires squealing, and disappeared in the distance.

The day, which had dawned sunny and hot, had begun to cloud, and a sudden burst of wind caused the front door to bang on its hinges and then swing open all the way. Mother and son swiveled their heads and looked at the house.

"I know I done closed that door," Snowda said.

"Well, I sure as hell didn't leave it open," Richard said.

He pulled his cell phone out of his pocket and punched 911 to report a robbery in progress. The dispatcher told them to stay in the yard until an officer came on the scene.

He arrived five minutes later in a flurry of sirens and flashing lights.

"Stand back," he shouted at Snowda and Richard, pulling his pistol and advancing slowly on the house. Officer Posey was young. He'd graduated from the academy less than three weeks before, and with any luck he'd collar the perpetrator before either of his two older colleagues on the force answered the call. He'd grown up watching *Cops* and *Robocop,* which is why he'd decided to go into the exciting field of law enforcement, but so far the only excitement he'd had was breaking up a party of surly, underage drinkers and capturing Old Mrs. Vandergriff, who'd wandered away from her daughter's house wearing nothing but a pair of faded pink slippers. The vision of the naked, shriveled old woman in the back of his squad car had haunted his dreams for weeks.

"Any firearms in the house, sir?" he said over his shoulder to Richard. Officer Posey held his pistol in front of him and noted with dismay that his hands were shaking.

"Well, now, no, not to speak of," Richard said. He scratched his head and appeared to be giving this question serious thought. "There's my daddy's old huntin' rifle. And of course the double-barrel twelve gauge. And then there's Uncle Rafe's German Luger, the one he took off a dead Hun in a ditch at Roncheres Wood. It's up in a shoe box in the hall closet but it ain't loaded, and even if it was, there's something wrong with the firing mechanism, it has a tendency to misfire, which might explain the dead Hun in the ditch at Roncheres Wood."

Officer Posey tiptoed across the sparse lawn, leaping onto the porch and flattening his back against the house, his pistol held against his chest just under his nose. He stuck one foot out gingerly and cocked it under the edge of the swinging door, giving it a sudden furious kick. At the same time he swung around into a ready stance in front of the opened doorway shouting, "Freeze!"

"Well, I'll be damned," Richard said. "Look at that boy go."

There was a slithering sound inside the house, like something crawling around on all fours, and then quiet.

"I said freeze!" Officer Posey shouted again, his voice edging toward hysteria. He shook like a Parkinson's patient trying to hold the gun steady.

"I hope the durn fool don't shoot hisself on my property," Snowda said. "What's the rules on something like that?"

Officer Posey took small mincing steps in front of the opened doorway, then stepped across the threshold and disappeared inside. There was a sudden flurry of movement inside the house and a wild cry of "You want a piece of me?" followed by an oath and the sharp retort of a pistol.

Snowda slowly swiveled her head and looked at her son.

"We might oughta told him about the parrot," Richard said.

News of the apprehension of Fred spread through the town like a brushfire.

"Did he shoot the poor bird?"

"No. It appears that Officer Posey couldn't hit the side of a barn with a scattergun, much less a parrot in full flight. The bird was so scared it hasn't said a thing since then, just sits with its head under its wing. The animal rescue says it's suffering from Post-Traumatic Stress Disorder."

This was at a meeting of the Ladies of the Evening Investment Club, an assorted group of Southern matrons who met once a month to drink blush wine, gossip, and pick stocks. Josephine, Fanny, Alice, and Clara were all members.

"Birds can suffer from post-traumatic stress?" Fanny said, looking around in wide-eyed astonishment at the other members, who had suspended their usual business to gossip about the Smolletts. "I did not know that."

"Hell, honey, birds are as smart as little kids," Maitland said, serving glasses of wine on a silver tray. "I had a friend once with a cockatiel that used to cuddle up and watch TV with him. It could whistle the entire theme song from *The Love Boat*."

"You're just here to serve the drinks," Fanny reminded him primly. A big yellow cat had wandered in and sat perched on her lap. "You're not supposed to join in the conversation."

"Sorry, dear," Maitland said, rolling his eyes comically. "Sorry, ladies."

They all laughed quietly. There were about twelve members present, including the aunts, Clara, and Alice. They were assembled in the front parlor and Ava wandered in to say hello, then followed Maitland across the hall into the library. She stood watching him work his magic at the bar.

"What do you say I mix us up a little something special?" he said in a low voice, giving her a wink. Across the hall the conversation had drifted from the Smolletts to the advisability of buying shares in the maker of the Medtronic pacemaker. (Sally Kirkman's husband had just had one installed.)

Maitland opened the top of a silver shaker engraved with his initials. "Where's Will tonight?"

"He's coming by for a drink before he heads off to Poker Night."

"Ah, a gentlemen's evening." He filled the shaker with ice cubes, then poured in gin, followed by lemon juice, sugar syrup, and a pinch of powdered sugar. He shook it vigorously for a couple of minutes, strained the liquid into two icy highball glasses, topped it with club soda, then floated a splash of cherry brandy on top by pouring it over the back of a bar spoon.

"Mud in your eye," he said, lifting his glass.

"*Na zdorovie,*" Ava said.

He sipped and closed his eyes. "Now, that's good stuff," he said, grinning at his own boastfulness. "We used to drink these at fraternity parties back in the twenties."

"What do you call it?"

"Singapore Sling."

Ava sipped quietly. The drink was sweet enough to disguise the sharp taste of the gin. She didn't normally like gin, but this cocktail was good. Quite good. "What was it like back then?" she asked Maitland. "I've seen the gangster movies, Jimmy Cagney and Edward G. Robinson and all that, but was it really that wild?"

"It was pretty wild. Looking back now it seems rather uncivilized. Bathtub gin, which by the way is vile, that's why we created cocktails, to mask the taste, and speakeasies and flapper girls. I remember how shocked my mother was when Alice bobbed her hair. She was up at Vanderbilt when she did it; she would never have dared do it at home. She'd been such a good sober girl up until that time, no trouble at all except for that summer when she went with Fanny down to Mobile and fell in with Zelda Sayre and Tallulah Bankhead. There was some trouble there, just girlish high jinks, and Judge Sayre got it all hushed up so that Mother never heard about it." He sipped his drink and looked fondly across the hallway at Alice, as if remembering his sister as a girl. "Still," he said, looking down at his glass. "No worse than some of the things others were doing."

"You were up at Sewanee in the twenties? Did you know Allen Tate and the other Fugitive Poets?"

"They were at Vanderbilt, not Sewanee. They were a little before my time but yes, I knew Tate. And Robert Penn Warren, of course. They were too studious for me, those Fugitives, with their New Criticism and constant harping on the classical forms of poetry." He grinned, his red face shining. He reminded her a little of W. C. Fields when he drank. She smiled, remembering how much trouble she'd had understanding him when she first came to Woodburn. Now she found his manner of speaking genteel and soothing. "A poet, I was not," he said. "I preferred more leisurely pursuits."

"Josephine told me the girls at Vanderbilt used to go around carrying teddy bears with hollow metal stomachs filled with gin."

"Vanderbilt was quite the Babylon in those days. A hotbed of radical thought, illegal booze, and jazz."

"Yes, but do you think it was worse than the nineteen-sixties, with the draft marches and the Summer of Love and LSD?"

Maitland's eyes sparkled mischievously. "Child's play," he said, raising his glass.

Ava laughed. Across the hall, Clara stood and gave a report on last month's meeting. They listened for a few minutes, then Maitland said, "Are you Russian or Polish or both?"

"I'm sorry?"

"Your toast. *Na zdorovie.*"

"Oh. I don't know where I got that," Ava said. "The movies probably. Or maybe Russian literature. I read a lot of Russian literature."

"Fanny and I always wanted to see St. Petersburg. Such a beautiful city. The architecture is fantastic. We always wanted to go but it was impossible to visit once the communists took over."

"It's never too late. Why don't you go now?"

He shook his head, staring thoughtfully at the liquor in his glass. "We're too old for travel. We like our comforts, our soft bed, our American food."

"But you traveled during your younger years?"

"Oh, yes, everywhere except Russia. Egypt, Europe, Japan. Africa was my favorite." Ava thought of the Ernest Hemingway photograph in the breakfast room, the three of them behind a downed water buffalo, Maitland looking every inch the brawny, big-game hunter. "We were always hurrying off to some exotic place or another in those days. Always stepping onto a train, or a motorcar, or a camel. Hurrying, hurrying."

"Making up for lost time," Ava said and instantly regretted it. Maitland looked past her at the crowd of women in the parlor, who all seemed to be talking at once. She could hear distant music playing, Ravel's "Boléro." Someone had left the radio on in the kitchen. Standing beside Maitland, Ava was suddenly aware of the size and strength of the man, of his wide shoulders and well-muscled arms, gone to fat now, but in his youth thick and sturdy as an Olympian wrestler. He was tall, and would have been an imposing figure back then, although it was easy to forget that now, looking at his wide, cheerful face and portly physique.

As if to remind her of this harmless geniality, he grinned suddenly and said, "Another dividend?" It was his way of asking if she wanted another drink.

"Yes, thank you." She sipped her cocktail, then added, "And by the way, I'm not Russian. I'm Irish on my mother's side and Polish on my father's. He died in an ice-fishing accident on the Detroit River when I was ten." There. She'd done it again. Told the same old lie. Only now she knew it was a lie.

"Oh, I'm so sorry."

She hesitated, then said, "Not really. My mother told me he died, and it wasn't until a few weeks ago that I found out he hadn't but had simply remarried and started another family. They live in Garden City. My father and his new family. It's a little blue-collar suburb of Detroit." She couldn't bring herself to tell him the truth about Frank Dabrowski, the fact that she had no idea who her real father was. She couldn't bring herself to tell anyone about that.

Maitland was obviously at a loss as to what to say. He busied himself mixing another shaker, then topped off Ava's glass and poured himself another one. "We used to drink these on hunting trips. My father owned a plantation in the Delta, and we used to go down there to hunt and play cards with some of his Mississippi friends."

Ava gave him a cynical look. "Mississippi friends? Let me guess. Faulkner?"

Maitland sipped his drink and made a wry face.

She'd said it as a joke but the truth gradually dawned on her. "Oh, my God!" she said. "You drank Singapore Slings with William Faulkner?"

Maitland grinned and shook his head. "Count Faulkner was a whiskey man," he said, tilting his glass. "I never knew him to drink gin."

Later, Ava helped Maitland serve finger sandwiches and appetizers to the club members while they talked business.

The investment club had been started ten years earlier by a school-teacher named Mary Beckham, who'd moved south from Philadelphia and married a local attorney. The members contributed $90 a month in dues, and stocks were picked by unanimous approval. Their unorthodox method of picking stocks based on "gut feelings" and gossip had given them a respectable 15.6% return rating. They were an odd assortment of professional women and old-money dowagers, newcomers and descendants of founding fathers.

Mary Beckham started the new business with a joke.

"What do you call a Yankee water-skiing behind an Alabama fishing boat?" She rolled her eyes and looked around the room. "Bait." She waited until the giggling had died down. "And I can say that," she said, grinning at Ava. "Because I'm a Yankee."

"We try not to hold that against you," Josephine said. She was drinking a Gin Rickey, as were Alice and Fanny. They left the blush wine to the Presbyterians.

Louise Singleton stood up first and gave her report on The Gap. "Y'all, retail is down," she said. "The Gap lost forty percent in one month, and Skechers wasn't much better. It went from $21.85 to $18.50."

"Well, no wonder. Have you been in The Gap and seen the clothes?"

"The colors are terrible! Tell me who can wear lime green and get away with it?"

"Or sherbet."

"You mean orange?"

"Do you know what orange does to my face? It makes me look all puffy and pasty."

"Well, those clothes aren't really for women like us," Josephine reminded them. "They aren't really geared for the mature crowd."

"Who're you calling mature?" Fanny said and everyone laughed.

"I tell you, the designs this year are just terrible. I took my girls in there and they didn't buy a thing. Not one single thing. And anytime the Truett girls go into a Gap store and don't buy a thing, you know it's not good."

"Lord, that *is* a bad sign."

"Armageddon," Josephine said mildly.

Mary leaned to touch Susan Truett lightly on the arm. "I'm so glad Mattie decided to go ahead and be presented at the Gardenia Ball."

"What a fight that was," Susan said, rolling her eyes. She sipped her wine, then set it down on the coffee table. "It almost killed her daddy when she said she didn't want any part of that old pagan ritual, that throwback to virgin sacrifice." Susan shrugged and settled her plate on her lap, glancing around the room. "You know how it is. They're so sweet as girls and then you send them off to college and they come back all educated and too cynical to participate in the old traditions."

Mary said, "That's funny, because in my house, I was the one pushing Katie to be presented. Evan, who was born and raised here, didn't want her to have anything to do with it."

"His mama must be rolling over in her grave," Weesie Hartman said. "Because she was the Gardenia Queen back in nineteen fifty-two or fifty-three, I think it was."

"Back in our day it really wasn't an option," Alice said, swirling the remnants of her cocktail in her rocks glass. "You just did it because it was expected of you. You didn't have a choice, and even if you did, you wouldn't have wanted to disappoint your mama and papa. I don't think young girls today know anything of self-sacrifice."

The room got quiet. Ava had the uncomfortable feeling they were all thinking about her. She was obviously the youngest woman in the room.

"What exactly are the criteria for being a debutante?" she asked politely.

"Well," Alice answered promptly, as if she found this a valid question. "In the old days, of course, you wouldn't have been invited to attend the Gardenia Ball unless your mother or grandmother had been presented. But things have changed now. They've become more— *democratic.* Girls are selected by committee vote."

"Was Darlene Haney presented?" Ava asked. She smiled as Maitland took the empty tray from her and hurried off to the kitchen.

The two women nearest Ava turned their heads to look at her.

"No," Alice murmured quietly, touching her mouth daintily with her napkin. "No, I don't believe she was."

Ava imagined that that must have been devastating for someone like Darlene. She felt a sudden twinge of pity for her. Ava hadn't spoken to her since the party at Longford—she'd been ignoring her calls—but she remembered Darlene's face that day in the Debs and Brides Shoppe as she helped young debutantes choose ball gowns. She remembered Darlene's grimace of cheerful and hopeless resignation.

Debutante balls, sororities, and Junior League meetings had never appealed to Ava. She had always avoided large groups of women who had the power to blackball her.

The room was quiet except for the dull hum of the air-conditioning system. Fanny smiled and raised her chin. "Well, I'm glad the world has become more democratic than it used to be. The old ways weren't always best, you know."

"History is all about perspective," Josephine agreed.

"You got that right," Clara said.

Ava smiled at her.

Boofie Crenshaw cleared her throat. "I say we sell the Gap stock and buy Harley Davidson," she said, trying to get them back on track.

Josephine cocked one eyebrow. "You mean the motorcycle company?"

Ava began to wander about the room, quietly replenishing everyone's wine.

"I think we should buy Harley Davidson and I'll tell you why," Boofie said, lifting her chin defiantly. She looked around the room then ducked her head and said in a more confidential tone, "You know Baxter Bell left his wife for a younger woman." Everyone stared at her, trying to make the connection. Boofie held her glass up to Ava. "I saw Celeste Bell in the grocery store last week, and she told me Baxter came to her last Christmas saying he wanted a Harley Davidson. I guess all the other anesthesiologists in town had one and he had to have one, too, and she said, 'No, you'll kill yourself on one of those things.' Next thing she knows, she goes to Destin with her tennis team and when she comes home he's moved out of the house and in with his twenty-six-year-old medical assistant. Celeste thinks now that it was one of those midlife crisis things men go through, and if she'd just said yes to the Harley Davidson, he'd still be sleeping in his own bed at night. Now I ask you," she said, looking boldly around the room. "How many men do we know on the verge of a midlife crisis?"

Her logic was irrefutable. Josephine asked for a show of hands of all in favor of dumping the Gap stock in order to purchase Harley Davidson. The vote was unanimous.

Karen Ashton stood up next, holding a small clipping from *The Wall Street Journal* in her hand. "It says here that AOL Time Warner is looking to buy out AT&T's cable unit. That would make AOL the largest cable Internet provider, so even though the stock has dropped from $30.55 to $24.19, I say we hold on to it and see if the merger happens."

"I second that," Boofie said, and Josephine asked for a show of hands.

Cheryl Ponsler said, "I know we talked last time about keeping Wachovia but I have to tell you, Mother has been dumping every bit of her Wachovia stock."

This got everyone's attention. Cheryl's mother, Lucille, lived out at the Suck Creek Retirement Village. She was hard of hearing and forgetful when it came to names and car keys, but she had an uncanny ability to pick stocks. "Mother was getting her hair done down at the House of Hair and she ran into Milly Stokes. Y'all remember Milly, her son, Buddy, was in my class at school. Anyway, Buddy works for Citigroup now—he's some kind of bigwig—and Milly told Mother that the bonuses were so big this year that Buddy is putting in a pool and taking the family to Europe for Christmas. So Mother is buying up every share of Citigroup she can get her hands on, and y'all know she usually does better than the brokers at picking winning stocks." She looked around the room as if challenging anyone to refute this, but no one did. It was Lucille who had urged them to buy Krispy Kreme two years earlier but they had instead heeded the advice of a broker friend who had advised them to buy tech stocks. When Krispy Kreme went public, it doubled within a few weeks and shortly thereafter issued a two-for-one split. No one liked to be reminded of the money they'd lost on that deal.

"If Lucille recommends Citigroup that's good enough for me," Susan said.

"Always listen to your mother," Boofie said. "I say we dump Wachovia in favor of Citigroup."

They all voted in favor. Ava finished pouring wine, then sat down next to Clara on the sofa.

"Now isn't this a pretty sight?"

At the sound of a deep masculine voice they all turned to find Will standing in the doorway. He grinned, his eyes seeking Ava in the crowded room.

"Oh, Will, do come and join us," Fanny said, rising and hurrying across the room to take his arm.

"Yes, we need a male perspective," Josephine said.

"You ladies seem to do just fine on your own," he said, smiling in that charming manner he had so that all the women in the room brightened instinctively and leaned toward him. He seemed so tall and straight standing there, the lamplight catching in his hair. "I just came to ask Ava if she minded me playing poker tonight."

The women seemed amused by this. Ava felt a creeping warmth in her face, wondering why he'd thought it necessary to ask her. Their evenings together had tapered off considerably since the party at Longford.

"I'm sure Ava wouldn't mind!" Fanny said, rising on her toes to kiss his cheek.

"I can't believe you would ask her! My husband would never ask me. He would just go."

"Young women don't know how lucky they are nowadays. Young men are so—*accommodating*. Why, I don't think Edgar has ever so much as made his own sandwich!"

Will continued to stare at Ava, a playful expression on his face. It was obvious that he was enjoying putting her on the spot. "So," he said. "Do you mind?"

"Hell, no. Not as long as you win. Not as long as you bring home a big pot of money."

He laughed, although the other women in the room seemed less certain of her answer. "It'll be late when I finish. Sometimes we play until the wee hours." Ava was afraid he would cross the room to kiss her but instead he winked and said, "I'll call you tomorrow."

"Okay," Ava said. "You do that."

Fanny walked with him to the kitchen. A moment later she returned, rubbing her hands together briskly, and resumed her seat. The conversation in the room, which had fallen to a dull hum, rose now to a low roar.

The blush wine was having its effect. Looking around the room, Ava noted several red noses and glowing complexions. Some of the women who had seemed staid and conservative when she first met them were now giggling like schoolgirls.

Ava remembered how, when she first came to Woodburn, she'd been intimidated by these women. And now, oddly, she felt at ease among them. Maybe it was the cozy, lamp-lit room or the Singapore Slings. Whatever the reason, Ava felt a sense of fellowship here that she would not have imagined possible. It was pleasant to envision herself years from now, sitting in a room like this, drinking blush wine and gossiping about husbands and investments, a confident, mature woman with a settled life and a large group of female friends. Maybe even children. And a handsome, accommodating husband who saw to it that she was not disturbed by the unpleasantness of life but instead kept cloistered like a princess in an ivory tower.

Ava had a sudden dazzling vision of this other self, the Ava she might become.

And then it was gone.

The investment club members were growing raucous. They had moved on, embarrassingly, from talk of accommodating younger men to talk of sex.

"That's right," Weesie Hartman shouted. "I know when I hear Edgar doing his impression of Maurice Chevalier singing 'Thank Heaven for Little Girls,' I'm in for it whether I want it or not."

The others hooted and covered their mouths with their hands.

"Look at Ava. She's blushing," Fanny said.

"More wine, anybody?" Ava said.

"Young folks don't like to think about old folks getting frisky, but we do!"

"Some of us are widows," Alice said. "Some of us have been widows so long we don't remember what frisky means."

"You're never too old for frisky!"

"What's your definition of frisky?"

"What's your definition of old?"

"Born ten years before Moses," Alice said.

"Getting long in the tooth," Josephine said.

"I don't know why y'all are talking about being old," Fanny said, giving her head a little shake. "I don't feel any different now than I did when I was sixteen years old." Josephine snorted and Fanny exclaimed, "Well, I don't."

"Do you want to know what old feels like?" Clara said, looking around the room. "Old is going to get your annual mammogram and discovering that the X-ray tech is someone you taught in school—*fifty* years ago."

"Don't you just love those annual mammograms?" Cheryl said.

"My husband said, 'What does it feel like?' and I said, 'It feels like laying your boob on a cold garage floor and having someone back over it with the car.' "

"I'm just standing there with my arm over my head," Clara continued. "Squashed between two plates, and the lady looks at me and says,

'Miss McGann, is that you?' And I said, 'Mary Montgomery, is that you?' And she said, 'Yes'm, you taught me world history back in high school.' And I'm trying to remember if I'd given her an A or an F because suddenly it seemed real important."

The room exploded in laughter and Ava rose and took a stack of plates into the kitchen. Maitland was standing at the counter mixing up a batch of his homemade mayonnaise. He was wearing his *Kitchen Bitch* apron.

"What's going on?" he said. "Do y'all need me to make up some more of those little sandwiches?" Above the bib of his apron, his red face shone happily.

"I don't think so. I think the meeting is winding down." Ava put her hands behind her and pulled herself up on the counter, her feet dangling, looking around the cheery room. There was something soothing and intimate about a kitchen, the heart of the house, the place where families gather around a table to break bread and forget their differences, if only for a short while.

The last time she'd seen Jake Woodburn he'd been standing in his mother's kitchen. She had not run into him since that day, and it seemed odd to the point where she had begun to wonder if he was avoiding her. And then she decided that he *was* avoiding her, and although she mentally shrugged her shoulders and washed her hands of him, she could not help but feel a vague sense of disappointment, too.

Maitland held the bowl of mayonnaise up for her to taste.

"Now that is good," Ava said. "You could bottle it."

He seemed pleased. "Do you think so?" he said.

"I do."

"I put a little stone-ground mustard in this batch, and I think it kicks up the taste a notch."

"Definitely."

He spooned the mayonnaise into a mason jar and carefully labeled it. Watching his meticulous preparations, Ava said, "Uncle Mait, do you mind if I ask you a personal question?"

"You can ask me anything, Sugar. I'm pretty much an open book."

Ava looked at her dangling feet. She traced the outline of the tiles in the air with her toes. "Why did it take you and Fanny so long to marry?"

He continued to smile, but his hands, she noted, shook with a delicate agitation as he put the mason jar down. Something dark, an expression of fear or remorse, passed quickly across his face, and was gone. He chuckled and shook his head, his florid face shining.

"Penance," he said.

She couldn't stop thinking of the words. Sometimes late at night when the work was slow, when she reached an impasse and the story felt heavy and cumbersome, she lay down on the bed and traced her fingers over the delicate carving. *Help me.*

Who had carved those words?

She felt certain it was Charlie Woodburn.

When she showed Will, he remarked scornfully, "That bed was built at Longford around the time of Napoleon. Do you know how many people have slept there? How many could have scrawled that?" His late-afternoon good cheer had evaporated the minute she mentioned Charlie. He strode angrily around the room, picking up items on the tables and setting them down abruptly. It was so unusual, this outburst, that at first Ava could do nothing but watch in astonishment.

"Why are you so angry?" she said.

"Because you make something out of nothing. You imagine things." He put his hands on the foot of the bed, leaning over so she couldn't see his face. Distantly they could hear the tinkling of barware as Toddy Time began. When he looked up again his face was calm, impassive. "Even if it was Charlie," he said evenly. "How do you know it wasn't the ravings of a man sunk in alcohol and depression?"

"I *don't* know," she said. "I don't know that."

"Then why are you implying that it's something more sinister?"

"I'm not implying anything. I'm just curious as to who carved it. And if it was Charlie, why did he carve it?"

"Someone's been filling your head with rubbish."

They were coming dangerously close to something. They stared at each other. Ava sat against the headboard, her feet curled under her. He stood, leaning his shoulder against the bedpost.

She said, "I had lunch with Jake Woodburn."

"So I heard."

"Is that what this is about?"

He pushed himself off the bed and went over to the window, staring out at the garden.

She said in a reasonable voice, "Jake didn't tell me anything. In fact, he didn't want to talk about Charlie at all. He has a rather misplaced sense of loyalty when it comes to your family."

"I don't want to talk about Jake," he said.

"Look, I'm sorry. I didn't mean to upset you."

A hummingbird hung suspended outside the window. From the library came the muffled sounds of conversation and laughter.

She had always been attracted to men who held a certain command over her, a stern masculine authority that made her willingly abdicate her own power. Anyone who knew her, besides Michael and Jacob, would have been surprised by this. People invariably described her as "strong-willed" and "self-sufficient," but it was an act on her part. A certain masculine tone of voice, a flicker of disdain, and she would go as limp and docile as a child. Michael and Jacob had had this manner of indifferent authority, and Will, she realized now, watching him turn and walk to the door, had it, too.

"They're waiting for us," he said.

"I was just curious about the carving," she said, trying to make him see her point. "I just wondered who might have done it."

He mumbled something she couldn't understand and went out, and it wasn't until later, as she drifted off to sleep, that she realized he had said, "For all I know, it could have been you."

Golden Girl

Ava continued to work on her novel every evening, although, in light of her argument with Will over Charlie Woodburn, the work took on a more sinister, secretive air. She knew now that she could never show him the novel. She could never openly betray his trust or that of Josephine, Fanny, and Maitland. And yet she couldn't stop writing.

She had begun to work in earnest now, sitting down at her computer every evening when the house was quiet. If the other members of the house knew of her nocturnal endeavors, they said nothing, other than to tease her about her new habit of sleeping late. She didn't care. Nothing mattered but the work, flowing between her fingers and the computer screen like an electric current. At night the house was hushed but for the periodic hum of the air-conditioning and the creaking of the ancient timbers settling around her. Caught up in the tragic story of Charlie Woodburn, she was unaware of time. Hours seemed to pass in a twinkling, and she was often stunned to look up and see that the bedside clock read four a.m. Often as she wrote, she became gradually aware of noises in the house—doors closing, footsteps in the hallway— but when she stopped writing and listened, the noises stopped.

She felt a connection to Charlie, and that connection was evidenced by the words that flowed from her fingertips onto the screen. And yet as the summer passed into the long hot days of late July, the work began to slow. She had entered the mid-book doldrums, the place where doubt and insecurity raised their ugly twin heads. It always felt to Ava a little like rolling a boulder up a mountain. Just before reaching the summit there was a moment of uncertainty, of breathless wondering: would the boulder roll back down and crush her, or would she be able to launch it over the precipice, where it would make its speedy, inescapable descent? With the story of Charlie Woodburn, she felt that she was being slowly, relentlessly crushed.

She felt stifled, confounded, unable to write anything she didn't delete the following day. It was frustrating to have come so far and now find herself blocked.

She had rewritten Charlie's character based on her conversation with Clara and Alice. She had made him more charming, more handsome, more popular and at ease with women. But something had happened. Some shift had occurred in the rewrite that made the story feel forced and false. Josephine was proving troublesome, too. She kept her secrets well. Despite appearing in several new chapters, Josephine had yet to divulge her lover. It was almost as if she was being coy, patronizing. Perhaps Ava had only imagined a secret lover after all.

Perhaps the story of Charlie Woodburn was beyond Ava's capability to tell.

That's what it all came down to, that same old fear and lack of faith she had struggled with for years. Did she have what it took to be a writer? Or was it just some girlish dream she had yet to outgrow? She had beat her head against this wall until it was bloody, and to come up against it now, when everything seemed to be going so well, seemed especially fatalistic. For the first time in her life she wondered if it was really all that important that she become a novelist. Surely a career as a copywriter would do just as well? Or perhaps she should just marry Will and settle down here in this quiet place where everything was simple and unhurried. Surely that life would do just as well?

No. She wouldn't think like that. She wouldn't give up, not yet anyway.

There was something with Josephine; she knew it. She had seen it in the scene she wrote yesterday, where Josephine, Charlie, and Clara stood in the garden and Josephine betrayed herself with a glance, an awkward movement, an affirmation that caused the other two to look away from her with swift, furtive expressions of pity.

Despite her frustration over the progression of her novel, Ava was thankful that another sleep episode had not occurred. The incident of the dark man by the window had left her shaken for days. A hallucination appearing after the initial paralysis had passed was something new, something she had not experienced before. She was afraid she might be entering a new stage of the disease.

But in the days following the strange appearance of the dark man, no other episodes occurred. As the days wore on, she found it easier to believe that she might have imagined the whole thing, the dark fleeting image brought on by her fright, a trick of the eyes, a subtle shifting of shadows and nothing more.

She spent her afternoons, while the others were napping, roaming the town looking for evidence of Charlie. She spent a great deal of time at the downtown library talking to the local historian, a retired schoolteacher by the name of Rachel Rowe. Rachel had not known Charlie—he had died before she was born—but she remembered her mother and grandmother talking about the scandalous elopement, and she was able to tell Ava about the boardinghouse where Charlie had lived before marrying, a rambling Victorian house that still stood not far from where Jake Woodburn currently had his furniture shop.

"Do you have any photos of him?" Ava asked her. They were sitting at one of the long tables near the research stacks, a large picture book on the history of Woodburn open in front of them.

"Of Charlie Woodburn?" Rachel frowned, her eyes narrowing. "No. I suppose I could check the microfiche. There may be a photo with an article in one of the old newspapers."

The next time Ava came in, Rachel beckoned to her and led her over to the large reader machine used to view the microfilms.

"I've found something you might like to see," she said.

Ava felt a quiver of excitement. She was suddenly afraid that the man she had pictured, the Charlie she had created in her imagination, might not match the real thing. She hoped she wouldn't be disappointed. She leaned forward, peering over Rachel's shoulder. "Were you able to find any of the Woodburn papers that mention Charlie?"

"No, unfortunately, all the Woodburn family documents were given to Vanderbilt years ago."

"Well, not all," Ava said, remembering that Will had checked the attic when looking for the original blueprints of Longford. "There may be some papers stored up in the attic at Woodburn Hall."

"Really?" Rachel looked at her with interest. "Do you have access to them?"

"Yes. I mean, I suppose I do. I don't know exactly what's up there, but I could check."

"You might want to look. Sometimes old photos fall to the bottom of a trunk and get lost. You might find some family letters that mention Charlie. People had a tendency to keep them in those days. I had a friend who did some renovations on a two-hundred-year-old house and found a box hidden in the wall containing a cache of letters. And they were pretty racy, too," she said chuckling. "For love letters of that day, anyway. Compared to now they seem pretty tame. Although I guess no one writes letters anymore, do they? It's all emails and instant messaging. How sad." She scrolled absently through the screen as she talked. "I did find one photo, and that's what I want to show you."

Ava laced her fingers together to keep them from trembling and dropped her hands into her lap. She sat quietly while Rachel wound and rewound the film until she reached the image she was looking for. It zoomed suddenly into view, dark and grainy, a photo of a group of men sitting around a long table in evening clothes. They were smoking cigars and wore what looked like laurel wreaths on their heads, facing the camera with the proud disdainful air that gentlemen of that period used when being photographed. There were no women present, but several black men dressed in dark suits and white gloves stood against the far wall.

The caption read "Gentlemen of the Commerce Club Gather for Annual Banquet." Underneath that was a list of names. Ava read through until she came to Colonel James Woodburn. And beside him, Mr. Charles Woodburn. An aristocratic old man with white hair and a long white mustache stared into the camera, and behind him, half hidden by the older gentleman, a younger man leaned into view. His face was bathed in shadow, and his features were indistinguishable. One elbow was propped carelessly on the table in front of him, and in that hand he held a thick cigar.

"Can you blow it up?" Ava asked.

"I can, but it doesn't make it any easier to see." The old man's face came suddenly into view, and Ava was shocked at his resemblance to Josephine. They shared the same proud, wary expression, the same high forehead and long blade-like nose. His head was tilted slightly up toward the camera, and his mouth was open as if he had been speaking or perhaps exhaling.

The young man behind him was still indistinguishable. His face was dark and blurry, but other details jumped suddenly into focus: the gold cuff link of his upraised arm, the smooth, slicked-back hair, a certain carelessness in the buttoning of his pintucked shirt, as if he found such formality absurd but necessary. But it was the dark blurry face with its inscrutable expression that most drew Ava's attention.

Staring at him, she shivered.

On the walk home from downtown, she couldn't stop thinking about that shadowy face. It was Charlie who had scratched *Help me* into the headboard of her bed. She was sure of it. He must have had some premonition of his death, some warning.

But *how* had he died? Was it really an accidental drowning, as the Woodburns seemed to imply? And if so, why would Josephine, Fanny, and Maitland refuse to speak his name more than sixty years later? Why were there no photos of him in the house? Grief was one thing, but a complete annihilation, a removal of any evidence that a person had ever existed, was something else entirely. It indicated—*what?* Revenge? Denial? Guilt?

She walked along the shady sidewalk in a stupor. The day was hot and humid, and she was glad of the overhanging trees. Their thick roots pushed up through the old brick sidewalk, twining around her feet like serpents.

Had Charlie set out to drink himself to death, and in an accident of tragic proportions, simply hastened the process, as Will had suggested? Or had he been murdered and, if so, by whom? There were several possible suspects with conceivable motives: the menacing cousins intent on avenging Fanny's honor; stoic Josephine, the defender of family secrets; or perhaps it had been Clara, as Darlene Haney had suggested, a woman familiar with all the poisonous plants of the garden, although Ava could not imagine what motive Clara could possibly have had.

The one with the most motive, of course, was Maitland Sinclair, the jilted lover. On the surface, jolly Maitland seemed an unlikely suspect, yet Ava had seen the youthful photos of him in his big-game hunting gear. She had glimpsed his face that night when she had asked him why it had taken so long for him and Fanny to marry.

And then there was his curious answer. *Penance.*

His adoration of Fanny was all-consuming. Some people would do anything for love.

Even murder.

She could see the imposing roofline of Woodburn Hall rising above the tall hedges. She was almost to the garden fence when her phone rang, startling her out of her reverie.

"Don't hang up," Jake said. "It's me."

The tall hedge surrounding the garden gave way now to the wide, sweeping lawn. Ava glanced at the house to see if anyone was out on the verandah but it was empty. She slowed her steps. A pair of rocking chairs faced the street, half-hidden by a row of glossy-green shrubs.

"Hello," she said, trying to keep her voice steady. She walked slowly, looking down at her feet, watching so she wouldn't trip.

"I've been thinking about you."

She'd been thinking about him, too. Because she hadn't been writing, she'd had a lot of time to think about how she might have been too hard on him the last time they spoke.

"Can you talk?" he said.

"Yes."

He made a sound that might have been a sigh. Or maybe it was just a bad connection. "I've been thinking a lot about what you said the last time we talked."

"Look," she said. "I was pretty irrational that day. Don't pay too much attention to what I said."

"No, I think you had a valid point. I should have opened up more about Hadley."

She didn't want to talk about Hadley. Not today anyway. "I took your advice," she said quickly.

"What advice was that?"

"I wrote a letter to Frank Dabrowski. You know, my father. Asking him why he hadn't ever sent me a birthday card or a Christmas present the whole time I was growing up. And do you know what he said?" *Dear God, what was she doing? Why did she feel compelled to tell him the most intimate, depressing details of her life?*

He was quiet, waiting for her to finish.

"He said he wasn't my dad after all! I had it all wrong! Even though his name was on my birth certificate, he wasn't my biological dad, and my mother told him it would be best if he just stayed out of my life. So he did."

"Damn, Ava. I'm sorry."

His voice was warm and sincere. She stood at the tall fence separating the sidewalk from the lawn of Woodburn Hall, clutching an iron paling with one hand. She was dismayed to find that she was crying.

"Are you all right?" he said.

She held her phone against one shoulder and rummaged around in her purse for a Kleenex. "I'm fine!" she said, then blew her nose.

"Do you want to go somewhere for a drink?"

"I can't. It's Toddy Time and I'm heading back to the house."

"All right. How about tomorrow?"

She wiped her eyes with the back of one hand. "Why don't you come over to Woodburn Hall? You can join us for a Singapore Sling."

"You know I can't do that."

"Are you afraid?"

"No."

She blew her nose again.

"Are you sure you're all right?"

"Allergies," she said. "I'm walking back from the library. I've been down to see Rachel Rowe. Do you know Rachel? The town historian? Anyway, she had a photo she thought I might like to see of your grandfather Charlie. I have a copy. Would you like to see it?"

He was quiet for a moment, then he said, "Sure."

"Did you know that your grandfather used to board at a house just down the street from where your shop is?"

"No, I didn't."

"I've got the address. I may go by there on Thursday."

"Ava," he said.

"What?"

She could hear movement in the background, as if he was placing his hand over the receiver. "Nothing."

"Maybe I'll stop by your shop while I'm in the neighborhood."

"I'd like that. What time?"

"Well, I don't get up much before ten."

"Sounds like a pretty sweet life."

"How about if I come by between 11:30 and 12:00?"

"That'd be great."

"Okay then. See you later," she said and hung up.

She was still snuffling into her Kleenex. Odd, how these crying spells seemed to come over her with no warning. She hoped her eyes wouldn't be red when she showed up for Toddy Time. Will was sure to notice. He noticed everything about her these days. His eyes seemed to follow her wherever she went, as if he suspected her of something and was trying to see validation of her guilt in her face. No doubt she confirmed his worst fears (whatever they might be) every time she felt the weight of those eyes and blushed.

She clung to the iron fence and blew her nose for the last time. At the edge of the lawn, under a glossy shrub, a white cat watched her warily, its tail twitching. She could hear distant voices. It sounded as if they were already gathered in the library for Toddy Time.

"Great," she said, checking her purse for eyedrops. She wished she hadn't teased Jake about coming for Toddy Time. She'd been trying to throw him offtrack, to hide the fact that she was crying, but she saw now that she might have seemed insensitive. She would apologize Thursday when she saw him.

He really was a nice guy. There was no reason they couldn't be friends.

Will was sitting on one of the long sofas when she came in, and he raised his glass in greeting. He seemed to trail her with curious eyes the whole evening. After dinner, he followed her into her room and shut the door.

"I'm sorry about the way things have been lately," he said, sitting in the chair by the window. His movements were stiff and awkward, and Ava saw how difficult this was for him. At Bard he had been open and friendly, but here in Woodburn he seemed, at times, clannish and cold. Not proud, but every bit a Woodburn. Able to switch off his feelings at the least provocation.

"You don't owe me an apology," she said quickly.

He put one hand up as if to stop her. "I don't want things to be difficult between us," he said evenly.

"I don't want that either."

He sat back, crossing his legs, resting an ankle on top of one knee. "It's hard to understand if you aren't from around here," he said. "People speak a hidden language. You don't always hear what's being said if you haven't learned to listen for it."

"Yeah, I figured that out," she said.

He played with the frayed hem of his jeans, taking his time before he began again. He had broken with tradition and dressed casually tonight. Ava had the feeling he had rehearsed this. "We're courteous, polite people, and we don't give ourselves away to strangers. There's so much history here, not all of it good, a lot of it terrible. And all our stories are mixed up together from having been in the same place for so long. They all overlap. And everyone has a different version of the truth. Their truth." He gave her a swift, earnest look. "Do you understand what I'm trying to say?"

She sat down on the edge of the bed, folding one leg under her. She said slowly, "When I asked you about Charlie Woodburn, I wasn't trying to be rude or hurtful. I was just curious. It's my job to ask questions, to try to figure out why people act the way they do."

He continued to play with the hem, wrapping his fingers tightly in the threads. "I know that, Ava," he said.

"I saw *Help me* carved on the headboard, and I wondered who could have done it. And it occurred to me that it might have been Charlie, that he might have had some kind of premonition about his death. Or maybe he suspected—someone."

He looked at her and Ava could see that he was angry, but he was fighting his anger. She had the sudden impression that he felt as if he was belittling himself, as if it should have been her apologizing, not him.

"I've been hearing these stories all my life," he said. "People in this town have always talked about my family. They say things that are untrue and hurtful. The thing with Charlie happened a long time ago, and none of it matters anymore, so let it go. I'm asking you. Please, just let it go."

She couldn't let it go. He had no idea how tied to this story she was, how dependent on it she had become. And she couldn't tell him why. She might never be able to tell him.

He sat watching her and she stared back helplessly.

Distantly, from somewhere deep in the house, she could hear the slow, somber music of Ravel.

She was having trouble sleeping, and when she did eventually fall into a restless sleep, her dreams were wild and nightmarish. She had begun to keep the lamp on all night, although she knew from experience that this did little to banish her dark fantasies. It was an old trick she had learned in childhood soon after the episodes of sleep paralysis had first begun.

She had suffered nightmarish dreams, but she had not had another experience of sleep paralysis, and for that she was grateful.

The night after Will came to apologize, she sat in front of her glowing computer screen, willing the words to come. They wouldn't, and after a while she stood, threw open the shutters, and raised the window. It was a beautiful night. Moonlight flooded the garden, and a chorus of crickets throbbed like a beating heart. Ava leaned her elbows on the sill and pressed her face against the screen. The air was hot and sultry, but occasionally a mild breeze stirred.

It was on a night like this, a moonlit summer evening, that she'd had her first attack of sleep paralysis. She was twelve, sleeping with the window open on a hot, muggy evening. She had lain awake long after she heard Clotilde go to bed, listening to the increasingly sporadic sound of traffic in the street. Far off in the distance she could hear the mournful wail of a passing train.

She fell asleep with her face turned toward the window but awoke suddenly in the middle of the night. She was lying on her back, taking short, shallow breaths. The room was a velvet blackness but, oddly, she could sense a light coming through the window. It was then that she realized that she couldn't turn her head to look, she couldn't move at all, lying stiff and wooden on the bed. There was a sense of something heavy resting on her chest; she couldn't quite catch her breath. But this was nothing compared to the gradual horror, the dawning awareness that *there was something in the room with her.* She could hear whispering. Out of the corner of her eye she caught the movement of several small, shadowy figures. They didn't move like humans; they skittered like crabs, and they were touching her cold skin with long, probing fingers and chattering among themselves, some strange language she couldn't understand. Her terror was so extreme she thought she might faint. She tried to scream but couldn't.

And then she could, screaming long after Clotilde had burst through the door and gathered her up in her soft arms.

Remembering this episode now, Ava shivered. She rose and began to walk around the room, stopping to stare at Clotilde's vase. She had not spoken to her mother since the letter from Frank Dabrowski had arrived but now, remembering Clotilde's comforting presence all those years ago, she said bitterly, "Don't think I forgive you. Because I don't."

Clotilde maintained a knowing silence.

Ava sat down on the edge of her bed. She could hear a soft tapping in the wall behind her, and it was then, while listening halfheartedly to whatever was making the sound, that a thought occurred to her.

She rose, went into the small office, and took down one of the ledgers from the glass-cased secretary. On the spine was written *1919–1920.* She opened it and began to read. The handwriting was more modern, more easily decipherable than the earlier journals she had studied. Colonel James Woodburn, the aunts' father, had continued his ancestors' habit of keeping farm journals, except that his entries had less to do with farming and more to do with the weather, business, and family events. She closed the journal and put it back, running her fingers over the spines of the books until she found the one reading *1927–1928.* Nineteen twenty-seven. The year Charlie Woodburn first came to town.

Ava opened the journal and began to read. The Colonel wrote in short, choppy sentences, in a rather somber, self-conscious manner.

April 22nd–fair day. Wind from the west. Met with Attorney
Atwood in the a.m. Lunched at the hotel with Jennings and Cates, who
are trying to sell me a lumberyard. Josephine has spurned another beau,
Harry Monroe, who she says has big feet and a cowlick, and is
therefore unsuitable. I fear she has inherited the Woodburn pride.
No man will ever be good enough for her.

It was here then, hidden among trivial notations about weather and
business, that Ava would find the clues to her story. She read on.

April 28th–Dinner party at the Randolphs. Returned home to find the
house in an uproar. Sweet Fanny observed a man beating a mule in the
street and went forth in a rage to put a stop to it. He replied impertinently
that it was his mule to do with as he pleased, at which point Josephine
intervened and offered to buy the animal. He asked how he was to get
home with a wagon and no mule, and Josephine made an offer on the
wagon, too. Thus I returned home to find myself the proud owner of a mule
Fanny and Celia have named Tulip, as well as a broken-down produce
wagon! I despair sometimes of ever finding these girls suitable husbands.
The fault is mine; they were raised without the gentle, nurturing presence of
a mother. Celia is sober and steady. She will do fine. But Fanny is
tenderhearted and silly, and Sister is proud and unforgiving.
She especially seems destined for spinsterhood.

And farther on, Ava found this:

May 7th–Saw C.W. in the street today. His resemblance to Old
Randal is uncanny. They say he's only recently come from New Orleans,
where he spent his childhood.

May 9th–Rain began around 7 a.m. A steady downpour all day.
Called John to bring the car around twelve in the afternoon. Had lunch
with C.W. at the hotel. Sister sick with a fever but will not allow Dr.
Atkinson to attend her. Stubborn girl.

Ava looked up, studying the dark square of window at the end of the room. Only two days after meeting Charlie in the street, the Colonel had had lunch with him. Which meant, surely, that Charlie must have made a favorable impression on his old kinsman.

She took the journal to bed with her. It was two a.m. when she finished the last entry and, rising, went into the office and pulled the last slim volume off the shelf. *1929.* The year the Colonel had died. The year Charlie Woodburn had eloped with Fanny. She padded back to bed with the book cradled in her arms. The entries here were less frequent, the handwriting less legible, as if in the last year of his life, the Colonel's eyesight had begun to fail. A short time later she came across this rather odd entry:

> *August 24th—I saw my beloved today. It was dusk, and she was standing at the edge of the garden in a long white gown, her hair undone. The dead are with us always. Their world touches ours, shimmering through. I am an old man, and I am weary of this life and ready for the next.*
>
> *Had a stormy meeting with Atwood yesterday and told him to draw up the deed. Tomorrow I will tell C.W. I hope to right the wrongs of the past by giving back to C.W. what is rightfully his.*
>
> *May our sins be washed away in the Blood of Our Redeemer.*

There were only six more entries after that one, the last in October, a week before his death. None of them mentioned Charlie.

The following morning Ava awoke early but lay in bed waiting for the others to leave the house. Fanny had a dental appointment, and Josephine and Maitland were scheduled to take her in at ten o'clock. They planned to make a day of it, having lunch downtown and then buying groceries, so Ava figured she had at least an hour to roam around in the attic looking for photos of Charlie Woodburn before the cleaning people arrived. She could have asked Josephine; she felt certain Josephine would have politely agreed to her exploring the house, but she didn't want to have to explain what she was searching for. She didn't know how to broach the subject, so in the end she said nothing, waiting until she heard the car pull out of the drive before rising and going to the window.

To make sure she was alone, she went to the hallway and called out, but no one answered. The mantel clock chimed ten o'clock. She stood for a moment, listening, then slowly climbed the staircase, letting one hand trail along the banister.

There was a peculiar stillness to the house, a heaviness, as if somewhere in the darkest corners a storm might be brewing. She thought of Fraser's comment that Will had been afraid of the staircase as a boy, that he had often seen the ghost of the Gray Lady standing there, and it was not too hard to imagine how this might be so. The staircase curved sharply to the left at the landing, and ascended for many wide shallow steps to an open central hall on the top floor. The sharp curve of the staircase, as well as the placement of a tall stained-glass window on the landing, caused the lower portion of the staircase to be bathed in shifting shadows.

Ava noted this now as she climbed, watching the way the swaying trees outside the colored window caused murky shadows on the stairs. It was not hard to imagine a child mistaking those shadows for a ghost.

She stopped and turned around, staring at the bottom of the stairwell. A slight breeze puckered the back of her neck. She remembered the entry in Colonel Woodburn's journal, the image of his dead wife standing at the edge of the garden in a long white gown. What was it he had written? *The dead are with us always.* Even now, if she stared long enough, she could see, out of the corner of her eye, a small dark-haired woman in a gray gown standing at the foot of the stairway.

But no, Fraser had said Delphine Woodburn always dressed in black. She was constantly in mourning for one of her dead children. Ava reordered the image in her mind and now the woman was dressed in a dark, flowing gown that pooled around her feet. Her pale face, gazing up at Ava, was set in lines of despair and grief.

Turning, Ava continued to climb.

Despite her lush imagination, she had a hard time believing in ghosts. The rational side of her wouldn't be swayed by something she'd never actually seen. Being raised by Clotilde, a woman who believed in reincarnation and divination, had made her a skeptic. And yet the imaginative side of her, the creative side that could imagine characters and dialogue and the way a landscape looked a hundred years ago, was willing to believe in an unseen world. Here, too, perhaps it was Clotilde's influence, her stories of gnomes and changelings and lonely wandering spirits, that had shaped her.

More than Ava cared to admit.

She reached the top of the stairs and stopped. She'd been up here once before, when Will first showed her around the house, but she hadn't climbed the stairs since then. There had been no need. She was comfortable on the bottom floor of the house. Her rooms were large and pleasant, and the other occupants of Woodburn Hall left her alone to work. Up here she felt like an intruder, a guilty thief.

She stood at the top of the stairway, listening. If anyone came home unexpectedly, if Will showed up unannounced, she'd decided that she'd say she'd heard a noise above her, and, knowing the house to be empty, had gone to investigate. She would claim to have been worried that one of the cats was trapped in a room and wreaking havoc. Standing there now, she thought she *did* hear a scratching sound coming from one of the rooms. But as she began to walk stealthily along the creaking floorboards, the noise stopped.

The ceilings on the second floor were lower than on the first, maybe nine or ten feet high. Two large bedrooms opened off the hallway to her left, separated by a bath. On the right was a large room, the old nursery where Josephine and Fanny had slept as girls, and next to it was a small, slope-ceilinged room where Will had slept as a boy.

"The nurse's room," Fanny and Josephine had called it, giggling.

At the end of the hall was a door, and behind it was a set of narrow stairs leading to the attic.

"You don't want to go up there," Will had told her the night he'd showed her the house. He had opened the door so she could peer up the narrow staircase into the darkness, but he had not stepped inside.

"Why not?"

"It's dusty and filled with broken-down furniture, and the light isn't very good."

Ava stopped on the threshold of Will's room, ducking her head inside. The bedroom was a time capsule. She imagined that it hadn't changed since Will left home for college. Led Zeppelin, The Melvins, and Soundgarden posters plastered the sloped ceilings, and in one corner a full-size cutout of Janis Joplin stood with several school ties looped pompously around her neck. A neatly made twin bed was pushed beneath the window, and on one wall a tall bookshelf covered in sporting trophies, photos, and tattered paperbacks stood next to a small maple desk. Above it hung a bulletin board plastered with cartoon cutouts and newspaper clippings.

Ava turned and continued to the end of the hallway, knowing that she had little enough time to explore the attic. Will's room would have to wait for another day. The housecleaners would be arriving soon, and she didn't want to be up here when they came for fear that one of them might say something to Josephine.

She stopped in front of the attic door, standing with her hand on the knob. Will and Josephine might not have minded her wandering the house, but they certainly would have objected to her looking for evidence of Charlie Woodburn, and this knowledge filled her with a sense of guilt and foreboding. And yet, she told herself, if they had been open about Charlie from the beginning, there would have been no need for subterfuge.

It was easier to blame them than it was to admit her own treason.

The attic door stuck, and she had to pull on it forcefully before it swung open. A sudden blast of hot, stale air greeted her. She peered into the gloom, trying to adjust her eyes, and fumbled in her pocket for her key chain flashlight. She flipped it on, and a thin beam of light shone weakly over the planked walls of the stairwell. She could see a string hanging from the ceiling, and she pulled it, switching on the overhead light. It was nothing more than a bare suspended bulb and gave off little light. The stairs were covered in dust, but there were footsteps clearly visible, no doubt from the day Will had climbed to hunt for the plans of Longford.

She stepped inside, leaving the door open behind her, and began to climb the narrow stairs. Her breathing was labored in the sultry heat. The light from the overhead bulb bled into darkness at the top of the steps, and the thin beam of her flashlight was barely enough to illuminate a few feet in front of her.

Will had been right. She didn't like it up here. It was dark and dusty, and the air felt as if it was too thick to breathe. She imagined mold spores growing on the dark beadboard walls and ceiling, poisoning her lungs. She stood peering into the gloom, filled with a vague sense of dread.

She understood why, as girls, the aunts had been afraid to play up here.

The room was long and narrow, and had a coved ceiling covered in dark pine. Along one wall, two dormered windows overlooked the drive and the back lawn. The walls were dark, too, giving the room a drab, dreary feeling that the light falling through the small windows could not dissipate. A tall bookcase stacked with medical journals and apothecary jars stood along the opposite wall. She remembered that Will's ancestor, Jerome, had once used the room as a medical laboratory.

At the opposite end of the room were several old leather trunks and stacked boxes, and beyond that, a narrow passage led into a large open room under the eaves filled with broken furniture and discarded household goods. Ava had no intention of exploring that space; it was too dismal and dank.

She concentrated on the boxes and trunks, which were mostly filled with moldy shoes and clothes, delicate hand-stitched linens and silks ravaged by time and insects. A tower of round boxes filled with ornate, wide-brimmed hats occupied her for some time. There was a treasure trove of vintage clothing here, although most of it had been left to rot.

She found several boxes of documents: old receipts, newspaper clippings, bills, check drafts, and household ledgers. But no letters and no photos.

She heard a car door slam and, going to one of the windows, she saw the Merry Maids van pulled up in the yard and two employees unloading mops, buckets, and a vacuum cleaner. As if sensing her presence, one of the women looked up, and Ava stepped back into the shadows. She remembered her first day at Woodburn Hall, when she, too, had felt herself observed from one of the upstairs windows. Perhaps the very one that she was standing behind now.

A delicate shudder touched her spine, and she turned away from the window. She was beginning to feel depressed by the room, weighed down by something indefinable. There was a peculiar heaviness in the air, an unpleasant odor of formaldehyde, mold, and something unfamiliar, something Ava didn't like to think too much about, an odor that seemed to linger in the dark, dank corners. She went quickly to the trunks and began to hurriedly repack the clothes.

It was while running her hands inside the bottom of the trunks, looking for forgotten letters, that Ava's fingers closed over something of interest.

She pulled out a small red leather book. Opening it, she read,

JOSEPHINE, HER DIARY: MERRY CHRISTMAS 1927 FROM PAPA.

There were very few entries, and none of them were dated. Most of the pages were filled with elaborately drawn cartoons of flappers, jazz singers, and college boys in raccoon coats and saddle oxfords. One cartoon showed a tall, dark-haired boy in a badly fitting suit, his bony wrists and ankles comically exposed, blowing on a clarinet in front of an audience of wild-eyed girls. The caption read, *The Sheik works his magic on a bunch of Dumb Doras. And how!*

Ava slid the diary in her pocket, and, closing up the trunks, she quickly descended the stairs.

She paused on the threshold of Will's room, hesitating even as she heard the shouts of the cleaning women below. And then, because she knew she would find what she was looking for, she hurried over to the bookcase. The photo she was searching for wasn't in sight, but she found it pushed behind a stack of *Mad* magazines, a silver-framed photo of Will, Hadley, and Jake standing in the shade of a graceful colonnade, their arms around one another. Will was the same slender boy she remembered from Bard, but Jake looked different. He wore a grave, obscure expression, and his face was turned coyly away from the camera, as if he were embarrassed, or hiding something. Both boys had their arms—protectively? possessively?—around Hadley.

She was beautiful, tall and blonde and lovely as Ava had known she would be, as she had already imagined her, gazing at the camera with an expression that seemed both artless and arrogant, a golden girl who knows the world is hers for the taking.

Courtship

Despite her resolve to keep her distance from Jake, she awoke Thursday morning with a fluttering sense of excitement, knowing that she would soon see him again. She rose early, dressed carefully, and set out for downtown around ten o'clock.

The morning was sweltering. Cicadas hummed in the trees, and from time to time a lone car passed along the street. Two people slowed down and asked her if she wanted a ride, Boofie Crenshaw from the Ladies of the Evening Investment Club, and Sally Stewart, who went to church with Josephine and Fanny and sang in the choir with Maitland. Ava waved and told them no, she was out for a little exercise. Beneath her feet the brick sidewalk rose and fell like the deck of a ship. She liked walking—it helped clear her mind—but today she had underestimated the heat. She had only walked a block and already her sleeveless blouse clung to her back. Ahead she could see a long tunnel of oaks and she hurried on, her sandals slapping against the bricks. It was cooler in the shade by maybe ten degrees, and she stopped for a moment to admire Mrs. Barfield's hydrangeas and catch her breath.

Rachel Rowe had given her the address of the Victorian house where Charlie Woodburn had boarded in 1928. According to Rachel, he had come to town that summer after spending his first year at Vanderbilt, and had clerked at one of the downtown businesses. Ava told Rachel about the ledger she had found, mentioning the Colonel's intent to "draw up a deed" that gave Charlie what was rightfully his.

"Really?" Rachel said, her eyes wide behind her thick glasses. "What do you think that might be?"

"I was thinking maybe Longford."

"Longford?"

"If Randal had married the Chickasaw woman instead of Delphine, then Longford would have passed to Charlie's ancestor and not the Colonel's."

"Well, yes, I suppose so," Rachel said. "But if the Colonel deeded Longford to Charlie, if there was a conveyance, you would have thought the Woodburns would have known about it."

"You would think so," Ava said.

"But then again, Charlie died pretty young. They may not have known. They may have just assumed the property was still in the family." Her voice rose, filled with a breezy enthusiasm. "I'll go over to the courthouse this afternoon and check the deed records. Although, you should understand, if you're right, that the Colonel's gesture may not have been as generous as you would think. Longford in the twenties was abandoned, and the house was falling into ruin, so the property probably wouldn't have been worth much." She looked at Ava, blinking. Her face was pink, and her hands, placed one atop the other on the desk, trembled slightly.

Ava gathered that this was the most excitement Rachel had felt in years.

Ava stood in the shade of one of the large oaks in front of Mrs. Barfield's wrought-iron fence, imagining the street as it must have looked in Charlie's day. It was not hard to picture him strolling along the dusty street on a summer day like this, dressed in a sacque suit with a bowler hat. Only in those days the street would have been brick like the sidewalk, and the houses on either side less crowded together.

Everyone would have kept a vegetable garden and a shed out back where cows and chickens were stabled. The houses would have sat on large lots much like the one Woodburn Hall sat on now.

She half-closed her eyes, peering through the fringe of her lashes, and the landscape changed again; wide fields stretched now on either side of the street, and the trees were smaller, more compact. A line of gas lamps stretched along a flat sidewalk that was smooth and unbroken yet by floods and tree roots. Ava squinted her eyes and waited, and a moment later she could see a tall dark figure striding toward her, weaving in and out of the shade. He appeared to be whistling, one hand shoved deep in a pocket and the other swinging free. Watching him stride toward her, noting the wide set of his shoulders and the graceful way he moved, Ava felt suddenly chilled.

"Hello, are you all right?" Mrs. Barfield said. She had come out on her porch, and noting Ava standing motionless at the fence, had walked to the edge of the steps.

"Yes. Yes, sorry, I was just taking a breather." Ava rubbed her arms where goose bumps had begun to appear.

"It's a hot one, isn't it?"

"Yes. But nice in the shade." They stood for a few minutes exchanging pleasantries and then Ava moved off. She took a right one block before reaching the square. The houses here were smaller and less ornate than the ones lining River Street. She checked the address she had written on a piece of paper, then walked another couple of blocks.

She recognized the house from a photograph Rachel had shown her, although the facade had changed slightly. It was missing one of its porches, and someone had removed all the gingerbread trim from the eaves. A man was building a swing set in the side yard and Ava called to him.

"Can I help you?" he said, standing.

"I'm sorry to bother you. Do you live here?"

He stood, wiping his brow with the back of one arm. "Yes," he said.

"This used to be a boardinghouse."

"So they tell me." He wore a pair of shorts and a sweat-stained T-shirt. A tool belt circled his waist, riding low on his hips.

"This is going to sound odd." She wanted to ask him if she could come inside his house, walk around the rooms where Charlie had once walked, see the room where he slept. The man seemed like a nice enough suburban dad but something in his protective stance, in the way he looked at her, friendly and wary at the same time, made her realize the impossibility of her request.

For some reason, she thought of Frank Dabrowski and the day she had pulled up in front of his little house in Garden City and a woman (his wife?) had come out and eyed her suspiciously. She had written Frank another hasty letter but had not heard from him since. Would probably never hear from him again.

She said, "A man by the name of Charlie Woodburn used to board here. Back in the nineteen-twenties."

"Sorry." The man shook his head. In the sky behind him, the sun slid behind a scrum of swiftly moving clouds.

"Never heard of him," he said.

It was only two blocks farther to Jake's shop, and Ava plodded on like a sleepwalker. It was only ten-thirty, too early to drop in on him, but she had nowhere else to go. The sun was almost directly overhead, and the heat remained fierce and steady, rising in waves off the pavement. The sidewalk here was newer, concrete bleached by the sun, and most of the houses had wooden fences instead of wrought iron. She passed a pair of children playing in a yard with a spotted puppy. At the corner, an old man driving a riding mower waved at her.

Jake's shop was in a row of small brick warehouses that stood a block from the square, and had been used, over the years, as storage for cotton, machine parts, and soybeans. The buildings sat across the street from a residential neighborhood, back in a grove of walnut and chinaberry trees. Ava waited at the corner to cross the street. A pickup truck cruised by slowly and the driver whistled and grinned. He slowed down but Ava stared at him defiantly until he shouted, "Be that way then!" and sped off.

She crossed the street and stopped, standing beneath the awning of Jake's shop in front of a wooden door sporting a brass kick plate. Now that she was here, she was having second thoughts. Will had made his feelings about Jake quite clear, and she didn't want any more trouble with him. And Darlene Haney, as well as Fraser Barron, had warned her about Jake's "bad" reputation. Her own feelings were suspect, too; the fact that she had found Jake so instantly attractive was probably not a good sign, given her past track record.

She hesitated in front of the door, gazing up at the sun-bleached awning. It seemed a flimsy excuse to visit him, bringing him a blurry photo of his unknown grandfather. He had, no doubt, seen through her ruse. She remembered the photo of him, Will, and Hadley that she had found in Will's room, the way he had tilted his face away from the camera, as though he was hiding something. She remembered what he'd said the last time they spoke, "I've been thinking about you," and it seemed to her now that there had been an edge of slyness in his voice.

To the left of the awning hung a sign that read *Thorny Shire Woodworks*. Underneath it were two massive iron-hinged doors that slid open on rollers. The doors were closed. The street was empty and quiet but for the drowsy whirring of cicadas and, faintly, from one of the houses across the street, the tinny blaring of music.

In that instant Ava made up her mind to leave. She would tell him something had come up; she'd offer to send him the photo. She had turned around and taken two steps toward the street when a voice behind her said, "I bet you get that all the time."

He was sitting in an Adirondack chair in the shade of one of the chinaberry trees in the alley, sipping on a bottled Coke. She hadn't seen him as she walked up.

"You bet I get what?" She had no choice but to slowly retrace her steps.

He made a move as if to stand but she quickly motioned for him to stay seated.

"Catcalls from strange men in pickup trucks."

"No. Not really. Not usually." She felt her face flush with embarrassment. Seeing this, he grinned.

"You don't know you're a traffic stopper?"

"It's just that everyone down here is so—friendly."

"That we are." He had drawn one leg up on the chair so that the arm holding the Coke rested on his knee. The chair was painted a bright blue, and had cutouts of crabs, starfish, and sea horses across the back. One leg of the chair was chained to the chinaberry tree. "So where were you going?"

"I don't know. I realized I was early and I thought you might not be here." She stared fixedly at the chair with its chain tether.

"My chairs have a tendency to run off if I don't secure them," he explained, noting her interest.

"Your chairs? Are these what you make in your shop?"

"They're some of what I make." He sat for a moment, regarding her steadily. He wore a pair of baggy shorts and a Lucinda Williams T-shirt, and his hair fell damply around his face.

She pointed at the shop sign. "I like the name," she said.

"It's from a Dylan Thomas poem."

"Yes, I know."

He nodded and grinned. "Do you want to see the rest of the shop?"

She glanced up and down the street. "Sure," she said.

He stood up. His movements were slow but powerful, like a cat unfurling itself in the sun. "Next time you don't think I'm here," he said, "just ring the bell."

The room was brightly lit by overhead skylights and smelled of pine and freshly planed wood. Sawdust and shavings littered the concrete floor. All along the back wall were neatly stacked shelves containing plastic bins and boxes. The interior of the shop was crowded with routers, planers, and various circular saws and, to her right, a pegboard wall was hung with miscellaneous hand tools. In the center of the room, where the light from the skylights was brightest, stood a wide, slightly raised platform, and on this platform rested a squat, thick-legged coffee table.

"It's my newest piece," he said. "Do you like it?"

"It's beautiful," she said, reaching out a tentative hand and stroking the table like she would an exotic animal. It was surprisingly cool in the airy room. The air conditioner hummed quietly, prickling her skin.

"I'm building it for a couple in Tribeca."

She walked slowly around the platform, admiring his work. "It's very masculine," she said. "Very geometric in its simplicity."

"Well, no one wants a crooked coffee table." He stood with his arms crossed over his chest, watching her intently. Ava had the feeling he was laughing at her.

"Sorry. I guess I don't really know much about hand-built furniture."

"Don't apologize. Don't ever apologize for saying what you think. It's what I like best about you. Your honesty." He grinned slowly. "Well, it's one of the things."

"Right," she said.

"No need to blush," he said, his smile widening.

"I'm not blushing."

Ava waved her hand vaguely at the door. "I was at the boarding-house," she said, "where Charlie Woodburn used to live."

"Down the street?"

"Yes."

His manner with her was different, more flirtatious than it had been that day out at his mother's house. It threw her off guard, made her wonder why he would have changed toward her in the weeks since then.

As if aware of her confusion he said, "I heard you and Will weren't dating."

"Who told you that?"

"A little bird."

"I told you before that Will and I are just friends."

"I had to make sure." He grinned, a long, slow grin, and the nearness of him, the thickness of his forearms, was enough to set off a vibration in the pit of her stomach. She thought suddenly of the photo she had found of the three of them, beautiful Hadley standing between the tall cousins. The two men who loved her.

She took the photo of Charlie Woodburn out of her purse and gave it to him. "I thought you might like to have a copy of this. Rachel Rowe found it. She was combing through old newspapers and found one photo but it wasn't very clear. You really can't see his features."

"Rachel Rowe. The town historian?"

"That's right."

He must have loved Hadley. He wouldn't have risked what he had if he hadn't loved her. Ava wondered what had become of her, whether she had married and settled down or gone off into the wide world to seek her fortune. Did he ever hear from her? Did he ever drink too much and send her a lonely email? She knew he would tell her if she asked and yet, oddly, she didn't want to know, she didn't want to watch his eyes change at the mention of Hadley's name as Will's had, become bitter and sad.

"You're right," he said. "You can't see him very well." He looked up at her. "Thanks." He slid the clipping into his back pocket. "Would you like something to drink? Iced tea, bottled water?" He pointed to a circular stairway at the far corner of the room. "I live upstairs."

"No, oh, no," she said quickly. "I don't want anything." She smiled, avoiding his eyes. His mouth was wide, generous, with a full lower lip.

He stepped around her. His arm grazed her shoulder, and she could feel the unexpected heat of his body against her skin. "Do you mind if I grab a couple of bottled waters?"

"Of course not."

"I'll be right back," he said.

On the walk between Charlie's boardinghouse and Jake's studio, it had occurred to Ava that Will might have been right. *Help me* could have been the scribbling of a desperate man; not the act of a man afraid of violent murder, but a man overcome with remorse or alcohol or depression. A suicide.

Who knew what baggage Charlie might have brought with him

from New Orleans? What demons he might have battled? It was so difficult to ascertain a man's true character glimpsed only through the eyes of others. And the Charlie who presented himself in her novel—how close was he to the real man? She seemed to have reached an impasse with his character. He remained as obscure to her now as he had from the very first sentence she wrote. Surely the Colonel had thought well of him. The Colonel's journal indicated an almost paternal obsession with his young cousin. A feeling of *obligation,* as evidenced by his willingness to pay Charlie's tuition at Vanderbilt and his cryptic message in his journal that he was going to give Charlie what was rightfully his, and thereby right the wrongs of their fathers.

But would Fanny's papa have liked Charlie enough to have him as a son-in-law? Or would the Colonel's prejudice against a social inferior, despite his many kindnesses to Charlie, have been clear to the young man?

It was obvious from Josephine's diary that she had detested Charlie. The cartoonish drawings of *The Sheik* were, of course, her ridiculing of Charlie himself. Ava had recognized him almost immediately from the descriptions she'd gathered from others: the dark, sullen face, the hollow eyes, the rawboned appearance of a country boy masquerading in a gentleman's clothes. Could Josephine's abject contempt of the man her sister married ultimately have caused him to lose himself in alcohol and depression? Was there a weakness in Charlie, a fatal flaw that only Josephine knew how to exploit?

Ava stood in the middle of the sun-filled studio, thinking about Charlie and waiting for the sound of Jake's footsteps on the stairs. He returned a short time later carrying two bottled waters. She noticed that he had changed his T-shirt and combed his hair. He gave her a bottle and took the cap off the other one. She was suddenly thirsty, and she tipped her head back, drinking greedily.

When she was finished, she put the cap on and wiped her mouth. "Did you ever hear of Charlie being sick?"

"Sick?" Jake's eyes were so dark she couldn't see the pupils.

"Depressed. Or maybe physically ill before he died."

"To be honest with you, I don't know a lot about Charlie. Most of what I've heard came from my mother or town gossips." He picked up a rag and began to rub the legs of the coffee table with tung oil. "People say that he was bad to drink, that he was an alcoholic, but maybe that's just their way of blaming the victim. You know. He was a bad guy, so he deserved to die. That kind of thing."

"I don't think he was a bad guy."

"Well, you're in a minority in this town." He continued his long, even strokes, then stopped. He stood, leaning his hip against the platform. "You seem interested in my grandfather. Talking to people, asking questions."

"I'm just curious about what really happened. I'm just trying to fit all the pieces together." She was nervous under his piercing gaze and took another long pull from the bottle.

He stared at her fondly but curiously, as if he was trying to see beyond her words to the meaning behind them. Her nervous gesture, her inability to look at him, gave it away. "You're writing a book," he said. "You're writing a novel about Charlie Woodburn." When she didn't answer, he put his head back and laughed so long and ardently that Ava finally had to say, "Hush."

He wiped his eyes with the back of his hand. He shook his head. "Does Will know?" When she didn't respond he said, "No, of course he doesn't." He sighed, folding and refolding the rag in his hands. "Have you thought about the repercussions? Have you thought about the response the Woodburns might have to a novel like that?"

"I try not to think about it," she said. "Because if I think about it, I won't be able to write, and this is the best thing I've ever written." She returned his gaze steadily. "I mean it. I can publish this novel."

He held his hands up. "Hey, I believe you. It's compelling stuff." He wrapped the rag around his knuckles like a prizefighter taping for a match. "But is it worth your relationship with Will and Josephine? Because I can tell you right now, they won't ever forgive you. They're not the forgiving kind. I know that from experience."

She knew he was right; she had known it ever since she began the novel but she'd been unable to stop herself. It had become an obsession. She couldn't stop now even if she wanted to.

He saw her resolve in her face and he didn't say anything else about Will. "I have to admit, the sickness angle is interesting," he said, "but it's not the truth. Charlie was covered in bruises when they pulled him out of the river. I've heard that from several different sources."

"There are a lot of boulders in that river."

"True. But one of the deputies who pulled him out told my grandmother that he looked like he'd been worked over pretty good."

"So you don't think it was suicide or an accident? You don't think he was ill before he died?"

"I never heard that he was sick. From what I know of Charlie, he was no suicide. He had too much to live for."

Ava's cell phone began to ring. She looked for her purse and he helped her, but it had stopped ringing by the time he found it over by the scroll saw. He held it out to her. She took it, their hands touching briefly. She checked the display, then slid it back into her purse.

"The aunts calling to check up on you?" he said mildly.

"No. Will."

He didn't say anything, pushing his hands down into his pockets.

"I better go," she said.

He walked with her to the door. She thanked him for the water, then stepped out into the fierce heat of midday.

"I'll see you later," she said.

He stood in the open doorway with his shoulder pressed against the jamb. "Thanks for the photo."

"Don't mention it."

She crossed the street and headed home, walking briskly, aware the whole time that he was standing in the doorway, watching her.

Whatever easygoing flirtation she had felt between herself and Jake had disappeared the minute Ava mentioned Will. Or that's how it had seemed anyway. He hadn't seemed all that sorry when she said she had to go. He hadn't tried to talk her out of it. Nor had he mentioned them getting together some other time. Walking down the shady midday streets, Ava realized this now with a stir of disappointment.

It was as if the mention of Will's name had thrown up some kind of barrier between them, as if whatever was promising and inevitable had faded away.

She walked with her head down, watching her sandals slap against the sidewalk. She knew she should call Will back but she didn't want to. They had barely spoken since that night in her room, had stopped going around together in the evenings. Now that she wrote at night, she had began to make excuses as to why she couldn't go out for movies and drinks, and after a while Will had stopped asking. He was pleasant and cordial at Toddy Time, but if they were alone together there was a cool distance between them. Their friendship, she was beginning to understand, would not survive her summer in Woodburn.

The sudden ringing of her phone interrupted her thoughts. It was Rachel Rowe.

"Hey," Rachel said breathlessly, when she answered. "I've been down in the deed room checking the books all afternoon, and I didn't find any conveyance from Colonel James to Charlie Woodburn. And I had a couple of the old deed dogs down there helping me, too, so I'm confident that there's nothing recorded. They say they've never heard of any such conveyance."

"What's a deed dog?"

"A lawyer who does title searches."

"Oh."

"I think our best bet is for me to go up to Vanderbilt and check the Woodburn papers. I might find some letter there from the Colonel to Charlie explaining the journal entry. Or I might find a deed. It may be something that was never recorded." She sounded as excited as a child on a treasure hunt, and Ava couldn't help but be affected by her enthusiasm.

"Do you mind going up to Vanderbilt?"

"Hell no," Rachel said. "It'll give me something to do tomorrow.

You get to be my age, you don't have a lot of ways to fill your spare time. This is perfect."

"Call me when you get back."

"I will. I'm just sorry you didn't find any photographs up in the attic."

"Yeah," Ava said. "I'm sorry, too."

After she hung up with Rachel she walked on, clinging to the shade as best she could. The heat coated her tongue and her throat like warm molasses. She was sorry now that she had chosen the hottest part of the day to walk to town. At that moment a white Ford Explorer came barreling down the street, the driver turning a blank face to Ava. The car skidded to a stop in the middle of the next block and Ava watched in wary annoyance as it began to back erratically toward her. The passenger's window slid down.

"Get in!" Darlene Haney yelled at her from the driver's side.

"No, that's okay, I'll walk."

"Get in, dammit! I don't got all day." Darlene's face was red, and she seemed agitated and tense. Her pleasant, docile mask had slipped. A tennis ball whizzed by her nose and bounced off the front dash, and Ava could see three shadowy figures bouncing around in the backseat. Her sons.

Darlene swung her arm over the backseat and someone yelped and said, "Dammit, Mama, it was Ridley who threw it, not me!"

Ava got in. The boys strapped into the backseat ranged in ages from four to seven, and went by the names of Stansbury, Ridley, and Bob. The two elder ones hugged the windows and the youngest, Bob, sat in the middle. Bare-chested, he had taken his T-shirt off and was attempting to strangle Stansbury with it.

"Lord help us," Darlene said, slamming the SUV into drive. "What I wouldn't give for a margarita."

"Are they okay?" Ava asked, nervously eyeing Stansbury, who was beginning to make loud choking noises, much to his brothers' amusement.

"Oh, they're fine. They're just playing is all." Darlene had just come from her mother's and she was in a sour mood. She put the music up loud in the back so they wouldn't have to listen to Stansbury.

They drove to the light and stopped. Darlene made a conscious effort to regain her composure, plumping her hair with her fingers and glancing at Ava with a forced smile. "So where have you been?" she asked sweetly.

"Nowhere. Just out for a walk."

"Really?"

"Yes."

"Been down to see Jake Woodburn's shop?" She glanced in the rearview mirror. "Come on, boys!" she said. "Y'all behave. Miss Ava won't like you if you're ugly. Bob, stop playing with Stansbury and put your shirt back on. If y'all are good, Mama will turn up the music. Would you like that? It's *Lynyrd Skynyrd.* Y'all's favorite."

"Darlene, the light's green," Ava said.

She pumped the accelerator. "Doesn't he have the strangest taste in furniture?"

"Who?"

"Jake Woodburn."

"His stuff is cool."

"Oh?" Darlene arched one carefully sculpted eyebrow. "Do you think so? No one around here buys it except for the Adirondack chairs. Everyone wants one of those, so now he doesn't make them anymore. Isn't that just like Jake?"

"I guess so. I don't really know him."

"Oh?"

"Freebird!" Bob shouted happily from the backseat, twirling his T-shirt above his head.

Darlene couldn't wait to tell Will Fraser she had seen Ava coming out of Jake Woodburn's shop. She would call him just as soon as she got home and got the boys fed and hosed off. Will probably wouldn't like it at first. He was sure to get angry, but she was certain he'd calm down eventually and realize she had his best interests at heart. Sooner or later, Will was going to learn to appreciate her loyalty. Sooner or later he was going to wise up and realize that there was only one girl in the world for him, and that girl was Darlene Smollett Haney. By God.

She gave Ava a sly look. "You know, Will was engaged once before," she said. "He was engaged to a girl named Hadley Marsh."

"I know all about Hadley," Ava said, wishing she'd never climbed into the car. She wasn't about to let herself be dragged into another of Darlene's ambushes.

"You do?" Darlene said brightly. "You know about Hadley? Who told you?"

"You did."

Darlene giggled. "Did I?"

"So did Will. And Jake."

"I can't imagine either one of them talking about her! Still, water under the bridge. Don't you worry. It was a long time ago. I'm sure neither one of them gives her much thought these days."

Ava ignored her implication. "She sounds like a great girl. If both Will and Jake were in love with her, she must be special. I'm sure I'd like her if I met her."

Darlene smiled. "Oh, really," she said.

"She sounds like someone I might be friends with."

Darlene snorted. "Obviously they didn't tell you everything."

"What do you mean?"

They drove for a while in silence listening to the boys sing "Freebird." When Ava couldn't stand it anymore she said, "Okay, tell me. So what happened to her?"

"Who?" Darlene asked innocently.

Ava swiveled her head and stared. "Hadley," she said.

Darlene smiled serenely. She glanced at Ava, then back at the road. "She's dead," she said.

"Dead?" Ava said. She stared stupidly at Darlene.

"She died in a car accident seven or eight years ago on her way home from visiting Will."

They didn't speak for the rest of the ride to Woodburn Hall. Ava kept her eyes turned to the window, trying to regain her composure in the face of Darlene's obvious bombshell. She didn't want to give Darlene the satisfaction of knowing she'd rattled her.

She had lied to Darlene. The truth was, she and Hadley would never have been friends. She had seen this in Hadley's photo, in her casual, arrogant expression. The popular girl and the shy, secretive class clown. A truce perhaps, a grudging appreciation of each other's gifts, but never a friendship.

She stared at the lush green landscape and thought of Hadley Marsh. A beautiful girl. A beautiful dead girl.

Ava could not put her finger on why this bothered her.

For supper Maitland had made a shrimp salad served in avocado halves and garnished with fresh tomato and cucumber slices. They were just finishing when Will came in.

"Let me get you a plate," Josephine said when she saw him, getting up from the table.

"No. I've eaten."

He was standing just inside the kitchen door. Ava could see from his face that Darlene had told him about her visit to Jake's shop.

Fanny looked at him wide-eyed. "Is something wrong?" she asked in a timid voice.

"I need to talk to Ava."

Ava stood up without a word and followed him through the house into her bedroom. She closed the door quietly behind them and sat on the edge of the bed while he paced up and down the room. He shoved his hands deep in his pockets and went to the window, standing with his back to her, looking out.

She said, "I went to Jake Woodburn's shop today."

He turned around and faced her, his eyes an icy blue. "I thought I made it clear that you were to stay away from him."

"You made it clear that you didn't like him. Who I hang out with, Will, is my own business."

He stared at her. A muscle moved in his cheek.

"Look." She put her hands out in a placating manner, palms up. "I don't want to fight with you over this. I went down to see Jake because I had something to give him. A photo of his grandfather that Rachel Rowe found in the library archives."

"A photo of his *grandfather*?" He looked at her incredulously, pulling his hands out of his pockets. "Is that what this is about? Are you pumping him for information about Charlie Woodburn? Because I can tell you right now, he doesn't know anything about Charlie. When we were boys he knew even less about him than I did."

"That may be true, but at least Jake's willing to talk about him."

"Of course he is! He'd talk about anyone if it would get your attention."

She looked down, dropping her hands in her lap. "I don't want to fight with you," she said.

"Then you shouldn't have gone to see Jake," he said coldly.

"Who I see is my own business. I don't owe you any explanations."

He looked at her a long time and when he spoke his voice was filled with bitter accusation. "You've made that very clear," he said.

"Jake doesn't try to hide anything."

"Oh, come on, Ava, you don't even know him!"

"Do I know you?" Ava said, looking up. "Do I know anything about you? How about Hadley?"

"I told you about Hadley!"

"You didn't tell me she was dead."

Outside the windows dusk fell, bathing the room in a purple light. He turned around and leaned his forehead against the glass. Crickets chanted in the shadows. When he faced her again, the anger seemed to have gone out of him. "What difference does it make?" he said. "It was a long time ago."

"Yeah. I hear that a lot down here." She pulled her legs up under her, leaning back against the headboard. "It obviously made a difference to your relationship with Jake."

His expression hardened. He shook his head stubbornly. "I don't want to talk about him."

"There's a lot you don't want to talk about."

"Don't keep bringing Charlie into this."

"I'm not talking about Charlie."

"Do you know he beat her?" he said softly. His eyes narrowed and he gave her a coolly appraising look. "Your hero, this dead man you spend so much time mooning over. He beat Fanny. Black and blue."

She stared at him, watching a range of emotions flicker across his face. Of all the possibilities in the story of Fanny and Charlie, this was one she'd never considered. "Don't change the subject," she said softly. "You always do that. You always try to throw me off the trail. As if you don't trust me with the truth."

"What truth have I not told you?" he said. "Besides the fact that Hadley is dead, although I still don't see why that should affect you. What else have I not been truthful about?"

"You told me you'd never seen a ghost."

He groaned and shook his head. He chuckled, a dull, mirthless sound.

"Fraser told me that as a child you were terrified of the staircase because you used to see the ghost of Delphine Woodburn standing there."

He dropped his chin and stared at her. "Oh, well," he said. "If you're going to bring the fantasies of childhood into it!"

"So, you did see her."

He regarded her coolly, soberly. "Not that I recall. No."

He had a clever way of remembering only what he wanted to remember. Ava supposed it was a useful trick.

"I don't know what's so hard about honesty," she said.

He stood very still, staring at her. Then, without another word, he turned and walked out.

She lay back against the pillows and turned her face to the window, watching bats flit across the darkening sky. She could feel Clotilde observing her from the mantel. The atmosphere inside the house felt heavy, depressive.

After a while Ava got up and called Fraser Barron to see if he wanted to go for a drink.

They met at a small English pub on the square called Churchill's. It was a restaurant, too, and the interior was crowded with families sitting at pub tables and in booths along the walls. Fraser sat at the bar. He was in one of his Poe moods, dressed in a dark gray sacque suit with a burgundy cape thrown over his shoulders. Ava indicated a booth in the far corner, and Fraser stood up and followed her, picking his way through the tables and flourishing his cape like a magician.

"I can't believe you don't have heatstroke in that outfit," Ava said, sitting down. Fraser stood for a moment, allowing everyone in the pub to get a good look at him.

"One must suffer for beauty," he said, sliding into the booth opposite her. "Look at you women and your high heels."

Ava stuck one sandaled foot out for his appraisal. "Note that I am not wearing high heels."

"No. But then you're different. We've established that."

A flustered-looking waitress brought them a couple of vodka tonics. Ava told Fraser about the argument with Will. She told him about meeting Jake at his shop.

"All alone?" Fraser asked casually. "Oh, dear."

"I mean, Will was furious. I've never seen him so angry."

"Someone probably told him about it before you had a chance to. He just got his male pride a little ruffled."

Ava crossed her arms and leaned against the table, ducking her head and leaning in close so she could be heard over the noise of the restaurant. "I want you to tell me what's going on between those two. Why does Will hate Jake so much?"

Fraser raised one eyebrow and sipped his drink, then set it down again. "You already know why," he said.

"They can't still be fighting over a girl who died years ago. There has to be something more to it than that."

"You mean Will hasn't told you?"

"There's a lot Will doesn't tell me."

"Well, that's a Southern *thang*." He ran one finger absentmindedly around the rim of his glass. "I think it has less to do with Hadley and more to do with the fact that Will thinks Jake betrayed him. He'll never trust him again. And now you come along and it's obvious Will has feelings for you. Don't blush and look away, you know he does." He grinned at her discomfort.

"Will and I are just friends," she said.

"Uh-huh," Fraser said. "Anyway, it doesn't matter. I think having feelings for you and watching Jake move in on you brings up a lot of baggage from Will's past. Stuff he'd rather not deal with right now."

"Oh, good Lord," Ava said. "I'm not dating either one."

"Look," he said, settling back and pulling his cape around him. "You've been in therapy, right?"

Ava looked around the pub. "Well," she said.

"Yes, yes," he said, snapping his fingers impatiently. "Of course you have. Anyone with any sense has been in therapy. I was in therapy even before I came out." He stopped and gave her a curious look. "You knew I was gay, right?"

Ava laughed.

Fraser laughed, too. "I know. I was never any good at hiding it, even back when I still tried. When I was fifteen, I'd come home from prep school and go shopping with Mother and she'd tell all her friends, 'Fraser has the best taste! Why, he's just like a woman!' We'd go to public high school football games and critique the cheerleaders, and it never occurred to her that I was gay; she just thought I was a little *odd*. Odd runs in our family. Look at the Captain. Mother was raised in a different time. Men lived by a different code then. They could drink, gamble, whore around, abuse the help and their own wives and children, and as long as they had the right pedigree, still be considered gentlemen. Hell, they could kill somebody and, as long as they did it for the right reasons, still be considered gentlemen. But homosexuality! That was a horse of a different color. That was impropriety on a grand scale. Hell, that was sin!"

In the booth behind them, a child stood on her seat and said shyly to Fraser, "I like your dress."

"Thanks," Fraser said. "I like yours, too."

"Mary Ann, sit down," her mother said sharply. "Don't you be bothering those people with your foolishness."

Fraser pushed his glass around, making little wet spots on the tablecloth. "When Mother caught me looking at the cheerleaders in the yearbook she said, 'Fraser, there's nothing wrong with you looking at pretty girls. You'll have a pretty cheerleader one day to call your very own.' I said, 'Hell, Mother, I don't want to *have* a pretty cheerleader. I want to *be* one.'

"She sent me to Father Nichols, of course, and he sent me to a therapist in Nashville, and that turned out to be the best thing that's ever happened to me. Because he got me talking about my past and about myself, and the more I talked the more I knew who I was and the more I knew how I wanted to live my life."

Ava raised her hand to tell the waitress to bring them another round.

"Here's the thing about being Southern," Fraser said. "You're raised to be polite. Yes, sir. No, sir. On the surface it's all moonlight and magnolias, but underneath it's miscegenation and tragedy and poverty and ignorance. Sure we pay lip service to history, we pretend to admire it, but the truth is, no one really wants to talk about it, not the dirty part anyway. We don't want to acknowledge all the bad things that happened. That gets swept under the carpet because it's fucking unpleasant, and no one wants to talk about unpleasantness."

His voice had risen as he talked. Ava glanced apologetically at the neighboring table. She dipped her head and said in a low voice, "Could we keep it down a little? There are children present."

He smirked, raising his glass. He took a long drink, then set it down again with a loud *thock*. "Coward," he said.

"Maybe. But I'm not hearing impaired."

"I thought you wanted to talk about the past."

"I do. But I want to talk about it quietly."

"We're tied to our history," Fraser said. "We carry it around like rusty chains. No one does suffering better than us, unless it's the Jews. Or maybe the Irish."

The waitress brought their drinks. Trying to prompt him, Ava asked, "How did Hadley die?"

"I'm getting to that. I'm going to give you the broad outline but I'm not going to give you details, because you need to go home and talk to Will about that. You need to get him talking to Jake. You need to get those two talking. Somehow."

"Have you ever been in love, Fraser?" That shut him up. He was quiet for a moment, tilting his glass and staring down into his drink like he was looking into a crystal ball.

"Of course I have. Many times. After college I lived in Atlanta with my significant other, Michael. Yes, I had a significant other. He was an architect and he was a lovely person. He was a cheating, lying bastard but he was lovely." He set his glass down and waved his hand in front of his face, as if clearing away smoke. "But we're not talking about me. We're talking about you. You and Will and Jake Woodburn."

"No. We're talking about *Hadley* and Will and Jake Woodburn."

"Okay, so you already know that Jake and Will went off to boarding school together thanks to Fanny and Josephine. It was at boarding school that Will met Hadley. I guess it was love at first sight, at least on Will's part. They dated all through high school. Jake took a year off after prep school and then went up to Sewanee. Hadley followed him while Will went to Bard. Will and Hadley got engaged sometime around their junior year. It was Christmas and there was a big engagement party out at Longford and everyone was there, even Jake. I guess Jake and Hadley had been carrying on for some time at Sewanee, so the engagement must have come as a surprise to him. Because not long after they announced it at the Christmas party, Jake dropped out of Sewanee and went to California. All that money Josephine and Fanny had invested in his education, and he just threw it back in their faces. It wasn't that long after Jake left that Will found out about him and Hadley and broke off the engagement.

"It almost killed Will when he found out. They had to bring him home in the middle of the semester because they thought he was having a nervous breakdown."

Ava could imagine Will's suffering and she was sorry for it. She hadn't really known him then. It was during the time at school when they hadn't seen much of each other.

"Hadley," she said, carefully folding the edges of her cocktail napkin. "Do you think Jake really loved her?"

"Jake?" He frowned and looked at her with surprise, as if trying to figure out why that mattered.

Ava wasn't sure why it mattered, but it did. Perhaps it would show Jake in a better light. Perhaps it would help explain his actions. Ava imagined the three of them standing arm in arm beneath the portico. There was no doubt that Hadley had been a beautiful woman. That she had captured the hearts, or at least the desires, of two near-brothers spoke volumes of her power over men. And yet, how to draw a true picture of this fateful love triangle? Had she wanted it to happen? Had she instigated it? Ava didn't know how to see Hadley as she truly was.

Death smooths the rough edges, obliterates the cruelties of the deceased. It makes heroes of monsters.

Fraser chuckled and shrugged his shoulders. "Who knows with Jake? He always had a certain charm with women."

"I don't think he would ever purposefully hurt Will."

Fraser gave her a sly look. "Why are you defending him?"

"I'm not defending him. I'm just pointing out that there are always two sides to every story. There may be something we don't know."

"Anyway, six months after the broken engagement Hadley was killed in a car accident. The rumor is, she was driving back from visiting Will, trying unsuccessfully to get him to take her back. And Jake and Will have been stuck ever since. Neither one can forgive and move on because neither one wants to talk about what happened."

"That's not true. I think Jake is willing to talk but Will isn't."

An Irish jig played softly in the background. They were quiet for a while, sipping their drinks.

Fraser shrugged. "You may be right. Will keeps himself bound up pretty tight. Somehow you've got to get him talking. You know as well as I do that the thing that works about therapy is talking."

Ava shook her head. "I'm no therapist. No one should accept psychological counseling from someone as fucked-up as me."

"He'll listen to you."

"Don't bet on it."

"Are we going to talk about denial then?" Fraser said mildly, setting his drink down. "Because I'm an expert on denial."

Ava said, "Shut up."

He giggled.

They sat quietly listening to the music. The waitress came and asked them if they wanted another drink and Ava hesitated, looking at Fraser.

"One more for the road," he said.

"It's a good thing we walked," Ava said, watching the weary woman push her way through the crowd.

"We'll probably have to take a cab home. Mother said it was supposed to rain."

He got up and went to the bathroom and when he came back, Ava said, "There's something else I want to ask you."

"Okay. Shoot." He settled himself in the booth, pushing his cape back from his shoulders with fussy movements.

"Did you ever hear anything about Charlie Woodburn beating Fanny?"

Fraser frowned and shook his head. "No," he said. "I mean, Mother rarely speaks of him, of course, no one does. But in the little I've heard her say, there's never been any mention of him being abusive. Just *unsuitable.* I think she would have mentioned something like that." He regarded her with bright, curious eyes. "Why do you ask?"

"No reason," she said, smiling at the tired waitress who had brought their drinks.

When she got home that evening, she went straight to her laptop and began to write. It was a cool, rainy evening. The rain had started around nine o'clock, and had continued, steady and undiminished, for hours, a soft, rattling accompaniment to the sound of her fingers striking the keyboard.

Whatever block she had been suffering from was lifted. As the dark house settled around her and the rain lightly shook the windows, she wrote in long, continuous sections about Charlie. He had changed. He did not reveal himself so readily now; he was secretive, cunning. There was a hint of avarice in his love for Fanny that Ava had not realized before. Fanny was his possession. His chattel.

Ava wrote until the early hours of the morning. The rain eventually stopped and a pale ribbon of moonlight streaked the glass. The old house shifted and creaked, while all around her the unsuspecting Woodburns slept.

For the first time in her life, Ava knew what it was to be part of a family, a group of people whose opinions mattered to her. She could not bear to think of Josephine and Will's faces if they should find out about her novel. She couldn't bear to think what Fanny and Maitland would say. Yet she couldn't help herself. She couldn't stop writing. She was like a medium receiving messages from the dead.

And they were everywhere in this house.

The next morning Fanny and Josephine were waiting for her in the breakfast room. The storm had broken in the night, and the air was cool and fresh. The breakfast room windows were open, a gentle scent of tea olive and honeysuckle wafting in.

Ava sat down at the table and Josephine brought her a plate of eggs, bacon, and toast that she'd been keeping warm on the stove. Fanny poured her a cup of coffee.

"Don't you just love how clean the air smells after a rain?" she said, smiling brightly.

"It was a quiet storm," Ava said, spreading pear preserves on her toast. "It stopped around three o'clock."

"Oh?" Josephine said, sitting down beside her. "Were you awake then?"

"Well, yes," Ava said. "I mean, I heard the rain stop. It had been drumming in the gutter for so long, and I guess I heard it stop and looked at the clock." She had crawled into bed around four o'clock and had promptly fallen into a deep sleep.

Fanny and Josephine glanced at each other. "I hope you aren't having trouble sleeping," Josephine said quietly.

"Oh, no. It wasn't that," Ava said, not wanting to tell them about her nighttime labors. She realized that they had obviously overheard her argument with Will yesterday and that's why they were still here at the breakfast table. They were waiting for her.

Fanny smiled nervously at Josephine. She put her elbows on the table and propped her cheek on one hand. "I think I'll wash my hair today," she said, to no one in particular.

Ava finished her eggs. She looked at Josephine, chewing thoughtfully. "Why are you still here? Don't you have bridge this morning?"

Josephine said, "We don't play in July. Too many Trump Queens off on vacation."

She and Fanny exchanged another swift look. Ava ate her breakfast, staring through the window at the deep green lawn and the glistening hedges. She had turned off her phone last night but this morning, thinking she might have missed a call from Will, she had turned it back on. She had been expecting him to call and apologize for their argument over Jake. Watching as the dial lit up, she realized there was no missed call.

"I hope you don't think we're prying," Josephine began, then stopped, touching her mouth delicately with a napkin. "Will is such a private person. He was always like that, even as a child. And so, naturally, there are certain—things he wouldn't have discussed with you."

She waited for this to sink in. Ava gave no sign of disagreement, and Josephine went on. "Jake was a handsome boy, handsome as—any of that side of the family. But like all of them, he was trouble."

No one said anything. The word "them" hung heavily in the air.

Fanny plucked at her hair. "He was a lovely boy," she said absently, her eyes fixed dreamily on the window. "He always had the nicest manners. 'Miss Fanny,' he used to call me in that teasing manner he has. So full of high spirits and so popular with the girls. Why, I remember . . ." She yelped suddenly and looked at Josephine, and Ava had the distinct impression that Josephine had kicked her under the table.

Josephine cleared her throat. "He was a lovely young man," she murmured. "There's no disputing that." She hesitated as if uncertain how to continue. "And it was unfortunate what happened between him and Will."

"Oh, yes, yes, it was tragic," Fanny said, her eyes wide and tender. "I worried so about Will during all of that. It almost killed him."

Josephine gave Fanny a piercing look but Fanny, oblivious, continued to stare sadly out the window. Josephine had obviously agreed to do much of the talking, but she seemed uncertain how to proceed. She appeared unwilling to mention Hadley. The dead girl seemed to haunt the occupants of the house like a ghost; her presence was felt everywhere, but especially in the long silences that fell across the breakfast room table.

"They were as close as brothers at one time," Josephine said. "But later they had—a falling-out. And Will has a good heart, he's a good boy, a good man, but like all the Woodburns he has a streak of stubbornness. He has a tendency not to forgive people who have hurt him."

Fanny sighed. "Just like Papa," she said. "So much like Papa."

"Having an unforgiving nature is not a good thing, of course, and we don't encourage this estrangement."

"But it takes two to tango," Fanny said wistfully. A big gray cat Ava had never seen before jumped up on her lap.

"Yes, whatever it is that drove them to—" Josephine hesitated, and Ava could see that she was trying not to mention Hadley, not knowing how much Will had told her and not wanting to get him into any trouble. "To quarrel," she finished lamely. "They'll have to work it out between them. Will and Jake. And they will eventually, I feel sure of it."

The backdoor slammed and Alice walked into the kitchen wearing a turquoise tennis suit and a pair of pink Keds. "Aha," she said. "I knew I'd find you two working her over."

"I'm beginning to understand now," Ava said, putting her fork down and looking around the table. "You heard us arguing yesterday. Or maybe someone called and told you they'd seen me coming out of Jake Woodburn's shop."

"Bingo," Alice said, pouring herself a cup of coffee.

"I think the important thing to remember," Josephine continued calmly, indicating with a look that Alice should sit down and be quiet, "is that in the past Jake went after a girl he knew Will was in love with. He betrayed his trust."

"What about Hadley?" Ava said. "She betrayed his trust, too."

Alice sat down on the other side of Fanny. No one said anything. It was obvious that they held Hadley to a different standard.

Alice stirred cream into her coffee. "He went after her even though she and Will had dated all through high school. And Will and Jake were cousins. You know that, right? Like brothers, really. I tell you, it was the talk of the town. And that's why people pay so much attention when they see you and Jake together." Ava opened her mouth to protest and Alice said quickly, "Not that anyone is suggesting that there's anything improper going on between you and Jake. I'm just saying that people see you together and they're *curious*. That's why they talk."

Fanny sighed and plucked aimlessly at an errant curl. She leaned her cheek on the palm of one hand. "He always wanted whatever Will had. If Will had a new suit, then nothing would do but for Jake to have one, too. If Will got a new camera, Jake would sulk until he got one."

The implication was that Jake would not have bothered with Ava if it were not for the fact that Will was interested in her. Ava didn't for one minute think that Fanny had meant to be offensive; still, the remark was insulting. And yet, the same thought had occurred to Ava herself on several occasions.

Josephine said. "I know there's nothing between you and Jake, but I wonder if it's wise to be seen around town with him."

"I was looking at his furniture," Ava said in a heavy tone. "In the middle of the morning. We weren't doing anything *inappropriate.*"

"Well, of course you weren't!" Fanny cried staunchly.

Josephine said quietly, "No one's accusing you of anything."

"Really? Well, it sure sounds like someone is. It sure sounds like someone is implying that I did something wrong. I wish people would mind their own business. I can't believe someone actually picked up the phone and called you to report something so ridiculous." Ava wondered if Josephine had ever had to warn Hadley Marsh of inappropriate behavior; but no, Hadley was a Southern girl. She would have understood the intricacies of small-town social conduct.

"It is one of the drawbacks of living in a small town," Josephine said agreeably. She turned her face to the window, giving Ava time to collect herself. "No one's saying either of you has done anything improper. I'm only bringing it up because I know how wounded Will would be if he saw you together."

Of course she was right. Ava felt a faint stirring of guilt. "Look," she said. "I went by Jake's shop because I'm writing an article on Woodburn and he's been very helpful with some of the information he's given me. He has a different perspective," she finished lamely. "Having lived outside of the South."

"An article on Woodburn!" Fanny cried. "Oh, Sister, isn't that wonderful?"

"Wonderful," Josephine said flatly.

"What's your angle?" Alice asked, leaning forward on her elbows. "Small welcoming Southern town versus big impersonal Yankee city?"

"Alice!" Fanny said.

"Ava doesn't mind," Alice said fiercely. "She doesn't mind if I speak frankly about Yankees." She patted Ava's hand. "She's one of us now."

"Gee, thanks," Ava said.

"Alice," Josephine said in a warning voice.

"No, Josephine, I will not be quiet." Alice's chin quivered and she looked defiantly around the table. "I'm sorry," she said. "But the whole South's being overrun with Yankees. They're always rushing here and there, driving like maniacs, throwing up shopping malls and subdivisions where there used to be nothing but green fields and trees."

"I think that's called progress," Josephine said archly.

"I don't care what it's called." Alice said. "It's mucking things up."

Josephine and Alice immediately launched into an argument over the good old days versus the present, with Josephine taking the side of progress and Alice arguing for the old agrarian society. Fanny leaned her chin on one hand and stared dreamily out the window as if she wasn't listening to either one. Ava was relieved that the conversation had shifted away from her "article" about Woodburn, and from Jake. Despite the fact that she agreed with them, in theory, that Jake shouldn't have gotten involved with Hadley, she couldn't help but feel oddly defensive of him. Certainly she could identify with him: a poor boy from the wrong side of the tracks who finds himself suddenly taken up by the aristocratic Woodburns, a family who could provide him with an education, a comfortable lifestyle, and therefore a brighter future than any he might have provided for himself. And really, was it any different with Ava herself? If Will had not provided her with the means to quit her day job and spend the summer down here rent-free, would she have ever had the opportunity to finish a novel? Not likely.

And the Woodburns had given her an even greater gift. They had given her the story of Charlie and Fanny.

"Progress brings jobs," Josephine said. "Without jobs all of our young people have to grow up and move away."

Fanny turned a hopeful gaze on Ava. "Do you think you would ever want to settle in Woodburn?"

"Oh, I don't know," Ava said vaguely. "I have my work in Chicago."

"Can't you write anywhere?" Alice asked sharply.

"Well, yes."

Fanny smiled tenderly. "Maybe you could spend part of the year living down here?"

"Don't be ridiculous," Josephine said. "She's young, and she lives in one of the most vibrant cities in the world. Why would she ever want to live in sleepy little Woodburn?"

This seemed to put an end to the discussion. Alice finished her coffee and stood up, stretching. "So are we finished warning Ava about Jake Woodburn? Because I've got things to do."

"Is that what this is?" Ava asked, grinning. "An intervention?"

"You'll only need an intervention if you take up with Jake," Alice said "If he sets his sights on you, there could be trouble."

Ava smiled, stacking her dishes. "Did you think to warn Hadley about him?"

No one said anything. Josephine stood and began to gather the dishes from the table.

"What was she like?" Ava asked, realizing she'd said the wrong thing but unwilling to change the subject.

"Hadley? She was beautiful," Alice said. "There's a photo of her and Will taken out at Longford. They used to go out there all the time while they were courting."

Ava said, "Courting?"

"It was all Will ever wanted," Josephine said. "Longford and a family. We used to go out there when he was a boy and he'd say, 'Aunt Josie, I'm going to have ten kids, five boys and five girls.' I guess it's common for only children to want big families."

Fanny shook her head sadly. "Poor Will," she said.

"I suppose he always blamed himself," Alice said. "For what happened to Hadley."

"It's in the past," Josephine said, glancing severely at Alice. "None of it matters now."

Outside the window a mockingbird sang sweetly. The sun slanted through the long windows, filling the room with light.

"Still, it was a tragic way to die. She was a beautiful girl. And so young."

"Such a lovely face," Fanny said dreamily. "So perfect on the outside."

And it wasn't until much later, alone in her room and waiting for her muse to find her, that Ava thought how curious that statement was.

Over the next two weeks, Ava worked with passionate and relentless determination. She had Charlie's character right now, she was sure of it, and that was propelling him toward his tragic end. She was still uncertain exactly who had done the killing, but she knew it had been murder. The story was unfolding as it should. It was only a matter of time before the true killer revealed him- or herself.

Caught up in her work, she had little time to worry about her social life. Jake didn't call. Will, eventually, did. She didn't press him, as Fraser had suggested she do. She didn't try to get him talking about what had happened between him and Jake. It seemed unimportant to her, and she was hesitant to break the uneasy peace that fell between them. It was easier to work when Will was appeased; it was easier to live undisturbed in the house with the aunts.

Will left her alone to work but when he did see her he seemed nervous, as if he realized that what was between them wasn't working but he was unwilling to let it go.

And Jake? Perhaps what everyone said was true; perhaps he was only a womanizer intent on conquest, and she had made it too difficult for him. Perhaps he had simply lost interest. Or maybe it was as he had intimated, that his guilt over once again pursuing Will's girl had proven too much for him.

Whatever his reasons, he didn't call.

It was all right with her. She had no time for anything but her work. Writing was the thing that drove her, the thing that gave meaning to her life. She realized that now. What had once been important she had put away for months, years while she worked dull day jobs in order to pay her rent. Because that was what happened if you weren't careful. You put away your treasure in order to live in the real world, and soon it became dusty, forgotten, something to be trotted out in blushing acknowledgment at cocktail parties. It became a hobby, like Will's music had become. The thing that had once given meaning to your life became diminished, small, something you could barely remember.

She could never be happy with the life Will offered. She saw that now. She could never be happy subjugating her life to his, disappearing into the role of wife, mother, keeper of the hearth. It wouldn't be enough for her. She was a writer. Her life turned on the rhythm of a sentence, a snatch of dialogue. Whole worlds opened at the thought of a young man, impoverished and alone in the world, returning to his ancestral home in search of love and redemption. Odysseus returning home to Penelope. Princess Sheelin returning home with the One True Pearl.

It was her mother's legacy to Ava, these stories. Writing was Ava's treasure, but the stories had been Clotilde's.

Every evening while the house slept around her, Ava worked. And then in early August, perhaps because of the strain she was feeling in her relationship with Will or the long hours she was working on her novel, the night terrors returned. She awoke on two consecutive nights to the sound of someone whispering her name. She lay there with her eyes wide, a sensation of dread prickling her scalp. The feeling that she was being watched, the sense that there was someone in the room with her was so intense that even after the paralysis subsided, she was afraid to turn her head to look. When she did, that first night, there was no one there.

But on the second night the feeling of vague unease continued, and as the paralysis waned she turned her head and caught something out of the corner of her eye, a dark fleeting figure that flickered and disappeared through the wall like a column of smoke.

Hippie Girl

Dear Ava—

I'm sorry to take so long with this. I've been thinking a lot about what I had to say and it seemed best to do it on the phone but I don't have your number. So I'll just have to write it. I'm not good at writing things down, so please forgive how messy this is. Also I can't spell worth a damn but you already know that.

I laughed when I read the part in your last letter about how Meg told you her and me met out at Boblo Island. I always called your mother Meg because that was her real name, Margaret Anne Govan. I never called her by any of those hippie names she liked to use. She was from Grosse Pointe, Michigan, and I'll get into all that in a minute. I have to write it down straight, just the way I'm thinking it. Otherwise I'll start to ramble and this will be twenty pages long.

The only time we were ever out at Boblo was when you were a baby and we went out there to hear Mitch Ryder and the Detroit Wheels. I met your mother at a Kmart parking lot. She was there with the Sunshine People. They were a bunch of hippies who traveled around the country in an old school bus painted with peace signs and flowers. They had parked their bus in the Kmart lot and they were *selling love beads. I walked by and saw your mother and it was love at first sight. I can tell you that. My heart just flopped around in my chest. She had long red-gold hair and she was wearing a white dress that fell to her ankles but it was kind of thin so I could see her shape right through it. She was the loveliest thing I'd ever seen.*

I was working at a machine shop in those days and I never looked back. I told my friends, you go on without me. I'm staying here. The Sunshine People took me in because that's how it was in those days. Flower Power and free love and all that shit. Excuse my French. It was, "Hi, how's it going, man? Want to go to California?" There were ten of us on that bus, six women and four men, and we were all a little in love with Meg. Dharma. That's the name she went by then, although I never called her anything but Meg.

She was a couple of years older than me. She'd been to college at Ann Arbor, although she'd dropped out without telling her parents when she hooked up with the Sunshine People. She was a rich girl, she was from Grosse Pointe, and her dad was a bigwig out at Ford. I don't know what her mother did. Spend money, Meg said. She was an only child. Raised in the lap of luxury with every privilege. There was bad blood between Meg and her dad; she never told me why, but she wouldn't talk about him, and maybe that's why she never saw her parents. I got a call years after we parted from some private investigator her dad had hired to track her down. He didn't get shit out of me. Bastard.

The six months I spent traveling around the country with your mother and the Sunshine People were the happiest days of my life. I won't lie to you. I still think of those carefree times now that I've got a mortgage and a wife and three kids to feed. Did I tell you I had three kids? Tom, he's sixteen, Ralphie, he's twelve, and little Lorie, she's ten.

Your mother was a storyteller. I guess you know that. We'd sit around the fire at night and she'd tell stories that made you shiver with fear or cry with sadness. She had a good heart. She was always looking out for others, always looking out for the underdog. She couldn't stand to see anyone picked on. Once outside a convenience store in Topeka she saw a man beating a tethered dog. She hit this guy in the back with a camp stove and knocked him down, and then she stood over him, flailing away with a bag of hot dog buns and shouting, "How do you like it, huh? How do you like it?"

It was the funniest thing I ever saw. She was small but she was crazy. I loved her. You have to know that. It wasn't my idea that we part.

Still, she was a difficult woman to live with. She had her own way of looking at things, and she didn't like anyone telling her what to do. She had her dark days, too, just like the rest of us. She used to cry out in her sleep, and she would wake up whimpering and wouldn't let anyone comfort her. Would just sit there with her knees drawn up against her chest rocking back and forth and whimpering, and if you tried to touch her she'd bare her teeth and hiss and claw like a scalded cat. I still don't know what that was all about.

When you came along, she changed. A lot of the wildness seemed to go out of her. You asked me if I knew who your real father was, and I have to say, honestly, I don't. Meg never told me. Still, I had my suspicions. I'm happy to talk about what I know, but I don't feel right writing it down in a letter.

Call me if you want to talk about this. My number's 313-886-5105.

Frank

p.s. Thanks for sending along a photo. Funny, how you look like her.

Coming as it did during a period of intense work on her novel, the letter only added to Ava's fairy-tale view of reality. Shut up in the old house, Ava found herself working feverishly every night, long into the early hours of the morning, the words *"Help me"* echoing in her head. Time seemed to move now in swoops and snatches; it had lost its linear arrangement. Perhaps it was the thick drowsy heat of August that made her feel as if she was moving through an underwater world.

"A rich girl," the letter had said. Clotilde had been "raised in the lap of luxury with every privilege." It was almost laughable. Certainly ironic. Ava thought of all the times she had done battle with irate landlords and debt collectors, the nights she had lain awake wondering if they would be homeless, if there would be money for school lunches and electricity bills. She thought of her ruined childhood, the stubbornly responsible character she had become so that her mother could remain carefree and childish. ("Oh Ava, don't fret. Everything will turn out fine—you'll see!") All those years of worry and want and desperation, when all Clotilde ever had to do was pick up the phone and call her rich father.

Ava walked over to the mantel and picked up Clotilde's vase. She held it above her head as if she might dash it against the floor. She said fiercely, "Why?" She said, "It wasn't fair."

She sprawled facedown on the bed, weeping for her lost childhood, her lost mother. Outside the windows, the clatter of the cicadas soothed her. The summer heat flowed through her drowsy limbs. After a while she fell into a fitful sleep.

She dreamed she was running through a dark forest. The trees were so thick she couldn't see the sky, and she was lost. There was something pursuing her—she could hear it crashing through the brush behind her—and as she looked down in terror she saw a red serpent underfoot. She couldn't help but step on it, and as she did, it swung around and sank its teeth into her flesh. There was a moment of excruciating pain, then she opened her eyes and noticed a light streaming through the trees, which were opening before her like a golden path.

She awoke with a start. The sky outside the window was a violet gray. She thought of the story Clotilde had told her all those years ago, the story of the Princess Sheelin who goes to the bottom of the sea searching for the One True Pearl. The girl who falls into a deep, mindless sleep until a messenger from her father wakens her and reminds her of her destiny. Reminds her who she truly is.

Somewhere out in the world there were Govan grandparents. Somewhere out in the world there was a flesh-and-blood father waiting for her to find him.

Two days later, she got a call from Rachel Rowe. Ava was on the verandah with Maitland and Fanny but Rachel sounded so excited that she excused herself and went into the house, closing her bedroom door behind her.

"Okay," Ava said. "Shoot."

"Well, you know how I've been going through the Woodburn family papers given to Vanderbilt? And let me tell you, that has been some chore. There are literally enough boxes to fill a semitruck, and most of them have been rearranged and pilfered by researchers and grad students."

"Rachel? What did you find?"

"I'm getting to that. There's a senior researcher there, Alice Atkinson, who I've known for years. She's very knowledgeable about the Woodburn collection, and she's the one who's been combing through documents with me looking for a deed from Colonel Woodburn to Charlie Woodburn. We literally went through every document and couldn't find anything. No deed, no letters mentioning Charlie other than the ones the Colonel wrote to the president of Vanderbilt recommending Charlie for admission. Nothing else.

"Just when I was ready to give up, Alice mentioned a couple of boxes in storage that contained odds and ends, family memorabilia, receipts, stuff they didn't know where to catalogue. I started going through the first box yesterday and within a couple of hours I had found it."

"A deed," Ava said, breathing slowly. "You found a deed giving Charlie Longford."

"No. Not a deed. A letter. From Colonel Woodburn's attorney." She hesitated and Ava could hear the shuffling of paper. "A Mr. Atwood. That was the attorney's name. Anyway, the letter was from him to Josephine. It was dated a few weeks after the Colonel's death. And there's a part that says, hang on, I'll find it." She was quiet for a moment and then continued, " 'Per our conversation in my office prior to the reading of the will and your later instructions, I have destroyed the document. The document,' " Rachel repeated, her voice trembling. "Get it? It must have been the deed they're talking about. The deed the

Colonel had mentioned in his journal. The Colonel had Atwood draw up a deed prior to his death, but it was never properly recorded. Or maybe never even signed. Maybe the Colonel was on his way to his attorney's office the day he dropped dead in the street. And later, when Atwood discussed the deed with Josephine, she instructed him to destroy it. Which would make sense because, from what you've said, she didn't like Charlie. She wouldn't have wanted him to inherit anything that belonged to her or her sisters."

"What was the date on the letter?"

"November 14. It was addressed to Josephine via a Mrs. Stillwell's boardinghouse."

"So it was after Fanny eloped with Charlie."

"Yes, a week or so after." They were both quiet a moment, then Rachel said, "Do you think Charlie knew about the deed? Do you think the Colonel told him about it before he died?"

"Yes. I do."

"Then that would mean that Charlie knew he'd been cheated out of something promised to him. And it might explain why he eloped with Fanny."

"Yes," Ava said quietly.

Rachel sighed. "There's a lot we don't know for sure, a lot we'll probably never know. You don't think we're reaching?"

"It makes a good story," Ava said. It made perfect sense, the pieces falling easily into place. Josephine's smoldering hatred of Charlie exploded into open warfare between the two of them. Charlie would have known he'd been cheated at the reading of the Colonel's will, although he may not have known who it was who cheated him, the Colonel or Josephine. It would not have mattered to him.

She remembered that Will had told her the Colonel was the last to use the plantation ledgers. He was wrong about that. In the final journal she had found a page at the end with a cryptic message written in a modern hand.

Goddamn them all to hell. Every last lying, cheating one of them. They'll rue the day they crossed me.

She felt Charlie Woodburn's presence everywhere in the house. She felt a connection to him, and that connection was evidenced by the words that flowed from her fingertips onto the screen.

And then one evening a curious thing happened.

She had fallen asleep with her head slumped on the desk, and she awoke suddenly and sat rigidly upright, listening. The room was frigid. Condensation fogged the windows. She had fallen into a deep sleep with no warning or recollection. The computer screen had gone black; the room was lit only by the dull glow of the lamp at the corner of the desk. She had been dreaming of something unpleasant, something that left an ódd sensation of a tingling scalp and raised hair at the nape of her neck.

She rose like a sleepwalker and extended her arm to turn off the lamp, and it was then, at the precise moment when the room was plunged into absolute darkness, that she felt, quite clearly and distinctly, someone take her hand.

1931

Woodburn, Tennessee

"You're a fortune-teller. Tell me my fortune, old woman."
"Beware of dark water," Martha said.

He could have had the other one, the other sister. He had known that from the night on the train, when he first played the jazz clarinet for an appreciative audience of planters' sons and bankers' sons, and, walking by her seat and leaning to speak to her, he'd seen her face flush. He'd known then that he could have her, if he wanted her.

And yet when the time came, he'd hesitated, which wasn't like him. She was too much like the Old Man, the one who'd cheated him of his inheritance, as their branch of the family had been cheating his since the days of the Old Patriarch, Randal Woodburn. He could have her, but could he keep her down, or would she figure out a way to outsmart him in the end, as her father had done?

Tuition paid at Vanderbilt and a handful of stained letters that would have secured for him nothing more than a clerking job in some dusty little town. The Old Man had promised more. He had promised Longford. He'd taken him home, introduced him to his daughters, taken him around to his club. Charlie had expected a stake, a pot of money he could take down to the gambling dens along Frenchmen Street and turn into something large enough to live on until his luck changed. He had already figured out what to do with Longford, although it was clear the Old Man hadn't seen much value in it or he wouldn't have offered it to him. But Charlie had seen its dilapidated state, its secluded location, and realized it would make the perfect juke joint and gambling den. Outside the town limits but not too far to make it a difficult drive.

But then the Old Man had died and he'd gotten nothing but paid tuition and a handful of dusty letters of reference. Then Charlie had had to rearrange his plans. He'd gone back to Vanderbilt feeling cheated, knowing he could have her, Josephine, if he wanted her. But not wanting her either. By then he was tired of it all, the whole charade of pretending to be someone he wasn't, of playing up to the spoiled rich sons of men who'd risen in life by cheating and stealing from the unwary and innocent, just as he was willing to do. Men who'd married for money, just as he was prepared to do. These men had done it for their children, for their sons, just as he was willing to do for his.

King. "Don't call him that," Myrtle had said. "Don't give a crippled boy a name like King." It had nearly broken his heart to hear her talk like that, a man who didn't think he had a heart left to break. A man who had never known what love and self-sacrifice was until he looked down into the innocent milky eyes of his little son.

Not that he felt that way about the mother, of course. He'd met Myrtle at a juke joint down by the stockyards, the kind of place drifters and drummers and hotel gadflies frequent to find girls who like to have a good time. It was during that long summer he'd spent living in Woodburn and trying to convince the Old Man that he was worthy of saving, that the Woodburn blood ran true and blue in his veins. The summer when he'd nearly died of boredom and had to break loose every once in a while down at the stockyards with a girl like Myrtle.

King was an unwelcome surprise, at first, a possible wreckage of his plans. But when he'd looked at his son, so small, so twisted in body and yet so fine in spirit, so much like the boy he, himself, must have once been before poverty and hardship took their toll, he'd known that he would do anything to make his life better. Anything. Even pretend to accept a life he didn't want to live. Even marry for money.

He'd gone back to Vanderbilt determined to have his revenge. But when he'd thought about marrying Josephine, he'd wavered. And several days later, when he'd gone up to Mrs. Stillwell's to check on Fanny and she, without ever considering the impropriety of her actions, had taken him up to her room and he'd seen the doll lying on her bed, he'd known with a cool certainty what he must do. He was surprised he'd not thought of it before. She had always seemed such a child to him. But now, watching her flitter about the room, he saw how pretty she was, how soft and yielding, so unlike the other sister, Josephine.

He could punish the older sister by choosing the younger one. Because he knew by now that Josephine loved him; he'd seen it in her foolish face. And it had been so easy, too, once he decided what he'd do, to include Fanny in his plans. All it had taken was a promise to take her home, back to Woodburn to the house where she had grown up.

And in nearly two years since then he'd had no reason to regret his choice. She cared nothing for the money; he could spend it as he pleased. And when the money ran out, he'd start selling off the furniture and fixtures, all the precious Woodburn possessions that made them who they were and him who he was not. Josephine might question his actions, but what could she do? She was helpless. Fanny was his wife. He could do with her as he pleased.

And therein lay another benefit to this arrangement, a benefit he had not foreseen. He could punish Josephine by lifting his hand to Fanny. She never said a word, just took it quietly, patiently, but Josephine went around the house with her eyes red and weary from crying at her helplessness. She would kill him if she thought she could get away with it. This brought him a certain grim satisfaction.

But he had to be careful, too. Fanny would let him beat her to death, and if he wasn't careful he might give in to this sweet urge one night and, in a drunken rage, do something he might live to regret.

She spent all her waking hours trying to decide how to kill him. It was amazing to Josephine now that she had ever loved him. Those days seemed so long ago; she was such a naive girl then, so unaware of the brutality of life. After the elopement she had stayed at Vanderbilt to take her degree in art history, traveling around that first summer to visit relatives because she couldn't bear to return home, where Fanny and Charlie had taken up residence. Charlie had never returned to school. He had tried to obtain money in exchange for the tuition Papa had agreed to pay, and when that didn't work, he'd simply spent Fanny's money. The cousins spoke of it incessantly the summer that Josephine traveled among them, gossiping about the money Charlie Woodburn was going through, the wild parties he threw, the gamblers and bootleggers said to frequent the house. In those days Josephine retained enough of her feelings for Charlie to defend him, to insist that Fanny would never have married, or stayed married to, a man of such low character.

But now she had graduated from Vanderbilt and come home and seen for herself that they were right. That it was even worse than they had imagined. Fanny, swollen and listless with pregnancy, spent most of her days sleeping in her room, her cat purring on her pillow. Charlie was drunk most of the time, sleeping the day away and waking just before evening. You would know he was up by the clink of bottles in his room. And he wasn't always alone either. Josephine had, on more than one occasion, glanced into the room behind him and seen the pale outline of a woman's arm nestled in the bedclothes. That had shocked her, as had the state of the house. So much had shocked her in those days before she'd become accustomed to all the ways human beings can find to degrade themselves. Now nothing shocked her.

Martha was too sick to cook and care for the house. She would not allow Clara to set foot inside, so Josephine took over the daily running of the house, refusing to hire outside help, afraid that the rumors already trickling through town would run rampant. That was how she discovered that some of the silver was missing, a sterling silver urn given to one of her ancestors by Lighthorse Harry Lee to commemorate the Battle of Paulus Hook, and a silver christening cup said to have been given to Randal Woodburn by his godfather, Thomas Jefferson. When she asked Fanny, she seemed confused and said vaguely, "Oh, I don't know. I'm sure they're here somewhere." There was a dark bruise on one of her shoulders. "Bumped it on the edge of the tub," she said blithely. "I'm as big as a horse now, and it's hard to get in and out."

Josephine believed her because she was naive in those days, and the terrible truth would not have occurred to her. But she was learning. In June she threatened to call the constable over a party that had dragged on into the small hours of the evening and Charlie, in a fit of rage, drove his fist into the wall beside her head. She had not flinched but it had taken every ounce of courage she had; the threat of violence hung so heavy in the air that she felt sick and light-headed.

The truth dawned on her gradually.

She went upstairs to Fanny's room and drew back the covers. Her sister's frail, swollen body made her weep.

"Hush," Fanny said. "He'll hear you."

Josephine went back down the stairs, raging, but he was gone, following the party out. She waited all night and when he did not return she went across the garden to the little cottage where John, Martha, and Clara lived. They confirmed what Josephine already knew, surprised it had taken her so long to realize the truth. When she began to rage, John reminded her quietly, "She's his wife. He can do with her what he pleases."

Going out again, Clara followed her and pushed a horrid-looking doll into her hand. It was made of burlap and covered in several strands of dark, silky hair. A hatpin had been driven through its chest, through the middle of a crudely drawn heart. "Show him this and he'll leave you alone," Clara said.

Josephine kissed her and gently returned the doll. "You keep it," she said.

She was glad now that she'd sent Celia to live with Minnie's family in Bell Buckle.

When Charlie got home two days later, he was not alone. He had the crippled child, King, with him, and the boy's mother. They sat in the breakfast room, a bottle of whiskey on the table between them.

They'd given the boy a glass of buttermilk and corn bread, and he was drinking out of Randal Woodburn's silver christening cup.

"That belongs to me," Josephine said, standing in the doorway.

Charlie glanced at her, his eyes narrowing as he looked away from the boy. "It's mine as much as yours," he said.

"No," she said, lifting her chin. "It's not." And when he didn't answer she said, "Get them out of here."

He stood so quickly she only had time to step back against the pantry door. He crossed the room in long strides, putting his hands on either side of her head and leaning in so close she could smell the whiskey and tobacco on his breath.

"You can't hit me," she said. "I'm not your wife."

"Thank God," he said.

"Thank God."

Later, as he climbed the stairs to Fanny's room, he looked at her and grinned, and Josephine felt her stomach clench with hatred and despair. She went to Papa's room then and rummaged around in the armoire for his shotgun, but Charlie had obviously taken it. He had probably sold it.

Now she spent all her time thinking about how to kill him. She could tell Maitland, who loved Fanny so much he'd never come home from Sewanee after she married, staying to gather one degree after another. Maitland would do it. Or she could tell the cousins, who had long hated Charlie for taking advantage of Fanny and squandering the family fortune and good name. They would do it themselves or hire it out to some gangster from New Orleans or Memphis.

But on her good days, Josephine knew she had too much of Papa in her to ever let someone else do her dirty work for her. She would do it. Still, she would need help. An accomplice. She sat down and wrote a long letter to Maitland, telling him what was happening.

The result, she knew, would be tragic but inevitable.

The Progress of Love

The incident of the strange hand stayed with Ava, hovering always at the edge of her consciousness as she went about her daily routine, dazed and stuporous. It had obviously been a hallucination brought on by the sleep disorder, yet it had seemed so real, the texture of the skin, the slight pressure of the fingers, that even now, thinking about it, Ava shivered.

The lack of sleep was beginning to affect her in odd ways. She was always catching shadows out of the corners of her eyes, hearing strange sounds in the house even during daylight hours: whispers, plaintive snatches of jazz, footsteps on the stairs. Twice, when she was alone in the house, she heard knocking and went to the front door only to find that no one was there. And yet she was afraid to see a doctor for a prescription, afraid the medication would increase the hallucinations or, worse, dampen her creative urge, slow the torrent of work that seemed to occur every night now like automatic writing. At the rate she was working, the novel would be finished by the end of August. She couldn't let anything interfere with its progress. She often had the feeling she was rushing toward something, some amorphous conclusion that kept her working relentlessly, regardless of its effect on her health.

And yet when Fraser invited her to go shopping with him and Alice in Nashville, Ava gratefully accepted. She was exhausted, and needed an excuse to get out of the house and away from her desk, away from the increasingly silent Will and his vague air of disappointment and regret.

They picked her up early one Thursday morning in Alice's antique Chevrolet. Ava sat in the backseat and listened absently as mother and son kept up a steady stream of banter like an old vaudeville act. They shopped for a while at the Galleria, where Fraser helped Ava pick out a new purse ("You look like a bag lady with that horrible thing you carry") and his mother a new dress and matching pumps ("Seriously, Mother, get out of the Keds and tennis suits!").

"I don't know what I ever did without you to tell me how to dress," Alice said in a deadpan voice.

"Suffered unfashionably, I suppose."

They stopped for lunch at a small tearoom in Brentwood. It was on a block of antique shops and clothing boutiques crowded with well-dressed shoppers.

"Hard to believe all this used to be farmland," Alice said with a heavy sigh, gazing around the room with an expression of dismay. "Nothing but rolling hills as far as the eye could see. Two of my great-great-grandfather's plantations, The Grove and Nott Hill, were not far from here."

"Back in the good old days," Fraser said to Ava, rolling his eyes.

"Well, they were the good old days," Alice said sharply, then chuckled softly. "At least they were for some of us."

"Yes, yes, Ava knows all about the long-vanquished Southern aristocracy. I've told her about the Captain and his lovely ways."

Alice gave him a stern look. "Fraser, you really shouldn't speak badly of the family."

"You see," he said to Ava. "We southern WASPs are not overly religious people but we do practice ancestor worship as devotionally as any Shinto practitioner."

"Oh, Fraser, really," Alice said. The waitress came and took their orders and brought them tall, frosty glasses of sweet tea.

"Did you talk to Will about making nice with Jake?" Fraser asked, helping himself to a basket of scones. Ava shot him a warning glance but he laughed and said, "Oh, don't worry, I told Alice about our conversation. I tell Alice *everything.*"

"I'll have to remember that," Ava said mildly.

Alice looked uncomfortable. She took the basket from Fraser with a little shake of her head. "Where are your manners?" she said, passing the scones to Ava. "Would you like one, honey?"

"No, thank you," Ava said. Her appetite had diminished over the past few weeks.

Alice set the scones down. "I hope you don't mind Fraser confiding in me," she said. "We are almost family, after all. At least I feel we almost are." She colored, then went on blithely. "There are no secrets between family."

"Really?" Ava said. "In that case, tell me what happened to Charlie Woodburn." ·

Fraser laughed loudly. Bright spots of color appeared on either side of Alice's nose. "What happened to him?" she repeated vaguely.

"How did he die?"

"Rather suddenly," Alice said valiantly. "He was so sick, throwing up blood and hallucinating. He kept seeing his dead mother everywhere. He wouldn't let anyone call a doctor, of course; he didn't believe in doctors. Stubborn and pigheaded up until the very end."

"I thought he drowned," Ava said.

"Who told you that?" Alice asked sharply.

"Will."

Fraser put his chin on his hand and gave his mother a slight, mocking smile.

"Well, yes," she said quickly. "He was found in the water, that's true. Out in the Harpeth River on the way to Longford. You know the Harpeth, it flows through town. There's a bridge at the end of the street where we live that actually crosses it." Fraser continued to smile at her, one eyebrow raised. Ava said nothing, waiting patiently for her to continue.

"Anyway, he was found in the river but there was an empty bottle in his pocket and he reeked of whiskey. Even after being in the water, he reeked. There was some conjecture at the time that he might have stumbled out of Woodburn Hall and, intoxicated, lost his way in the dark and fallen into the river. In those days there were no streetlamps at the end of the road, only a one-lane bridge, and he may have become disoriented and fallen in. That would explain him being found down-river near Longford."

"You say he was hallucinating the week prior to his death?"

"Yes, he was very sick. I saw him. It was truly dreadful. The hallucinations could have been brought on by fever. Or by delirium tremens, I suppose."

"Had he had these episodes before?" Ava asked.

"I really don't know. Understand, at the time, his elopement with Fanny was considered scandalous. His living under the same roof as Fanny and Josephine was even worse. My mother wouldn't allow me near that house. I had to sneak over to see them. And Josephine, well, poor Josephine suffered terribly, because how could she expect to make a good marriage after all that scandal? They were so isolated, the two of them, shut up in the house alone with Charlie. No friends, no family, no visitors. Just the riffraff Charlie associated with. And he was a vio-lent man. He carried a pearl-handled derringer like the riverboat gam-blers used to carry. I was terrified of him."

This was not the Charlie Woodburn of Ava's novel. He had been misunderstood and mistreated by life, forced into a role he was un-trained for in a society that constantly devalued him. Ava had imagined him as a lonely, Christlike figure, yet she knew that truth was subjec-tive, that it was only natural that Alice, Maitland's sister, would see Charlie differently. She remembered Will's assertion that Charlie had beaten Fanny. But that could have been something constructed later by the family to explain his murder. To justify it. Somewhere between the man Alice remembered, the man Will had been told about, and the man Ava had imagined lay the real Charlie Woodburn.

Ava said, "Celia had gone to live with a cousin after her father's death, but why didn't the cousins keep an eye on Fanny and Josephine, too? Why did the family turn their collective backs on them?"

"Because Charlie wouldn't allow them to set foot in the house! He was Fanny's husband, and in those days that meant something. He could do with her as he pleased, and no one could lift a finger because they were legally married. He would have thrown Josephine out, too, if she'd been less determined, but she would never have agreed to leave Fanny."

"What about Clara? She was in the house with them, too, wasn't she?"

"She lived in the cottage out back with her parents, Martha and John. But Martha was sick by then. She couldn't come up to the house and work, and John wouldn't allow Clara in the house. Charlie seemed to take particular pleasure in tormenting her. He would curse her and threaten to take a horsewhip to her father, who was a proud man, a prominent member of the African-American community."

"You said Charlie was a violent man. Did you ever hear of him physically abusing Fanny?"

"Good Lord," Alice said, gazing at her with an expression of alarm. "Of course not. Josephine would never have allowed that. Maitland would never have allowed it." She took a long drink of iced tea, set her glass down again with a slight frown. She dabbed her mouth with her napkin. "Of course, such things did happen in those days but mainly among the—" She paused. "Mainly among other families, but not those along River Road."

The waitress brought their food and they ate for a while in silence.

Fraser touched his mouth with his napkin and smiled at Ava. "You did a very nice job of changing the subject but you still haven't told us how your talk with Will went."

"I don't really want to talk about it."

"That well?"

"Fraser, be quiet," Alice said.

Fraser waved his hand at the waitress and ordered a round of gin and tonics.

"It won't work," Ava said. "I don't like gin."

"Well, Missy, we're going to sit here until you tell us, so you might as well spill it." Ava stared at him obstinately until he said, "Okay. I'll start. What did Will say about your secret visit to Jake Woodburn's wood shop?"

Ava was dismayed to feel her face flushing. "I've already told you. He wasn't happy about it. And it wasn't a secret visit."

Alice chuckled.

"Now we're getting somewhere," Fraser said.

"He doesn't much like Jake, for obvious reasons, and he doesn't want me hanging out with him."

"The obvious reasons, I suppose, have to do with Hadley Marsh. What does he say about her?"

"Not much. He admits that she's dead."

Fraser giggled. "That's a start," he said.

"But other than that, he'd prefer not to talk about her."

"Well, of course he does," Alice said. "It was so tragic." She waved one hand vaguely and picked up her iced tea. "All of that."

"Tragic because they both fell in love with Hadley or tragic because she died?" Fraser asked.

"Both," Alice said, regarding him evenly over the rim of her glass.

"What's Jake's story?" Ava said, folding and refolding her napkin in her lap. "Has he ever been married? Girlfriend?"

"He keeps to himself, which makes him all the more desirable," Fraser said. "I think he turns down invitations and refuses to socialize because it makes him more mysterious."

"But *could* he socialize? Would he be accepted?"

"Of course," Fraser said. "He went to the right schools, he has the right pedigree. No one cares anymore that his branch of the family crawled out of the woodpile."

Alice sniffed. "Well, some care," she said.

"*Most* don't care," Fraser said. "Those old social customs that kept his grandfather down don't apply anymore, thank God. I think Jake's criticized more for the fact that he doesn't seem to give a damn about dinner parties and joining the country club than for his obscure beginnings. By holding out he makes society feel bad about itself. How great can those things be if someone like Jake doesn't want to join? And he's a great-looking guy, you've seen that for yourself," he said, slanting his eyes at Ava. "But he has a tendency to love the ladies and then leave them, which, of course, makes everyone nervous. No husband wants a guy as good-looking as Jake Woodburn on the loose."

"So he has dated women in town?"

"He's not gay, if that's what you're asking. Unfortunately."

"Fraser, please," Alice said, looking around at the other tables with an air of apology.

The waitress brought their gin and tonics.

Ava thought of the photo she had found in Will's room. "Hadley must have been some girl to have both Will and Jake fall for her."

"Well, she was gorgeous."

"Of course she was."

Fraser laughed. "Don't say it like that," he said. "You don't need to feel intimidated by Hadley Marsh. She didn't have your depth, your strength of character, your *loyalty*. Did she, Mother?"

"Oh, heavens no," Alice said. "There's no comparison at all."

Ava made a wry mouth and Fraser laughed again. "Loyalty" was not a word they would use to describe her in the future. Not if her novel was ever published.

"You two are polar opposites," Fraser said, continuing his comparison of Ava to Hadley.

"Apples and oranges," Alice agreed, happy now that the waitress had brought their drinks.

Working late at night in the dark, sleeping house, Ava was vigilant now, listening for the creak of footsteps, quiet sighs, vague knockings behind the walls. She no longer switched on the lamp. She had not touched it since that evening when it felt like someone, or something, took her hand. She was accustomed to the occasional late-night hallucination but the horror of that moment had imprinted itself upon her mind in ghastly detail. She would not risk it again.

She wrote now by the light of her computer screen, crawling wearily into bed in a room illuminated by its dull, glowing light. The writing continued unabated; nothing seemed to interfere with that. She was quickly approaching the climax, and she knew now with a fair degree of certainty who had killed Charlie. It had come to her in the days following her trip to Nashville with Fraser and Alice. Some offhand comment made by Alice had brought the murderer's motive suddenly and clearly into focus. From that point on, everything fell into place. It was all so clear now. She was astounded that she had not seen it before.

Toward the end of August, she got a call from Jake.

"I have something for you," he said. His voice sounded curt, distant.

"Oh?"

"A photo."

"I'm listening."

"My mother found it in some old things she had." And when Ava didn't respond, he said more soberly, "A photo of Charlie Woodburn."

Ava was quiet, bracing herself. In light of her novel's ending, she wasn't sure she wanted to see it. But how could she refuse? "I'd like to see it," she said.

"Come by the shop tomorrow afternoon," he said, and hung up before she could say anything else.

The Traveling Wilburys were playing "End of the Line" on the CD player when Ava stepped into Jake's workshop. Light slanted through the tall windows set at regular intervals along the brick walls. There was a pleasant scent of pine and cedar in the air. Jake was standing at his worktable in the center of the room, hand-sanding the legs of a delicate-looking chair. He glanced up at Ava as she came through the door.

"So you made it," he said. His hair was darker, longer than she remembered.

"Yes."

"Do you want something to drink?"

"No. Thanks."

"Let me finish this and we'll go upstairs." He went back to work, covered, as usual, by a light dusting of wood shavings. Ava wandered around the shop admiring his work, stopping to examine ornate fragments of fretwork and scrap.

Jake seemed absorbed in what he was doing, yet she had the feeling he was very much aware of her, following her progress with guarded eyes.

"I'll be done in a minute," he said. His hands moved along the chair legs as gently as a lover's caress.

This thought made her stir; she roused herself and said, "I don't want to keep you. Do you have the photo?"

He stood and wiped his brow with his wrist. "Are you in a hurry?"

She raised one hand, vaguely indicating the door behind her. "I have work to do," she said.

He tossed the sandpaper down and strode toward her, walking in such a purposeful and determined way that she stepped back instinctively, striking the edge of a table with her hip.

He put his hand out to steady her. "Careful," he said.

"Thank you," she said politely, formally.

He looked her in the face. "I had thought, after our last meeting, that I might see you again," he said.

"I had the impression, after our last meeting, that you did *not* want to see me."

"It seems we've misread each other."

"It would seem that way."

He let her go, and walked ahead of her toward the narrow iron stairway in the corner of the room. She could still feel the warm pressure of his fingers on her arm.

"Where are you going?" she said.

He turned and looked at her. Their eyes locked. "The photo's up here. In my apartment." She hesitated and, seeing that, he grinned suddenly and put his hand on his chest.

"I'll be on my best behavior," he said. "I promise."

She followed him up the circular stairs to a small, neat apartment above the shop. The room was filled with his whimsical furniture. A low sofa stood along a brick wall, opposite a galley kitchen. On another wall hung a pop-art print of a beautiful woman's face. Hadley.

"Very nice," Ava said stiffly.

"Do you like it? I did it years ago." She swiveled her head and looked at him but his expression was bland, noncommittal. He went into the kitchen and took two bottled waters from the refrigerator.

Ava stood carefully examining Hadley. She seemed to be staring at Ava with a sly, mocking expression as if she found her presence here highly entertaining. Looking into her eyes, Ava felt as if she was intruding on something intensely personal, as if she was the brunt of some private joke.

Jake tapped her lightly on the shoulder and she startled, taking a bottle from him.

"I can't stay long," she said in a wooden voice.

"Oh. Well, then, I won't keep you." His manner changed abruptly and he set his water down on the coffee table and went into the bedroom to get the photo.

Whatever ease she had felt between them had disappeared under Hadley's sly, knowing gaze. Why, despite everything that had happened, had he kept this reminder of her? Was it an act of defiance or one of tenderness? She turned and walked over to the window, staring down at the leafy street.

He came back a few minutes later carrying a faded black-and-white photograph. She sat down on the sofa and he sat down beside her. He passed her the photo. She stared down at it, feeling a catch in her throat. The photo showed a tall, earnest-looking young man with dark swept-back hair. His face was startling in its resemblance to Randal Woodburn, the patriarch. All but the eyes, which were dark and filled with an intensity bordering on mania. He was dressed in evening clothes and there was an air of studied elegance in his pose, something compelling and yet false, too.

"Handsome devil, wasn't he?" He was so close she could feel his breath on her cheek, warm and sweet.

"Where did you find this?"

"My mother found it in my father's things."

"I don't suppose I can have a copy."

"Take this one," he said. "I don't need it." He leaned forward, resting his elbows on his knees. His T-shirt stretched across his wide shoulders, exposing his back, and she could see the faint line of downy hair at the base of his spine.

"What did you mean?" he asked.

"Sorry?"

"Downstairs." He turned his head and looked at her. "When you said you thought I didn't want to see you again."

She was quiet for a moment, thinking how best to begin. "I don't know. You seemed to change when Will called. As if you were suddenly sorry I was here."

"Baggage," he said. "Not knowing if I was stepping in between Will and someone he cared about. Again."

"I told you we were just friends."

He smiled, nodding his head. "So you did," he said.

"I had the impression you wanted me to leave."

"You were wrong."

The windows of the room had no shutters or blinds, and the sun fell through unimpeded, the crowns of the tall trees outside making lacy patterns on the glass. Books spilled out of the bookcases and were stacked in piles on the glossy wood floor. There were no rugs. The room was clean and neat but spare. A bachelor space. Ava stared at the photo, aware of the faint traffic sounds on the street and the dense silence that drifted between them. It was shocking, looking into a face she had seen so often in her imagination.

"Have you told Will yet that you're writing a novel about his family?" He leaned back cautiously, his shoulder nearly touching hers.

"It's not about his family. Not really. I mean, there are some similarities."

"Have you told him?"

"No."

There was a hole in his jeans just above one knee and he poked his fingers in and began to pull threads through the opening. "Because if you're hoping to build something with Will, if you're planning—" He stopped and continued to shove his fingers into the frayed hole, pulling loose threads free.

"I'm not planning anything with Will," she said. "We're friends. That's all."

"They'll consider a novel about Charlie Woodburn a betrayal," he said calmly, as if he hadn't heard her. "It doesn't matter how you write it or how it ends. They'll blame you for bringing up the buried past."

"I know that."

"No matter how pretty and charming you are." There was a faint cleft in his chin, visible through the stubble of beard. "No matter how fetchingly you blush."

"I'm not blushing."

He grinned slowly.

"Besides, isn't it hypocritical of you to warn me about betraying the Woodburns, given your past history?"

"Do as I say, not as I did." He leaned over and drank from his bottle, then set it down again on the coffee table.

Neither one moved, sitting companionably in a silence that seemed less awkward now. Outside the window the sun slid behind a ridge of clouds, causing a swift succession of shadows to fall across the floor. On the wall to their left, Hadley stared benignly, smirking.

"She was very pretty," Ava said.

"I suppose so."

Jake put his arm across the back of the sofa. She could feel the warmth of his hand, just inches from her skin. "Does Will ever mention Hadley?"

"He doesn't like to talk about her."

He smiled, his eyes fierce and black. "No, he wouldn't. He's not much of a talker."

Ava felt disloyal talking about Will. "I don't think he's particularly happy about your—estrangement, as Josephine calls it."

"Well, he hasn't exactly tried to do anything about it."

"Have you?"

"Yes. At first. I tried for years."

She was quiet for a moment, looking down at the photo of Charlie. "I think he feels guilty, not only over the trouble between you and him, but also over Hadley's death."

"That wasn't his fault. That wasn't anyone's fault but Hadley's."

She slid the photo into her purse. "Did you love her?"

He sighed and shook his head. "I suppose I did," he said.

"So you weren't just going after her because she was Will's girlfriend?"

He met her gaze, giving her a long, searching look. "If you believe that you must not think very highly of me."

She could feel the heat of his arm like a phantom limb, an extension of herself. "Sorry," she said, looking down. "I know you wouldn't do that." The sun was back, glittering along the floor. In the street a truck passed, rattling the windows. "What was she like?"

"Hadley? Well, there was the person she wanted you to see and then there was the other one."

"I'm not sure I understand."

"No. You wouldn't," he said fondly, and he touched her now, lightly squeezing her shoulder. The shock of his touch was palpable, arousing. "She was from Birmingham, the youngest of six. Her father was a housepainter."

"A housepainter?" She gave a half-laugh, an expression of surprise. "She went to boarding school. I would have thought she was part of the ruling elite."

"She was a scholarship kid. Like me. There were a lot of us, and we tried desperately to fit in but in the long run, of course, we didn't. I was lucky. I could bring friends home to Woodburn Hall. Will and I told everyone we were orphaned cousins being raised by our great-aunts, and of course that was true except for the fact that my mother was still alive. I saw her when I was home, but I never took friends from school home with me. You know how you care about things like that when you're fifteen. I was lucky Will and Fanny and Josephine let me pretend to be one of them."

"You *are* one of them."

He laughed. "You haven't been here long enough to understand that I'm not. I'm an impostor. A cuckoo in a magpie's nest."

"Fanny and Josephine are genuinely fond of you."

"And I so wanted to be one of them."

"Did they like Hadley?"

"Of course, everybody liked Hadley. She made herself very— agreeable. It was a knack she had. And she was impressed by the Woodburns, too, the family, the history, the money."

"So what happened between you two?"

He put his head back against the sofa and looked at the ceiling. His profile in the slash of sunlight was strong, austere. "Have you ever been in love?"

"Yes." She hesitated. "Twice."

"In the beginning we were just friends. When she first came up to Sewanee that's all it was. But over time, things changed. There was an attraction that we both tried to ignore. Things had always been rocky between her and Will. From the very beginning. So when she came to me and told me they had broken up, I believed her."

"And you started dating her then? Thinking she and Will were broken up?"

"Yes."

"You can't be blamed for that."

"I never asked Will. I never saw fit to question what Hadley was telling me. I don't know. Maybe I didn't want to know." He lowered his chin, gazing out the window. "That night at the Christmas party at Longford when they announced their engagement, I was shocked. She hadn't told me anything, she hadn't warned me. We'd never dated openly at school. She'd been very careful about that. She knew I wouldn't tell Will. She was very matter-of-fact about the whole thing. It was the money, of course. She'd grown up poor, and the money meant a lot to her. And the funny thing is"—here he stopped and looked at her with bitterness—"the funny thing is, I didn't blame her. I could understand the lure of power and wealth. I felt complicit in the whole thing, and it made me sick with shame. That's why I couldn't stay around. I dropped out and headed to California."

"But if you kept your relationship secret, then who told Will?"

They exchanged a long look. "I did," he said. "After six months out in California I began to see her differently. I realized she wasn't the girl I had thought she was. The girl Will thought she was, and I knew he deserved better. So I called him."

"You did the right thing."

He shook his head. "Will didn't see it that way," he said. "He probably thought I still had feelings for Hadley and was hoping to get something out of it. The truth was, the only thing I felt for Hadley, and myself, was disgust. Will was too proud to ever forgive her. She begged him not to, but he broke it off with her, and then six months later she was killed and he couldn't hold on to all that rage and hurt he felt for her. So he put it on me." He stared at the print of Hadley. A muscle moved in his cheek. "I guess I don't blame him," he said.

A hummingbird hung suspended outside the window, its delicate beak tapping the glass.

"So why do you keep her face on your wall?"

"To remind me of my fucking mistake."

He put his hand on her shoulder and she let it nestle there, warm and comforting.

After that, there wasn't much left to say. She could see him so clearly as he must have been as a boy, young and hopeful and believing for the first time in a future brighter than any he had ever imagined for himself. Imagining a life with a girl like Hadley.

He leaned back against the sofa, studying her. "Will you go back to Chicago?" he asked.

"I don't know." And it wasn't until she said it that she realized she wouldn't be going back. A new life here in this place, a thought that three months ago would have seemed inconceivable, seemed now to carry a certain weight, an incontrovertible authority. She could imagine herself holed up in a little cabin like his mother's, overlooking a wide sweep of rolling hills, churning out novels about people who understood the joys of living in a place where nothing much ever happened. If you didn't count murder, tragedy, undying love, and familial revenge.

"It grows on you," he said. "It seeps into your blood when you least expect it, and before you know it you're hooked. I went out to California, which for all intents and purposes is paradise, and after a while all I could think about was kudzu and sweet tea. I missed going out to the drive-in on Friday nights. I missed people smiling and saying 'Good morning' and telling me their life stories in the grocery store line."

She laughed. "That's a pretty good description." She was aware of his hand on her shoulder, the weight of it, the gentle pressure of his fingers.

"So I take it wedding bells are not imminent?" he said.

She looked into his eyes. She felt breathless. Light-headed. "What are you talking about?"

"Between you and Will."

"I don't know why everyone is so eager to marry me off to Will."

"I'm not."

Looking at him she felt a familiar stirring deep in her chest. "I should go," she said. He said nothing but as she tried to rise, he put his hand on her arm and kissed her. It was as natural as falling, that kiss. A sensation of letting go, drifting.

"I've wanted to kiss you from the first day I saw you," he said.

Later, they heard the front door slam. They rearranged their clothes and Jake stood up. "Damn," he said. "I forgot to lock it." He went to the stairway and called, "I'll be right down."

Ava stood up, running her hands through her hair. "Who is it?"

"I don't know."

Her face was pink, and when he saw her, he laughed and pulled her into his arms. The door slamming again was like a pistol shot.

They went downstairs.

Whoever it was had gone. The sky had darkened and, looking up through the skylight, Ava could see swiftly moving gray clouds.

"Whoever it was doesn't appear to have stolen anything," Jake said, looking around the shop. He wrapped Ava in his arms, resting his chin on top of her head. "You don't have to go," he said, nuzzling her ear.

"I *do* have to go," she said, pulling away reluctantly. "I'll call you."

"We'll have a date," he said. "Dinner. Maybe a movie. Hell, I might even take you dancing at the Cimarron Ballroom."

They were almost to the front door when it swung open violently and Will stood there, outlined against a bone-white sky.

Behind her Jake said jovially, "Look out!"

Ava had enough sense to step aside as Will rushed past.

It took two burly welders Ava hailed from the building next door to break up the fight. Both Will and Jake were bleeding from the mouth and breathing hard, their shirts torn in front.

"I should have done that a long time ago," Will shouted, as he was being pushed toward the door by one of the men.

"You should have!" Jake began to laugh, so the other man let him go. He wiped his face with his sleeve and called to Will, "What took you so long?"

"You always wanted what you couldn't have."

"And you always had too much."

"Asshole."

"Fucker."

"I'll see you then."

"Whatever."

"Bye."

"Bye," Jake said.

It was then that Ava realized it wasn't about her at all.

W ill didn't say anything to her on the long drive home. She had agreed to let him drive her because it seemed the only fair thing to do.

"Look, Will," she said, but he stared fixedly through the windshield and she saw that she would get nowhere with him.

The rain had begun, falling in windy gusts, splattering the glass. He let her out and drove away without a word. Ava tried to call him several times over the next two days but he didn't answer his phone. Josephine stopped her in the hall one night and with a quiet, resigned air told her that Will had gone to Chattanooga to visit some friends and wouldn't be home for a few days.

"Oh," Ava said.

"How's the work going?" In the dim light, Josephine looked much younger, and it was not hard to imagine her as she must have been in the time of Charlie Woodburn. A tall, handsome woman.

"It's going well."

"Is there anything I can get you?" Her expression was studied, polite, cold.

"No. Thank you," Ava said.

Jake called several times but Ava didn't answer her phone. She felt that she couldn't talk to him again until she'd talked to Will. She owed Will that much at least. And there had been something in Josephine's expression that night in the hall, an indication that her hospitality was almost at an end, that drove Ava to immerse herself in her work.

She finished the novel. One night, it just ended. The relief she felt was indescribable. She had expected emotional fireworks and soaring sensations of accomplishment, but not this quiet feeling of relief. She printed out the manuscript in its entirety. She arranged it neatly in a box on her desk. It wasn't finished, of course. There were months of rewriting that would have to be done before she could begin her search for an agent. But it was enough for now. It was farther than she had ever gotten before.

She began to pack her belongings. She had no doubt that Will was steeling himself, strengthening his resolve to come home and send her packing. She didn't blame him. And because she didn't blame him, and because she felt that she owed him that much, she emailed him a copy of her manuscript.

She emailed a copy to Jake, too. But with him, her intentions were different. With Jake it was more a desire to impress him, to show him what she was capable of, that drove her.

Something I've Been Meaning
to Tell You

"Frank? It's Ava."

"Ava? Oh. *Ava.*" There was a moment of silence, followed by the sound of a hand placed over the receiver, and then a breathless, "Let me get someplace where we can talk."

Ava imagined him trying to hide from his wife. She thought of the sharp-eyed woman she had seen standing on his stoop the day she had driven to Garden City. She heard the sound of a door closing and then Frank said, "How are you? I'm so glad you called. I was afraid I'd never hear from you, and I didn't have your number so I couldn't call you." His voice shook slightly. With nervousness, she supposed, or perhaps fear. There was no telling what she might say to him.

"I'm sorry I didn't call earlier. I've been working this summer and I haven't had a lot of time to myself." It sounded so false and insincere that she trembled, saying it. She had rehearsed this conversation for weeks but now that it was finally here she felt tongue-tied, awkward.

"That's okay. What do you do, Ava?" he asked politely.

"I'm a writer."

"A writer? You mean like books and shit?"

"Yes. Novels."

"Wow. Cool. I guess I'm not surprised. You were always a smart baby. I remember that. And like I said, Meg could tell a good story. She always had her nose in some book. She had you reading before you were four."

"How do you know that?"

"Oh, well, you were just a baby when we broke up, but for a few years after that I'd get letters from wherever you and she had landed. We parted on good terms; there was never any bad blood between us. I just wanted a wife and she didn't like being one. Settling down seemed to drive her crazy. Anyway, sometimes she'd send photos of you and she'd tell me how you were doing. You were always smart, and she was so proud of that. She called you an old soul in a young body. You know how she was."

Ava felt a wincing pain under her ribs. Amazing how grief could settle on you when you least expected it, cold and heavy. "When was the last time you heard from Clotilde? From Meg, I mean. With news about me."

"Oh, well, she was real good for a while there about writing. I sent money. Every penny I could spare. But then I got remarried, and me and Sharon started having kids and I guess Meg just figured it was better if she butted out. I guess she didn't want to cause any problems with my new family. Not that I ever asked her to," he added quickly. "I was always glad to hear from you two."

"So from the time I was ten or so?"

"Younger than that. There was a long time when I didn't hear anything. And then I guess it was when you started college that she called. I had to fill out some forms for your financial aid."

"Frank, I want you to know that I didn't know anything about you. If I had, I'd have gotten in touch."

"Oh, listen, I understand. You don't need to worry about that."

"No, really. It's important to me that you know that. Clotilde, Meg, was a good mother but there are some things she did wrong. She made some big mistakes. Like telling me you were dead on my tenth birthday."

"Dead? How'd she say I died?"

"In an ice-fishing accident on the Detroit River."

He laughed. "Sounds like her," he said. And then, as if noting her silence, he said, "You're right. She shouldn't have told you that."

"I still have nightmares."

"Sometimes adults think they're doing the right thing even when they're not."

"Yes."

"I want you to know you're welcome in my home anytime. I've told Sharon. I've told the kids and they're dying to meet you."

She swallowed hard, blinking. "Thank you, Frank."

"Don't you live in Chicago?"

"I'm spending the summer in the south. In Tennessee."

"Maybe when you get through down there you can come up here and visit."

"I'd like that." Outside the window, the late-afternoon sky was gray and rainy. Clouds of mist rose in the distance. "Frank. You said in your last letter that you might know who my real father is."

"Well, yes, I did but I've been thinking about that, Ava, and after everything you've been through, I'm not sure I should say. Because the truth is, I don't really know. I'm just guessing."

"That's okay, Frank. I understand. And I appreciate you trying to protect me just the way Clotilde did but the thing is, Frank, you reach a point where you don't want to be protected anymore. You want to hear the truth. Do you know what I mean?"

He sighed loudly. "Yeah," he said. "I do." He was quiet for a moment and Ava could feel his hesitation.

"Frank?" she said.

"Okay. I'm going to tell you this but you have to understand, I don't know whether it's true or not."

"It's all right," Ava said. "Just tell me what you know. I'll sort out the truth later on."

"Meg always wanted children. She used to say she wanted a house full, and that was one of the things she and I used to dream about while we were roaming around the country with the Sunshine People. We used to dream about settling down and having a house full of kids. We'd live in the country and she would bake her own bread and home-school the kids and I'd be some kind of organic farmer. Which is kind of funny when you think about it because I don't know shit about farm-ing! But we were just kids ourselves, and we were dreamers, which makes what happened later with your parents so sad."

Ava said, "Parents?"

"See, I traveled around with Meg and the Sunshine People for about six months, and just before we broke up, Meg told me she couldn't have children. She had that disease where the tissue grows inside your stom-ach."

"Endometriosis," Ava said woodenly.

"Yeah, that's it. Anyway, we parted, and two months later Meg shows up on my doorstep with a four-month-old baby she claims was hers and says we have to get married. She had an affidavit signed by two hippies stating that they'd seen Meg deliver the baby, and we hired an attorney to get your birth certificate issued. I knew she was lying, but I was crazy about her and I was willing to do anything she said as long as she'd marry me."

"Oh, my God," Ava said. There was a viselike tightness in her chest. A ringing in her ears.

"My guess, it was the two in the affidavit. I don't remember them, but there were people coming in and out of the group all the time, and they all took those crazy names. It was probably just some young kids who joined the Sunshine People and then realized they were too young to care for a kid of their own. You know how that happens some-times."

"Of course," Ava said. She could feel needle pricks at the back of her throat.

"In a case like that, Meg would have been the first one to step for-ward."

"Frank, do you mind if I call you back later?"

"Oh, sure, that's fine. It was really good talking to you. I mean it, Ava. This means a lot to me."

"To me, too, Frank. I'll call you later." She hung up.

The news was so shocking she could not fully comprehend it. And yet somewhere inside her head the calm, still voice protested that she had always known.

Clotilde was not her mother.

There were no tears this time, just an overwhelming feeling of despair and confusion. She lay in bed listening to the rain.

What had Clotilde been thinking? What had she been looking for all those years they spent on the run? Or better still, what had she been running *from*? Why would a woman who cared so little about living a conventional life take and try to raise a child who wasn't her own?

A bright flash of lightning lit the sky, briefly illuminating the garden.

All her life Ava had told herself, for better or worse, *I am my mother's daughter.* Her whole life had been a lie. A prettily fabricated story. The tiny scrap of self-awareness she had clung to so desperately was gone.

There were no words to describe how bereft she felt, how alone.

A distant rumble of thunder rattled the glass. Gradually she became aware of the knocks and scratchings of the old house. She could feel it breathing around her, the rhythmic rush of the cooling system like a thudding heartbeat.

Eventually she fell into a restless sleep. She awoke several hours later to the sound of voices in the hall. The rain had stopped, and moonlight flooded the room. Outside the window a vague line of silvery clouds sailed above the trees. The voices in the hall were loud, angry. A man and a woman.

She had been dreaming of another time. She was a child, barefoot and dressed in a white pinafore, running along a dusty road. The red serpent was in this dream, too, only this time it didn't bite her. Instead it bit its own tail so that it made a perfect circle, a hoop, and she ran beside it unafraid, laughing and rolling it along the dusty road.

The photo of Charlie Woodburn faced her on the nightstand. She stared into his dark, unfathomable eyes.

It was on a night such as this that he had died.

It took her a moment to come fully awake and realize that the man's voice was Jake's. Ava got out of bed and went to the door, opening it a crack. He and Josephine faced each other in the dimly lit hallway.

"Why have you come?" Josephine said.

"To see Ava." He stood just inside the front door.

"You shouldn't be here. You made your choice."

"It's not always black or white, Josephine. Sometimes there are shades of gray."

"Why do you always want what he wants?"

"You can't choose who you love. You, of all people, should know that."

"Don't speak of things you know nothing about!"

He turned, pulling the door open on its well-oiled hinges. "Tell Ava I'll wait for her outside," he said, going out.

Josephine stood, a tall, dark shadow at the end of the hall. She leaned, slowly and deliberately, and switched off the porch light. Then she turned, walking like a sleepwalker down the dim hallway to the staircase.

Ava slipped on her sandals, then went to the mantel and picked up the vase containing Clotilde's ashes. She opened her door and stood listening to the faint overhead sounds of Josephine preparing for bed.

Jake was not on the porch when she went out. She called to him and a moment later he appeared around the corner of the house, moving swiftly across the lawn.

"Where have you been?" she called softly.

"Throwing gravel at your window. I knew when she turned off the porch light that she had no intention of telling you I was here."

He came up the steps, his pale shirt glimmering in the moonlight. "What've you got there?" he said.

"Someone I used to know."

They walked together down the darkened street toward the river. There was no light except for the moon and the occasional flickering of a gas lamp in front of one of the grand houses. If he was curious about the vase, he didn't say anything besides offering to carry it for her, which she refused.

"You have a bad habit of not answering your phone," he said, breaking a long, moody silence. His exchange with Josephine had obviously upset him.

"I didn't want to talk to you until I had a chance to square things with Will. I felt I owed him an explanation at least."

"Listen, the other day. It wasn't about you."

"I know. You don't need to explain."

"Unfinished business," he said, looking at her.

They walked on. She shifted the vase in her arms and said, "These are ashes. I used to think they were my mother's."

Something in her tone warned him. He stopped, and she stopped, too, facing him. A lone streetlamp cast a spindly glow. At the end of the street they could hear the rushing river, swollen with the rain. She hugged the vase to her chest and told him everything.

When she was finished he whistled softly and said, "Wow. Now there's a novel."

She smiled faintly. "Yes. I suppose it is."

"So you have no idea who your parents are?"

"I suspect, knowing Clotilde, that they might be the two listed in the affidavit as having witnessed my birth. She's not the type to have snatched a baby from a Kmart parking lot. She would never have wanted to cause anyone pain."

"I'd start with the two on the affidavit. Will you try to find them?"

"I don't know. Maybe later. It doesn't matter right now. All I want to do is grieve Clotilde's passing."

"That's understandable."

"Because for all intents and purposes, she was my mother."

"Of course she was."

"And I did love her."

"And she loved you."

"Yes," she said, and began to cry.

Afterward they walked to the bridge. He held her hand, the gentle roar of the river growing louder. A deafening chorus of frogs sang in the thickets lining the banks. The moon hung over the water like a lantern.

"So what are you going to do?" he asked.

"About?"

"Everything. Your novel. Your life."

"I'm not really sure. I'm opening myself to possibility."

He grinned, his teeth glimmering in the darkness. "I like the sound of that."

They reached the narrow wooden bridge and walked out into the middle, leaning against the wire railing. Dark water rushed underneath, thick and oily in the moonlight.

"Will you go back to Chicago?"

"No. That life's over."

"I'm glad."

"Me, too."

He leaned on his elbows, looking down at the rushing river. Pale boulders rose out of the darkness, dimpling the surface. "I read your manuscript. That's why I've been trying to call you. That's why I came over tonight to see you. It's incredible. I couldn't stop reading. I would never have seen Josephine and Clara like that, yet the way you described it happening makes perfect sense."

"Well, it's my story. It's my version of the truth."

"Will isn't going to like it, though."

"I sent it to him, too, but I haven't heard from him."

"You will." He put one arm around her shoulders and pulled her close, nuzzling her hair. "So what will you do now?"

"I don't know. Look for a day job, I guess. But nothing that involves writing. That was the mistake I made before, choosing a job where I had to be creative so that by the time I got home, I was too tired to write. Maybe I should look for work as a forest ranger or a lighthouse keeper. Something physically demanding that still leaves time for solitary creative endeavors."

He laughed. "The forest ranger thing is a possibility but there aren't too many lighthouses here in the mountains."

"True," she said. She grinned, looking up at him.

He kissed her nose. "My mother's looking for a stable hand. It's part-time but I bet you could talk her into letting you stay in her old trailer. It's about a mile from the house, and last time I was out there, it was in pretty good shape."

"Wow, I've never really thought about living in a trailer."

"Stick with me, kid. The sky's the limit."

"I may have to rethink the whole marriage to Will Fraser thing."

"There's a lot to be said for never having to worry about money."

"I'll say."

"But then again, money doesn't buy happiness."

"Who says?"

He shrugged and looked at the sky. "Someone who obviously didn't have any."

"That's assuming I ever *do* marry. She looked down at the dark oily water. "Which given my temperament and demanding career will probably never happen."

"Probably not."

"Still, you never know. The right man might come along."

"If you're lucky."

"I haven't been too lucky up to now."

"That could change."

"And then there's your reputation."

He took the vase from her gently and set it down on the bridge. "My reputation?" he said.

"Ladies' man. Heartbreaker."

He grinned and pulled her roughly against him. "You can't believe everything you hear," he said, and kissed her soundly.

When she was ready, she took the lid off the vase and scattered the ashes in the river. A faint earthy smell of decay and roses filled the air.

She said, "Goodbye, mother." She thought, *I am an orphan.*

But that wasn't true, really. She had parents out there in the world just waiting for her to find them. If she wanted to. If she decided later that it was necessary.

"From what you've told me about her, she would have loved this place," Jake said.

"Yes," she said. She climbed off the bridge and, filling the vase with wildflowers, nestled it among the rocks at the edge of the river. Moonlight flooded the clearing. "This is where I'll come when I want to visit her."

She climbed up the bank and walked out onto the bridge where Jake waited for her. Despite the sadness of the occasion, she was filled with an odd feeling of hope and optimism. She looked up at the moon floating over the water. She thought, *I am my mother's daughter. I am my father's daughter. I am neither.*

I am.

She laughed. "I've always wondered, what is the meaning of life? But now it dawns on me that I've been asking the wrong question."

"What's the right question?"

"What is the meaning of *my* life?"

"Ah," he said.

That night, she slept the sleep of the dead. When she awoke the following morning, sunshine flooded the room and the sky was blue. Josephine and Fanny were gone but they had left a note on the kitchen counter, with instructions on where to find breakfast. Ava had the feeling they were avoiding her, which only strengthened her resolve to move out. She would get a hotel room, if she had to, until she talked to Jake's mother about the trailer or made some other arrangements. She had no job, very little money left in her bank account, and she had, quite possibly, burned her bridges with the Woodburns but she wasn't worried. She wasn't fearful. All that was in the past.

It seemed to Ava that her whole life had been ruled by fear. Fear that her mother would leave her, that they would starve or be homeless, that no matter how hard she worked she could never escape the wolves at her door, their ravenous howling.

Her search for her father had been a distraction, she saw that now, a way of staving off the wolves. She had been looking for a protector, a savior, first with her mythical father, and later with her lovers. But there were no saviors, there was only herself. Maybe that was what Clotilde had been trying to teach her with her stories. To be unafraid and strong.

To do whatever was necessary.

She showered and went into her room to finish packing. Around ten-thirty there was a knock on the door and Ava, startled, said, "Yes?"

Will stood in the doorway holding two coffees in a takeaway tray. He looked tired and unkempt; there were dark crescents beneath his eyes. "I brought breakfast," he said. "Or at least coffee."

She stood at the desk, stacking the box that held her manuscript on top of her laptop. "How nice," she said, making room for him.

He set the tray down carefully on the desk and passed her a cup. She took it, smiling.

"It looks like you're packing."

"Yes."

"Where will you go?"

"I'm not sure yet."

"But not back to Chicago?"

"No."

They sipped their coffee companionably, gazing out the opened shutters at the wide blue sky. The house was quiet. Neither one wanted to begin.

"You read the manuscript?" Ava asked finally.

He sighed. "Yes."

Outside the window, a fat bee tapped repeatedly against the glass. In the crowns of the tall trees, leaves fluttered on an errant breeze.

"You can't think my family will be happy about this novel," he said.

"It's not really about your family." He gazed at her forlornly until she looked away. She said, "It's fiction, Will."

"You've made Josephine and Clara murderers."

"Not Josephine and Clara. Lillian and Rose."

"You can't just change the names! Everyone will see through that."

"I'm not saying it's the truth. I'm not saying it's what really happened. It's just the way my story evolved. It gave them the most motive to kill Charlie."

"If you publish this my family will be a laughingstock in this town."

"What is it you expect me to do, Will?"

They had reached an impasse and they both knew it.

He sipped his coffee, carefully avoiding her gaze. "I suppose I blame myself," he said. "If I'd been more open about Charlie from the beginning, you wouldn't have been so curious. But it's hard, Ava. That's not the way I am. I can't just open myself up the way some people can. And down here, you're raised a certain way. You're taught to keep some things private, family matters especially. It's just the way it's done."

"Everyone worships the past but no one really wants to talk about it."

He sank down on the edge of the bed. "I wasn't trying to close myself off from you. That was never my intention."

"I know, Will." She stood looking down at his bowed head.

"And you're right. I haven't been honest about a lot of things."

"It doesn't matter. You don't have to explain."

He looked up at her. "Humor me," he said coldly. His eyes slid away from her, coming to rest on the box holding her manuscript. He sat quietly staring as if contemplating a plunge into deep, frigid water. "You asked me once about the Gray Lady. The ghost. You asked me if

I'd ever seen her and I said no. That wasn't true. I did see her. Or at least I thought I did. Several times when I was a child. A small, smoky figure standing on the landing beckoning to me."

"What did you do?"

"I cried. I wouldn't go upstairs without Josephine to hold my hand."

"Did you tell her?"

"Yes."

"What did she say?"

"She said, 'Don't be afraid. She's one of us.' "

Ava put a hand out and touched his face.

"I wanted it to work with us, Ava."

"I know." She sank down beside him. "And we'll always be good friends. But I could never make you happy. You know that. I don't want the same things you want. I'm nothing like Hadley."

"Hadley?" He laughed harshly. "Thank God you're nothing like her."

She blinked, confused. "But I thought after the other day at Jake's that you must still love her."

"I didn't love her, but Jake did."

"Will," she said gently, shaking her head. "You were engaged to her but you didn't love her? You dated her for four years but you didn't love her?"

He got up without a word and went out.

She was still sitting on the bed when he returned a few minutes later with a large cardboard box in his hands. He sat down on the edge of the bed with it on his lap, took out a framed photo, and gave it to Ava.

"Here's a photo of Hadley when I first met her, when I thought she was the most beautiful girl I'd ever seen." He reached into the box and took out a faded pressed carnation, frail and dry as old paper. "Here's the boutonniere from our first dance, where I caught her in the cloak-room with someone else." He laid it down on the bed and took out a small velvet box. "And here's the promise ring I gave her that she returned to me the summer before she went to Europe. It was the most miserable summer of my life, lying up there in my room imagining her in the arms of English schoolboys." His voice had become increasingly bitter as he spoke.

"And here's a photo of her the following fall when she returned to school and we agreed to see other people, which meant that I moped around and watched while she went through a steady stream of boyfriends."

He picked up a photo of himself, Hadley, and Jake standing in formal clothes in front of a stone chapel and passed it to Ava.

"Of course, my own cousin, a boy who had been almost a brother to me, who had attended the same school, the one person I trusted above all else. Even I didn't imagine that she could be capable of that. But she was. They were."

His expression was anguished, sullen. She gave him back the photo and he placed it, facedown, in the box. "I swore I'd never forgive them."

Ava didn't know what to say. She sat with her hands in her lap, staring at the bright patch of blue sky beyond the window.

"What you saw the other day wasn't about me and Hadley. It was about me and Jake." He was quiet, folding the flaps of the box down. When that was done he set it on the floor at his feet. He said hesitantly, "I may have been wrong about Jake. I realize that now. Maybe he left school and went to California to give Hadley and me a chance to be together. Maybe he thought he was doing the right thing. I know he loved her. He didn't know her like I did."

"She told him you two were broken up. She lied to him from the beginning."

He stared at his hands. A moment later he lifted his head and gazed out the window. The light slanting through the glass accentuated his pallor, the deep shadow along his cheeks where he hadn't shaved. Ava had a sudden desire to touch him, to comfort him, but she was afraid he would misunderstand her actions.

"The sad thing is, all that anger wasn't necessary because I didn't love her anymore. I realized that after I found out about her and Jake. I guess I saw her then for who she really was. It was an ideal I loved, not the real girl, but I was too young to know that."

Ava slid her hand into his and he looked down at it gratefully.

"When she came to see me not long after I broke off our engagement, I told her how I felt, all the cruel, hurtful things I'd wanted to say to her for years. When she left, she was crying and I didn't care." He looked at Ava, his eyes wretched, bleak. "I've always wondered—was I responsible for her death? Was she crying so hard she couldn't see the road? Or did she kill herself, knowing that I'd have to live with the guilt the rest of my life, knowing that Jake would have to live with the loss? Because she was capable of that. She was capable of throwing her life away in one final act of spite."

Ava put her arms around him and he buried his face against her, holding her fiercely. She stroked his hair.

She said, "I'm sorry, Will. I'm so sorry."

Later, she went out to take a call from Jake's mother and when she came back in, Will was standing at her desk holding the photo of Charlie Woodburn.

"Is this who I think it is?" he said.

"Yes."

"He looks like Jake."

"A little."

"Was it Jake who told you about Josephine and Clara?" His voice was cool and noncommittal. He seemed less agitated over Jake now, as if whatever had stood between them all these years had diminished. Or maybe it was simply the act of telling her the truth about Hadley, the act of confession that had changed everything.

"Jake didn't want me asking questions about Charlie any more than you did. He knew it would upset you and the aunts, and he doesn't seem to care what happened. It was something Alice said that got me thinking that it could have been Clara who killed Charlie. She said that

Charlie used to torment Clara by threatening to horsewhip her father. It was a time when a white man could do whatever he wanted to a black man with little fear of retribution. So maybe Clara believed Charlie's threats enough to poison him to protect her father. I knew she couldn't have done it alone. She would have had to get his body to the river, and that's when I started thinking about Josephine. I found her diary, and I knew how much she hated Charlie. How much she wanted to be rid of him for Fanny's sake. And she loved Clara like a sister. She would have been willing to do anything to protect Fanny and Clara."

He set the photo down carefully on the desk. She shrugged, smiling faintly. "It wasn't too hard to imagine Josephine and Clara on one hot, fateful day finally taking matters into their own hands and getting rid of Charlie Woodburn."

She waited for him to say something. He stood with his hands hanging down at his sides, facing her across the room.

"There's something between you and Jake, isn't there." He said it as a statement, not a question.

Ava met his eyes. "Yes," she said.

He nodded once, looked around the room. "You don't have to be in a hurry to move out of here, you know. No one's evicting you."

"I appreciate that."

"Will you move in with him?"

"No." She told him about the trailer Jake's mother had offered to let her use.

"I know the place well. Jake and I used to have wild parties out there." He smiled. A look of sadness passed swiftly across his face. "It's the perfect place for a writer. Quiet, secluded." He gave her a brief, devilish grin. "I think it even has indoor plumbing."

"Thank God." She made a comical face. She folded one leg under her and sank down on the bed. He walked over to the window and stood looking out with his hands clasped behind his back.

"He misses you, Will. You and Fanny and Josephine. I think he's lonely for all of you but he doesn't know how to make it right. Maybe you could see him. Put it all behind you once and for all, because I do think he's sorry."

He didn't turn around. "We'll see," he said quietly.

They went into the kitchen and made sandwiches, then took them out on the verandah to eat. The sky had begun to darken. Several fierce gusts of wind rattled the windows. It was the way August was down here. Blue skies in the morning and rain every afternoon.

They sat in two rocking chairs with their plates and glasses resting on a small round table between them.

Will gazed across the lawn, his feet tapping lightly against the floorboards. "I want you to know that whatever happens, we'll still be friends."

"I'm glad," she said. The rain began, falling softly. "Do you think Josephine and Fanny and Clara will feel the same way?"

"Well," he said, chewing thoughtfully. "You might want to wait until they're dead to publish."

"Yeah. I thought about that." And it was true, she had thought about putting the manuscript away in a drawer and taking it out later to see it with fresh eyes. To see if it was still as good as she thought it was.

"Of course, that's just an idea," he said. "It's a fine story. A damn fine story about a Colorado cattle baron and his violent offspring. It's got it all: greed, love, murder, even a vengeful family ghost." He grinned at her and she smiled gratefully. "You've got it wrong though, about Clara and Josephine."

"You don't think they killed Charlie?"

"Neither one is capable of that."

The rain began to fall more forcefully, drumming along the roof and gutters. They sat quietly rocking, listening to its melancholy music.

He said, "You've also given Josephine a lover in your story, which is pretty far-fetched."

"Is it? She was an attractive woman, and she never married. Alice says it was the family disgrace of Fanny's elopement that kept her from marrying. I imagined her being in love, and I imagined Charlie putting an end to the affair just by his presence in the house. Certainly Josephine hated Charlie. You can see that in her diary."

"Well, in your story that's fine. But in reality I don't believe it ever happened. And another thing," he said. "I don't for one moment think my great-grandfather James meant to give Longford to Charlie Woodburn. How did you come up with that?"

She told him about the journal entry and the letter Rachel Rowe had found.

"So you're saying that if Josephine had not ignored her father's wishes, if she had not ordered the deed destroyed, then Longford would belong to Jake today and not to me?"

Ava said nothing, staring out at the rain.

"I don't believe it," he said.

She got up, went into the house, and came back out with Josephine's diary and a file folder filled with letters and documents Rachel had found. She set them down on the table between them.

"This material is yours. Do with it what you want," she said. "I've told my story. I've made all the pieces fit. The historical truth doesn't matter. No one will ever know what really happened to Charlie Woodburn."

A sudden blast of wind swept the porch, jangling the chains of the porch swing. Shivering, Ava rose and went to fetch a sweater.

On the threshold of her room, she stopped and stood, very still, staring. The pages of her manuscript lay scattered across the bed and floor as if tossed by vengeful hands. Thinking the wind might have blown them, she walked stiffly across the room to the windows, but pulling back the shutters she was startled by her pale, frightened reflection in the glass. A shiver of fear and trembling possibility rose up her spine.

The windows, she saw, were tightly latched.

1931

Woodburn, Tennessee

Pain was part of love.

Fanny had learned that all those years ago watching Papa suffer following Mother's death. She had learned it blindly following Josephine. And she had learned it, too, married to Charlie Woodburn, had learned to take his anger and sorrow into her own body as she did the Eucharist, to submit gracefully to the terrible fury of his despair. He knew of the suffering quality of love, too. She had heard him cry out for his dead mother at night, his hair dark against the pillow, his face in sleep so boyish and innocent, and she had comforted him, holding him to her breast until he woke and, in disgust, pushed her away.

She had seen that same suffering in his face as he watched his son, King, toddling on crooked legs across the verandah, pulling himself up by grasping his father's trousers in his tight little fists. How tender Charlie's face became when he looked at King! And he would feel the same way about their own son, too. She put her hands there now and felt the child move, trailing one tiny foot across her swollen belly.

Her own poor child who would never know his father. Fanny knew this now. She had dreamed it the other night. Papa had come to her in her dreams, holding a bowl of spiky fruit in his hands.

It was sad, of course, but inevitable. Some things are not meant to be.

Was it only two days ago that Charlie had climbed the stairs after his fight with Josephine in the kitchen? It seemed a lifetime ago. Fanny had been sleeping but had heard his footsteps on the stairs, waking with a start and preparing herself for the inevitable. Their voices, raised in anger, had been part of her dreams, and that's how she knew that they'd been quarrelling, that's how she knew Charlie would come seeking retribution.

She was unprepared for the depth of his anger, and as he stepped into the room and she saw his face, she put her hands instinctively to her belly. He crossed in several quick strides, and Tom Penny, on the pillow beside her, arched his back and hissed. He leaned down and picked up the cat by the scruff of the neck, and Fanny, frantic now, rose and began to claw at his face. Surprised, he looked down at her and laughed. It was at that moment that Tom Penny turned and sank his teeth and claws into Charlie's arm, and with a shouted oath, Charlie flung the cat against the wall. It hit with a sound like a ripe melon breaking. Fanny leapt up and ran to Tom Penny, kneeling and cradling his broken body in her arms, and Charlie, surprised by her tears, stood for a moment, breathing heavily.

Then, without a word, he turned and left the room.

She buried him in the garden where she had buried the other Tom Pennys, six neat little graves in a row. Then she took her shears and her gloves and her basket and went to the corner of the old stable, where she knelt and picked several spiky balls from the castor bean plants. She went inside the stable, plucked out the seeds, cut them into small pieces with her shears, and put them in a bowl, careful not to get any on her skin, and when she'd finished she took the bowl into the house. She could hear Charlie in his room, moving around. She could hear the clinking of bottles, and she went to the stove and scrambled bacon and eggs in a big frying pan. She put the eggs on a plate and mixed in the tiny seed pieces, then crumbled the bacon on top the way he liked it.

She called to him to come for breakfast. They were alone in the house, just the two of them. He sat down and began to eat, and when he had finished, Fanny took the plate and fork out and buried them with the gloves and the shears behind the stable, just like she had seen Papa and John do with the rats all those years ago.

The following day he was too sick to rise. Fanny offered to make him some broth and he said weakly, "You do it. I don't trust that sister of yours." And she went into the kitchen, and when the broth had cooled she dropped in pieces of the seeds and took it in to him, sitting beside the bed and feeding him carefully.

Josephine came in and said, "Should we call the doctor?" and Fanny said, "No, he'll be all right. He has a sensitive stomach is all."

"From all the drinking, no doubt."

"No doubt."

"Our reading club meets tonight."

"You go," Fanny said. "I'll look after him."

By evening he'd begun to hallucinate, thrashing about in the bed, and when Fanny went in to him there was blood on his pillow and on the sheets. She cleaned him up and changed the sheets, then went out into the garden to bury the spoon and the bowl she'd used to feed him the broth. When she came back into the kitchen, he was standing there, fresh blood trickling down the corner of his mouth onto his nightshirt. The kitchen was dark but for a slash of moonlight coming in the long windows. Faintly in the distance, a gramophone played "Boléro."

"Mama?" he said, weaving on his feet.

He fell onto the floor and lay staring up at the ceiling, blood bubbling on his lips. "I'm sorry," he said.

She wiped his mouth with the hem of her dress. "I know," she said gently.

Deep within the house she could hear the muffled chiming of the clock.

He was too heavy to move, and she sat for a long time waiting for Josephine to come home and help her. She must have dozed, awakening to footsteps coming up the front porch, then down the hallway, and she thought, *Those are too heavy for Josephine.* And then she thought, *Papa?*

"Fanny?" Light flooded the room and Maitland stood in the doorway. "Oh, my God," he said, bending down to where Fanny sat, blinking, with Charlie's head in her swollen lap. "What happened?"

She told him. Everything. When she had finished, he rose without a word and went into Charlie's bedroom to get his clothes. He dressed Charlie, then wrapped him in a quilt, dragging him out the kitchen door while Fanny pulled the car around.

The moon had risen high in the sky by the time they got to the river. Maitland switched off the lights of the car and they coasted across the narrow bridge. The water was dark and foamy. Several large boulders gleamed in the moonlight, and there was no sound but the rushing of the water and the wind moaning in the trees.

Maitland poured whiskey from a flask all over Charlie's clothes and into his mouth and jammed the empty flask into Charlie's pocket. Then he pushed him over the edge, the quilt unfurling from the bridge like a flag. He stood for a moment, looking down, then bundled the quilt in his arms and went back to the car.

Fanny stood at the railing looking down at Charlie, who had landed faceup in the river and was beginning to float, partially submerged, with the current, his face, in the moonlight, pale and waxy as some monstrous exotic flower.

About the Author

CATHY HOLTON, the author of *Beach Trip, The Secret Lives of the Kudzu Debutantes,* and *Revenge of the Kudzu Debutantes,* was born in Lakeland, Florida, and grew up in college towns in the South and the Midwest. She attended Oklahoma State University and Michigan State University where she studied creative writing. She lives in Chattanooga, Tennessee, with her husband and their three children.